MW01172013

Mystic Highlands Love Story

Also by this Author:

Arianna A Tale from the Eleven Kingdoms

Mystic Highlands Love Story

GC Sinclaire

Copyright © 2019 by GC Sinclaire

Copyright © 2019 by GC Sinclaire

All rights reserved. No part of this publication may be reproduced, distributed, or transmitted in any form or by any means, without prior written permission.

Printed in the United States of America

GC Sinclaire
Gig Harbor, WA 98329
www.gcsinclaire.com

Publisher's Note: This is a work of fiction. Names, characters, places, and incidents are a product of the author's imagination. Locales and public names are sometimes used for atmospheric purposes. Any resemblance to actual people, living or dead, or to businesses, companies, events, institutions, or locales is completely coincidental.

Mystic Highlands Love Story/GC Sinclaire-- 1st ed.

Print Edition ISBN 978-0-9977915-6-3

E-Book Edition ISBN 978-0-9977915-7-0

Print Edition ISBN 978-0-9977915-5-6

E-Book Edition ISBN 978-0-9977915-4-9

Library of Congress Control Number: 2018915129

Dedicated To:

*All my wonderful
readers and the Divine*

Map of the Mystic Highlands

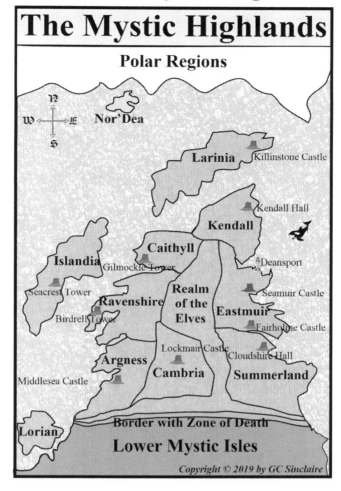

This map shows the locations of all the Highland Clans, the main castles, as well as the realm of the Zidhe. It also shows the polar regions where the elves created their emergency sanctuaries. The Mystic Highlands are the Northernmost regions of a collection of islands called the Mystic Isles.

Contents

The terminology, as well as measurements, are different in the Mystic Highlands. I have, therefore, taken the liberty to convert some of them to make it easier to follow this engaging tale.

Acknowledgments

A very special 'THANK YOU' to all my amazing friends and family who loved and supported me during the creation of this book. I much appreciate all your input, your ideas, and your patience. You were always there for me whenever I needed you and often listened to me talk about the book for hours. I love you.

Also, thank you, Rhonda Mackert and Robbi Baskin, for your help with the editing and your valuable comments! Thank you, Christopher Boscole, for your support, for your music, for expanding my emotional horizon, for showing me how beautiful love can be. You were the inspiration for some of my characters, gave me much-needed insights, and without you, none of this would have been possible. I will always love you.

The cover took shape over several months. Thank you, David Aldrich, for being there to advise me and help me. Thank you, all my artistic friends and family for helping form it with your comments and tips.

Last, but not least:
A huge thank you to the Divine
for sending me this story in a dream
and helping me write it.

Publisher GC Sinclaire, Gig Harbor, WA 98329

Part 1

Frankonia

Ki'ara

High up in the Frankonian Mountains, in a dilapidated castle surrounded by dense, cloying fog, Ki'ara was huddling under the covers to stay warm. She was happy to be traveling home in a couple of days. Her apprenticeship was over, much to the disgust of the wizard she had been sent to study with. Argulf had nothing left to teach her she wanted to learn, his dark magic he could keep to himself. The young lady was tired of being his meal ticket as well as having to clean up after him.

Argulf had not been prepared for her rapid and sudden assimilation of his knowledge. He had tried hard to deny her the diploma she had more than earned. The wizard had come up with all kinds of enchantments and tasks for Ki'ara to perform, most of which he had never taught her. To the incredulous man's surprise, his up to then mediocre student had passed every test he had set before her with flying colors. In the end, the infuriated sorcerer had stormed off in a huff.

Now that she was leaving, the young lady was anxious as well as excited. Disjointed thoughts continued to race through her troubled mind. What would it be like for her this time? What kind of a reception would she get from her siblings? Would she be able to find a way to see Conall without losing her family? So many questions and no real answers! Only time would tell.

It took a while, but, finally, she relaxed enough to slip into sleep. Not long after, Ki'ara started to dream. She was back in the Highlands, her beloved home. Looking around, she realized that she was at Seamuir Castle, the seat of the MacClair Clan, in her bright and airy bedroom. Her maid, Liana, was assisting her in getting ready for a wedding in nearby Deansport. The young lady was genuinely looking forward to the event.

Any celebration in the Highlands was always a lively affair. Due to the convenience of each realms magical gates, folk could come from all over to attend the festivities. It usually turned out to be great fun. Ki'ara had missed these get-togethers. She had been off studying for a while and was thrilled that she would get to see many of her friends as well as her favorite uncle.

For this special occasion, Ki'ara had taken great care with her dress, jewelry, and hair. With the help of Leana, the girl's unruly mane had been braided and twisted into a real work of art. She looked beautiful in the floor-length, midnight blue gown. Diamonds sparkled at her ears and throat, and she was wearing her favorite ring, a gift from Conall, the man whom she had loved for as long as she could remember.

Adding a touch of color to her cheeks and lips, Ki'ara regarded herself in the mirror. She could not think of anything to add to improve her appearance, and neither could her resourceful maid. Just then, the clock struck the hour. It was finally time to go! Giving her tresses one last pat, the young lady headed out the door, danced along the corridor, and then gracefully waltzed down the broad stairs.

It was so amazing to be back where she belonged, especially on such a bright and joyful day! Ki'ara could feel the warm sunshine on her upraised face as she stepped out the entry. She paused on the landing and closed her eyes for a moment. A deep sense of contentment and happiness filled her entire being as she took in her surroundings. She could not help but smile. How wonderful it was to be home!

Ki'ara was jolted out of the peaceful tranquility she had been feeling when abruptly everything around her changed. The warmth of the sun she had been enjoying a few seconds ago was rapidly bleeding away. Her environs turned dark, and the air suddenly felt charged with danger. To make matters worse, her brother's face appeared out of the black clouds looming above. It hovered menacingly above her where bright blue sky had been but a minute ago.

The girl cringed at the sight of this angry visage. Fear rose up within her when she saw the cruel set of Ragnald's mouth and the unbridled malice in his eyes. She did not miss the pure hatred in his piercing gaze. His hand appeared out of the mist, and he began to laugh, ugly and mean, as he aimed a large ball of fire straight at her heart.

Being a competent sorceress, Ki'ara immediately drew on her powers to create a defense. Her shields snapped around her in an instant like a cocoon. Not a moment too soon! Flames started to rain down, burning everything they touched, rapidly creating a hazard for anyone near.

She should have been safe within her protective orb, but to Ki'ara's dismay, first one cinder, then another got through and burned her arms and face. She noticed that others were beginning to force their way in. Her shields were in danger of collapsing!

Ki'ara realized that she was in trouble. This was no ordinary fire! She could sense that this blaze was fueled by her brother's fury as well as all the magic of the land. It had all the power behind it he was able to wield as the Lord of Seamuir Castle. Her shields were almost useless against it. She would have to try to outpace it! Without a moment's hesitation, the young lady took off running, trying to save herself from the inferno.

Ragnald's cruel laughter rung in Ki'ara's ears as she raced towards the drawbridge of the castle, fleeing for her life. The blaze was hot on her heels. Her alarm increased further when she realized that she continued to lose precious ground. She could feel the heat getting closer and closer!

To regain her lead, Ki'ara tried to increase her speed, but her elegant gown got in the way, and she tripped. Almost instantly, the fire was upon her and began to engulf her. The young lady screamed in agony as the flames began to scorch her flesh. She collapsed to the deck of the drawbridge surrounded by the violent conflagration.

As her hair and dress burned around her, the pain grew beyond what Ki'ara could bear. She could not help but let out a scream. Big mistake! When the hot air scorched her lungs, she suppressed her shriek instantly, but it was too late. The damage had been done, and she could barely breathe.

Tears rolled down her seared face only to evaporate in the heat of the flames. Using her hands, Ki'ara had managed to minimize the harm to her eyes. Everything was blurry, but at least she could still somewhat see, and this allowed her to frantically search for an avenue of escape.

She still could barely believe it! Her brother, who was supposed to protect and care for her, was killing her! What had she ever done to him? Why did he hate her this much? What could she possibly do to save herself? To get out of this situation alive? There just had to be a way, all she needed to do was to find it! Ki'ara looked around desperately. There had to be something that would help her survive!

Blurred by the heat of the inferno enfolding her, Ki'ara noticed the water in the moat underneath the drawbridge. Being imbued with the magic of the land, it might extinguish the blaze! The girl gathered the last of her strength and pushed the terrible pain aside. If she could only make it to the edge and let herself drop into the cold fluid, she might yet live!

Ki'ara almost blacked out from pure agony as she ever so slowly inched her way to the side of the wooden span and over. She seemed to be falling forever, but finally, her burning body hit the still water below. The pain from the impact was enough to almost make her lose her senses. It took all her will to stay conscious.

The cool liquid extinguished the flames but barely eased the horrible agony of her crisped flesh. She had no strength left to swim and therefore tried to just float. Time after time, she started to sink. Using her powers, she frantically called out for help. If someone was close enough, they might be able to come to her aid!

Just as she started to go under again, the magic of the land responded to her desperate plea. This was completely unexpected! It flooded her body, surged through her veins, and eased the terrible pain. In awe, she watched the burned outer layers of her skin flake away to reveal smooth new dermis beneath. Her lovely red hair, which had been burned down to her scalp, grew back lustrous and long.

Gradually Ki'ara's strength started to return, but she was still very weak. Furthermore, her mind felt a bit foggy from the shock of the trauma she had gone through. Very slowly, she began to swim for the far side of the moat, all the while rejoicing in the flow of power restoring her to her former healthy self. It felt heavenly to be almost whole again!

She had escaped for now, but where was Ragnald, and what was he up to? Ki'ara could not see him from down here in the moat, and that worried her. He could appear at any moment to finish what he had started! The shape she was in, she would not be able to defend herself from another attack. She would have to rely on help from the outside.

Ki'ara turned to the magic of the land flowing through and around her. She sent it her boundless gratitude for the timely saving of her life. The girl could tell by the flow of love which she received in response how pleased it was to be so acknowledged. Would it continue to help her, defend her? She hesitantly asked for protection from her guardian who had almost succeeded in murdering her.

Ragnald had committed an unforgivable crime. Not only had he abused his powers, but he had also violated the sacred oath he had taken when he became a lord. It was her brother's sworn duty to shelter all members of his family and clan. According to the laws set down by the elves long ago, with this despicable act, he had forfeited his right to rule. Would the magic take her side against him? Ki'ara sure hoped so!

A sense of quiet reassurance was her answer, and a new awareness along with an incredible flow of power entered her being. Ki'ara realized that things would never be the same. She had been granted the magic, all of it! Instead of Ragnald, she was now intimately tied to the land! Never again would she have to fear her brother, she was the power now, was 'The MacClair', lord of the clan. This was a turn of events she had not anticipated!

Feeling ultimately more confident and much more restored, the young lady strengthened her stroke. She was slowly but surely getting closer to her goal, but it appeared to be taking her forever to reach that far side. Had the moat always been this wide? It felt like she had been swimming for such a long while!

After what seemed like an eternity, finally, her hands touched the walls bordering the channel. Ki'ara let out a sigh of relief. Now to deal with the next problem. How was she going to get out? She had these new powers but was not yet sure what exactly she was able to do. The girl concluded that she would have to rely on her instincts.

The channel had been created as a very effective defensive measure. It had been designed to keep enemies, who had fallen or had been pushed in, from getting out. The stones were smooth and well-jointed. They gave little purchase to Ki'ara's searching fingers. It would not be easy climbing up, but she was sure with the magic behind her, she would find a way. Could she make the water lift her to safety?

Suddenly, a pair of hands came down from above. They grabbed the young woman by the arms and pulled her from the moat. For a moment, Ki'ara was utterly frozen so great was her terror. Was it her brother? Was Ragnald going to try yet again? Was he here to make sure she ended up dead? What should she do?

In an instance, a sense of calm flowed through the panicked girl. It was the magic quietly letting her know that she was safe. Once the fear subsided, Ki'ara remembered that the power he had once yielded was now hers to control and not his. Ragnald could no longer harm her!

Next thing she knew, she was pulled close to a man's chest. He was holding her so tightly that her face was pushed firmly into his shirt. This was making it hard for her to catch her breath and prevented her from determining his identity. The way he was pressing her against him felt like he was never going to let her go.

Ki'ara had not been hugged like this since the day her parents departed! Her gut told her that this was a friend. Trusting her instincts, the young lady let go of her trepidations. The strong arms around her felt protective and so very safe. For the first time in a long time, she felt completely at home. Who was this man who had come to her rescue? With her nose buried in his shirt, she was unable to see his face, but he did smell familiar, a wonderfully clean scent of lavender and horses with a touch of the sea.

She vaguely remembered this odor but had not been around it for a very long time. It had been part of her childhood, almost forgotten in the many years since. Ki'ara tried hard to recall who this fragrance had been associated with. At first, it eluded her completely.

Her mind had not yet cleared, and she was still drained from her recent ordeal. Finally, it came to her, and she gasped. Could this truly be possible? Could this be him? Conall, Lord of the StClouds? Her friend, the one and only man she had ever loved and wanted?

Pulling up her arms, Ki'ara pushed against the man's chest until she could move her head back. Finally, she could look up at his face. Slowly his handsome features came into focus. Their eyes met, and she could feel herself melting. As if drawn by a magnet, he started to lower his head, getting ready to kiss her.

Ki'ara looked up at her rescuer as his mouth descended towards hers. He seemed to be moving in slow motion. The young lady was overcome with relief and awe. Her love had come to her rescue! He was here, with her, after all this time! How long had it been since she had last seen him?

Too many years! Ki'ara's heart contracted with longing as well as pleasant anticipation. Her stomach felt like a kaleidoscope of butterflies had taken up residence and were flying about madly, her soul was vibrating and overflowing with love, just like it had always done when he was near.

Ki'ara relished the devotion shining in Conall's soulful brown eyes. She saw her own yearnings reflected in his. After all this time, here they were. Finally, together again! The happiness she felt flooded her entire being and made her feel warm and tingly from her head to her toes.

What came next was the stuff nightmares are made of. Just as the StCloud's mouth neared hers, had almost touched her eager lips, he was abruptly torn away from her. Ki'ara watched in dismay as the man she so utterly loved was flung into a deep chasm that had suddenly appeared beside them. Immediately, she used spell after spell trying to save him, but her efforts were in vain. The powerful sorceress only succeeded in using up all her magic until she could not even cast the most basic of spells.

The exhausted Ki'ara watched in horror as the one she loved continued to drop further and further away from her. The StCloud just kept on falling, nothing she had tried had worked. Conall was rapidly disappearing into the bottomless void. Once he was gone from her sight, she could still weakly hear the echo of him calling her name. Disconsolately, the young woman collapsed beside the yawning abyss.

All those enchantments Ki'ara had cast in her attempt to save Conall had burned out her powers. She could not even sense the land anymore. Where that connection had been, there was now only an immense emptiness. Tears were streaming down her face as she curled into a tight ball. She knew that he, as well as the magic, were gone forever, she could feel it in her very soul. The grief which tore through her body took her breath away, and the world around her faded into oblivion. Darkness engulfed her, and she lost consciousness.

When she came to, Ki'ara found herself alone, in a sea of white. She had lost all that mattered to her, the man she loved as well as her bond with the land and its magic. She despaired at the thought that Conall was gone from her life and that she would never see his handsome face again, feel the warmth of his embrace, hear his beloved voice.

How could fate be so cruel? It was too much for her to bear. How could she spend an eternity without him? Ki'ara could have survived without her powers but not without him in the world! As long as the StCloud had been alive, there had been hope!

As if sensing her anguish, the mist began to move closer and closer. It coiled itself around Ki'ara, tighter and tighter. It constricted around her defenseless form, making it difficult for her to breathe. As it enveloped her, the fog began to squeeze the life out of her. The girl started to suffocate. The light in front of her eyes slowly grew progressively dimmer.

Having lost the one man she had loved since she was a child as well as her magic, Ki'ara gladly let herself slide into the oblivion at hand. She, who had always found some way to persevere, surrendered without the slightest attempt to fight for her life. Her heart was broken, her hope gone, her will defeated, her soul longing for release.

Without Conall and powerless, immortality seemed more like a curse than a gift. Ki'ara would be at the complete mercy of Ragnald, a fate worse than death. As far as the girl was concerned, she had no reason left to go on. This thing, whatever it was, might as well have her!

Just as she was about to let herself be taken into the darkness and perish, a rough, urgent lick on her face jarred her awake. Ki'ara sat up, gasping. Tears were rolling down her cheeks, and her entire body was spasming with the force of her anguish. Despairing sobs shook her whole being and chocked off her breath.

Several minutes went by before she grasped that it had all been a dream. It took a while longer for the pain of her loss to lessen just a little. A feeling of unreality still lingered, and she lit the candle on her nightstand in an attempt to chase the last remnants of the nightmare away. Slowly, her breathing started to calm, and the sobs to subside.

Then, suddenly, something else occurred to her, and terror engulfed her. Would she have actually died if her faithful friend had not woken her? The thought made her shudder. Ki'ara had never experienced anything like this before. This dream had felt evil, all wrong and oily somehow.

The big, tawny cat stopped licking her and sat down beside her. Ki'ara could just barely make out the buff shade of his throat, chest, and belly. She estimated that the large male was almost eight feet long from nose to tail. He was lighter in color than some of the other cougars she had seen in warmer and more humid climates. The fur on his back and head appeared almost silver-gray instead of reddish-brown. The flickering light played over his slender, well-muscled body, and even as distressed as she was at that moment, she could not help but think how beautiful he was.

Gently, but insistently, Taryn pushed his head against her chin. The girl wrapped her arms around him and buried her face in the soft fur of his neck. She held on to him tightly and allowed the tears to flow freely. Her instincts told her that he had just saved her life!

Chapter 1

De'Aire Chateau

It was her last day at the castle if the weather permitted. An exasperated Ki'ara had taken refuge on her balcony. Argulf, the owner of the stronghold and her latest teacher, was furious with her. She had upset HIS plans for her future, and he felt bested and betrayed. He could not believe that a mere girl had outsmarted him. The wizard was utterly puzzled how she had learned so much and in such a short time when he had been trying to hold her back as much as he could.

Had Argulf honestly expected her to spend year after year doing his bidding and taking his abuse? Just so that he had a steady income? Talk about self-centered! Ki'ara had seen the writing on the wall shortly after she arrived and had been determined to return to the Highlands as quickly as possible. She had worked hard to achieve this.

That her teacher would not be happy with her success was something the young woman had been expecting, but that he would react this badly had surprised even her. Ki'ara was tired of the ugly confrontations which had ensued every time Argulf, and she had crossed paths in the last few days. Usually, she had managed to avoid him quite effortlessly but not lately. He continued to seek her out wherever she went. If only the fog lifted by morning!

For the last few days, the mountains had been completely socked in. Getting lost out there would be inevitable. Since the weather was not conducive for Ki'ara to escape outdoors, her room and the balcony were safe places to be. The wizard would not invade her chambers even if he were dying to find out how she had managed to absorb so much knowledge in such a short time.

Mist hung over the tall peaks and cast the deep gorges into murky shadows. It surrounded the small, secluded fortress located high up among the mountaintops. Not only was the old edifice far removed from any other human habitation, but, in the thick haze, it seemed to be floating in a sea of impenetrable, suffocating white. How glad she was to be leaving here soon!

Ki'ara took in the total isolation of the stark, crumbling structure. It definitely had its own beauty. The ancient fort had been constructed right at the edge of a steep cliff dropping down almost 2000 feet to the river valley below. Some parts of the building looked as if they had been glued to the side of the sheer wall, and the stone of the small stronghold blended in with the rock of the mountains. It was hard to discern where one began and the other left off.

De'Aire Chateau was a dark and dreary place in the winter and only marginally more pleasant in the summer. All year long, it was whipped relentlessly by the frequent storms coming in from the sea. On occasions, these tempests would bounce back and forth between the tall crags, dumping massive amounts of rain or snow.

Then, for days on end, only muted light would weakly illuminate the dwelling's dusky gray ramparts. Getting down the mountains during such times was impossible and, if one was not well enough prepared, food, candles, and wood could end up being in short supply.

One thing was sure. The tired old castle had seen better days. Once, it had been a bustling place and home to a fair number of people despite its remoteness.

That was before Argulf acquired the fort. Now, due to its present owner's rude and reclusive nature and his total neglect of anything but his enchantments, it was a pale shadow of its former self.

✦⋆⋆✦

Coming into a sizeable inheritance from a deceased uncle had made it possible for Argulf to obtain the castle. The previous owner had died, and his young widow wanted no part of the desolate place. She was only too happy to leave the mountains behind and move down to the coast where it was warmer and more populated. Therefore, she had sold the place cheap.

Once the papers were signed and the money exchanged, Argulf had taken over the castle along with its staff. It soon turned out that he had no regard for either. The retainers' repeated pleas for repairs had fallen on deaf ears.

Again and again, the old magician had absentmindedly assured the servants that he would take care of things and then had promptly forgotten all about it. When the situation had become untenable, most of the help had left. By the time Ki'ara arrived, only those too old and feeble to find other employment still worked there.

✦⋆⋆✦

The young sorceress was noble-born, one of the powerful, almost immortal Zidarians from the far north. She was a tall, slender woman. Ki'ara's waist long, somewhat curly hair shone like bright copper in the sunshine. Her startling green eyes, set into a face with clear skin and delicate facial features, were the color of a mountain lake with moonlight reflecting off its waves. Her inner beauty matched her appearance and was so evident that most people instantly liked her.

By rights, she should have never been sent to a dwelling such as this. She should have been afforded a certain standard of living but, thanks to her unkind guardian, her oldest brother, Ki'ara was no stranger to hardship. This was not the first unpleasant place she had been sent to under the guise of furthering her magical education.

The young lady had spent her childhood far to the north in the Mystic Highlands where the winters were long and hard and the summers short and frequently chilly. She had been to many disagreeable locations since, some hot and humid, others cold and plagued by snow for months on end.

Still, nothing could have prepared her for a place such as this. Due to the total neglect by its owner, De'Aire Chateau was now more of a ruin than a proper place to live. To make matters worse, the weather was inclement for most of the year.

༺✦༻

Within days of her arrival, Ki'ara had gotten a fair sense of how much the few remaining servants suffered under these hostile conditions. The rundown keep was an abysmal place for anyone but especially the elderly and frail.

Living here had not been easy for the young woman either. Since it was trying for someone in the prime of her life used to harsh weather conditions, she figured that it had to be more than difficult for the aging staff of the castle. Her heart went out to these people who had been nothing but kind to her from the beginning.

Ki'ara soon realized that most of the habitable rooms in the old stronghold were cold and drafty, even at the height of summer. Heating was kept to a minimum since most goods had to be fetched from the lower reaches, including the wood. Often only her magic kept the girl comfortable. Never in her life had she been so grateful for this gift, and she pitied the servants who had no such powers.

Both men and women alike would bundle up in multiple layers of clothing in a futile attempt to stay warm. Nonetheless, they froze when icy winds howled through the passes. Most ended up limping and barely able to move.

⁂

Once Ki'ara had realized the true extent of their plight, the girl had felt bad for the castle's elderly inhabitants. She had decided that something had to be done. Since Argulf was not taking care of the fort, she would take things into her own hands. She had always enjoyed helping others and had acquired a host of skills in the process, she had just needed to figure out when she could work on this project.

Some days Argulf had been so involved in some secret experiments that he had completely forgotten about her, but usually, he had kept Ki'ara busy from morning until late in the night. That had left her little time for anything else. She had, however, gained the concession from the ill-tempered wizard that she could have an hour for her daily exercise, an absolute must as far as she was concerned.

The young lady had argued that she could get much more accomplished if she took proper care of herself and took time to decompress. She had seen her walks in the mountains as vital for her health and happiness, as a source of grounding. They had also kept some of the homesickness at bay. The wizard had finally relented and, with much grumbling, had allotted her some time each day. It was often the only occasion she had to enjoy a few minutes of peace, but it did make it more challenging to do much else.

Where there is a will, however, there is always a way. With the help of the servants, Ki'ara had examined the entire structure closely. She had come up with a detailed plan of what needed to be done to make the place more comfortable. Next, she had created a list of her restoration projects. Every task had been sorted by priority and by how much time it would take to complete.

Whenever she had a few extra minutes, and every evening after Argulf sent her off for the night, Ki'ara had worked on the castle. She had started with the kitchen and the bedrooms housing the staff. Bit by bit, she had improved the living conditions in the old fortress.

⁂

Argulf and his laboratories occupied the sheltered and best-preserved sections of De'Aire Chateau, and he had not been willing to relinquish even an inch of his space. The servants' quarters, on the other hand, were in some of the most exposed and decrepit parts of the stronghold. Ki'ara had deemed them unfit for human habitation, but there was nowhere else to house the retainers.

The sorceress had felt strongly that the crumbling section should have been condemned, right along with the rest of the castle. It had not been up to her, however, and she had seen no other option but to use her magic and skills to rebuild that segment of the fortress.

It had not been easy and had taken several months, even with the help of the grateful staff. From the very first day, these caring people had gone out of their way to make Ki'ara welcome. The girl had felt strongly that giving them a warmer place to sleep and a room they could shelter in during some of the blizzards was the minimum she could do to repay them for their kindness.

The competent sorceress had used her knowledge of ancient buildings combined with her powers to repair and fill in the worst of the gaps in the old stone walls. She had paid for the supplies to reinforce most of the crumbling supports and had strengthened failing walls, all things the owner of the fortress should have been attending to but was too preoccupied to address.

The young woman and the servants had stuffed straw, mixed with mud or moss, into the remaining openings to tighten things up further. She had assisted them in fixing the leaking windows and drafty doors. Together, they had continued to improve conditions bit by bit, but there was a lot left to be done.

<hr />

Since De'Aire Chateau was always cold, Ki'ara had been determined that the elderly staff should have at least one place where they could get warm and take refuge during the worst of the storms. Therefore, one of Ki'ara's first priorities had been to make sure that the kitchen, located in the basement, would stay cozy no matter how much the wind howled outside.

Ki'ara's repairs had saved all their lives the first winter she spent there. An especially fierce blizzard had battered the fortress for more than two weeks. During those days, the temperature in the castle had continued to fall steadily, a little more with each passing minute.

The old building had literally frozen from outside in, and the sound of cracking rock had been terrifying. With every hour, the ice crept further in, covering walls and many a surface. Even Argulf's sheltered chambers became too frosty to occupy.

Only the kitchen had remained warm thanks to Ki'ara's repairs and her magic. She and the servants had quickly taken to sleeping there. Before long, the usually so aloof wizard had decided to join them. Naturally, he had claimed the best spot right next to the hearth for himself and, he had brought his most important experiments with him.

On most days, the atmosphere in the castle was strained and unhappy. Due to his complete disregard of their persons, the servants had no loyalty to Argulf. Most of them despised the selfish man. They had shared with Ki'ara that the upkeep of the fortress had never been on the sorcerer's priority list. When he had moved in, he had taken care of a few things, but since then, he had wholly neglected the castle.

From what Ki'ara had been able to fathom, shortly after arriving at De'Aire Chateau, Argulf had gotten involved in a mysterious project. He had kept it hidden from everyone, including his student. All that secrecy had made the young lady more than a little suspicious right from the start.

Ki'ara remembered having so many questions shortly after beginning her apprenticeship. Why was the wizard acting so peculiar? And, of what nature were his endeavors? Since he was so far away from civilization and the law, was it possible that Argulf had crossed the line? Was he practicing the forbidden arts? Could that be the reason he was so obsessed? Could he be exploring some evil enchantments to increase his own power? To make more of a name for himself?

Argulf considered himself an authority in all things magic. Within a month, Ki'ara had concluded that it would be just like him to somehow self-justify some abhorrent experiments. She had come to believe that the conjurer's lack of a moral compass made it entirely possible that he was casting spells that had been outlawed for excellent reasons.

On those occasions when Argulf forgot about her, Ki'ara had sensed a muted air of wrongness emanating from his private laboratory. The usually sloppy man had even cleaned up after himself making it impossible for her to determine the exact nature of his enchantments.

After the first such occurrence a couple of weeks after her arrival, Ki'ara had decided that it would be prudent to keep her eyes open, be cautious, and remain alert at all times.

The elderly servants were just as wary of Argulf and had been immensely grateful for Ki'ara's assistance. In turn, they did anything possible to ensure that she was as contented as they could make her. On her very first day at the castle, the young woman had been invited down to the kitchen. At that time, it was the only marginally warm room in the entire chateau. After riding for days in the cold mountain air, the girl had appreciated even that small amount of comfort.

From then on, she had shared the servants' daily meals. Ki'ara had loved the hot cup of chocolate that was always waiting for her after her work on the castle was done, and she appreciated the company. In a way, she was less lonely here than she had been at her home. She would miss the easy camaraderie which had developed between her and her new friends over the months.

Argulf was surly and no pleasure to be around. He would have never even considered sharing a meal with his lowly student. Therefore, Ki'ara would have been terribly isolated had she not had people to talk to, to eat with. It had made the young lady feel less alone and part of a sort of family. The retainers, in turn, had made sure that the girl understood that she had been adopted as one of their own. She had always been welcome among them.

Nobody had cared that she was a sorceress as well as a highborn lady or that she was much younger than they. The housekeeper, Milla, a woman well up there in years, had quickly taken to treating their lord's apprentice like a cherished granddaughter. She had been the one who had always fixed those delightful cups of hot chocolate.

Being part of an extended family again had felt wonderful to Ki'ara and had reminded her of happier days. Life had been so full of fun and joy before her parents' departure. Having people who loved her had warmed the young woman's heart and had made being away from the Highlands that much more bearable.

Leaving her elderly friends behind was one of the things which dampened her delight about the upcoming departure. Ki'ara would miss them sorely and knew that they felt the same about her. She was determined that someday, when she had a home of her own, she would find a way to repay these compassionate people for all the kindness and love they had shown her.

Chapter 2

The Zidhe

Thinking of the Highlands and Argulf reminded Ki'ara of her ancestors. She was a Zidarian, part human, part Zidhe. People like the greedy wizard had been the reason the fey had settled in the far north and why they and the other Highlanders wanted little to do with the rest of the world.

The more the young lady traveled, the more she appreciated her home. Their society was very different compared to the other places she had been. In her opinion, clans were a wonderful thing, as was the connection her people had to the land. Ki'ara felt truly blessed that the Highlanders had managed to preserve and safeguard their unique way of life. Her thoughts drifted to the tales from her childhood.

Long ago, the Zidhe or Le'aanan, also called elves or fairies, were scattered all over the Arillian Continent. The largest number of them resided in the more temperate and fertile regions. Here they built beautiful cities and created a thriving society. Being kind of heart and generous, they invited the other races to join them. For a long time, elves, dwarves, humans, giants, and a few others coexisted in relative peace.

The Le'aanan gladly shared the bountiful lands and their cities with this multitude of different folk, all living and working side by side. Treaties were signed, and rules laid out to help keep order among these varied peoples. A pact was endorsed in which everyone agreed to help each other and to pull together in times of need.

For the greater good of all, the Zidhe used their magic abilities to shape the world around them. They were responsible for much of the planting, growing, and harvesting. Their farms supplied fruits and vegetables to the other races, and the healers among them provided any medicinal assistance they could to the sick and injured. In return, the elves received whatever available goods they required.

At that time, the cold and barren northern reaches, including the Mystic Highlands, were only sparsely occupied. They had become home to those who preferred living away from the hustle and bustle of everyday life as well as those who just did not fit into a peaceful society. Life was hard for those individuals.

Matters were much different further south. Here, money played no role, and the barter system worked well for the growing civilization. Taking care of all the farming would have been too much for the elves all by themselves. They were assisted by individuals from several races who had an interest in agriculture and wanted to learn from their knowledgeable associates.

Having such an intimate connection with the world and all its creatures made it abhorrent to the fairies to kill another living, breathing being. They wanted no part of it, even if it was for the good of some of their neighbors. Since the Le'aanan did not partake in animal flesh, their helpers ran the ranches and handled the raising and slaughtering of livestock.

The elves would, however, assist with the healing of an injured beast in times of need. They hated to see anything suffer, person or animal alike. More often than not, the rehabilitated creature ended up spending the rest of its life on one of the Le'aanans' farms as a spoiled pet, something the other races observed with amusement.

For many centuries, the peaceful coexistence was an ideal state for the Zidhe and their fellow citizens, but eventually, things began to change. At first, the differences were subtle and almost too imperceptible to notice. With each passing year, however, the underlying discontent among the sworn allies grew.

There were few births among the elves. Being immortal, the fairies did not procreate as quickly as most of their shorter-lived brethren did. As time went by, the populations of the other races steadily increased. Soon, they vastly outnumbered the Zidhe in their own cities as well as out on the farms.

One of those allies who multiplied the fastest were the humans. They were also the most aggressive with their demands for more food and housing as well as frequently the least prone to help in return. The other races had a hard time keeping up with all the goods needed, and this caused resentment to gradually rise.

With so many individuals surrounding them, the Zidhe began to feel more and more crowded. They sensed the growing disgruntlement, and it made them progressively more uncomfortable. After several violent incidents, the healers among them started to withdraw into some of the more secure buildings in the centers of their cities, and the elves out in the country moved to those farms which were easier to defend. They left their helpers in charge of the others. The Le'aanan no longer felt safe.

༺✦༒✦༻

The buildings the Zidhe had erected were graceful and beautiful to behold. The elves had constructed their cities on hills so that they could be seen for miles around. The houses whitewashed facades shone brilliantly in the sunshine and were a magnificent sight even from a distance.

The pink and white marble used for some of the walls glowed and had been shaped into intricate designs by the Le'aanans' magic. Ornate gas lanterns lit up the streets, and the stunning gardens surrounding the dwellings were lush and full of flowers. The greens and rich hues of the blooms contrasted pleasantly with the light-colored residences.

༺✦༒✦༻

With the Zidhe's withdrawal, this began to change. Just as soon as the elves vacated one building, it was taken over by the growing masses. This, in turn, made the fairies even more uncomfortable, and more of them moved to Le'aanan occupied sectors. Soon there where entire blocks held solely by humans and the other races.

Within weeks, these sections of the cities began to decline. The love and care which had imbued the houses with their radiance began to fade. In the yards, the vegetation died of neglect or was killed off to make room for the new inhabitants' things.

It did not take long for the once glorious neighborhoods to start resembling overcrowded slums. Unhappiness and crime gained a firm foothold in those areas. Hunger was not far behind.

༺✦༒✦༻

With the continued decline of the existing order, the once prosperous society commenced unraveling.

According to the ancient agreement, the fairies and their helpers took care of the fields and livestock in return for other goods. They were the ones who organized the supply of food for their allies.

With the alteration of the populace's composition, however, the other races began to see the deliverance of sustenance as their right and not as an exchange of services. To the detriment of the Le'aanan and their associates, the barter system their society had been built on began to break down.

Once, each able-bodied individual, except for the very young, had contributed wares or labor. This had changed with the steady growth of the populations, especially the human one. There had been enough food available to carry a few extra mouths for a while and plenty of people to do all the work but no longer.

The surplus had allowed parents to pamper their adolescent children, and many of them became overindulged. Not having to worry about where to get their next meal left some of the young ones with time on their hands. They became involved in other activities besides learning a skill. For them, the pursuit of pleasure and ease continually gained in importance.

With each passing year, more of the fledgling generations lost interest in the trade of their parents. Valuable knowledge was no longer handed down from father to son or mother to daughter.

Skills were lost, and the maintenance of the general infrastructure fell by the wayside. The breakdown of the system had truly begun.

Thinking back to those days of old and the fate of the once thriving society, Ki'ara thought it incredibly sad that it, along with most of those once magnificent cities, was in ruins now. She had traveled through some of the areas and had been stunned by the beauty of what was left of the ancient architecture. She would have loved to have seen these buildings in their glory. What a sight they must have been!

Chapter 3

Argulf the Great or How to Best a Wizard

Standing at the rail of her balcony, Ki'ara's thoughts wandered back to her present situation. Before long, the events of the night before came to her mind. That nightmare had left a lasting impression, and she shuddered at the mere memory of that terrible dream. It had taken her a long time to calm down once she had awoken, and just the recollection was enough to make her physically ill to her stomach.

Ki'ara had been genuinely grateful that she had not been alone. As the minutes had ticked by, the loud purring of her large friend had done much to soothe the young woman. The horror of the nightmare had started to fade, and with it, the pain of losing Conall yet once again. The gut-wrenching sobs and shudders had begun to slowly subside.

After a while, the closeness of the animal pushed tightly against her had done its magic. Ki'ara had grown calmer with each passing moment. What a horrible dream that had been! It had felt so terribly real! Could it have been spawned by her brooding about what would happen once she got back to the Highlands? Or, had it been something else?

Feeling her apprehension, the cat rubbed up against her. Absentmindedly, the young woman started running her fingers through Taryn's soft fur. His purr increased in volume, echoing through the fog. She stood there for a very long time, her unseeing eyes on the shapes created by the drifting mist, her hands gently stroking her friend.

Ki'ara was deep in thought. She was trying to make sense of the nightmare which had shaken her so severely. Could it be an omen of things to come? A warning? She hoped not, but fear gnawed on her insides. The dream had left a lingering feeling of unease and had affected her to the very core of her being.

It had been bad enough that Ragnald had broken her engagement to Conall and had forbidden her contact with the one Zidarian she had intended to spend her life with. At least, as long as the man she loved was alive, Ki'ara still had the hope that someday things would change, that there could be a chance of sharing his life, to become Lady StCloud.

The sorceress had been born into one of the nine ruling Highland clans, the MacClairs. The StClouds were their immediate neighbors to the south. Even though they were no longer royalty, the families were highly revered, and the lords held enormous power over their people. Most did not abuse this, and exceptions, like her oldest brother Ragnald, were rare.

Every Zidarian was intimately connected to the land, and the nine reigning families had the most magic in their blood among all the Highlanders, an inheritance from their Zidhe ancestors. Being part elf allowed them to live for more than a thousand years. They were, therefore, for all intents and purposes, immortal.

When Ki'ara had reached her twenty-first year, she had physically stopped aging. As did all the mix breed children, she would continue to mature emotionally and, under the usual circumstances, would have remained under parental or a guardian's guidance until she reached her 30s birthday.

Being a Zidarian, her body would remain healthy and full of vitality until well after she turned one thousand. To spend all this time without Conall was something Ki'ara could not even consider. Just the idea that something could happen to the one person whom she so desperately longed for filled the young lady with immeasurable dread.

Spending an eternity without the possibility of being with Conall was an existence without light, a life without love. It was bad enough that she was forbidden to see him and was continually being sent so far away from him and the Highlands!

The girl could still hardly believe that her brother had sent her here to this desolate place! Had he known what this castle was like? Or had he been deceived as well? From what Ragnald had told her, he had thought Argulf to be a first-class conjurer, and that had been his reason for hiring him.

The reality was much different. The master of the castle, the wizard Argulf, was one of the most self-centered, ignorant, and conceited people Ki'ara had ever met. In the magic mirror, he had appeared regal, tall, and imposing. The resume she had been shown had been filled with impressive achievements and abilities, most likely figments of the overactive imagination of a somewhat delusional man.

When Ki'ara arrived, the old sorcerer had tried hard to give off an air of exaltedness and grandeur. He had even worn shoes with blocks glued to the bottoms to make himself look taller and more majestic. The wizard's floor-length robe had been marginally clean but so wrinkled that it looked like he had slept in it. His frequent tripping over the hem had also made him appear even less dignified.

Argulf's had attempted to dye his stringy, greasy mane, but, somehow, the magic had gone wrong, and the hair had looked more purple than black. The beady, dark eyes he had shrewdly scrutinized Ki'ara with had reminded the girl of a rat. The wizard's beak of a nose had purple veins all over it from drinking too much. His mouth with its thin lips had been turned down into a frown, and his face set in a permanent scowl.

The image she had seen in the mirror had looked nothing like this and had most likely been a glamour. Once he had started talking, Ki'ara had realized very quickly that Argulf was nothing but a fraud and not a very nice man either. When she boldly met his gaze, the wizard's stare had turned even colder and more calculating. He definitely did not like to be challenged!

All in all, the short, pompous man had reminded the young woman eerily of an overgrown rodent. If he could not even get a simple spell like his hair color right, he had most definitely misrepresented himself. Ki'ara had figured correctly that Ragnald would be furious when he found out.

The MacClair had called to check up on things. Not that he really cared about Ki'ara's well-being, he just liked to remind her who was in charge. As if she could forget that! Ragnald had talked to Mathus, the tutor he had sent along to keep her in line. The irate man had given her brother an earful about the terrible conditions he was being subjected to.

Ragnald had been livid, and Ki'ara had almost been allowed to return home. The wizard had chased them all from the room and had talked to her brother alone. Somehow, Argulf and the MacClair came to an agreement, and she had been ordered to stay.

It had taken little time for Ki'ara to comprehend the true extent of the situation at De'Aire Chateau. She had observed everything around her with great interest, and within minutes, she knew beyond a shadow of a doubt that life at this castle would not be pleasant.

The young lady had realized that the egotistical wizard did not care how his people fared or that the castle was falling apart around him. He was so busy with the various magical exploits that he paid little attention to anything else.

Most days, Argulf had kept his new student, already an accomplished sorceress, busy with trivial tasks. To her exasperation, he had treated her as he would any lowly apprentice.

The peevish wizard had made Ki'ara fetch and carry ingredients for his experiments, clean up after him, and see to his comforts. She had actually been somewhat amused when one of the first things he had ordered her to do had been to fix the color of his unkempt mane.

The young woman had turned his hair a beautiful shade of black with an ease that had set the magician's teeth on edge. Argulf had hated her instantaneously since he had spent days trying to fix the problem.

As she had anticipated, life at the fortress had been far from enjoyable. Ki'ara had enough understanding of people to realize that the cantankerous man was unable to face himself and his own shortcomings. Therefore, if something went amiss, it had to be someone else's fault.

He, after all, was infallible and never did anything wrong!

Every time an enchantment had not gone according to plan, which was fairly often, Argulf had yelled at Ki'ara. He had blamed her for the mistake, even if she had not actually been present!

⁘

During the first few months Ki'ara had spent at De'Aire Chateau, Argulf had entirely ignored that he was being paid to teach her. He knew that he had agreed to take her on as his trainee but could not bring himself to share his knowledge with her.

Instead of training her, the spiteful wizard had treated Ki'ara like his maid. Argulf had gotten a perverse satisfaction from watching her clean up after him instead of assisting. Having the girl make his bed and mop the floors was also great fun as was sending her hustling to fetch him all kinds of items. Most of the things the peevish man sent his apprentice for were of no consequence, and he did not even need them.

Eventually, however, Argulf had figured that for his own good, he needed to make at least some pretense of teaching the woman. Her brother was an important and rather powerful man and would not take it well if he was getting nothing in return for his gold.

From then on, the wizard had allowed Ki'ara to assist him in simple spells but had sent her away every time he worked on something more complicated. Argulf was determined to keep his student back as much as possible for as long as he could get away with. From what he had seen, she knew enough magic already!

Why would he want to add to her knowledge so that she could surpass him? Not that there was much chance of that, but why take the risk?

⁘

Convinced of his own preeminence and cleverness, Argulf never realized that Ki'ara was learning from perusing his library as well as from watching him. Even clearing his cluttered workbenches supplied her with valuable information since the sorcerer was sloppy at best. The young lady had enough magical proficiency to draw her own conclusions from the spills she disposed of every day.

When Ragnald had demanded a progress report, Argulf had decided that he needed to test his pupil. Naturally, he had expected Ki'ara to fail since the exam, approved by the brother, had consisted of spells the wizard had not yet taught her. He had intended to claim that the young woman was just slow and needed more time. Why give up the goose which laid the golden eggs? Having money for extras was nice!

As usual, things had not gone as planned. Ki'ara had proven to be much more skilled than Argulf had anticipated. Any task he had set her, she had completed perfectly and with ease. This had perplexed and infuriated the vain man.

How could she know these complex enchantments? Not from him, that was for sure! How had this stupid girl managed to advance so fast and without him to help her?

When the wizard had been contacted by magic mirror a few days later, he had realized that Ragnald was not overly happy with the results of the test either. The lord had not voiced this directly, but Argulf had seen the fury in the MacClair's eyes. Did the Highlander not want his sister home any time soon? The conniving magician had instantly seen an advantage.

Acting on his hunch, Argulf had begun to lay out a long course of study, enough for many more years. Ragnald had started to look more and more pleased. The two had agreed that such a comprehensive education would benefit the young lady immensely. She was immortal, after all, and had plenty of time.

As part of the deal, the lord had insisted that all topics had to be covered in as much detail as possible. Ragnald claimed that he wanted his sister to be thoroughly familiar with each subject and all facets of magic. Nothing less would do for a lady of her standing, and the knowledge would greatly benefit the clan.

The wizard was no fool but rather sly as a fox when it came to looking out for himself. Having Ki'ara at De'Aire Chateau was a definite plus. Argulf had every intention to keep her at the castle for as long as he could. He had deemed the agreed-upon curriculum safe. After all, it was only a drop in the bucket of his vast knowledge!

Since he was being paid to do so, the sorcerer believed that it would not hurt to share at least a small amount of his immense wisdom with the girl. Especially since Ragnald had agreed to increase the monthly stipend and add a hefty bonus for every year his sister stayed at the castle!

⁓⁂⁓

After his successful negotiations with the MacClair, Argulf had poured himself a couple of drinks to celebrate. He had felt like the cat which had eaten a canary or maybe even two. The sorcerer had been so thrilled!

He had been convinced that he had managed to secure a steady income for many years to come, something which had escaped him so far. If he had read the feelings of the lord correctly, there was a good chance that he might manage to keep the girl indefinitely!

⁓⁂⁓

Feeling like a real teacher for the first time in years, Argulf had gone over the curriculum with Ki'ara. Acting duly impressed, she had agreed with him when he told her that it would take a long time to cover it all. The young woman's respectful and almost deferential behavior had fed the wizard's ego even more.

Feeling very full of himself, the sorcerer had boasted that this course of study was only a fraction of his enormous store of information and that not even her long life would be enough to learn all that he knew.

The lady had looked at Argulf in awe and had told him how lucky she felt to have been sent to such an educated enchanter. He had entirely missed that she was being sarcastic.

✦

Ki'ara had acquired good people-skills over the years, something which served her admirably now. She had been aware of both her brother's and Argulf's motivations and had no intention of spending one day more than she absolutely had to in this dismal place.

The girl had decided that the true state of her competency had to be a secret until she was ready to reveal it and had learned all she cared to.

The young woman had known only too well that pompous and self-important people are easily manipulated. All one had to do was feed their egos, give them appreciation and admiration, and avoid criticism of any sort at all cost.

Using the insights she had gained over the years, Ki'ara had quickly come up with a strategy for dealing with Argulf. The man was exceedingly vain and loved to hear himself talk. She had decided to use his weaknesses against him.

✦

Watching the shapes in the mist, Ki'ara remembered one of the stories her father had told her. Long ago, her ancestors had also found themselves in a situation where they had to deceive those around them.

Had the elves not done so, they might still be virtually enslaved by their once friends and might even have become prisoners in the lands to the south.

Without the Zidhe, the Highlands would not be the remarkable place they had become, and Ki'ara would have never been born.

Chapter 4

The Exodus

Every Zidarian child was told the tale of the elves' flight from the south. Their elders felt that it was vital to keep that history alive so that it would never repeat itself. Ki'ara had always loved the stories and had pestered her parents endlessly to tell them to her again and again. They now gave her solace and helped to lessen her guilt.

As her people's history showed, at times, deception was a necessary evil to assure one's survival. This did not necessarily make one a bad person. The situation just left one no better option, and the price for a direct confrontation was beyond what one was willing to pay.

Had Ki'ara directly confronted Argulf and her brother, she would have been banished from the Highlands, would have been left homeless, and penniless. A high cost for rebelling against her guardian. Life as she had known it would have been over. For the elves so long ago, it would have meant war with their neighbors, possible enslavement, and the death of many a person. Peace-loving and kind, this was not something they were willing to chance.

The Zidhe were compassionate and caring individuals. They did not like to see anyone in distress, hurt, or going hungry. Therefore, they took on more and more of the burden of keeping their once thriving society healthy and fed. To their dismay, the situation continued to deteriorate with no change in sight.

To the beleaguered elves, it seemed that their once friends were growing progressively more spoiled and lazy. What upset them the most, however, was the squandering of food. A fair part of the fruits of their labor was being wasted and left to rot out in the streets while fresh goods were being demanded.

With so many mouths to provide for and so little respect for what was being supplied, resources became increasingly stretched. The Le'aanan expended more of their magic to encourage plants to grow faster and the fields to remain fertile. They had to work harder and harder and could have used additional help.

The Zidhe's pleas for assistance fell on deaf ears, and the misuse of food continued unchecked. The elves and their helpers were dealing with more labor and a decreasing workforce. Some of their aides grew tired of the hard work and quit. One day, this reached a point where the Le'aanan could no longer keep up. A storm had wiped out a good part of the harvest, and there were no reserves left.

All of a sudden, many of the less prudent folk went hungry. The discontent, which had been smoldering just below the surface, erupted in full force. The ties, which had bonded these varied peoples together, finally snapped. Each group was blaming the other for the debacle. The first race to exit in disgust were the dwarves. It did not take long for others to follow, leaving the cities mostly to the humans and the few Zidhe remaining within.

Even with fewer mouths to feed, the situation did not improve. Nothing the elves did was enough to please their ever more demanding neighbors. Dissatisfaction grew among the masses, and the Zidhe were treated with less and less respect. They were being pushed into a position of servitude instead of being the masters of their own lands.

Adding to this already volatile situation were the problems created by the exodus of most of the other races. A vacuum in the administrations of the realms and cities had been created by the departure of some of the previous government heads. Suddenly, no one was sure who was in charge.

✦⋆✦

Few of the Zidhe had ever been involved in the running of things. Their trusted allies had dealt with this obligation. Therefore, they were unaware that a change was occurring, especially since they were busy dealing with the feeding of the remaining population and the ministering of the sick. The elves did not realize that there was a problem until it was too late.

A scramble for power had taken place. In the end, a mostly human ruling class filled the open positions. One of their first actions was to seize control of the dispersal of food. A new barter system, governed by a few enterprising and powerful individuals, was introduced. It was corrupt from day one.

The self-made lords began to take control of the towns. They started to hoard goods at the expense of the common people. The more they amassed, the greedier they seemed to become. To survive, one had to stay in their good graces, which was often not easy to do.

Anyone who desired to eat had to comply with the bidding of this new ruling class. The chiefs handed out food as payment for those jobs they wanted to have done. In the process, they gained more and more power. Weaker and unwanted individuals ended up hungry and being shoved to the fringes of the social order.

With the change in administrators, greed and selfishness had firmly established itself in the once so civilized society. This gave rise to poverty and oppression and pushed many to the brink of starvation.

Being this close to all this seething humanity with its squabbles, problems, and incessant demands finally became too much for the Zidhe who loved nature and harmony. All they wanted was to live in peace once again, far away from their neighbors.

Due to the treatment and threats they were receiving, the elves had lost all trust in the people they had once considered friends. They called a secret council, the first one of its kind they had ever held in all those long years. Extensive precautions were taken to ensure that what they were about to discuss would not reach unwanted ears.

The Le'aanan were intelligent and intuitive. At the meeting, they examined and evaluated their present situation carefully. Being keenly aware of the strengths, shortcomings, as well as the needs of their neighbors, they came to the valid conclusion that they were in trouble.

The talents of the Zidhe were vital to the continuously growing society. They and their trainees were the ones doing most of the labor. The elves figured that, if they stated their intent to move on, it would not go over too well.

The role they played in this floundering society was far too important for anyone to want them to leave. The Zidhe could not even blame their neighbors. They had allowed themselves to be pushed into a position where they commanded little respect. The humans would not want them to depart and might end up forcing the elves to stay against their will.

The fairies felt enslaved enough as it was. They and their devoted helpers did all the farming and ranching. As of late, they did so mostly without receiving the goods they required for themselves and to keep things running smoothly. They resented being made to feel that their requests were a huge imposition instead of part of the bargain.

More and more often, there was not even a thank you forthcoming when deliveries were made. It was all taken for granted. Since the elves were grossly outnumbered, however, they needed a plan.

It took a lot of discussion, but finally, a course of action was hit upon that all the Zidhe could agree on. They would use their neighbors' weaknesses against them and in turn, help those who now found themselves oppressed and despised.

Just as quietly as they had arrived, the Le'aanans' leaders slipped back out of the council and set in motion the events which would ultimately lead to their freedom.

As part of their plan, the Zidhe looked for the poorest of the poor, the ones oppressed and desperate enough to grab at any straw offered to them. Those who were willing, they brought out to the farms and into the healing centers as their new students. They gave hope to these outcasts and gained their loyalty by treating them with respect and kindness.

The elves and their associates began teaching some of these unfortunates how to fertilize the fields, when to harvest the crops, and how to take care of the livestock. Others they trained in the healing arts. To win their liberty, the Le'aanan shared much of their wisdom.

As their apprentices became more proficient, the Le'aanan out in the country prepared to surreptitiously disappear. On the agreed upon date, the Zidhe simply slipped away in the dark of the night. They used their magic to pass through the lands unnoticed and began the long trek to the far north.

Those of the elves' helpers who wished to remain took over the farms. The process went smoothly, with barely a hitch. Life continued as it had for many a generation, just the individuals running things were different. Their neighbors never even noticed the change and remained clueless for the time being.

Exiting the cities was a little more tricky. It would be easy for the humans to confine the fairies within the walls of the towns or in their homes if they caught wind of their plans. Then, only the Zidhe's magic and possibly the use of force would allow them to leave. Harming others was not something they wanted to do. This escape, therefore, required especially careful planning.

In preparation for their departure, the Le'aanan had been marginalizing their role as healers by passing on most of the medical chores to their students. This ensured that their absence would go unnoticed, at least for a while.

Just to make absolutely certain, however, and to give the majority of the Zidhe a chance to get cleanly away, a few individuals volunteered to stay behind for a bit.

During an especially violent downpour, created and fed by the magic of the fairies, most of the remaining Zidhe quietly walked out of the gates unseen. Some of their helpers had volunteered to assist and were hidden close by with horses and wagons. Using their powers to move undetected through the tempestuous twilight, the group of healers started on their clandestine migration to the far away Highlands.

Only one or two of the more prominent Le'aanan were left in the cities to keep up appearances. This allowed their friends and families to get a good head start. After a few days, those individuals' time to depart came as well. One cloudy, moonless night, the last of the Zidhe slipped away to follow the others. Only their most powerful sorcerer lingered to make a deal with the humans as well as the rest of the races.

The elves' helpers and their trainees, who had been looked down upon and despised by their peers, were now fully in charge. They suddenly found themselves with the keys to the coffer.

From the Le'aanan, these individuals had not only learned how to take care of the fields and the animals, but they had also been shown how to defend what was now theirs. Faced with their greedy neighbors' demands, the elves' co-workers were very grateful that they had been taught the skills necessary to protect themselves and their homes.

Many of the homesteads were now virtual fortresses, ready for a siege, and in a position to barter. Their new owners were determined to stand their ground and to keep others from oppressing them ever again. The Zidhe had made sure that their grateful replacements had bargaining power.

Most of the food procurement, except fishing and some hunting, was now in the hands of the elves' aides, and their neighbors' lives depended on these farmers, ranchers, and healers doing their jobs well. The knowledge and training these underdogs had been gifted with had gained them status and the Zidhe their freedom.

Several days later, most of the Le'aanan were safely away. Only their leader, Geradian, remained. He was the strongest and wisest of them all with amazing skills and capabilities. The Zidhe's connections to the land went deep and, unbeknownst to even his people, much of its magic would be accompanying him to their new home in the north.

The elf was a tall, handsome man with long, dark hair and a slender build. His bright green eyes were piercing and seemed to see right to the very core of a person. Not much got past him. Geradian was highly intelligent and intuitive but also kind and compassionate.

What made him so ultimately suited for dealing with the elves' once friends, however, was his ability as a shrewd negotiator and an astute reader of others' emotions. Many years of experience as a circumspect leader had taught him much.

Being few and able to work better with the land than their once allies, the fairies did not require as large an area to thrive. Their magic allowed them to flourish where not many others could.

The elves had enough of their old comrades. All they wanted from their former associates was an agreement to be left in peace from now on at the places of the Zidhe's choosing.

⁖⁘⋈⁘⁖

Geradian was not happy that his people had to depart these beautiful and warm environs because of the humans' greed and corruption. This made him so much more determined to secure a home where the Le'aanan would never have to leave again.

As the representative of the Zidhe, Geradian called all the races together for a council. It was to be held at the next new moon, on a flat hill far away from any of the large cities.

The shrewd man had chosen a place well out in the plains, surrounded by farms and ranches loyal to him. If trouble brewed, he had an army.

Word of this meeting was carried across all the lands, and grudgingly the chiefs appeared. After dealing with some initial protests, Geradian cleverly sold the other races on the elves' desires. He cunningly gained some crucial concessions by appealing to his former associates' pride as well as their greed.

Wanting only the Highlands and some small sections far to the north, Geradian proposed that the other races could share the lands to the south. The Zidhe would relinquish any claim to these regions and make their main home in the far northern reaches of the Mystic Isles. That area was a cold and barren place of little value for farming and such.

Most of the assembled folk regarded these ranges as uninhabitable and had no objections to the Le'aanan taking them over. Only the humans, as the main beneficiaries of the fairies' presence, tried to object. Geradian's assurances that the homesteads were in good hands and that healers and herbalists had been trained to replace his people appeased them a little but only for a brief moment.

Once the land issue had been settled, Geradian dropped the next bombshell. The Le'aanans' insistence that the farmers and ranchers were to be treated with respect and goods bought from them and not stolen infuriated the realms' crooked administrators once again. They were too used to taking whatever they wanted and deeply resented this encroachment on their total control.

Having to make such a concession was more than a little unwelcome. Some of the enraged officials started shouting at the elf and anyone attempting to calm them.

They tried to convince some of the chiefs to take their side and stand with them against the proposal brought forth by the Zidhe. This was in vain, however, since most of the other leaders secretly rejoiced in their plight.

The power-hungry thugs were finally forced into compliance with all the terms of the deal. In the end, they not only lost control of the food supply but also of significant portions of what they saw as their lands. A binding agreement was hammered out and signed, and a majority vote ratified the terms.

Having achieved his objective, it was time for Geradian to follow his people. Taking only what he could carry, the elf, along with a few of his associates, began the long trek north. He would miss the sunshine and the warm weather, but not most of the people he had once called his friends.

The humans happily moved into any houses left vacant by the departure of the Zidhe. They established regular markets where they could trade their goods and offer their services. Things went reasonably well until the increase in mouths needing to be fed caused trouble again.

The dwarves, tired of all that upheaval, hid under the mountains and had little to do with the rest. They had enough of the squabbling and petty disagreements. Most of the other races also kept to themselves. Life went on, and folks adjusted.

It took only a generation or two before the kind magical beings who had built the once magnificent cities the throng of humanity now inhabited began to pass from memory. They and the other races who had once shared these lands started to slip into legend.

That all the peoples had once lived side by side and shared a common interest, and a thriving civilization, was soon all but forgotten.

Ki'ara had always felt that this loss of a large part of the south's history was infinitely regrettable.

Chapter 5

Necessary Deception

To Argulf's surprise, Ki'ara had turned out to be an exceptional student, easy to get along with, and a real pleasure to teach. She was respectful, paid keen attention, and never reacted with boredom to even his most lengthy lectures. When he tested her, she passed easily but never with the stellar marks she had gotten on her first exam.

After a couple of weeks, the wizard had started to feel at ease during their lessons. Before long, Argulf had even revised his opinion of his pupil. He had decided that she was nowhere near as brilliant and as competent a sorceress as he had first believed. As a result, he had stopped seeing Ki'ara as a threat to himself and had discontinued his practice of choosing his words as judiciously.

One of his biggest weaknesses was that Argulf loved to hear himself talk. Without being aware of what he was doing, the sorcerer divulged more and more of the knowledge he had so carefully hoarded and had been so protective of. Having this young woman hang on every one of his words was a balm to the wizard's soul, and it made him feel very important and powerful.

As a result of the girl's undivided attention, Argulf puffed himself up and became even more self-important. He would strut back and forth in front of Ki'ara's desk like a peacock, continually looking for more things to say to impress his eager student. He was completely unaware that he was being skillfully played.

Believing that the girl was nowhere near intelligent enough to make sense of his cryptic references and hints, he went into more detail about his various projects. He never even realized how often he unwittingly slipped up and supplied Ki'ara with information on his illegal experiments.

Knowingly, Argulf would have never told a soul what he was up to in his secret chamber. He kept the room under lock and key at all times. No one was permitted to enter unless invited. His student had been allowed in to clean, but only on rare occasions, and under the sorcerer's strict supervision.

The wizard never suspected that this and the secrets he had inadvertently shared were enough to give the brilliant young lady a general idea what he had been up to.

⸙

Ki'ara had learned long ago that she could learn a lot from just listening. People usually ended up telling her much more than they intended. Often, it took very little to encourage them, just a well-placed question here and there, a few thoughtful comments and an attentive facial expression. Over the years, she had perfected this to an art.

The young lady would imperceptibly guide the conversation with carefully phrased questions and give the appropriate response at just the right time. This had worked well on Argulf and had gotten the chatty wizard off on the desired tangent time after time. Her rapt attention did the rest, and he just kept on explaining the subject in excruciating details.

Argulf would have been aghast had he realized what he was doing, but Ki'ara was an expert at steering the dialog back to a safe topic. He never noticed his slip-ups. The haughty wizard had been supplying the girl with more than enough information on his experiments, and she had no further desire to find out the details of the horrible things he had done.

If what the wizard had revealed about the nature of his most secret tests was correct, he had gone well beyond just occasionally crossing the line. He was practicing forbidden magic. Argulf would be arrested if anyone found out what he had done, and Ki'ara felt very strongly that he needed to be reported and stopped.

This was Frankonia and not the Highlands. The young sorceress was not sure of the best way to proceed or even who to talk to about putting an end to the atrocities, but she was determined to find out. The dark arts and their practitioners were something she disliked intensely since their disrespect for life went against everything she believed in.

Had Ki'ara been aware of the contents of the dungeons and the true scope of Argulf's crimes, she would have seen herself forced to take action right then.

It was part of Ki'ara's nature to be polite and friendly to people, even to such an overinflated and unpleasant person like Argulf. She believed in tolerance and in treating others with respect and kindness. There was little to like about the smug wizard, but to her, he was still a fellow living being and deserved fair handling. The necessity to mislead him to shorten her stay at the castle did not sit well with the lady.

Remaining at De'Aire Chateau for many more years, away from the Highlands, was not something Ki'ara had wanted to do. She had figured out what her brother and Argulf had agreed on and had devised her own strategy.

Good thing the arrogant wizard was not the most brilliant of people, or her plan would not have worked quite so easily. Without realizing it, Argulf was actually helping her to get back home. He might be a very unpleasant man and a criminal to boot, but Ki'ara had no liking for her chosen course of action.

Keeping the full range of her abilities from the sorcerer and getting him to talk by playing on his overinflated ego was something the girl would have preferred to avoid. It made her feel two-faced and untrue to herself. To appease her own conscience, she was extra friendly and helpful to the old scoundrel, something he took advantage of on a regular basis.

It felt wrong to treat the wizard such but the spells he had intended to teach her over the next few years, Ki'ara had learned in the first three months. Had Argulf caught on how rapidly she was learning and how much she was reading beside the books he gave her, life would have become exceedingly unpleasant very fast.

To achieve her goal of returning back to the Highlands, Ki'ara had to surpass Argulf in knowledge as well as in abilities. Her brother and the sorcerer had to be kept in the dark until the girl had managed to learn all that she wanted from the old wizard. Since he had an overinflated sense of his skills and no clue as to hers, it was not really all that difficult.

Deception like that was not to her taste, but it was the only viable option at her disposal since she was dealing with not just one but two men trying to keep her at De'Aire Chateau.

Ragnald had been Ki'ara's official guardian since her parents' departure from Seamuir Castle and Eastmuir, the MacClair clan's ancestral lands. Unfortunately, until very recently, this had placed him in complete control of her life.

Ki'ara had seen no other choice but to do what she was told. While her brother was in charge of her life, she had to obey him if she ever wanted to return to the Highlands and her home legally. The banishment which would have been the result of her defiance would have broken her heart.

It was, therefore, in her best interest to treat Argulf with deference, feed his immense ego, and not to let on the true extent of her powers, even if it did make her feel guilty that she was milking him for all of his legal magical knowledge.

The wizard was not the only one she needed an edge over, after all. The more power she had, the more she honed her skills, the better were her chances of surviving the next time Ragnald attacked her.

Argulf was most certainly not in the same class as her brother. He was nowhere near as cruel, at least not to her. Ki'ara had been able to get an occasional concession out of the sorcerer. He had backed down when she had really wanted something. Ragnald just did as he pleased.

The young lady had long since come to see that the old wizard was actually a very lonely, miserable, and misguided man. She did not think that he was even aware of the harm he was doing with his illegal spells. Often, Ki'ara had felt pity for him. He had so thrived on her attention.

Once the sorceress had gotten Argulf started on a subject, he had kept talking for hours. It had been easy to keep him engaged with some well-phrased questions and to elicit even more information.

To further her agenda, Ki'ara had made certain to always come across as innocent and a little naïve. She had realized that to achieve her objective of returning home, she had to remain as non-threatening as possible or Argulf would become aware that he was systematically telling her almost all that he knew.

Ki'ara could sense that there were secrets he was holding back, even darker things, but her gut had told her that this was information she would not care to have. She had made sure to gently redirect the wizard whenever he got started on those topics.

The fog around the keep had gotten thicker. Ki'ara could barely make out the door to her room from where she was standing on the balcony. She kind of enjoyed the sensation of just her and Taryn in this sea of white. There was something restful about it. Over the last two years, she had spent some of the precious minutes she had to herself observing this remarkable phenomenon.

Being part of nature for those few moments had helped her let go of the guilt she was feeling. At least, she had been able to be mostly herself around the servants, but she had decided to hide the true extent of her powers.

Not one of them would have ever voluntarily given her secret away, but, as Ki'ara well knew, Argulf had ways to extract what he wanted to hear. He also lacked empathy and compassion and would go to great length to get what he sought. The girl was confident that the vindictive wizard would gleefully pass any bit of information he could glean on to her brother.

Why could her family not act more like her friends here at De'Aire Chateau did? What had happened to

Ragnald to make him such an unpleasant man? Did her brother even feel love for anyone in his family or his clan? Maybe for Lyall, his closest sibling, but not for the rest, not even for his own father.

Ki'ara had been observing her guardian closely for years now. She had been trying to understand what had shaped Ragnald into such a cruel person. The more she had learned, the more wary she had grown. Of one thing she was absolutely sure. Her brother did not have her best interest at heart.

Chapter 6

Dawn of the Highlands

Thinking of Ragnald always made Ki'ara miss her parents and life as it used to be. She had a pleasant childhood and had been well-loved by Mikael and Ali'ana. How much had changed since then! The young woman's heart filled with longing to just live in peace. This brought her thoughts back to the Zidhe. The elves had to give up their beloved home to escape an untenable situation. Would her fate be similar?

The places the Le'aanan had asked for and were granted in the covenant were a few small outposts in the polar regions and the mostly uninhabited Mystic Highlands. These lands encompassed the northernmost parts of the Mystic Isles and included several adjacent islands.

The Highlands consisted mainly of barren hills and mountainous areas. Moss was by far the most predominant vegetation, and only some highly adapted animal and plant species called the place home. Few humanoid individuals had chosen to live there due to the harsh climate and dire conditions.

The Zidhe imbued chosen areas in these Highlands with their magic. In the very center of this remote place, in the vast caldera of a long-dormant volcano, they built their new city. Every fall for the first few years, a good number of the Le'aanan migrated back to the town from the outlying settlements. They spent most, or all, of the hostile winters in its welcoming shelter.

Using their ability to shape the world around them, the fairies created energy domes over some of the secluded valleys and the bowl-shaped crater. Tapping deep into the earth, they encouraged heat to rise and warm the frigid air. Soon these zones grew pleasantly balmy, and life became much easier for the hardworking elves.

The Le'aanan had carried specimen and seeds with them from their former homes and from along the way, which they planted in their sheltered spaces. They nurtured the sprouts and encouraged them to make this barren place their own. The somewhat hardier types of vegetation from just a bit south of the border, the elves bred to become stronger and more resilient so that they could survive outside the heated domes.

With each passing year, new plant species took root and began to grow and spread across the Highlands. Life gained a foothold in areas that had been barren or covered in moss until then. The soil of the region slowly improved, and the vegetation became stronger and increasingly more abundant.

When the first forests started to grow, they began to temper the once so extremely hostile climate. The few scattered animals which called this once forsaken place home began to thrive and multiply. For the first time since their creation, life started to prosper in the Highlands as well as on the adjacent islands.

The power, skill, and persistence of the Zidhe were such that they were able to achieve this despite the severe northern weather and the terrible winters. The areas of the Highlands where they had chosen to settle turned from desolate valleys and barren plains into prized fertile lands.

To make travel more comfortable during the long winter months, the elves decided to build roads protected by magic as well as tunnels that connected their outlying farms and settlements with the city.

The Le'aanans' society began to thrive once more.

Having lived in the pleasant and temperate regions further to the south, the Zidhe's new home was already close enough to the genuinely hostile polar regions for their taste. After their past experiences, however, many felt anxious that they had nowhere left to escape to. They were determined to never be caught unprepared again.

The Highlands had taken enough work and many years to make them habitable. Anything further north, including the places they had been assigned by the treaty, would be far worse. The elves were aware that it would take tremendous power, time, and ingenuity to flourish in an environment dominated by snow and ice for most of the year.

The Le'aanan could survive in the arctic but did not like the idea of living predominately under domes and in the limited areas where they could find a source of heat. To them, to be always in a shelter felt wrong. They needed to feel the wind on their faces, touch the soil, sit among the trees, and care for wild creatures.

Their connection to nature was vital for the elves, and most of them feared that they would end up feeling confined and cut off, that they would lose their link to the magic within them. Many believed that a place without forests and a multitude of animals and flowers would not feed their hearts and souls. It just was not home.

Geradian, always the voice of reason and able to see possibilities where others could not, finally had enough and proposed an expedition into the north. After their experience with the other races, he was determined to have a backup plan for his people just in case the unexpected occurred. The man was pleasantly surprised when, despite all that grumbling his elves had done, he immediately had a number of volunteers, among them his own wife, Jenna.

It took a few months to acquire and provision several sturdy boats. When all was in readiness, thirty years to the day after their arrival in the Highlands, Geradian sent some of his Le'aanan out to explore far up into the polar regions. Their mission was to evaluate the lands they had been granted and locate places which could be made habitable, were defensible, and had resources of some sort. An essential requirement was also that it had to be reasonably simple to hide the site. Banks of fog were an excellent ally for that.

The Le'aanan scouts ranged far and wide, and the most promising they found was an unnamed volcanic island a good way to the north. The ocean there was not as cold as they had expected. A strong current from the south brought warm water into these icy regions, moderating the weather for the coastal areas and making the land much more habitable than many of the locations they had thus far been to.

The isle also had plenty of fresh water as well as hot springs, and the sea around it was teeming with fish. Being of volcanic origin, the soil was rich and fertile, and there were many spots perfect for the placement of domes. Steam was issuing from the ground in some places which could be used for heating. The differences in ocean temperatures could be exploited to create a barrier of mist which would hide the island from possible invaders.

The Zidhe were charmed by this rugged and beautiful place, and they named it Nor'Dea. It had so genuinely appealed to the explorers who found it that they wanted to go back. Most of them volunteered to become part of the advance party. From their description, Geradian felt it would be ideal for creating a refuge, and his people agreed. It made the top of the list.

***

Some of the other scouts had also found places they liked, which fulfilled the requirements. The Le'aanan, therefore, picked five of the most promising spots. While continuing their work on the Highlands, they built outposts in each one of those locations. The elves decided that their highest priority, however, was to be given to the island Nor'Dea.

Domes were created over part of this landmass, and the steam from the volcanos used to heat them. Tunnels were blasted to allow for travel from one habitation to the other even in the depth of winter when ice and snow covered the region. Houses were built, and more Zidhe brought in to help with the project.

The second stage was the planting of trees and other vegetation. Within just a few years, whole forests grew in some of the domes. Others protected fields and farms and gave shelter to the imported animals.

The Le'aanan did everything they could to make all the sanctuaries on the island as pleasant as possible. They, however, were in for a welcome surprise. Not only was the isle beautiful and served their needs admirably, but it also had an additional benefit. For some unknown reason, those who stayed on Nor'Dea to help maintain the refuge found that their birthrate increased. That was huge!

After this momentous discovery, the number of volunteers who wished to help settle Nor'Dea soared. More homes were built to hold all these helpers. With time, the island became a popular destination for the more adventurous Zidhe as well as all those wanting a child.

Despite having their sanctuaries on the five outposts, the Le'aanan felt it was best to be prudent. Therefore, the immortal elves made the conscious choice not to farm all their regions. Remembering the past, they decided it was best not to tempt their neighbors and to keep themselves apart from the other races. The memory of the secret exodus from their homes was still too fresh in their minds.

As far as the Zidhe were concerned, this was the place where they would make their final stand, even if they did have a backup. They would not allow others to run them off these lands. The Highlands were theirs and would remain such. Any trying to take this region from them would do so at their own peril.

Being realists, the elves knew it would be almost impossible to keep enterprising humans entirely out of their lands unless they took action. Therefore, they came up with a plan. Never again would they allow a situation like the one they had experienced before their exodus. The Zidhe were determined to not let themselves be used as they had been by their once allies down in the south.

The Le'aanan had chosen to have only limited contact with their immediate neighbors, but it had been enough to realize that the few other persons inhabiting the region were of a different sort than their once friends.

Life had been really tough here before the elves' arrival, and it had molded these people.

Many had escaped from the temperate areas when their once peaceful society had collapsed. Few had come to the north out of choice, and some were criminals hiding from justice. It gave them a common bond with the Zidhe since they had all fled here for one reason or another. This was not only the elves' place of refuge but their fellow Highlanders as well.

To keep the peace, some ground rules would have to be established. The Zidhe decided to call all the people together for the first meeting of the folk of the Highlands.

Chapter 7

Memories

Watching the shapes in the wafting fog was just too mesmerizing, and Ki'ara could not bring herself to go in. She would have loved to go down to the kitchen to spend this last evening with her adopted family, but that was not an option. The previous few days, Argulf had shown up there each and every time. He had made all of them uncomfortable with his prying questions and tantrums when the girl gave him an honest answer that he did not want to hear. She just could not face that tonight, two confrontations in one day were enough!

The outraged wizard did not want to believe that Ki'ara had learned so much by studying hard and paying close attention to his words and his experiments. She had come to understand that Argulf would never be able to accept that she had assimilated most of his 'immense' wisdom that effortlessly.

The vain man could not face the truth that he was not the fantastic sorcerer he thought he was and that his student was now more powerful and knowledgeable than he. Consequently, he had gotten it into his head that the girl had to have cheated, and he was determined to figure out how.

Earlier that day, Ki'ara and her friends had been having a peaceful lunch when Argulf had shown up. He had become so nasty towards the young woman that Milla and the others had intervened. The furious housekeeper had gotten right in the wizard's face and had given him a piece of her mind. The other servants had taken up positions behind her, backing her up, and occasionally adding a few words of their own. Seeing that he was not getting anywhere, the furious sorcerer had stalked off in a huff.

Things had gotten really out of hand, and Ki'ara was worried that the vindictive wizard might fire his staff if they stood against him again. None of them had a place to go or family to take them in, and she was not yet in a position to care for them. Therefore, staying in her room was safer than taking the risk of more unpleasantness with that ill-tempered man.

***

Ki'ara went inside to fetch a blanket and a warmer jacket. She made a nest for herself and Taryn right there on the balcony, next to the wall. Curling up with the big cat, the young lady got more comfortable by leaning up against the wall of the decrepit building. She watched the pure whiteness drifting by and started to relax just a bit. The fog reminded her of home and off the long voyage ahead.

The sorceress did not like leaving her friends at the old castle behind. The housekeeper and some of the other servants had become more of a family to her than her three brothers had ever been. Ki'ara would especially miss Milla, who had treated her with such love and affection. The jovial, rather rotund, woman had always been there for her when Argulf had been especially nasty and hard to get along with that day or when the girl just wanted some company.

The elderly housekeeper had treated the lonely young woman with such warmth that she had felt truly cherished. She had pampered Ki'ara at every opportunity. The nightly cup of hot chocolate had been only a small part of that. Milla had also been right there with the sorceress when she had worked on the castle, helping or just watching to make sure that her darling did not get hurt or overextend herself.

Ki'ara just wished that she would have been able to do more to repair De'Aire Chateau. With the old fortress being in such bad shape and of considerable size, she had been able to do only so much. It had taken a lot of magic to stabilize the crumbling walls and form them back into something which provided some shelter.

Aware of the scope of her repair project, Ki'ara had tried to achieve as much as possible as quickly as she could. She had often exhausted herself and had only stopped when Milla said enough. On the upside, all that use of power had made the sorceress stronger every day, just like working a muscle.

During a gale, the old building often became as cold as ice. Only the kitchen, in the basement of the castle and carved into the rock, stayed nice and warm on those occasions, especially since the sorceress and her friends had tightened up the walls in the surrounding rooms with mud and moss.

The sleeping quarters had been the other primary focus for Ki'ara's repairs. In the rest of the castle, the wind seemed to be ever-present. The cracks and holes in the disintegrating walls ensured that it had free reign about the structure. Strong gusts whistled along happily in the corridors and halls and found their way into just about every nook and cranny in the ancient edifice.

The energetic breezes blowing about the old fortress loved to tussle Ki'ara's long hair. They would playfully tug strands out of her coiffure no matter how much she tried to keep it neat. She finally gave up and left it unfastened, the way she preferred to wear it in the first place. Initially, Mathus, her tutor and brother's enforcer, had protested, but when his charge refused to obey, he eventually gave in.

Those sneaky drafts found their way all throughout the fortress. During particularly severe storms, wafts of freezing air had managed to intrude even under the covers of Ki'ara's bed. She had to use her magic to keep them at bay. As much as she was loath to leave her friends, she was really looking forward to turning her back on this desolate dwelling.

The one person Ki'ara would most certainly not miss was Argulf. He easily ranked among the worst of the teachers her brother had hired over the years. The man was bad-tempered, uncaring, and had definite delusions of grandeur. From what she had observed, the wizard saw all others as incompetent and far inferior, and he really believed that only he had the keen intellect required to ponder and understand the enchantments needed to perform the most powerful magic.

After a bit of a rough start with the sorcerer, Ki'ara had observed everything he did closely. She had chosen to never point out his errors or the flaws in his spells, something Argulf reacted violently to. It had taken only once for her to adopt this strategy.

When she had first arrived, Ki'ara had made the mistake of drawing the wizard's attention to a blunder in one of his experiments. It had not gone well. Argulf had lost his temper and had cruelly berated his pupil for several hours before storming off to his chambers. He had even screamed at her for several days after and had made her scrub the laboratories until they were impeccably clean.

So instead, if at all possible, Ki'ara had taken to inconspicuously fixing the experiment or enchantment even if she had to tolerate the wizard's gloating at his success. It was still preferable to the nasty old man yelling at her.

※※※

Being outwardly docile and compliant was a survival tactic Ki'ara had been forced to adopt since her parents' departure. It had served her well with the self-centered wizard. The young lady had realized quickly that Argulf was not interested in imparting his knowledge to her, and she had felt blessed that her previous training had put her in a position where she did not need his explanations.

Ki'ara had been patient and quiet, but one day the arrogant wizard had pushed her too far. She had been in the middle of an enchantment when, out of the blue, Argulf had started screaming at her. The usually oblivious cad had noticed that she had slightly altered the formula, and he was irate. How dare she do things differently from the way he, her wise and powerful teacher, had written them down?

That it would have never worked using the methodology the wizard had laid it out did not matter. Letting him rave, the young woman had calmly and successfully finished the spell. Then, she had turned to Argulf and had coldly set him straight. He had been resentful but had shown her a bit more respect after that.

※※※

Despite the environs and her disagreeable teacher, Ki'ara worked hard on staying as positive as possible at all times. This was not always easy here at the chateau. Nor at home for that matter, not since her parents had left. How drastically her life had changed since that day!

When she was little, Ki'ara's mother would tell her that she had sunshine in her soul. Ali'ana claimed that was the reason her daughter was always so happy. The girl feared that in these last few years, the rain had found its way in on many an occasion. Had it not been for her innate ability to let the beauty of nature feed her heart, she might have despaired.

There was much to lament about the ancient castle, but it did have some good points. When the sun was shining, the view from Ki'ara's chamber was spectacular. Then, the pure white of snow-covered mountains contrasted with the pink and grey of sheer granite cliffs plunging thousands of feet down to dark green vales where lively streams danced through fertile meadows.

On exceptionally clear days, far off in the distance, she could just barely make out the sea, a sight which always filled her with longing. A brilliant blue sky with puffy white clouds, however, never failed to lift her spirits, and even De'Aire Chateau had a certain timeless charm in the bright sunshine.

This day, however, all the majesty around the castle was well hidden. The imposing mountains and lush valleys had secreted themselves behind dense veils of fog, which reminded Ki'ara vividly of home and the mist-covered moors of the Highlands. To her, this ever-changing whiteness had a magnificence all of its own.

In the diffuse light penetrating through the haze, the ancient fort appeared mysterious and like something out of a dream. Its neglected appearance was hidden by the pale vapor. As Ki'ara watched, the thick fog drew in even closer, creating the impression that the dilapidated building was vanishing completely. Before long, it had gotten so solid that all except the young woman's immediate surroundings had wholly disappeared.

Ki'ara remained sitting on the balcony of her room, lost in thought. She was staring out into the sheer whiteness with blind eyes. This fog took her mind back to Seamuir Castle, the place where she had grown up. That fortress was not so very different from this one in some ways, but it did overlook the sea and was far less secluded and in much better condition.

How much she missed it! Yes, it was dreary as well, not unlike this lonely place, but at least it was home. She could walk on the moors, ride down to the sea, or go sailing at the port. Her father had always kept a small boat there for her. She had been allowed to take it out anytime she pleased just as long as she remained in the shelter of the bay.

Where were her parents now? Were they happy? She sure hoped so. Ki'ara had never understood the reasons for their sudden departure. The explanations they had given their family and the clan had made little sense. And, why did she have to stay behind? Until then, they had always taken her wherever they went!

Placing her in the care of her oldest brother had turned out to be a nightmare for the girl almost as soon as the gates of the castle closed behind Mikael and Ali'ana. Ki'ara had quickly realized that she would have been better off practically anywhere but home. Why leave her at the mercy of their cruel son? She knew that there had been other and more suitable options.

Her parents could have fostered Ki'ara with her uncle, Iain. He would have been happy to take her in and had told her so multiple times. Or, even better, she could have stayed with Conall, the Lord of the StClouds. He had always treated her with respect, tenderness, and love. He had been her folks' closest and trusted friend and would have made a far better custodian than Ragnald.

In Ki'ara's opinion, Conall would have made a great guardian. Who better to look after her? The lord had been her intended husband, after all. He would have had her best interest at heart, unlike her brother who seemed to hate her for some unknown reason. How could her father have been so blind? And, why had her mother allowed this? What had her parents been thinking?

Growing up, Ki'ara had often been allowed to visit with the StCloud all by herself. His castle, the ancestral home of the StCloud Clan, Cloudshire Hall, had been like a second home to her, and she would have gladly stayed there. How different her life would have been had she been placed into Conall's care!

Just the memory of the man whom she still loved with all her heart brought a flush to the young woman's cheeks. Living with the StCloud would have been very interesting and fun. Conall had asked for Ki'ara's hand in marriage on the day she turned 11, and her father had gladly agreed. What a fantastic party that had been! She would probably be the StCloud's wife by now had it not been for Ragnald!

Ki'ara and her parents had been invited to Cloudshire Hall for the weekend of that birthday. Conall had gone all out. When they had arrived, she had been surprised to see the fortress tastefully decorated with vibrant flowers and large and small banners. The StCloud had presents waiting for her and had invited her friends.

The lord had known her so well that he had always managed to find gifts that he was sure would charm and bring pleasure to Ki'ara. He had been her closest friend despite their difference in age. Conall had wanted this celebration to be exceptionally memorable since this was to be an extra special day. He had been planning the event for several weeks.

When darkness had approached that evening, the servants had lit the many lanterns hung all over the fort and grounds. The colorful lights had illuminated the house and garden, giving the entire place the look of an enchanted fairytale castle. Ki'ara had been beyond delighted.

As the sun set, the orchestra hired just for the occasion had begun to play a lively tune. The StCloud had bowed formally, and hand in hand, they had walked to the middle of the festive courtyard. Together, they had led the first dance. She had absolutely loved it. Conall had made her feel like a princess, and he had been her handsome prince. It had been like a dream, and she had been so happy.

When it got a bit chilly outside, the party had moved indoors. Tables had been set up all around the walls of the great hall in a horseshoe shape with the ones in the far center on a raised dais. This had left the middle of the room for the dancers and entertainers.

After a few more songs, it had been time for the feast. Ki'ara's attentive partner had guided her to the place of honor next to his chair. Once everyone had been seated, Conall had clapped his hands. The doors to the hall had been thrown wide to reveal the servants lined up in rows of two, each holding a tray. They had been waiting to serve them.

A multitude of colorfully decorated dishes had been presented and placed on the tables to the applause of the guests. It had been a truly sumptuous meal the cooks had prepared and had included all of Ki'ara's favorite foods. She had tried to do justice to this abundance of choices but had soon reached the extent of what she could eat. Instead, she had busied herself talking to Conall.

When the dinner had been concluded and the dessert plates cleared, the StCloud had risen and had walked around the table to stand in front of Mikael MacClair. He had bowed to her father and had formally asked him for his daughter's hand in marriage. With a huge smile, her dad had granted the request. Ki'ara had thought she would faint and had jumped to her feet with excitement. Becoming the bride of this brilliant man had been the best birthday present of all!

Solemnly, Conall had returned to her side. He had gotten down on one knee before her and had gently taken her hand. Then, he had very formally asked her to become his wife. Ki'ara had tears of pure happiness rolling down her cheeks, and her voice had shaken with emotion when she had whispered a breathless "Yes." The girl was usually not at a loss for words, but that one word was all she had been able to say at that moment.

Receiving her acceptance, the StCloud had reached up and had gently wiped away Ki'ara's joyful tears. Then, he had presented her with the most beautiful ring she had ever seen. Two diamonds, side by side, set into an infinity symbol to represent their union for all eternity as well as the joining of two equals. The band was decorated with her favorite gemstones, aquamarines, emeralds, and small sapphires next to each diamond.

Ki'ara had instantly loved it. To her, it had been the most stunning and gorgeous ring she had ever seen, especially since it bound her to Conall. She had held out her hand and had allowed her fiancé to gingerly slide this treasure on her finger. For the rest of the night, she had been on cloud nine.

To this day, she remembered thinking, 'I am the luckiest girl alive! I am officially engaged to my very own knight in shining armor! The day I turn 18, I will become his wife! He is such an exceptional man, and I can still barely believe it! This is a dream come true!'

With a smile that had lit up the room, Ki'ara had met the StCloud's loving gaze and had bent down to kiss him for the very first time.

Sitting on the balcony, curled up with her large feline friend, Ki'ara remembered that night as if it had been yesterday. How ecstatically happy she had been! She was certain that she would be married to Conall by now had her parents stayed just a few more years or had they made better arrangements. The thought filled her with deep sadness, and the well of pain inside her soul threatened to engulf her.

Of all the beautiful jewelry Conall had given her, she had been able to save just a few things. At least Ki'ara still had her cherished engagement ring. For that, she was grateful, it reminded her of a time when she had been filled with joy, and life and her future seemed bright and full of promise.

Believing that no place at Seamuir Castle was safe for her beloved treasure, she always carried it with her but kept it well hidden. If her brother, or the tutor for that matter, ever laid eyes on it and realized what it was, it would be gone in an instant.

Had it not been for her instincts, Ki'ara would have lost this gift right along with some of her other prized possessions. On the day her parents departed, a nagging suspicion had told her to conceal the ring along with anything else she could hide. Something had prompted her to put another band on her finger. The feeling had been so intense that she had followed it, even if it had made no sense at that moment.

Just a few minutes later, the new Lord MacClair had come to her chamber. He had stormed in like a madman. Ki'ara had feared for her life, but on that occasion, he had a different agenda. Her brother had collected every single item he had suspected of coming from her fiancé.

Carelessly, he had thrown it all in the middle of the room. Then, as she watched in horror, he had used his magic to gleefully destroy these mementos of a happier time.

Had Ki'ara not followed her gut, Ragnald would have taken the ring from her along with the rest. It had felt like her brother had wanted to wipe Conall from her life. And that had only been the beginning. The sadness rising up inside her at the memory threatened to overwhelm her, and she started to cry. She still had no understanding of all this hate and why her fate had changed so completely.

Ki'ara had loved the StCloud with all her heart since she was a small child. He was much older than she, but when one is immortal, such things do not matter all that much. It had been her parents' desire for the two of them to marry as well as her own.

Mikael and Ali'ana had wished for this wedding from the moment their infant daughter was born. They had intended to forge a union between the MacClairs and the StClouds because they had felt that it was about time to put the last little remnants of hostilities, going back hundreds of years, to bed once and for all.

After the two had left, everything had changed for Ki'ara. Did her parents even know what had happened?

Almost anything would have been better than placing Ki'ara under the guardianship of her oldest brother Ragnald, Lord of Seamuir Castle, and the ruler of the MacClair Clan. By leaving her with him, her parents had very effectively destroyed their youngest child's world. One of the first official acts of the new clan leader had been to break his sister's engagement with the StCloud. He had forbidden her to see or talk to the man ever again.

Next, Ragnald had started sending the heartbroken girl off to distant places like this one. The explanation he gave to their brothers, the council, and the clan had been that she needed to be exposed to as many diverse forms of magic as possible so that she could provide the best service to their people. The actual reason was very different. Ki'ara knew that the lord could not stand the sight of her. He had told her as much.

Studying with so many different teachers had gifted the young lady with a wide-ranging education and a number of skills. It had taken away, however, one of Ki'ara's most important ties, her connection to the Highlands and the people of the clans.

The separation from her parents, the one place she truly belonged, and the man whom she loved felt like a constant deep ache in her heart. Ki'ara missed her former life and, despite her cheerful nature, sadness had become a frequent companion. Now that her time here at De'Aire Chateau had reached its end, the girl was looking forward to going back to her home, but she could not help feeling apprehensive.

Argulf had been the latest in a long list of more or less competent sorcerers. Instead of their aptitude, the location seemed to have been the deciding factor in their selection. The more remote and out of the way, the longer the travel time, the better her brother appeared to like them. There had been much better instructors closer to home.

Usually, it did not take the young woman all that long to learn all these second-rate magicians had to offer. Argulf was fairly incompetent, but he did have some knowledge that had interested her. He had been clueless about her carefully hidden progress and had believed that he would have this student for many more years.

About a week ago, to his utter frustration, the surprised sorcerer had realized that he had nothing left to teach his apprentice. This had never happened to him before. The infuriated magician had, therefore, rudely told his talented pupil that it was time for her to leave. He wanted Ki'ara out of his life and quickly so. He had been bested, and the girl was a constant reminder of his failings.

Not knowing how Ki'ara had achieved such an incredible feat was driving Argulf to distraction. He just had to figure out how she had done this. All that vast knowledge, all those enchantments, how could it now all be hers? Could this happen again with the next apprentice? What could he do to prevent this?

The incensed wizard was totally mystified. How could Ki'ara have gone from a good but not stellar student to having such skill? He had purposely put the brakes on, had taught her as slowly as he could, and here this girl knew all those things he had never intended to share with her in the first place!

How was this possible? Had she used some sort of a spell? The questions were driving the sorcerer mad, and he had taken to confronting Ki'ara at every occasion. He was determined that she was going to tell him.

Spells and enchantments came naturally to Ki'ara. Her abilities far exceeded Argulf's. The wizard had been allowed to see just enough for him to release her from the apprenticeship but no more. He would have been amazed had he been aware of the actual skills of the young lady.

Over the years, Ki'ara had experienced similar reactions from other teachers who had resented her capabilities, but none had been as blatantly rude about it as Argulf. To keep the peace, she did what she could to avoid the resentful man. When they did meet, however, the looks he shot her were filled with pure hatred, and his angry questions would rain down around her.

This was her last day, and all Ki'ara wanted was a few hours without having to deal with that man before the long journey in the morning. Besides, what was she going to tell him? Not the truth, that was for sure! The overconfident Argulf would have never believed her!

⋅⋅⋅ ⋅⋅⋅

The pace at which Ki'ara could assimilate information would have astounded the arrogant wizard as well as her brother. The girl, however, had kept this concealed from those around her from childhood on and had every intention to continue to do so. She had started hiding her gifts on the advice of her parents, Liana, and Conall, who were the only ones who had some idea what she was capable of doing.

People fear that which they do not understand, the unfamiliar. Ki'ara had seen this time after time. Why she was so unique, she did not know, only that she was. Beyond her powers, she did not really feel any different than anyone else. She most certainly had no need to put herself above others like Argulf.

As much as Ki'ara loved her friends here, she had not shared this secret part of herself. Argulf had no morals and would stoop to anything to get his way. The girl would not put it past the wizard to use some sort of an enchantment to find out what they knew. It was safer for them and for her if they were kept unaware.

⋅⋅⋅ ⋅⋅⋅

The real menace in her life was her brother. It was in Ki'ara's best interest to keep her skills carefully hidden. She was only too aware that her life may depend on this deception one day.

If Ragnald underestimated her powers, it would give Ki'ara a much-needed advantage if he ever decided to attack her again. She could not count on her brother

Gawain or someone else willing to help being around the next time the MacClair took it in his head to try to murder her.

Ki'ara was so tired of all that family trouble. She wished that Ragnald could see that there was no need to act like a tyrant. It was a shame, really, that he had not inherited more of the peacefulness which was such a huge part of the Zidhe's persona.

Chapter 8

A Daring Plan

The first meeting of all the Highlanders so long ago had been a spectacular event. Ki'ara admired the Zidhe for the feat they had accomplished. Gathering so many individuals who had really preferred to live alone in one spot had been neither easy nor without peril. The invitations had, therefore, been accompanied by a compulsion: appear and be civil. None had been able to refuse to attend, and they had been made to behave. Nothing else would have done for her peace-loving ancestors.

Being told that the Highlands now belonged to the elves and why had caused quite a stir among the assembled masses. Many had vociferously voiced their protests, but the Le'aanan had made sure that their new associates had understood that they were all refugees and that they had one common goal - survival. Each person had been given a choice: Help defend the Highlands or leave.

It had taken a fair bit of explaining, but finally, this mixed lot of humans and others had begun to comprehend that their existence depended on stemming the influx of people from the more temperate regions.

The Highlanders had eventually recognized that the Zidhe were in the same boat they were in and that they were valuable allies. The elves had incredible magical powers at their disposal, and they had offered to use these in the defense of their home.

If the lowlanders had been allowed to stream in and multiply like they had done everywhere else, the consequences would have been dire for the Highlands. None of the northerners had wanted this.

To preserve their way of life, an alliance had been formed to safeguard their lands and keep the southerners where they belonged.

⁘

Having won the cooperation of the other inhabitants of the Highlands, the Zidhe had set their daring plan into motion. To protect the southern boundary, the fairies had encouraged a strip of land, as well as the sea next to it, to become even more hostile than ever before. From that time on, deformed trees, carnivorous plants, and bubbling moors ended in a broad band where nothing at all grew or lived. This zone of death marked the border.

Animals and plants never seen before had begun to appear on both sides of this barren strip. They had been bred to help bar the way north. Large, vicious carnivores continued to roam the region in search of those who dared to set foot into their territory. Not many who ignored the signs put up as a warning survived.

Ghostly beings haunted the area and often drifted into the adjacent lands to the south. All those who laid eyes on them were filled with terror at the sight. To ensure that their army of specters kept growing, the Zidhe had cast an enchantment that turned any being killed in the death zone into a wraith, bound to protect this protective strip from that day onward.

⚜

All these precautions had been only the start. Everything the Zidhe and their new allies had been able to imagine had been brought into play. Within a few months, it had become almost impossible to survive a trip across these cursed lands or to sail across the sea near them unless you were one of the people and carried the special charms which allowed for safe passage.

Most of the time, the defenses lay dormant, but the moment any uninvited foot or ship touched the barrier, it snapped to instant awareness. Then, there was a high price to pay.

So far, only a few of the trespassers had managed to flee back to the south. The stories they had told had been frightening beyond compare, an additional deterrent for most reasonable folk.

⚜

With their fortifications in place, the Highlanders and the Le'aanan had hoped that anything which could be done to dissuade possible invaders had been implemented. They had figured that time would tell, but for the moment, they had been satisfied with their protections.

Only those Lowlanders who had been granted permission by the Zidhe to cross these frightful lands had managed to do so unscathed. They had, however, not been able to do so alone. If they had not waited for their guide, they had done so at their own peril, not a smart choice. Most who had tried to make their way north by themselves had not survived.

For a long time, relative peace had reigned in the Highlands. The few individuals who had lived there had become very grateful for the Zidhe's arrival. Over the years, their lives had taken a drastic turn for the better. All they had to do was to stick to the rules.

⚜

The non-elves of the Highlands had been a rough bunch. Outcasts from their societies, members of multiple races, pushed to the brink of civilization for one reason or another, hated, and despised. In the hostile environment of this region, they had grown self-sufficient and more than ready to defend what was theirs.

Newcomers had not been welcomed among them and had a hard time finding acceptance. Few had made it through the barrier or had even tried anymore. Stories of ghosts, monsters, and people being eaten alive in the lands north of the border had spread far into the Lowlands. It had kept all but those most cunning and desperate away.

Fearing the creatures roaming the border as well as all other inhabitants of the Highlands, the Lowlanders had finally built a protective wall well back from the boundary. The few gates they had installed were heavily guarded and discouraged most comings or goings. They had kept the throng of humanity confined to the south.

Their neighbors to the north had been more than happy with this new deterrent. They had seen anything that had stemmed the flood of people from spreading towards them as a gift from the gods.

⚜

The majority of the dwarves who had come north had withdrawn into the mountains and had built new underground cities. Some had gone along to the polar sanctuaries to help with mining and tunnels, a most welcome assistance. Nearly all the other races had preferred to live off in some far corner and had kept to themselves. Only the humans had remained nearby, and the Le'aanan had been determined to observe them closely this time. They had never expected that this might have unforeseen consequences.

Having learned from their past experiences, the Zidhe had decided to be more cautious. To keep an eye on their region, they had established several remote habitations which had also served as guard stations. The elves had wanted to make sure that whatever happened on their lands, they would be the first to know. They had seen it as vital to keep a watch on their mostly human neighbors.

In their previous home, the Le'aanan had shared their space with the other races, had been friendly with them. They had, however, hardly ever interbred with their neighbors. Having relations with an outsider had just not been done and had been heavily frowned upon.

In the Highlands, this had changed. The freezing nights, along with the elves' outlying security posts, had led to unexpected results.

The long, cold winter months in the elves' remote settlements had gotten lonely. Only a handful of Zidhe had remained to guard the outposts, the rest had returned to the city. At times, when the storms had reached especially frightening proportions, some of the humans living in the Highlands had been allowed to take refuge in these protected valleys.

The elven males were handsome and well built, the women slim and beautiful. Stuck in one spot day after day, they had soon grown bored and had been delighted with any diversion. They had usually been only too happy to grant shelter to their neighbors. After all, what better way to keep these people in their sight than having them right there with them?

Huddling together in the dark of winter with a willing maiden or young man for days on end, the unexpected had happened. An initial attraction had led to bonds forming, and things had gone from there. As a result, mixed children had been born.

⸻❧⸻

At first, humans and fairies alike had despised these half-breeds. Life had been hard for them and their parents since they had been being shunned by both races. Even their families and friends had often wanted nothing more to do with these individuals once they had discovered their indiscretion. The outcasts had ended up forming small groups of their own.

Who could have foreseen that these despised mix-breeds would one day become the saviors of all the Highlands in their greatest moment of need?

⸻❧⸻

South of the border, in the meantime, a disaster had been brewing that would change the fate of the half-breeds forever. Conditions had been steadily deteriorating. The human population in the cities had expanded to the point where many had no longer been able to find a place to live, let alone work. Hunger and despair had grown among the masses. There had been just too many of them.

What had made conditions so much worse had been the influx of folk from the surrounding rural areas. Tired of the hardships of country living, men and women, often with their entire family, had left their small farms to go make their fortune in the cities and towns. This had further reduced the supply of available food.

Far from the heaven they had envisioned, these unfortunates had ended up fighting for survival. As the situation had grown ever more dire, many had begun to believe that they had no chance for a decent life in the southern reaches.

The unknown lands to the north had started to look rather appealing to these unlucky people. Trying to escape servitude and toil, ever-larger groups had begun to stream into the areas just south of the wall.

At every gate, the camps had steadily grown. There had been no way to get enough food to them, and the assembled people had ended up starving. In addition, due to the unsanitary living conditions and close quarters, diseases had broken out.

Out of desperation and in a vain attempt to save the rest, anyone who had been unfortunate enough to fall ill had been arrested by the guards and had been taken through the gates and north. They had been brought as close to the barrier as the soldiers had dared go. Here they had been left, sick and unarmed, with no hope of survival.

After dark, the Zidhe's creatures had come. They had crossed through the death zone, drawn by the nearness of would-be invaders. Weaponless, the abandoned people had no way to defend themselves. They had soon fallen prey to the monsters. Night after gruesome night, the elves' beasts had feasted well.

The situation had grown more volatile with each passing moon. The large encampments south of the wall had been ripe with dissent. The whole area had been like a powder keg ready to blow.

All that had been missing had been someone to come and set a torch to the fuse.

Chapter 9

The Last Night

Despite his awful behavior, Ki'ara could not help but feel compassion for the arrogant sorcerer. When she had arrived at the castle two years ago, he had been so full of himself. Argulf had strutted around like a peacock, oblivious and uncaring of anything or anyone around him. Everything was about him, his wants, his needs, his greatness. The girl had immediately realized that she was dealing with an extraordinarily conceited and narcissistic man.

Until a week ago, Argulf had been so very sure of his own superiority. Especially, since he had managed to acquire such an important student, the Lady Ki'ara, one of the fabled Highland magi! This remarkable person had been sent to study with him, the most eminent among all living magicians! To the vain man, this had been further confirmation of his elevated status.

The self-important wizard had been wholly convinced of his own preeminence. He had believed that he was the best enchanter of them all, far above everyone else, even the part-elven witch-breeds, as Ki'ara's people, the Zidarians, were called in these parts. Nothing, not fact nor fiction, had been able to deter him from that even when he heard that the Highlanders had incredible abilities, were almost like gods.

Argulf had been extremely confident that he was infinitely more knowledgeable and powerful than anyone but especially a woman. In some of his more rational moments, which were far and few in-between, he had to admit to himself that it was possible that some of the male Zidarians might have skills close to his. His mind, however, could not even wrap itself around the possibility that this might also apply to his student.

The self-assured wizard had been beyond certain that the girl was far beneath him. After all, no mere female could ever be as competent a sorcerer as he.

On the day Ki'ara had begun her apprenticeship, Argulf had enlightened her that she could spend a lifetime with him and never learn all that he knew or even all that he had by now forgotten. The girl suspected that this claim had been one of the reasons Ragnald had chosen him as her teacher. To the horrified magician's total dismay, it had taken her less than two years to match and surpass him.

A magical missive requesting an audience had gone out to Ragnald. When they had connected by mirror the next day, the incensed Argulf had demanded the girl's immediate removal. Her brother had been very disgruntled with this unwelcome turn of events.

It had required a fair bit of convincing before the displeased ruler had grudgingly agreed to arrange for his sister's way back to the Highlands. The lord had expected Ki'ara to stay much longer and was far from happy that she would be returning back home so soon.

The officious note the MacClair consequently sent to Argulf made it abundantly clear that he was hugely disappointed. In the lord's opinion, the haughty wizard had grossly misrepresented himself. Ragnald, therefore, believed that he was entitled to a full refund plus some extra for damages.

The sorcerer's furious tirade when he read this unwelcome message had been heard all the way down in the kitchen.

Ki'ara had been at the receiving end of the ill-tempered wizard's rage many a time. She knew only too well how nasty he could get. Being aware of the even more foul mood the missive had put Argulf in, Ki'ara had taken great pains to avoid encounters with the incensed wizard, but all her sneaking about had been in vain.

These last few days, it had become almost impossible to spend time with her friends. Every time she had slipped into the kitchen thinking that she had gotten past Argulf, he had shown up within minutes. Ki'ara had finally given up and instead had spent her time repairing more parts of the castle. Milla had made sure that she had stayed fed.

Using her powers, Ki'ara had shored up additional sections of the crumbling walls and had patched up areas of the leaking roofs. This would make life a little easier for the servants who had been so kind to her and would allow them to move about the building in a bit more comfort. They and her four-legged friend were the main things she would miss about this unhappy place.

In preparation for her departure, all Ki'ara's belongings had been packed. The efficient Milla had overseen the process and had made sure that everything was ready to be stowed on the horses for the long ride down the mountains. The young woman's tutor Mathus, an annoying and somewhat unpleasant fellow, would accompany her, as always.

Her brother had hired the man to keep an eye on Ki'ara whenever she was away from home. The girl could not help but think that it was too bad that she could not sneak off without the little toad! It would serve him right to be left behind in this dreary old place!

As it was, it would take several days for Ki'ara, Mathus, and the stablemaster to reach the port. The trail down the mountains was perilous and slow going. Without a local guide, it was easy to get lost or run into trouble. Even as enraged as the fuming sorcerer was, he was too afraid of her brother to dare to send them out there alone.

Ki'ara was looking forward to the ride. The views from the paths were spectacular when the weather was clear. Also, it would feel marvelous to be out in nature and away from the oppressive air of the castle and its sullen master. She could not wait to turn her back on the place.

While making their way to the harbor, Ki'ara would have plenty of time to think. She was looking forward to that. The trail was too narrow for two to ride abreast. This made conversation almost impossible, so for most of the day, she would not be subjected to her tutor's constant complaining.

The destination of their trip down the mountains was the town of Mercede, the busiest seaport in the region. The sizeable sheltered bay of Mercedeas made for a deep natural harbor suited for large ships. Even in the fiercest of storms, it provided a safe haven from the howling winds and pounding waves so prevalent in this part of the world.

The growing shipping industry had brought prosperity to the region and its people. Sailors liked their drink and were quite fond of women. The vessels required provisions, sails needed to be fixed, timbers replaced. A whole new industry had been created by this demand. Unfortunately, crime had increased right along with the influx of wealth.

Pickpockets and such the sorceress could handle. From what she had seen on her way to the chateau, Ki'ara expected that getting down out of the mountains safely would be the biggest challenge on their journey. Once she and her companions reached Mercede, finding the docks would be easy.

The masts of the tall ships, towering above everything else, would lead the way. Then, it was just a matter of weaving their way through the throngs hustling and bustling about in this busy little city without running afoul of muggers and thieves. This was an easy feat if one had magic to protect oneself and one's possessions.

✦✦✦

The young lady was filled with happy anticipation about getting down to the shore. How much she had missed the sea! She had never done well far from the water, a trait she shared with many of her people. With every mile traveled, she would be getting closer to the ocean with all its familiar sights, sounds, and smells.

The *Sea Witch,* her very own ship, would be picking Ki'ara and Mathus up and ferrying them home. To be out on the water once more, to smell the fragrant sea air, to feel the spray on her face would be pure bliss after all this time spent so far inland.

✦✦✦

Ki'ara's thoughts returned to the moment. By now, night was falling, and the white world around the dilapidated castle had begun to dim. The fog drew in even closer until the girl could barely see a handspan in front of her face. Tiny drops of moisture clung to her hair and clothes and covered her cheeks with their dew.

Looking around and noticing how little she could see of the balcony made Ki'ara feel like she and Taryn were the only beings alive in this sea of mist, isolated from the rest of the world, just her and her cat. His purr of contentment vibrated around her, and she watched silently as the light faded into darkness.

When a few ice-cold droplets found their way down her back, Ki'ara shuddered. Her thoughts had started to wander again. Firmly, she brought her attention back to the moment. Reaching out, the sorceress embraced the white oblivion, became one with the world. For one last time, she allowed her spirit to glide over the majestic peaks and dive down into the deep valleys.

Soaring along, Ki'ara gingerly touched the mind of the sleeping eagle who had become a friend of sorts. The big bird had taken to flying right over the castle early each day. She smiled at the memory of the morning he had landed on the balcony. She had only been here a few days and had been feeling especially alone. He had come to cheer her up with his antics. Blowing him a gentle kiss, she sped on.

The young woman's spirit headed up and over the cliff. It raced around the old fortress onto the small plateau behind it. Part of this mesa was taken up by the run-down stables; the rest held a now thriving garden. When she had first arrived at the chateau, a few struggling plants had been trying to sprout there, lovingly tended by the castle's very own gardener.

The old man had been doing his best but had little luck until Ki'ara came along. She had helped him build a small greenhouse, and with her magical encouragement and protection, a few of the vegetables and herbs had finally grown. The girl smiled at the memory. She had enjoyed those hours of close connection to nature and had found them incredibly grounding.

Passing the stables, Ki'ara headed on. The path leading down from the mountains started from this shelf as did another heading further up and around to the next gorge. Wanting exercise, the young woman had taken to exploring them both. Out hiking had been how she had met Taryn.

On one of these lonely treks, Ki'ara had made a friend, a large mountain cat. From that day on, it had joined her whenever she had set out for a walk. After a while, her new companion had begun to stay close to the castle. Every day, the big male had waited patiently for her to appear. He had become quite tame, and even the servants had become used to his presence.

During one especially wicked winter storm, the cat had followed Ki'ara inside. He seemed to like it and had stayed, sleeping next to her bed or on it whenever she let him.

The catamount had made himself at home in the castle. A small hidden door in the wall to the garden was usually left open for him, allowing the cougar to come and go as he pleased.

After a few weeks, he had seldom been gone for very long. Her friend would go out hunting and then return back to the fortress, sometimes bringing fresh meat. Such a treat was always much appreciated, and he and the cook got along very well.

The more time he had spent at the castle, the more domesticated the cat had become. He had started to behave like a pet. On those nights when the icy winds had raged relentlessly outside, and the bowl of water on Ki'ara's dresser had frozen over, he had slipped under the covers with her. He had cuddled up next to the girl to help keep her warm. She had been grateful since their combined body heat had made even the coldest of nights easier to bear.

Ki'ara had named her new friend Taryn - king of the rocky hill. He had taken to following her wherever she went. Being a typical cat, he had quickly figured out the warmest and most comfortable places in the castle. The kitchen became one of his favorite haunts, especially after the cook made him a nice soft bed close to the fire.

Having the ghost cat as a companion as well as her other friends had helped the young woman feel just a little less lonely. Taryn got along well with everyone except Argulf and Mathus. The castle's servants had promised to look after the feline once she was gone. They had grown to love him almost as much as she did.

Argulf, the cat had learned to avoid. The cranky old magician would have been less than pleased had he known about this new resident in his castle but, being preoccupied with his magic and person, the man had walked past the bulky animal several times and had never even noticed him sitting there.

The sorceress was grateful for the love she shared with this wild creature. Over the last few months, they had formed a close bond, and she would truly miss him. She knew that a part of her heart would remain behind here with him in these mountains.

As if sensing her thoughts, her large friend moved closer to her. Taryn started to impatiently push his head against her hand until Ki'ara relented and began to absentmindedly stroke his smooth back. She was both sad and exhilarated about leaving but also quite anxious about returning to Seamuir and her brother's control.

An exasperated nudge finally startled Ki'ara out of her reverie and brought her wandering mind back to the balcony. It was almost fully dark by now and so foggy that she seemed to be sitting in a sea of dark gray.

Slowly Ki'ara pried her cramped fingers from the blanket. She had never even noticed that she had gripped it this tightly. The girl rose, and the two made their way into her room, side by side, with the girl's hand still resting on Taryn's sleek head.

While pouring herself a glass of water, Ki'ara heard the loud growl of her stomach. The young woman realized for the first time just how hungry she was and how many hours she had spent out on her balcony lost deep in thought. At noon, she had left the kitchen without finishing her meal once Argulf had shown up, and breakfast had been interrupted by him as well.

A sudden knock startled the young woman, and she could not help but feel panicked for a moment. Was this Argulf again? Had he chosen to pursue her in her private quarters now as well? Somehow, she did not think so. That was one rule she had firmly established from the very first day. "Who's there?" Ki'ara called while making her way towards the door.

"It's me, Milla!" came the cheerful answer, and the girl happily unlocked the door to let her in. To Ki'ara's surprise, the housekeeper was not the only one standing on the landing waiting to enter. All her friends had come, and they had brought dinner and extra chairs! A board and a tablecloth were spread over her bed, and soon a virtual feast was laid out.

Once everyone was comfortably seated, the housekeeper held her hand up for silence. For the occasion, she had fixed her long grey hair in a neat bun, and she was wearing her best dress. Milla looked very festive at that moment and entirely in charge.

The elderly woman looked at Ki'ara with so much affection that the girl felt her heart soar. Having companions such as these simple, kind people was such a pleasure. Here, there was no deception, no hidden agenda, no pretense, what you saw was what you got. She really liked that about them.

"We figured you were hungry after the master made such a scene in the kitchen and thought that a little party would cheer you up, pet! Since this is the only place you are safe from that horrible man, we decided that we would come to you!" Milla told her with a huge smile.

"To Ki'ara," she proposed raising her glass. The others raised their drinks and gladly picked up the toast. "Ki'ara!" they shouted as one. The girl had tears in her eyes as she returned their salute and took a sip. She then raised her own goblet. "To all of you and to friendship! Thank you for everything!" Big smiles erupted all around as each took a swallow of their wine.

Within minutes, everyone was eating and talking. How much Ki'ara would miss these people's kindness and loving company! The young woman was determined to find some way to make them part of her household as soon as she could. Would she have to break with her clan to achieve this? She hoped not.

Since Ki'ara and the tutor would be setting out on their journey in the morning, her friends left after a bit so that she could get some sleep. The way down the mountain was strenuous, and she needed to be well-rested for the ride.

✦❧✦

The girl was looking forward to the trip with eagerness but also apprehension. The same questions kept churning in Ki'ara's mind. What would await her this time when she returned to the Highlands? How would Ragnald treat her? Would she have to play her trump card and break her ties to the lord of the clan?

Declaring her a legal adult was at least one thing her father had done right. It made up a little for all the harm her parents' leaving had caused. Sadness flooded her heart. Would she ever see them again? Ki'ara sure hoped so! Excitement and fear battled within her as she got ready for bed.

Taryn insisted on curling up next to her once she got under the covers. He seemed to sense that she was leaving and had been sticking closer than usual to her all day. Ki'ara wrapped her arms around him and buried her face in his soft fur. The sound of his breathing lulled her to sleep.

Ki'ara's last thoughts were of the Highlands and of how much damage one unscrupulous man could cause. Was Ragnald just as ambitious as Ulric?

Chapter 10

An Ambitious Man

Many years ago, a lordling named Ulric decided to set his sights on the lands to the north. His invasion of the Highlands had never been forgotten. Not only did his exploits cost the lives of many an innocent soul, but the heartless noble and would-be conqueror also changed Ki'ara's people's entire way of life.

Ulric was a monster in human form. He callously took advantage of folks' hopes for a better future to further his own desires. In his mind, he was the emperor of the Highlands, they just did not know it yet. Only, a couple things stood in his way. The north's present population, and the lethal border area. The cunning lord, however, had a plan how do deal with them both.

At the time the lordling showed up to gather his army, living conditions south of the wall had become so dire that the deadly barrier was no longer the effective deterrent it had once been. The camps near the gates grew larger every day as more people, driven by desperation, found their way there. Hunger, disease, and hopelessness reigned among the assembled masses.

Along came Ulric, the ruthless son of a harsh and self-serving southern lord. He was a real chip off the old block, just as cruel and vain as his father. In his mind, he was a powerful warlord, a conquering hero.

The coldhearted scoundrel saw the lands to the north as his first step to the ultimate prize – the rule of the Mystic Isles and beyond. All that he required to set out on his quest was a safe way to get his army of trained fighters through the barrier.

The gathered throngs at the gates were just what this depraved man needed. Ulric filled their heads and hearts with visions of a better life, promised them a bright future in those wide-open lands up to the north. The men signed up in droves to take part in his upcoming campaign.

The deceitful lord and his companies of experienced soldiers and mercenaries armed and trained these unfortunate people. What these clueless recruits received were only rudimentary instructions, just the absolute basics, and nothing which would genuinely help them to survive the dangers they would be facing.

Most were farmers, many in poor health. Ulric had decided to take them all, sick, lame, or old, he did not care. These desperate men were grateful to be given a chance, any chance, and they worshipped their new leader. He was their savior, their hope for a better quality of life for themselves and their families. This made them putty in the heartless aristocrat's hands.

When the impetuous rogue felt that his new troops were ready, he forced the guards to open the gates. Without a moment's hesitation, Ulric forged his way north into the barrier lands. He had no concern for his vast army of farmers and craftsmen, nor did the ambitious lord give a second thought to the women and children he had allowed to tag along.

This was most likely the worst prepared force one could think of. Ulric was well aware of this, but he just did not care. He was good with losing a large number of them, to him they were all expendable, he just needed his trained fighters.

The lord's attitude said much about him as a future ruler. Ulric would have been a tyrant without pity nor compassion for his people, without morals, without a real sense of humanity. Who would want to be governed by one such as he?

⁂

The young lord had come to conquer, to pillage, and to oppress. Ulric had no intention of coexisting within the present order; he wanted the realm all to himself. He intended to enslave the Zidhe and to clear the Highlands of all other inhabitants except those who were willing to serve him. He was determined to put an end to the barbarians squatting on what he saw as 'his' lands.

The ambitious man had visions of creating a vast empire, starting with the areas here to the north. He planned to force the elves to use their magic to build him a palace the likes of which had never been seen before. From there, he would reign over the region until he had built up a substantial army. Then he would make the Zidhe fashion weapons for him, so he could ride out and conquer the south.

The lord felt that it was high time that he got what he deserved, his very own throne. He intended to make a name for himself, be admired, and even feared. His father would finally be proud of him, and his peers would pay for the sneers and slights he had had to endure over the years.

One thing was certain, no sane person would have taken such a sorry bunch of people into the dangers to come. By the time Ulric and his 'army' reached the northern extent of the boundary lands, their numbers were significantly reduced. Of the vast group which had set out with such hope and determination, less than a thousand remained, and many were injured.

The calculating warlord had allowed the men he recruited at the wall, mostly homeless peasants and tradesmen, to bring their wives and offspring along for a good reason. He callously had used his inexperienced followers and their families as protection for himself and his hired fighters.

Even then, his main troops barely made it into the Highlands alive. Merely by chance had a fair number of his experienced soldiers survived, but still, he had lost many. Of the significant force Ulric had started with, only the most lucky and skilled warriors still lived.

Their leader was not pleased. He would have preferred to have more men than he now led. Being confident of his own superior tactical abilities, however, Ulric decided to continue with his campaign anyway. He firmly believed that the inhabitants of the Highlands were uneducated savages. How hard could it be to overcome them?

The moment the invading army had crossed into the barrier, alarms had gone off in the homes of the elves. The Le'aanan had gone to investigate and had found a vast number of people heading their way. Immediately, they had set a watch on the group and had sent out a call to arms across the region. Soon warriors streamed south to defend their homeland. They met up with the elves close to the border.

The arriving Highlanders had been horrified when they realized how Ulric was using his people. The elves had already jumped into action and saved as many of the remaining families as they could. These lucky ones suddenly found themselves back at the wall, their minds filled with the horrors of what they had seen and lived through. Most quickly headed south to get as far away from that nightmare region as they possibly could.

Ulric's use of innocent lives to further his agenda appalled and infuriated the elves and their allies. The Highlanders decided that this unscrupulous lord would pay for his crimes. A plan to deal with the invaders was hatched, and the Zidhe used their magic to guide the intruders to a place where their own forces would have the strategic advantage. There, the enemy would be met head-on, and a reckoning dealt out.

Judging from the way Ulric had treated his people, the defenders knew that they could not expect mercy if they were captured. They could well imagine what the cruel noble and his troops would do to any who had the misfortune to fall into their hands.

This enemy was on their land, ready to conquer. The Highlanders saw no option but to fight to protect their homes.

⚜

To minimize their own casualties, the northerners had decided that they would rely on their skills and strengths once the two armies collided. The Le'aanan knew that using their powers in close combat was not always a safe choice. It could get some of their own forces killed right along with their opponents. To the elves, all life was precious, and they would have preferred to harm none.

This lord, however, seemed to be unbelievably heartless and brutal. From what the Zidhe had observed, all he cared about was his own life and, he was blinded by ambition. The elves were confident that he would not see reason and decided that it was not worth trying to negotiate with this despicable man.

Ulric would have to be taken care of, one way or the other. The Le'aanan and their allies prepared an ambush for these brazen intruders.

✦❦✦

Even though the Zidhe's border strip with its traps and creatures had done its part by dwindling down the numbers of the invading army, a sizeable force of well-trained warriors had managed to make its way through. Most of the ones who had perished or disappeared had been the unskilled soldiers and their loved ones.

What Ulric had not counted on, however, was the determination of these 'savages' to defend what was theirs. The cruel warlord and his men were about to be met by an army of Highlanders of all races, among them a frost giant or two, several trolls, and a good number of dwarves. They had come to put a stop to the lordling's atrocities once and for all.

It was late morning when the southern lord and his men reached the valley the Zidhe had chosen for their ambush. Ulric's captain, a veteran of many wars, took one look at the narrow gorge. His alarm senses began to tingle. The mercenary's experience told him that this was a perfect place for a trap. He quickly rode up to his lord and voiced his misgivings.

The seasoned soldier's words fell on deaf ears. As usual, the noble completely ignored him. The young aristocrat was so arrogant, so full of himself, and so convinced of his own superiority and intelligence that he looked down on all others. Ulric seldom listened to advice, even from those far wiser than him.

Only his father did he grudgingly respect, and on occasion, the cad had reluctantly paid heed to his sire's words. His mother, he had actually loved since she adored him and never contradicted his wishes. As far as she was concerned, whatever her darling wanted, he got.

Ulric was the youngest and closest to the lady's heart. She had spoilt him terribly. All the other boys preferred to keep company with their father and wanted little to do with their overly clingy mother. In her eyes, her favorite child had been the smartest and most handsome of all her children, and she had filled her son's head with misguided ideas of his greatness.

Feeling invincible and highly superior, Ulric had made up his mind long ago about the world around him. Before he had even left his home and had all the necessary information, he had scoffed at the competence of the savages he had come to defeat. Not even the heavy losses in the border region had shaken his ill-founded assumptions.

The lord was completely and utterly convinced that these northern primitives were too dumb to defy him, let alone overwhelm him. He was wholly confident that they lacked the coordination and cunning necessary to muster up an efficient defense against his well-trained soldiers. Ulric was sure, therefore, that the worried mercenary was imagining things.

After all, they had not seen a single person since they started on their trek north from the barrier! It seemed as if these lands were entirely uninhabited, ripe for the taking.

Therefore, against the advice of his captain, Ulric waved his troops onward. Seeing how his men eyed the steep walls with concern, he rode to the front of the column. Without a second thought, a moment's hesitation, or any prudent precautions such as sending out scouts, the self-assured lord led his apprehensive fighters into the vale.

The Highlanders were ready and waiting for the invaders. Everything had been carefully thought out and prepared in advance. They had been working all night. Just as soon as the last soldier of the attacking army set foot into the valley, the trap was sprung.

Suddenly, a massive rockfall tumbled from the tall cliffs behind Ulric's troops, cutting them off from any retreat. The exit was blocked, forcing the army onward. As the soldiers looked around nervously, arrows began to rain down from above. Panic ensued, and many a mount reared up and shook off its rider. A desperate rush towards the far end of the valley began.

The captain immediately took charge. His voice rang out over the din calling the few men left astride on their horses to him. A stampede was ensuing around them. Those soldiers who could made their way over through the mass of frightened animals and people. The officer placed them in battle positions around their stunned lord. Ulric was looking about in disbelief. He was being bested by savages! How was this possible?

The mercenary commander gave the order to head for the far end of the vale where he hoped they could exit this death trap. Arrows were still picking off men left and right. The group started to race down the gorge in a tight formation. The loyal soldiers had their shields raised to protect Ulric from the hail of missiles from above. They had almost made it when a second rockfall cut off their escape. All hope was lost!

⚜

The young noble had by now recovered his faculties. He had been stunned for only a few moments by this sudden turn of events. Then, his natural arrogance had reasserted itself. Ulric, once again, took over command from the captain. The incredulous officer had had just about had enough of his witless employer.

The exit and entrance areas of the valley were enclosed by sheer cliffs, but in a small space in-between, the slopes were not as steep. This is where Ulric now led his men, all the while shouting challenges at the Highlanders. He dared them to come down and fight.

It did not take long for the warriors from the north to oblige him. The battle which ensued was bloody and ferocious. It lasted for hours. By midafternoon, the invading force had been drastically reduced. Finally, the Highlanders managed to surround the haughty lord and his few remaining fighters.

At this point, the Zidhe came forward and asked for the southerners' surrender. They assured the exhausted soldiers that they would be shown mercy if they laid down their arms. Hesitantly, the mercenaries began to lower their weapons since yielding meant they got to fight yet another day. In a situation such as this, that was usually how it was done.

With Ulric, though, one never knew. Their employer had proven to be totally unpredictable, did not follow the rules, and was deadly when crossed. Did the standard operating procedures apply? The warriors were not sure what to do, and even their captain was looking at his impetuous lord for guidance.

❦

The exhausted troops were ready to give up, but not so their leader. He would have none of this. Ulric decided that he would not concede defeat to these despicable savages. What would his father say?

The proud aristocrat figured that if he capitulated now, he would be the laughingstock of his peers. Taken prisoner by a horde of primitives, how would that look! They were not even a proper army! He would never be able to live down such a disgrace!

"We will never surrender!" he shouted, therefore. "I will fight to the last m…" The young noble's voice broke off in mid-sentence. Ulric looked down at his chest in disbelief. Two bloody arrowheads were protruding through his jacket. Blood squirted from his mouth as he began to crumble to the ground.

Slowly, the captain and the last surviving craftsman lowered their bows. When their lord had started to scream his defiance, they had exchanged one quick glance, then a nod. Both hated shooting anyone in the back, even Ulric, but desperate times called for drastic measures. They had raised their bows in unison and fired.

As far as the mercenary commander was concerned, too many people had already died for this rogue. He and his men were not being paid enough to perish here this far from home. It was time to put a stop to Ulric's insanity. They were done following orders from this insolent cad!

The Highlanders had been taken as much by surprise as Ulric and so had the bedraggled remains of the greatly diminished southern army. Instinctively, all raised their weapons. The soldiers were utterly confused. Who should they aim at, their captain who had just shot their lord or the savages surrounding them?

Fearing that things could get out of hand and get them all killed, after all, the officer took command. He ordered his flustered troops to stand down. The problem was that these were not only his men but other fighters Ulric had acquired. The captain was not certain where their loyalty laid but knew that they were used to obeying.

The commander's sharp order rang out again. The soldiers looked at each other helplessly. Should they obey the guy who had just executed their employer? After some initial indecisiveness, they complied. The captain had always taken much better care of them than Ulric and could be trusted.

The mercenary stepped forward. It had been a fair fight, and his party had lost. If they played this right, he and his men might survive. At least that was how it had always worked before.

Did these Highlanders know those rules? There was only one way to find out. The captain bowed to his enemies. He placed his weapons on the ground and raised his hands. The rest of the troops rapidly followed suit.

This time, there had not been a moment's hesitation. Most of the southerners were injured and just happy to still be alive. Now that Ulric was gone, the exhausted warriors did not intend to keep fighting for a cause that had been lost before it had even begun.

The Highlanders greatly appreciated the battle skills of their prisoners. Those of Ulric's men who did live due to superior capabilities or pure luck, as in the craftsman's case, were given a choice, leave or remain here in the north as honored members of their society.

The elves figured that experienced fighters such as these were hard to come by and could play a vital role in any future defense of the land.

The soldiers were assured, however, that if they did want to return south, the Zidhe themselves would guide them back to the wall. Seeing this as a golden opportunity to make a new life for themselves, most decided to stay, even the craftsman. After all, what was there to go back to?

Chapter 11

The Journey Begins

Ki'ara had plenty of time to reminisce on their way down from the peaks. The first day was very uneventful. She was bringing up the rear of their little column. The stablemaster, Hugo, her tutor, Mathus, and she traveled mostly in contemplative silence. Talking while riding single file turned into shouting, and that was never a good idea up here in these mountains. The sound alone could trigger a rockslide.

The horses were well familiar with the trail. Mostly, they were contentedly following Hugo's black mare, and only on occasions did Ki'ara have to concentrate on guiding her mount along. A few times, they came across spots where the path had been damaged by rockfalls or partially washed out by rain. Here, they had no choice but to dismount and carefully lead the animals over these especially tricky places.

The young lady wished that she could have brought Taryn along. She had grown very accustomed to his company and missed him already. Ki'ara had wrestled with her conscious for days and, in the end, had decided that it would not be fair to take the catamount away from all that he knew. How would he fare in the Highlands, so far away from his home? And, during the long sea voyage north?

Cats were not fond of water to start with and then nothing but ocean for days on end? How could she do that to her faithful friend just because she wanted him with her? It would have been selfish. Ki'ara loved Taryn too much to do something which might harm him. So, after weighing the pros and cons of the situation, she had decided to leave him behind and set him free, even though it was breaking her heart.

To prevent Taryn from following her, Ki'ara had asked the cook to keep him confined for a day or two. When they had left this morning, the sky had looked like it would rain later that afternoon. The young lady assumed that the water would wash away their scent. If the catamount could not track where she had gone, there was a better chance that her large companion would stay where he belonged, up in the mountains.

⋆⁕⸎⁕⋆

It had been hard to say goodbye to her friends and her cat, but now that they were on the way, she could barely contain her excitement. She was finally leaving that gloomy castle behind and going back to the place which had been calling to her without cease. How much she had missed the Highlands, her friends and family, and the people of the clans! Seamuir Castle might not be as beautiful as Cloudshire Hall, but it was home.

Hopefully, her interactions with Ragnald would be more pleasant this time. Ki'ara preferred to avoid confrontations with her oldest brother, they tended to turn ugly and had, at times, been downright dangerous for her. On one occasion, he had lost his temper and had almost strangled her. Why her father had ever made him her guardian, she was unable to comprehend. Mikael should have known better.

It had been many years since the young lady had last seen her parents. As was so often the case, thinking of their departure led her mind to some of the unanswered questions regarding Mikael and Ali'ana. They had left the castle and Eastmuir without revealing their destination and under somewhat mysterious circumstances. To Ki'ara's great disappointment, they had never returned, nor had they sent word of any kind.

As far as she knew, her mother and father both had more Zidhe blood than human. Ki'ara had always wondered where they had gone and why. She had sensed panic in both during the time they had prepared to leave. Her parents had quickly packed some of their things, put the affairs of the realm in order, and had left just as soon as they possibly could. Had they have gone to live with the elves in their beautiful city?

༚༝ཏ༚ཊ༚ཏ

In the past, a few people had been granted special permission to reside among the Le'aanan. Had her parents been allowed to do so? Mikael had always wanted to go there; for him, it would have been a dream come true. He had been fascinated with the elves, their history, and their home. Her father had told her the stories of her fairy ancestors whenever he tucked her in bed. How much she had loved those tales!

Ki'ara never got tired of hearing about the people whose blood ran so predominantly in her veins. It was thanks to this heritage that she, a Zidarian, was virtually immortal. She was honored to be a descendant of the Zidhe and hoped that one day she would get the chance to visit and explore their beautiful lands.

Mikael had always told Ki'ara that she had inherited many of the strengths and traits of her kindred. He had drilled into her head that if she was ever in trouble, all she had to do was to reach for the magic singing in her blood. It would help her, just as it had the elves in the past. Knowing this had given her solace.

The sorceress felt so connected when she was in the Highlands, so part of all that was, of the land. Whenever she was elsewhere, she deeply missed this bond. Ki'ara had been wondering for years if that gift would also work for her far from home. The magic seemed to have stayed with the Le'aanan when they had moved to the Highlands.

Had it accompanied her? Ki'ara had experimented a little wherever she went but had never felt the same kind of kinship with the land anywhere but in the Highlands nor that deep contentment she felt whenever she was home.

The Zidhe had gone through so much to make a place for themselves where they could live in peace! This brought her thoughts to the well-remembered stories.

The combat which followed the Highlanders springing their trap and engaging Ulric's army can only be described as bloody and brutal. The northerners were defending their home, the intruders were fighting for their very lives. Both parties were desperate and needed to win.

The outcome of the encounter had hung in the balance for a long while since the two forces were almost evenly matched. The mix-breeds, men and women alike, had been the deciding factor. They had taken the disorganized rabble of fighters who had heeded the call to defend their homes as well as the peace-loving elves and had forged them into a force to be reckoned with, one which had a chance to prevail.

The mix-breeds' prowess in battle and organizational skills had finally tipped the scales in favor of the Highlanders. The difficult life of the outcasts had taught them well. Without them, the north would have had no chance to overcome Ulric's seasoned army, and the invasion would have been a resounding success.

୰ℳ↝

Over the years, any child with 'tainted' blood had ended up as a pariah, the parents in disgrace. No one had wanted or accepted them, not even the kind-hearted Zidhe. Therefore, these unfortunate individuals had banded together with others in the same predicament. They had located places where they could exist in relative safety and peace and had built secure fortifications.

The exiled groups had been in dire need of safe shelters since a few individuals had gotten it into their heads to persecute them. In the view of some, this mixing of races was an atrocity. These zealots had felt that it was their holy duty to exterminate the 'abominations' from the face of the earth. Any biracial family they had come across was pitilessly murdered, men, women, and children alike.

Being outcasts and hunted, the mixed ones had been forced to fight to survive. It had become their way of life. The families had always been on guard and ready for an attack. To protect themselves, they had formed ever larger groups they called clans and had settled in places which they could successfully defend. Here, they had built the first strongholds.

The clans' social order had been very unlike the rest of the non-elven Highlanders. Following the example of the Zidhe, they had elected chiefs, and all had worked together for the benefit of the clans. To give every individual a better chance to stay alive, training in self-defense had begun just as soon as a toddler was old enough to hold onto a weapon.

Most youngsters had become capable and well-disciplined soldiers before they had even reached their teenage years. They had been used to fighting as a group and under a leader and not like a mob like the rest of their neighbors. Much of their time had been spent honing their battle skills. Having to defend themselves against their fellow landsmen, they had become fierce warriors.

Their abilities had served them well in the battle against Ulric. The mix-breeds had been the ones who ended up taking charge. They had led the rest of their people to victory. At first, there had been some grumbling, but once the outcasts' prowess in battle had become evident, the Highlanders had grudgingly done as they were told. Survival, after all, was a good thing!

⊱✿⊰

The greedy lord setting his eyes on their lands had achieved what nothing else could. It had united the peoples of the Highlands. Together, they had defeated the invaders. In that union had lain their strength, and the desperate battle had formed a growing bond between the different races and groups.

The Highlanders, including the Zidhe, had realized that there was safety in numbers. Had they not fought together, Ulric would have succeeded in his quest to become the lord of the realm. He would have killed or enslaved them all. This lesson had left a lasting imprint on many a mind and had been passed down from then on to each following generation.

⊱✿⊰

The outcasts had been given the name 'Zidarians' in honor of their Zidhe ancestors. They had made such an impression on their fellow countrymen that more and more individuals, mostly humans, began to settle around their nine fortresses. All had been made welcome as long as they were willing to fit in and adjust to a life with shared responsibilities.

The newcomers had liked the state of things at the fortresses. Here, there had been order, medical assistance, and help if needed. All had worked for a common good. It had been a much more comfortable existence than scratching out a living somewhere on their own.

Many had petitioned to be admitted to the clan and had done their best to integrate themselves into the mix-breeds' culture.

The folk, who had once been hunted and despised, had rapidly found themselves at the center of a changing society. Miraculously, their neighbors had not only accepted them but had wanted to be part of their world.

The Zidarians were being admired for their skills with weapons but also for the close-knit groups they had formed. After a bit of initial hesitation and discussion, new members had been admitted all the time. The clans had started to expand rapidly.

As the burgeoning society had prospered, the mix-breed chiefs had gained power right along with the increase in responsibilities. They had made sure all were treated fairly, regardless of race or gender. Having been outcasts themselves, they had no intention of keeping such prejudices alive.

The elves, approving of this development among their neighbors and realizing that an official governing system was needed to keep the peace, had decided to make the nine leaders kings. They had sent a missive to each clan with the news. Never had a message been more surprising or welcome. The celebrations which had followed had gone on for several days.

That they, who had been the underdogs for so many years, would ever rule over their fellow Highlanders none of the Zidarians had ever thought possible.

The lords, suddenly finding themselves in charge of large areas and responsible for a fair amount of people, had come to realize that a plan was needed to better defend their land. If it was left up to just one group or another, they might not be strong enough, and disaster might befall the Highlands.

Therefore, one of the first acts of the new kings had been to call a gathering. Zidhe, dwarves, and human alike had heeded the call. Even a couple of giants had attended. This get-together became known as the 'First Council of the Highlands.'

During that meeting, many an idea had been born and then discarded or had given rise to a brand-new proposal. Progress had been slow but steady. At this point, all the northerners had been aware that things could not continue as before. The battle with Ulric had taught them that. Their way of life had to change if they wanted to keep their lives and their homes.

The Highlanders had understood that it was vital that they banded together. They all had different skills, and had needed to learn from each other, get better organized. They had to be prepared to respond more quickly. The days of separate groups living here or there had to end if they wanted to survive.

✦✦✦

Out of the necessity to safeguard their homes, the 'Highland Nation' had emerged. Covenants had been signed for mutual assistance. Laws had been agreed upon, and a council created. A truce had been declared between all Highland races. From that day on, no mix-breed or any individual of any race would have to fear persecution because of his or her blood.

There had been some minor disagreements as can be expected, but about one thing they had all been in accord. Never again could a foreign noble be allowed to bring an army onto their soil. Once had been enough.

The Highlanders had been determined to never forget the valuable lessons they had gained from that bloody encounter.

The new nation's first priority had been the defense of their borders. And, who better to teach them than the Zidarian lords?

Chapter 12

A Strange Feeling

Ki'ara and her companions, Mathus and Hugo, had set out that morning in sporadic sunshine. It had actually been a rather pleasant day for traveling. In the early afternoon, however, dark clouds came boiling over the horizon. Gusty winds started to roar down the mountain passes and buffet the travelers. Then the rain, which had been threatening for hours, finally arrived. First, it sprinkled only lightly, but before long, the downpour began in earnest.

Mathus reacted the way he usually did when things got a little uncomfortable. He started complaining loudly. Then, the tutor stopped his horse dead in its tracks, blocking the path. Ineffectively, he attempted to get to his raingear, which was securely strapped on the saddle behind him. To reach it, all he had to do was to turn around and untie it.

The man twisted and contorted himself as much as he was able to, but it was not quite enough. He could not see what he was doing and kept fumbling unsuccessfully with the fastenings holding on his waterproof cloak. Try as he might, Mathus could not get them to budge. True to form, he was muttering angrily under his breath instead of concentrating on what he was doing.

Ki'ara realized that they would not be moving along anytime soon unless she helped. With an exasperated sigh, the young sorceress dismounted and assisted the grumbling man in putting on his rain gear. Even then, he still refused to continue on but whined unhappily about being wet and having to ride in such horrible conditions. It took her a bit, but she finally managed to convince the peevish man to proceed down the trail.

After that, the weather just kept getting worse. All three riders huddled miserably under their oiled cloaks while the rain pounded the mountains around them. They were moving very slowly to make sure none of the horses slipped on the wet rocks. Before long, rivulets were running across the path, making travel even more perilous. The danger of landslides was increasing with each moment since the soil was unable to absorb such a large amount of water.

The heavy deluge seemed to go on for hours. Small waterfalls had started to develop here and there along the path. The trio was now moving at a snail's pace for safety's sake. Just when Ki'ara thought the violent barrage would never stop, the sun broke through the clouds and illuminated the world around them. She let out a huge sigh of relief that for the time being, the rain was over.

The downpour had lasted for most of the afternoon and evening was approaching fast. Dark shadows were creeping across the impressive massifs and filling the deep valleys. Orange hues lit up the peaks and touched the snow-covered mountains far off in the distance, setting them aflame in a kaleidoscope of color. The view was stunning and managed to jolt Ki'ara out of her reverie. With great appreciation for the majestic beauty around her, she watched the sun dip further towards the horizon.

Hugo, the stablemaster at De'Aire Chateau, had been assigned as their guide. To keep the castle adequately supplied, the old man traveled this path every few weeks, mostly alone. He appreciated having Ki'ara along but had never cared much for Mathus.

Argulf had been unwilling to have any of his servants make an extra trip just to take his exasperating student down to her ship. Ki'ara could not really fault him for this, it was a long way after all. Hugo, therefore, would pick up the castle's regular supplies before heading back up. This combined the two tasks very efficiently and had been the reason for their delay in departure.

Ki'ara was happy that it was the stablemaster who was leading them down to the harbor. Not only did they get along well, but the man was familiar with all the best places to camp for the night. He was an expert at reading the mountains and good at avoiding the dangers around them. She had gotten to know him well and trusted Hugo wholeheartedly.

As it was, the inclement weather had significantly put them behind schedule. Ki'ara realized that they should have reached their first rest stop by now. The incessant rain had severely slowed their progress. With an eye on the fading light, the old man hurried them along.

It was a while before Hugo guided their party onto a side trail leading into a deep, narrow crevasse between two mountains. Carefully, they made their way along the tight, dark passage until it widened once more, and they arrived at the entrance to a small valley. Taking advantage of the confined space, someone had built a rather sturdy gate. Ki'ara was pleased to see that this was where they would be spending the night.

The protected gorge had plenty of overhangs to shield the horses in case the foul weather returned. Steep cliffs, enclosing it on all sides, prevented anyone and most creatures from coming in from above. And, best of all, it had a small wayfarer hut which promised welcome shelter from the cold night air as well as the elements.

Mathus, only concerned with his own welfare, immediately dismounted. He raced into the building, leaving his horse standing where it was. He never even asked if he could be of assistance. The stable master watched the tutor's disappearing back through narrowed eyes. Shaking his head, he snorted with disapproval.

'We are all wet and tired, and not only he! Has this lout never heard of lending a hand with the chores? Does he think he is too good to take care of his own mount? Or does he expect his mistress to do it for him? Just because the lady is kind does not give that rascal the right to take advantage of her!'

These and other irritated thoughts were going through the usually easy-going man's head. Ki'ara had noticed Hugo's angry reaction. When he turned back to her, she met his eyes and shrugged her shoulders. There was not much she could do about this.

Mathus was her brother's paid watchdog, and complaining about him had never accomplished anything before. Nor did getting upset over his rudeness. The tutor was already more pleasant than he had been in the beginning. This was not worth getting into a confrontation with him over.

Instead, Ki'ara helped the old man unsaddle and rub down the horses. They stowed the luggage and most of the gear in a small shed attached to the hut. Working together, it did not take them long to have the animals feed and secured for the night.

Hugo thanked the girl for her aid. He had known that she was kind and generous, but this had been entirely unexpected. None of the other apprentices his master had had over the years would have ever even thought of doing such a thing! The stablemaster would miss her smiling face down in the kitchen. She had been a ray of sunshine in their otherwise dreary lives.

After one last look around to assure themselves that all was in order, Ki'ara and her companion picked up the bedding and made their way towards the hut. It was getting colder by the minute, and the pair was getting chilled in their wet clothing. It was time to start a fire to warm themselves up, cook dinner, and have some hot tea.

⊱•❧•⊰

Ki'ara and Hugo had almost reached the shelter when suddenly, the sorceress froze. The hair on her neck and arms started slowly standing up. Something had caught her attention, but she was not certain what. She was convinced, however, that some sort of menace was near. Sending out her senses, she checked for possible dangers.

Her companion had been watching her curiously. Hugo was used to such conduct from Argulf and the many apprentices he had traveled with over the years. When a frown found its way onto Ki'ara's lovely face, however, the old man started to get concerned. He knew this young woman, and she did not spook easily. "Lady, are you alright? Something out there?" he asked worriedly.

His words seemed to jolt Ki'ara out of her trance. "I do not know, Hugo. I thought I felt something, but I am not sure what. I am not able to pinpoint any specific threat, but still, I have this vague sense of unease. It will probably turn out to be nothing. Let's go inside and get a fire going to warm up!" she responded, absently rubbing her arms since she was freezing all of a sudden.

The stable master was a cautious man and had long since learned to heed his own instincts as well as those of others. Knowing Ki'ara and trusting her gut, he was convinced that there was a good reason for the young sorceress' misgivings.

"Right after we bar the entrance and set the alarm!" Hugo replied. He had never seen the young woman react like this and was certain something was out there. Otherwise, his level-headed companion would not have responded like that.

Just as Ki'ara and Hugo finished with the gate, the sun dropped below the horizon. With the fading light, temperatures began to fall even more sharply. The two hurried to the hut, they needed to get warm. This high up, it was always frosty during the night. One needed heat, blankets, and shelter to make it safely through the long, cold hours until the morning arrived.

Hugo soon had a roaring fire going, and its life-giving warmth started to flood into the chilly cabin. Mathus stumbled over and rudely pushed the old man out of the way. The stablemaster tripped as a result of this unexpected shove and would have hit his head on the hearth had Ki'ara not caught him. She carefully helped him back on his feet. The usually calm young lady was furious.

As always, all the self-centered tutor cared about was his own comfort. Nobody or nothing else seemed to matter to him. No wonder her brother's lackey had been fired from his last employment and had to flee to the north! Had he wholly forgotten that they needed Hugo to safely reach the port? Leaving the horse had been one thing, but this was another. Mathus had gone too far!

Ki'ara had enough of his crude conduct. It was time, yet once again, to put this insufferable man in his place. "Mathus, what is wrong with you? How dare you treat Hugo like that? He could have been hurt! How do you think you are getting off this mountain then? Are you able to think of anything besides your own comfort at this very moment?" she spat in a low and tightly controlled voice.

Being such addressed, the tutor reluctantly turned around to face her. He took in the young sorceress' angry, narrowed eyes which seemed to be spitting fire. He was aware that she was much more powerful than he and vividly remembered the last time he had pushed Ki'ara too far. The outcome had not been in his favor.

In a show of submission, Mathus lowered his eyes. He was not prepared to pick a fight with this very irate lady right now. The tutor had other and far scarier things on his mind. Besides, in any straightforward duel, he was sure that he had no chance against her. There were more effective ways of dealing with this impudent girl. Direct confrontations had never been to his liking, he usually looked for a backhanded way to get even with someone.

"Hugo needs to cook our food on that fire! We are all hungry and cold, not just you! Step aside and apologize for your actions!" Ki'ara ordered in a voice that did not brook a refusal.

Seeing no other option, the spiteful cad did as he was told, but he was fuming under his remorseful facade. Mathus swore to himself that once they arrived safely back in the Highlands, he would come up with something to make that witch pay for this humiliation!

Once the trio had eaten, the tutor immediately plopped down onto one of the four beds. He was still angry and wanted nothing more to do with either of his companions. Before Ki'ara and Hugo had even finished cleaning up, Mathus' loud snores were filling the hut. All the young woman could do is shake her head in disbelief.

Her brother's watchdog was unpleasant at best, but traveling with him was always a challenge. His incessant complaining and rude behavior severely tested her patience each time. Ki'ara was looking forward to reaching the ship. Once they were on board, she could avoid the insufferable man. He usually became seasick and stayed in his cabin for most of the passage, giving her some welcome relieve from his presence.

⚜

In preparation for the night, Hugo banked the fire and, to get it going again in the morning, he and the girl stacked kindling and wood near the hearth. Finally, all was ready for the long, dark hours.

Ki'ara was tired from the challenging ride and glad that it was time to slip into bed. She had been unable to sleep well the evening before partially due to her worrying about Taryn and the friends she was leaving behind.

Her dreams of an impending doom of one sort or another had not helped either, and neither had her apprehensions about returning to Seamuir.

The mattresses here in the hut were hard but still better than sleeping on the cold ground. Hugo and Ki'ara each took a cot and rolled themselves into their blankets. It took only a few minutes for the stablemaster's soft wheeze to join Mathus' obnoxious snorts. The gangly man's annoying sounds filled the whole hut and reverberated off the rafters.

How could she possibly sleep with all that noise going on? Ki'ara sighed. This was going to be a long trip! Her thoughts turned to the Highlands, and the stories her father had told her at bedtime.

Regardless of their bloodiness, they had always been a comfort to her. Maybe these old and familiar tales would help her nod off despite all that awful racket!

✦✦✦

The ones who benefited most from the battle with Ulric's ill-fated army were the mix-breeds. They had fought like the heroes of legends, gaining the admiration of Zidhe and humans alike. Even the warlike dwarves had to admit that they were a force to be reckoned with.

The almost immortals were now collectively known as Zidarians. Any with at least 50% elven ancestry qualified for this distinction. The more Zidhe blood an individual had, the more magic he or she could wield and the longer the lifespan.

Since each ruler needed a successor to pass his reign down to, weddings ensued, often between members of different clans. This created new bonds. In due time, the first heirs were born. Interbreeding with humans was discouraged in the purest Zidarian families but was widely accepted among those with less elven blood.

✦✦✦

Being able to use magic as well as fight like berserkers, the mix-breeds stood out from the rest of the Highlanders. They had proven themselves as great warriors and as utterly fearless and cunning. In addition, they had incredible healing powers and could live for more than a thousand years.

During the combat, the outcasts had quite naturally slid into leadership positions due to their prowess. The respect they had gained resulted in huge changes. The nine ruling Highland clans were the direct result of the battle. The same people who had once despised the Zidarians now acknowledged them as kings and asked them for advice. Even the Zidhe had formed a close alliance with the mix-breed rulers.

So many people had ended up asking for admittance to the clans that the Zidarians had been outnumbered by humans within years. Houses had been built close to the fortresses, and, as their numbers had increased, these communities had grown into small cities and towns. Outlying farms and fishing villages had petitioned for entry as well. Thus, the areas governed by each group had continued to steadily increase.

To keep the peace, the elves divided most of the rim of the Highlands and the adjacent islands into nine kingdoms, one for each ruling family. Some regions were set aside for the other races. The center, a strip along the border with the south, and several valleys leading down to the sea, the Le'aanan kept for themselves.

The Zidhe's lands became known as the 10th kingdom, and rumors had it that it was a truly wondrous place.

The Zidarians had been hunted and despised most of their lives. They had yet to adjust to peace and to overseeing so many people. A considerable part of their lives had been spent on weapons training and the occasional fight. Old habits die hard, and therefore it did not take long before squabbles erupted over border regions between kingdoms.

The Zidhe decided that the only way to put an end to the quarreling was to allow these skilled warriors to do what they did best, just under controlled circumstances. They would hold a joust to settle some of these disputes. Each king would fight for the right to keep the area in question and to establish which one of them was the best fighter of all. The champion at the end of the day would become the primary arbitrator at the council meetings.

The new lords happily agreed. The rules were set down, and the tournament began. The winner, a man from what would become the clan of the StClouds, gained a sizeable piece of land and an honored position.

His realm he named Summerland due to it having the longest summer and most pleasant weather of all the nine kingdoms.

Chapter 13

Mathus the Annoying

It was the second day of their ride down from the mountain chateau. Again, the morning had started out sunny, but with each passing hour, the sky was becoming more and more overcast. The wind had started to pick up, and the temperature continued to drop. At least it was not raining, and for that, the young sorceress was immensely grateful.

In spite of Ki'ara's alarm the night before, their travel so far had been uneventful. She had, however, noticed that Hugo was keeping a much closer eye on their surroundings than he had the previous day. The sorceress remained watchful herself. Something unpleasant had spooked her, had been out there, of that she was sure, but she had no idea what.

Their biggest problem was Mathus. Ki'ara's tutor did nothing but complain every chance he got, but especially when they finally made camp for the night. The young woman and the good-natured stable master let out a huge sigh of relief when the obnoxious man eventually fell asleep.

Both Hugo and Ki'ara were tremendously grateful that the path was so narrow that they had to ride single file. Who would want to listen to that whining all day? It was bad enough for the few minutes they had to tolerate his constant grumbling whenever they stopped.

Usually, Ki'ara avoided her guardian's watchdog as much as she could. She had not liked the man from the first day Ragnald had assigned him to her. Mathus' task was to accompany her to the homes of the various teachers she was sent to study with and to report her progress, as well as her compliance with Ragnald's rules, back to her brother.

The tutor was supposed to make all the travel arrangements, look after her, and act as her chaperone. As part of his job, he was to help Ki'ara any way he could and ensure that she was treated with respect and fairness. That at least had been the official version the sly lord had sold to the council.

The reality was much different. The MacClair's lackey had been discourteous and rude to Ki'ara from the very beginning. He had threatened and verbally abused her. She was the one who ended up dealing with all the arrangements for their transportation. The young woman had minimal choice in the matter. To keep the peace and avoid unpleasant repercussions, she was forced to cater to the sullen man instead of him taking care of her.

Ragnald was aware of all this and, if anything, encouraged Mathus to handle his sister with contempt and disrespect. He had genuinely enjoyed himself the first, and only time Ki'ara had complained about the way she was being treated by the ill-tempered tutor.

The MacClair's attitude had told her beyond a shadow of a doubt that she was on her own and that no support of any kind would be forthcoming from her uncaring guardian.

✦✦✦

Mathus was blindly faithful to his harsh lord. Not being a member of the clan and not even a Highlander, his loyalty belonged solely to his master. Not that the tutor had much of an option. It was Ragnald's decision whether he was allowed to stay at Seamuir Castle and in the north, something the man desperately desired.

Having to return to the south was a fate Mathus was trying to avoid at all costs. He had successfully managed to hide from his present employer that he was a wanted criminal on the other side of the border. The conduct towards his last student had so enraged the child's father that he had filed charges against the belligerent tutor.

Since the justice system was not the most efficient and just to make sure that Mathus got what he deserved for emotionally and physically harming his son, the outraged lord had also put a price on the abuser's head. A pretty high one at that, paid for on his delivery dead or alive. The tutor had barely managed to escape his pursuers and had no intention of ever going back.

Therefore, whatever his present lord wanted, he got. Mathus took his cues from his employer. Having seen the intense dislike Ragnald had for Ki'ara, the tutor had correctly assumed that he did not have to be respectful or kind to his new pupil. No punishment would be forthcoming for treating this girl any way he pleased!

✦✦✦

Mathus was not a very pleasant person. He lacked compassion and empathy and had disliked most of his students intensely. The man had been deeply resentful that they got to sit in the lap of luxury while he had to kowtow as well as try to teach these arrogant little twerps. Who gave them the right to look down on him?

One day, his temper had gotten the best of Mathus. All that resentment and anger boiled over. He had just lost it and had beaten the small boy so severely that he had passed out. The tutor had seen the writing on the wall and had fled the estate before his crime was discovered.

The depraved man had left the bleeding and unconscious child laying there to be discovered by his mother many hours later. He had not even bothered to throw a blanket over the boy to keep him warm. It had been days before his victim regained consciousness, and he had never been the same since.

His present charge was much older than Mathus' usual pupils and a girl at that. In the beginning, this had tempted the corrupt man, but his life depended on keeping this job. Ragnald might let him get away with some things, but even he had to answer to the council, and they would have taken offense at such an act.

⊱⋅☆⋅⊰

Having a cad such as Mathus as her watchdog had not been a good situation for Ki'ara. She had little choice but to tolerate the tutor's lack of respect, his spying on her, and his strict enforcement of all her brother's unpleasant rules. After a while, she had found ways to work around her disagreeable companion and to marginalize him.

The young sorceress grew very inventive in her methods of avoiding her brother's henchman, and she was determined to stay away from Mathus as much as she possibly could without getting in trouble. Tolerating his occasional presence was unavoidable since it meant that she would have a somewhat more pleasant visit back at her home.

⊱⋅☆⋅⊰

Ragnald had made sure that his sister clearly understood the consequences of disobedience. She was to do precisely what the tutor told her or else. It did not matter what he asked of Ki'ara, she was to obey. There had been a long list of unpleasant punishments for noncompliance. By that time, the lord knew only too well what would hurt his sibling the most.

Spending the entire time as a prisoner in her room while at Seamuir had not appealed much to Ki'ara. She loved being outside, and she liked being around people. The threat of losing the freedom to walk on the moors, of being denied companionship, and having to stay all alone in her chambers for days on end, had very effectively kept her in line for a while.

All this had changed when Mathus had finally pushed Ki'ara too far. When the nasty man had started going out of his way to make her life as unpleasant as he possibly could, the sorceress just had it. She decided that she would rather face the consequences than allow herself to be treated this way on a daily basis. Enough was enough!

Ki'ara had very firmly but politely put the man in his place. She had told him that she would report his behavior to the council. He would be lucky if all that happened to him then would be his banishment from the Highlands. Abusing a Zidarian, a member of the immortal ruling families, was a severe offense and punishable by death or lifelong confinement.

The uppity cad had been terrified. This confrontation had not been what he had expected. Mathus had utterly misread the girl and had figured that she could be easily intimidated and kept under control. It had worked so far, and her own brother was on his side after all!

❧❦❧

Like all bullies, Mathus was really a coward at heart. Faced with his pupil's anger and determination, he had started backpedaling desperately and had begun to apologize profusely. For the first time since the tutor had joined her, Ki'ara had gained the upper hand.

Mathus knew how his lord rewarded failure. Ragnald would not only kill him but make him suffer unbearably. In the end, he would be begging for death just to put a stop to the horrible pain. The tutor had been a witness to such a punishment once. It had been for a very minor offense while this would be huge.

By then, Mathus was more afraid of Ki'ara's brother than anyone else. If Ragnald found out that his servant had lost control over the young woman, there would be hell to pay. And worse yet, what if his master was called in front of his peers to explain why he, her guardian, had allowed his employee to mistreat the sister he was charged with protecting?

Seeing that the man was sufficiently intimidated, Ki'ara had put forth a proposition to him. She had suggested that in return for her silence and cooperation, Mathus would leave her alone. They would pretend to her brother that nothing had changed and continue to travel together, just as before. They would, however, treat each other with respect and some consideration whenever they were away from the castle.

The tutor had been beyond relieved at this elegant solution. This would actually mean less work for him, and he was safe from being deported or tortured to death. Mathus had quickly agreed. Life had been much better since then for the young lady, even if she did have to put up with his annoying whining whenever they traveled.

⋆⁂⋆

Ki'ara was just about to fall asleep when she realized that something was niggling in the back of her mind yet again. She was immediately wide awake. Using her magic, she scanned their surroundings. Were they in some kind of danger? Was someone trying to sneak up on them? This was two days in a row, and the sorceress was determined that this time she would figure it out.

When her initial sweep yielded no results, she extended her keen senses further out. There! She had detected something! Just as soon as Ki'ara focused on her target, however, it vanished. For a brief second, she had been able to make a connection, but it had disappeared the moment she gave it her full attention.

The contact had felt familiar, similar to Taryn's but different. The catamounts were also referred to as ghost cats for a good reason. Stealth was a significant aspect of their nature, but this being had disappeared too fast, had evaded her searching mind too effortlessly, and it had seemed more menacing and darker than her friend.

✦⟡✦

Except for an occasional great sadness, Taryn's vibrations had usually felt friendly and full of light to Ki'ara. She had often wondered what had happened to him. Had the cat lost someone he loved? Could this have been one of the reasons he had moved into the castle and had bonded so tightly with her?

Ki'ara was almost convinced that what she had sensed had been some sort of a feline. Could it have been her friend, and she had misread the aura? The interaction had been so very fleeting before the beast had shaken off the connection. In her mind, the young lady went over what she had perceived at that moment. She tried to recall exactly what she had felt.

No, it had not been Taryn. The sorceress was now sure of that. 'It would have been wonderful if it had been him, if he had managed to follow me!' She could not help thinking with a slight touch of guilt. How comforting it would have been to have him near! Ki'ara missed him so much already, but she knew that it would be selfish to rip him out of his familiar surroundings, no matter how much she wanted to take him along.

If the catamount did show up, she would have to do her best to send him back home to the high peaks, if at all possible. The thought alone filled Ki'ara with great sadness. Parting with her beloved companion a second time would be even harder than leaving him in the first place.

All of a sudden, a terrible truth dawned on the young woman. There was something out there, and it was dangerous not just to her and her companions but also to Taryn!

With that thing prowling around, Ki'ara sincerely hoped that her friend had remained safely up in the mountains!

Chapter 14

Ghastly Accounts

With her mind so full of worry about Taryn and that creature haunting the mountains, Ki'ara had a hard time falling asleep. The young woman wished that she had been able to gather more than a hint of what she was dealing with. The unknown is always the scariest since the mind is expert at conjuring up all kinds of possibilities. Usually, these figments of one's imagination were worse than the real thing. The sorceress sincerely hoped that this was also the case here.

To lull herself to sleep, Ki'ara fell back upon her favorite bedtime stories. They had always helped to calm her in the past. The girl loved hearing about the Zidhe and had nothing but admiration for the inventive elves who had been instrumental in keeping the Highlands safe all these years.

Ulric's invasion had been a rude awakening for the Le'aanan and their allies, and they had taken action to ensure that this would not be repeated. Together, they had come up with a cunning plan which they had hoped would deter future forays into their lands. For its execution, they had managed to enlist the aid of some of the captive warriors from the southern army.

Those few of Ulric's fighters who had decided to go back home for one reason or another had told a terrifying tale. They had spoken of horrible creatures that stalked you in the night and pounced on you unexpectedly during the daytime. They had shared their memories of innocent-looking glades that would rise up and swallow an entire army without leaving a trace.

"But worst of all are the people of the north," one of the returning soldiers had said with a shudder. "Lightning flashes from their swords and lances. They strike you down before you can even get close! They are terrifying, truly horrendous!"

"No! That's not the worst!" another warrior had objected. "The worst is their faces! I had never seen anything like that! Their faces is so gruesome they will give nightmares to the most seasoned of fighters! I sees them, every night, in my dreams!" he had continued, turning a deathly shade of white at the mere thought.

"Them northern hordes, them fought like demons! And not just them men! Them womenfolk howled like banshees coming after ya! Them rip your heart out with their bare hands given half a chance!" another man had recalled. He had been shaking with fright.

"Us and our lord, we never had a chance! Just a few of them brutes could take on an entire huge army and win! Them devils are completely peculiar and mad as hatters! Them have no humanity, not even a smidgen!" he had continued quite vehemently.

The soldiers' accounts had been further reinforced by heads of the dead thrown over the wall in the dark of the night, and corpses piled high at the gates. Such a foul deed had not been much to the Highlanders' liking, but with the elves' magic, it had been easier and faster than burying all those bodies to prevent an outbreak of disease.

For Ulric, the invading army's ruthless leader, the Highlanders had reserved a special fate. His body had been impaled on one of his own lances and was now dangling from a large oak close to the wall.

The lord's corpse had been strategically placed too high to reach from the ground. By now, the guards had become so terrified that they had refused to go out of the gate, cross that bare strip of land, and cut down the tree. Therefore, Ulric had remained where he was, food for the birds.

People had climbed up to the top of the wall for days to see the spectacle of the once so high and mighty aristocrat swinging in the breeze. He had become a most morbid attraction, and bets had been made how long it would take before the crows finished off what was left of him. With a lord being treated such, the onlookers had ended up wondering what those beasts from the north would do to them if they were unlucky enough to be captured.

Watching the lordling swinging from the tree had quickly taken on a slightly carnival-like air. Folk had a grand time sharing the grisly stories of the ill-fated Ulric and his soldiers. Seeing a welcome business opportunity, enterprising traders had set up their stalls and had begun to peddle their wares within hours. These merchants had helped carry the tales to even the smallest of hamlets.

As planned, the ghastly accounts the defeated warriors had brought home had spread like wildfire. Soon, they had been whispered wherever people gathered. No one had dared to speak of the horrors out loud, not even in the light of day, for fear of drawing them near. They had been just too deliciously gruesome, however, not to share them with all willing to listen.

The consensus that it would be terrible if those invincible brutes ever came south of the border had gained momentum. As the stories were passed from person to person, they had been embellished a bit here and a bit there. New atrocities had been added to the continuously growing list, and all these adulterated narratives gave birth to the legend of the barbarian devils.

The tales became ever more frightening and brutal with each new telling. Soon, they had little resemblance to the actual reports given by the soldiers. Dread spread swiftly far south of the border.

⁂

The legends of the northern devils had struck terror into their southern neighbors' hearts, just as the elves and the Highlanders had intended. To accomplish this, the Zidhe had implanted a few enhanced memories into the willing minds of those returning home to the south.

It had been done with the fighters' permission, and they had been encouraged to add some details of their own. In return, the soldiers had been well paid. Those men who had used their rewards wisely never had to fight or work again as long as they lived.

⁂

For additional protection, however, the Le'aanan had strengthened and improved the barrier. Never again could an army such as Ulric's be allowed to make it across. The ambitious aristocrat had come too close to his goal of taking over their lands.

Also, all the deaths of the innocent men, women, and children that depraved lord had caused had weight profoundly on the Highlanders' minds and hearts. Even the possibility of such a tragedy happening again had to be prevented. Of that, they had all been in agreement.

Thus, as a further deterrent, the elves had added a thick barrier of impenetrable, magical fog designed to keep people out in a more humane way and prevent them from entering the death zone. It reached within easy viewing distance of the wall and was sentient enough to alert the Zidhe to even the smallest intrusion.

Any unwelcome visitors setting foot into the mist would rapidly grow confused and lose their orientation. They would walk around in circles until exhausted only to finally exit at a spot far from where they had first started. They would be tired, hungry, and thirsty but safe.

The guards who had to watch this stark whiteness from the top of the wall were the ones who were most affected by its presence. They could not help themselves. The roiling clouds soon took on all kinds of terrifying shapes and appearances. The shifting patterns and glowing spots, which resembled eyes staring back at the soldiers, were bad enough during the day but terrifying at night.

Knowing the stories, imagination took over from there. Many a brave man had run screaming from his post, often causing panic among his comrades who were already on edge. As time went by, it became harder and harder for the southerners to find people willing to work as sentinels on top of the wall.

The elves had been delighted to hear of this resounding success and that the enchantments feeding the fog managed to put fear even into the boldest of hearts.

The Highlands became known as a cursed place, best avoided. They were said to be magic riddled and not fit for regular folk to inhabit. Its people were seen as brutal savages devoid of love and compassion. Rumors had it that they had to be some sort of mix-breeds with beasts or the spawn of demons, utterly inhuman.

The terror the gruesome tales inspired had served well to keep the Lowlanders out for many, many years now but made traveling abroad a challenge at times. For the Highlanders, it was best to avoid notice.

Ki'ara had gotten very good at using a glamour, which made her appear as fully human. This allowed her to dodge possible unpleasantness on her journeys south of the border.

Chapter 15

A Hard Time Sleeping

That night, sleep was a long time in coming. Both Hugo and Mathus were snoring, but Ki'ara was wide awake. Her senses were very astute, but try as she might, she could no longer detect the source of the disturbance her mind had brushed across earlier. This had never happened to her before and made the young sorceress very uneasy. What exactly was out there, and how did it avoid being detected?

By now, they were a good way down the mountains. If all went well and the rain held off, they should reach the harbor late in the afternoon on the day after tomorrow. Traveling along these treacherous paths was the most challenging part of the trip. The view was stunning at times, but this was a dangerous place.

Even under ideal circumstances, the journey from the castle down to the sea took almost four days. The ride up to De'Aire Chateau had taken even longer. The *Sea Witch*, Ki'ara's very own beautiful clipper, should be waiting at Mercede Harbor to deliver her home. It would take another three weeks to reach Deansport. As usual, the young lady could not help feeling anxious about what life would be like this time when she returned.

Thinking of Ragnald always made Ki'ara sad. She understood that no one was perfect. Unpleasant traits could be found in individuals of all races. Some of her fellow Zidarians were not above being greedy and breaking the laws. The young woman had no illusions about that, but why did one of the worst offenders have to be her very own brother?

In an ideal world, people would treat each other with kindness, compassion, and respect. They would love their relatives and friends. Many Zidarian clans actually had bonds like that, but for some, the reality was much different. Her own family was a prime example of that.

The young sorceress could understand only too well why the Zidhe had separated themselves from the rest of their neighbors. It was nice to have one place away from such foolishness!

⚘

As the years passed, the population had begun to increase even in the Highlands. The clans were prospering, and houses and farms were spreading further and further across the realms. These lands were the elves' last refuge, and they were determined to defend the parts they had claimed as their own.

The Le'aanan had left most of the coastal areas to the clans, and that was where they were expected to remain. Some of the other races, like the giants, had headed further to the north, some even up into the artic. The dwarves had taken up residence under the mountains and had little care who lived above them. The majority of folks had found places to settle and care for.

The elves made sure that their neighbors respected the privacy they had requested. To keep people out, the Zidhe had fortified the boundaries of their realm with a compulsion that turned away any would-be trespassers. Few were allowed to enter their sanctuary, but at times, they did make exceptions.

To gain admittance, one was required to submit a written petition. Those who intruded unbidden and without a good reason seldom returned. The few outsiders who had found shelter in the kingdom of the elves could claim extraordinary circumstances. No one else had been welcomed nor would be, and the Le'aanan had made sure that all were aware of their wishes.

⚜

Many years ago, the Zidhe had called a second meeting of all the Highlanders. They wanted to make absolutely certain that the rules and their desire to be left in peace were firmly understood. Therefore, the elves had sent out messengers with invitations. These envoys had traveled to every clan as well as to the furthest islands that were part of the realm to deliver their missives.

The Le'aanan had requested that as many people as possible attended. They had promised great food and entertainment, always a draw for any Highlander. The elves had figured that if all went according to plan, the numbers should reach well into the thousands.

When the time had come, the Zidhe had prepared a large valley close to their realm for this momentous occasion. They had set up three magic gates to make traveling easier, had erected tents and had brought in supplies, had selected a camping area for each group, and had tried to anticipate all their various friends' immediate needs. Surrounding the clans' living areas, they had created corrals which supplied ample fresh water for the horses.

Then, the elves had added the finishing touch. Being well familiar with their guests often fiery dispositions, the Zidhe had cast a spell on the whole dale, which had helped to keep the assembly as harmonious as possible. They had no delusions and had understood only too well that one could not bring so many warriors into one place and not expect them to fight unless something was done to prevent such endeavors.

⊱✿⊰

Folk had begun to arrive from all reaches of the Highlands when the designated day drew near. As the Le'aanan had bid, only a few individuals had been left behind to guard the homes and to keep things up and running. The promise of a feast and a party had been enough of a draw.

The gates had been busy day and night. They had even backed up at first when the arriving people did not move off quickly enough. The Zidhe had assigned a few guards to keep traffic from stalling and to speedily send the newcomers towards their designated spaces.

Had it not been for the network of such doorways all over the Highlands, bringing these many individuals together would have been a logistical nightmare.

⊱✿⊰

Thanks to the elves, gates were located at strategic spots in each realm. They were easily reached from the main castles but never too close just in case of a hostile incursion from one of the neighbors. These shortcuts were primarily meant for official business and connected the nine kingdoms to each other and to the council's main chambers. The gateways allowed the lords to attend meetings and events no matter where they were held.

To prevent sudden invasions by opportunistic Highlanders, only one carriage could pass through at a time. The travelers were required to state their name and destination to the gatekeeper. He or she was intimately linked with the magic and the only one able to dial in the desired location, lock it in, and open the portal.

An alarm went off at any nearby fortress whenever someone entered the realm. A magic mirror could then be used to determine if friend or foe was on the way to their doorstep. The system had been built by the Zidhe long before the meeting and had been functioning perfectly for many a year.

It had been a great way to bring everyone to the assembly and the following party.

Thoughts of her home had finally managed to calm Ki'ara, and she slipped into a restless sleep. To keep Mathus, Hugo, and herself safe while she rested, the sorceress had placed a web of protection around their immediate area. If there were an attempt of an intrusion, she would be instantly alerted.

During the night, the young woman awoke several times when something tested the gossamer strings of her defensive shields.

Chapter 16

A Dark Presence

The young sorceress awoke with a start. Once again, she had the feeling that something was close by, creeping about just outside her shields. Using her powers, Ki'ara searched the area. She could not detect anything concrete, just a hint of lingering malice. This was definitely not Taryn; his vibrations were not sneaky and dark.

Judging from the hint of pure evil she had been able to sense, Ki'ara was confident that she had no desire to meet the thing stalking them. Carefully, the young lady slipped out of her blankets. She was still tired, but the situation needed her immediate attention.

The enchantress crouched for a moment, her hands touching the earth to ensure grounding. She extended her senses in all directions in an attempt to get a better feel for the menace. That the presence continued to evade her was beginning to annoy her.

Ki'ara could detect traces where the creature had been but not the being itself. There was no doubt that a presence was near, but try as she might, she could not pinpoint its location. The very air seemed to hold a sense of alarm that was being carried along by the wind. They were being watched; she was convinced of that. Feeling those eyes on her made the sorceress skin crawl.

Ever so quietly, Ki'ara awoke the stablemaster. Keeping her voice as low as possible, she shared her suspicions with the old man. Hugo would not be able to assist much in their protection, and neither would her tutor, but it would help to have them alert. If they were attacked, the young woman would have to use her powers to defend them, that was unquestionable.

Good thing that she was so well trained! From what she had perceived, Ki'ara only hoped that she would be strong enough to defeat whatever was out there.

The emanations of the creature made it likely that it was up to no good. Ki'ara decided that she would make it much harder for this thing to follow them from now on. Gathering her powers, she began to raise stronger shields. Just as she was about to slam them shut, she became aware of a bright presence racing down the path towards them. Taryn! He had followed them after all! And, he was in trouble!

The mountain cat had been running full out, most likely all night long. Taryn was so focused on the scent he was chasing that he was paying little attention to anything else. Until that moment, he had been one of the top predators in these high peaks with little to fear. Now, however, the menace Ki'ara had been unable to locate a few minutes ago boiled into full presence. It had homed in on him!

The sorceress feared that her faithful companion would stand no chance against this kind of a threat. Her friend would die if she did not do something and quickly, so instead of closing the shields around herself and her group, Ki'ara shaped them into a sphere with a long cord attached to it.

Taking careful aim, she flung the orb around the distant feline. Just in the nick of time! The young sorceress gasped when the impact of the evil presence reverberated down the thin thread. That entity, whatever it was, had tried to pounce on her friend and had met her shields instead! Had Ki'ara been but one second later, she would not have been able to save him!

The sense of pure hatred and malevolence shocked the young woman, and she shuddered. The creature, however, did not like the contact with her bright essence either. It reacted as if burned. The instant it reared back from the protective orb, Ki'ara acted. She simply vanished the globe and cat both and reappeared them in front of her.

⁕⁎⁕

At first, the catamount was disoriented by this sudden change in location. For a few moments, he continued shaking his head as if trying to clear it. Finally, his eyes focused on Ki'ara, and his whole demeanor changed in a flash.

Taryn was ecstatic to see his mistress, to have found her again. Rearing up, he placed his large paws on the girl's shoulders and started to exuberantly lick her whole face. Ki'ara allowed this for a bit, but she had no time for extended greetings right now.

The sorceress' immediate priority was their protection and to get them away from their present location.

⁕⁎⁕

Ki'ara had known about bandits frequenting these mountains, but she had never heard anyone speak of an evil presence such as this haunting these passes. What was that thing, and where had it come from? What kind of abilities did it have? Those were questions for later; right now, she needed to ensure their safety.

After placing more shields around the camp, Ki'ara helped the stable master. Together, she and Hugo got the horses ready for the day. They packed up and prepared everything for a quick exit. Taryn, in the meantime, had curled up on her blankets and had fallen soundly asleep.

Waking her tutor, the sorceress left for the last possible moment. After her recent encounter with that evil entity, Ki'ara needed just a bit more respite before dealing with Mathus. And, she needed some time to try to figure this out. What kind of being was this? What was it after, and where had it come from?

Ki'ara thought back on the impressions she had gathered from that brief contact. Since she loved to read, she was well versed in magical creatures. Her first thought had been that this was a dragon, but that had not felt right. She was sure it was not a wraith either nor anything natural. So, what exactly was she dealing with here?

The entity had tasted of magic, perverted magic as such, twisted and dark. They would have to stay on the alert from now on and take turns sleeping the next night. Good thing her powers had been so well honed, but using them for hours on end would still drain her. Ki'ara realized that she might need all her strength just to get them safely down to the harbor if this being continued to hunt them!

⚜

Mathus was less than pleased to be awoken so early. He started to complain loudly before the sorceress ever had a chance to explain to him what kind of danger they found themselves in. Ki'ara finally had enough and shut him up with a spell. Patiently, in a voice barely above a whisper, she laid out their situation.

"Now, can I release the gag? We need to get out of here and do so quickly. I need your cooperation if we are going to live. Do I have that?" Ki'ara asked gently but firmly, never taking her eyes off the man.

During her explanation, the tutor had gone as pale as a ghost. He nodded but would not look at the young lady. He was behaving even more shifty than usual. It immediately aroused Ki'ara's suspicions. She figured that there was something he was trying to hide.

"You know something, don't you?" she probed. With a resigned sigh, Mathus began to speak. "I am not sure, girl, but I have my suspicions. If it is what I fear, it will kill anything and anyone it encounters, indiscriminately. Our only hope is that you are stronger than it or that we can stay ahead of it. I believe it only lives a limited time."

So, he did know something! And, he was being reluctant about sharing this information with her, very unlike his usual self. The man loved to brag about his prowess and knowledge and could sing his own praises for hours!

Ki'ara's instincts told her that Mathus knew precisely what they were dealing with and who had sent it but was trying to avoid divulging the truth for some reason. Was he covering his own tracks?

"Do you have any idea what it is or who created it?" Ki'ara inquired more forcefully. She was watching Mathus carefully for signs of deceit. Sure enough, once again, the tutor would not meet her eyes.

"I have no proof, only a vague suspicion, and you do have my full cooperation, I swear! I am rather attached to my life, after all! What do you need me to do?" Mathus responded. He was saying all the right things, but his eyes kept shifting away from her gaze. He was still not being totally honest.

"I need to know everything you know about it, or suspect! All of it, Mathus!" Ki'ara countered. Her voice had taken on the edge of command.

"Alright, alright! I will tell you all I know!" he relented, looking profoundly offended. "It is only a hunch, mind you, but I heard the old wizard mumble something about a dragon wraith, so I looked it up," he began.

"It is a fearsome creature, brought into being through dark magic. If it does not feed, it only lives for a few days, hours. The reference claimed that a fair bit of power is required to create one and that it takes a somewhat skilled wizard to fetch it into this world, or a lucky one," the tutor explained, looking grossly affronted. He hated sharing this arcane knowledge.

"According to that book, it can be given directives by its maker, such as to kill someone. Unfortunately, it will also slaughter everything else it encounters. It is a truly horrific thing! Do you think that you can protect us from it?" Mathus finished. She could see the fear in his eyes, and the tutor's face had turned an even more deathly shade of white.

The young woman had been carefully observing the man's every gesture and facial expression. He had given her valuable information but not necessarily all of the truth. When Mathus had mentioned the old magician, he had been looking away. She was sure that he was hiding something, but right now was neither the time nor the place to force it out of the self-centered scoundrel.

꧁꧂

Once the tutor had been helped on his horse, they were on their way. So far, Ki'ara had been able to shield their group successfully from the monster's detection, but she could sense it searching for them. Did the old wizard really hate her this much for surpassing him? Somehow, that just did not seem right. The sorceress' gut told her that Mathus was much more involved than he claimed.

Ki'ara knew what Argulf's magic tasted like and thought that she should have been able to detect it on the creature. The vibrations it gave off, however, were unlike anything she had encountered before, very chaotic and jumbled, hard to make out.

There were some underlying similarities to the wizard's power, but this monster was utterly alien to her. It almost felt like it was a mix of different energies all jumbled together. It, she suspected, had been fashioned by someone or something entirely different. Was Argulf involved? Anything was possible, but Ki'ara was convinced that there was more to the story.

Chapter 17

A Boisterous Meeting

The travelers rode all day with Taryn contentedly padding alongside his mistress. There was no way he could go back up the mountains with the dragon wraith out there. It would have meant sending him to his death. Ki'ara would just have to take the cat home to the Highlands and hope for the best. It would not be easy, but she was glad to have him with her. He was far more helpful in a fight than either one of the men.

When Ki'ara had said goodbye, she had tried to explain to her beloved companion why she could not take him along, why she was leaving him behind. Not only was her own situation at Seamuir Castle quite difficult but, in the girl's opinion, her friend belonged among the tall peaks of the mountains. There, he could be wild and free, unlike on the ship or in the castle.

It seemed that this reasoning had made no impression on Taryn. At the first opportunity, the ghost cat had made up his own mind. He had slipped out on the cook and had raced down the path following the faint trace of Ki'ara's passing. He had been determined to find her and, disregarding his own safety, he had moved at a breakneck pace down the trails.

As happy as the young lady was to be reunited with her companion, she could not help thinking that it had been a good thing that the Highlanders had been a bit more cooperative with the elves when they were invited to that meeting so long ago!

Once the designated day had arrived, it had taken a fair bit for the multitude of individuals to get settled and for the last of the attendees to reach the isolated valley the Zidhe had chosen for the gathering. Stragglers had continued to arrive until the very last moment.

There had been a lot of excitement, comings and goings, and a few small arguments but also a lot of hilarity. Some individuals had gotten there so late that they had no time left to stow their things but had to head straight for the meeting! Leave it to a Highlander to wait until the very last minute!

⁓⁎⁎⁎⁓

On the morning of the council, all the attendees already present had been called to assemble. Once everybody had been comfortably seated, the meeting had begun. Using magic to amplify their voices, the Zidhe had spoken of their concerns. They had suggested that a pact should be signed by all peoples. The elves had felt that it was time to settle things once and for all so that no questions on boundary locations remained.

Having almost lost their own homes during Ulric's invasion, the other Highlanders had been able to understand the fairies' fears only too well. Some of the lords actually shared their concerns.

Over the years, the borders between kingdoms and regions had been moved around a fair bit. Many of the rulers had felt that it would be nice to have them fixed and to put a stop to the disputes and occasional land grabs.

※※※

The Le'aanan had prepared the magical contract ahead of time. It had been designed to bind them as well as their neighbors and had to be validated by the representative of each of the clans and the various groups. To make sure everyone had understood what they were signing, Geradian had read it out loud and had explained each point in detail.

The boundaries of the lands of the Zidhe had been readily agreed upon by all the folk of the Highlands. It had been a little harder, however, to get everyone to consent to keep the peace among clans as well as races. In some individuals' minds, some lingering hope to add to their territory had still remained. Also, raiding had become something that kept the young men busy, out of everyone's' hair, and it did bring in profit.

It had taken a while for all the objections to be voiced. In the end, the elves' demands had been grudgingly approved. This had put an end to the occasional incursion into each other's realms, something the clans, as well as the dwarves, had genuinely enjoyed.

After this significant hurdle, no one had a problem with the next point of the pact. Everyone had agreed that from that day forward, they would aid each other in times of need as well as assist in defense of their home.

The very last item on the fairies' list had been a gentle reminder to the rest of the Highlanders that they were living on lands that had been deeded to the Zidhe. They were welcome guests, but still guests.

All had accepted this fact. The clans and their neighbors had acknowledged that they would behave accordingly. None of them had wanted to be the ones facing eviction.

Once the contract had been signed and all points settled, it had been time for the eagerly awaited celebration.

✦❈❈✦

As promised, the Le'aanan had arranged for an elaborate feast. On top of this, each clan had contributed some of their specialties and had brought along their own distinct brand of drink. This had been the very first gathering of its kind that the Highlands had ever seen. The Zidhe had intended it to be memorable, and it was.

With the official part of the council behind them, it had been time to relax and to get to know each other better. New alliances had been formed, and long-standing grudges buried. Old friends had become reacquainted, and bonds strengthened.

✦❈❈✦

It had turned out to be a grand party. Wine, spirits, and mead had flown freely, and there had been plenty of food. Since the Highlanders loved a good feast, they had most certainly enjoyed themselves at this get-together. The boisterous revelry had gone on long into the night.

When folk had started on their way home the next day, they had been in good spirits. Many had been more than a little hungover, but such a thing was always taken with humor here in the north.

As the elves had surmised, nothing pleased the peoples of the Highlands more than some lively merrymaking with good company and plenty of drink!

✦❈❈✦

Ki'ara's horse stumbled, which brought her mind back to the present. The small group was doing their utmost to avoid attracting the dragon wraith's attention. Sounds can carry far in the mountains, so the sorceress and her companions had done everything possible to prevent any noise.

On Hugo's advice, the horses' hooves had been covered with burlap to deaden the clattering, and all items which might jingle had been carefully packed. Ki'ara was using her magic to hide their trail from the monster, and her shields were wrapped tightly around them. After a while, keeping up this protection became so automatic that it required little effort on her part.

Riding along in complete silence, each was preoccupied with their own thoughts. Ki'ara's mind once again turned to the Highlands.

———————

With the barrier reinforced, the Highlanders had managed to successfully keep their land separate from the Lowlands. Few, if any, hopeful immigrants ever found their way north anymore, and even if they did, it was rare that they received permission to stay. Mathus had been one of the lucky ones but was entirely at the mercy of his sponsoring lord.

Over the years, the magic the elves continually imbued their own lands with had begun to spread beyond the borders of their kingdom. By now, it had infused most of the Highlands and had taken on a life of its own. Those able to tap into were capable of incredible feats. The more Zidhe blood a person has, the greater their power.

The ruling Zidarian families had therefore made sure that their lines remained pure and were always looking to add more elven blood. They allowed inbreeding with humans for their clan members but never for one of their own children. The mix-breeds intended to retain their elevated positions as chiefs and did not want to weaken their magic. They were proud of their heritage.

The power, however, came with a caveat. To maintain the connection to the magic of the land, the rulers had to use it to care for the clans as well as their realms. They had to make sure that their people prospered, were happy, and free. The chiefs could do as they wished as long as they harmed none and worked for the greater good of the Highlands.

Transgressions against this unwritten law might be tolerated for a little while but, eventually, they would catch up with the wielder. The punishment, at times, had been much harsher than the crime. Therefore, most Zidarians stayed well within the law and would never even think of taking the chance of losing it all.

✦✦✦

For an immortal, to have his magic removed is the worst fate imaginable. Not only did one suddenly feel deaf, blind, and totally disconnected from the Divine, but remaining young forever was gone as well. Depending on how long a Zidarian had lived, rapid aging leading to death was one of the costs.

Without their powers, however, most would welcome the end. Being able to sense one's surroundings, to feel the pulse of the land, to be one with the Highlands was a precious gift the Zidarians cherished more than life itself.

The mix-breeds could not imagine being without this connection and treasured it deeply. Most would never knowingly do something to put it at risk. The strongest bonds of all were a privilege of the leaders, the lords of the clans.

✦✦✦

Nowadays, the chiefs of the Highland races were always called 'Lord.' The ruler could be a man or a woman, it made no difference. To some of the ladies' disgust, they had not been able to get their fellow Zidarians to budge on this matter. No amount of complaining had even the slightest effect. If at all, change came slowly in the north.

Life in the Highlands had been mostly quiet ever since the memorable meeting called by the Zidhe. There were, however, some brief exceptions, not unexpected, given the fierce nature of the inhabitants.

Many years ago, a war had broken out among the clans. After several bloody battles, the elves had had enough and stepped in. Something had to be done. The kings in question had been ignoring all the rules set down by the pact. Such conduct could not be tolerated!

The Le'aanans' punishment had made sure that the Zidarians remembered that this kind of behavior was against the contract they had signed. The elves had informed the lords that there would be even more unpleasant consequences if it happened again. Peace had been reestablished, and the warring parties had returned to their realms.

As part of the penalty for going to war, the Zidarian rulers had no longer been permitted to call themselves kings. It had been a constant and painful reminder that they were guests in these lands. The majority of the deposed monarchs had been wise enough to cherish the reprieve they had been granted.

Most of the lords had felt grateful that they had been allowed to remain in charge and to keep their homes, even if they had lost their precious titles. They had retained the privilege of governing their clans with almost the same authority but, from that point onward, had to also answer to the council of lords. A small concession in the scheme of things since they had been the ones who had broken the contract.

The wiser lords had actually figured that they had gotten off lightly. It could have been a lot worse. The Zidhe had been well within their rights to show all their unruly neighbors the door. Some, however, had seen the loss of their crowns as a terrible insult. Hate and resentment had reigned in their hearts. Ki'ara's own grandfather had been one of those few.

After the Zidhe's intervention, the Zidarians had adhered to the pact much better than the elves had ever expected. So far, the fairies had seen themselves forced to interfere again only rarely.

The Le'aanan were pleased that most of the realms were thriving. They appreciated the attempts of the lords to be more peaceful and to get along with each other.

In every bunch, however, there is always the one who is the exception. The Zidhe had been watching the new Lord MacClair quite closely for some time now. They had decided that if Ragnald violated the laws yet again, action would have to be taken.

Chapter 18

Continued Deception

Evening was starting to fall. By riding hard all day, Ki'ara and her companions had managed to stay ahead of the fearsome dragon wraith. As dusk began to approach, she noticed her tutor getting even more nervous than he had been all day. His face was ashen, he was sweating profusely, and his hands were shaking uncontrollably.

Ki'ara concluded that Mathus was deathly afraid. He was looking around anxiously and jumped at every sound. The longer she watched him, the more confident she grew that he knew what they were facing. "Leave it to that man to hold back information even when our lives depend on it!" the young woman mumbled under her breath. This kind of foolishness was alien to her.

'Mathus knows something he has not told me. What is he hiding? And, why? I can only imagine, but I bet that thing gains more strength at night like many evil creatures! We had better find shelter and soon,' the sorceress thought to herself.

Using her powers, Ki'ara cast about for a protected, as well as defensible, location. Usually, it was Hugo's job to take them to a safe haven for the night. She believed that the place where they had slept on the way up was not much further. If she remembered the layout correctly, however, it would not do in their present situation.

Her keen senses found a deep cave not too far away, but it lacked a second exit. If the monster caught Ki'ara and her companions in there, they would be done for. She had been able to hide their presence all day but felt that sleeping anywhere without another way out would be too much of a risk. The place just smelled of a trap, and her instincts warned her that this was not the right spot.

A protruding ledge with ample space underneath was another possibility. It was more exposed to the elements but just seemed safer. Unlike the cavern, it was a little way off their path but more to her liking. A deep fissure in the rock, just wide enough for the horses to get through, extended from the back. The crevice was located a bit to the left of the middle of the shelter. It made a perfect emergency exit.

The incline up to this cavernous retreat was rather steep. Ki'ara figured that she and the men would have to dismount and guide the horses. She only hoped that Hugo and Mathus were up for this. Neither was as young as they had once been, and the tutor was not a friend of physical exertion.

Being hard to approach would yield an additional advantage. It made the place all the more defensible. The hollow went back far enough to supply them with adequate protection, had excellent visibility, and provided them with a way to escape.

Since they were now further down the mountains, the nights were no longer as cold, so sleeping out in the open was relatively feasible. Not too pleasant but survivable. As far as Ki'ara was concerned, this space would serve their needs admirably, but she was sure that Mathus would find plenty of reasons to complain.

Hugo, the stable master, was in the lead, and Ki'ara needed to get past him. She quietly commanded Taryn to stop the horses at the next place where it was possible for her to maneuver around the two men. Once the young lady was ahead, she pointed in the direction of the shelter. Putting her hands together and tilting her head in the universal gesture for sleep, the sorceress got the point across to her fellow travelers without uttering a single sound.

Both men nodded their understanding. They seemed relieved, especially Mathus. It looked like he could not wait to get off this path. It was evident that he was utterly terrified. The question was why? Ki'ara regarded the tutor through narrowed eyes. She had never trusted her brother's lackey to start with and now even less. She decided that he would need to be watched closely.

Ki'ara doubted that her tutor was directly responsible for the creation of this monster. He was pretty attached to his own neck and was a coward to boot. Mathus would not do anything intentionally that placed him in danger. Had he accidentally done something he should not have? Her gut told the sorceress that this was quite likely. The man was, after all, not the most competent magician. He was only a very minor wizard with limited training.

One fact, however, kept nagging at Ki'ara. How did the tutor know precisely what they were dealing with? Very interesting! What was Mathus' involvement in all this?

Once they reached their shelter, it did not take very long for Ki'ara and Hugo to agree on how to set up camp. They decided that they would have to do without a fire this night since it would act as a beacon for the specter. The light would be visible for a long way in the dark.

Having amassed a significant amount of knowledge about the different types of magical beings, the sorceress suspected that even a small blaze would draw this creature like a moth to the flame. She decided that she preferred a cold meal to facing off with that nightmare in the dark.

For once, Mathus seemed to agree, and to Ki'ara's immense surprise, he was not even complaining. This was so unusual for him that it was definitely not a good sign. The girl's unease increased even more.

Hugo led the horses to the right side of the cleft. This area was more extensive and better suited for their mounts. He and Ki'ara unsaddled, watered, and fed them. They made sure that the animals were taken care of before seeing to their own needs. Then, they set up what they would need for the night and dinner.

Mathus had no interest in helping, nor was he able to. He was almost completely paralyzed by fear. Like a sleepwalker, the terrified man had stiffly gotten down from his steed. He had clumsily untied his blankets and had staggered off, leaving his mare standing untended.

The tutor had made his bed as close to the wall as he could and as far away from the open-air and cleft as possible. Without so much as a glance at his companions, Mathus had crawled under the covers. He had even refused to come out for the meal. While they were eating their food, the other two noticed that his entire body was shivering uncontrollably.

Ki'ara took pity on him. After exchanging a glance with Hugo, she walked over and bent down towards

Mathus. He flinched when she placed a comforting hand on his shaking shoulder. "Are you alright? What are you so afraid of?" she asked in a whisper.

"That thing out there! It wants me, don't you see! I can feel it coming closer! We are done for! We will never be able to make it out of these cursed mountains alive!" Mathus answered, getting more hysterical by the second. He was starting to raise his voice, putting them all in danger.

Ki'ara briefly touched the man's forehead and sent him into a deep, peaceful slumber. She made certain that he would not wake until late the next day unless she willed it otherwise. Getting an extra blanket, she wrapped it around his resting form to ensure that he stayed warm. With her tutor in a magical sleep, there was one less thing she had to worry about.

"You heard?" the young sorceress asked Hugo in a low voice once she had taken care of Mathus. The old man nodded. "Don't trust him, lady. That one, he knows more than he be telling. Me sees him sneak around the castle late at night. He thought we was all asleep. Down to the dungeons, he went," Hugo whispered with a shudder.

"That be a wicked place, lady, pure evil! Master puts all his old spells and experiments in there. I bet he has something to do with that monster!" the old man said in a hushed tone. He was angrily pointing at Mathus.

"What we going to do, lady? How we going to get down to the harbor? How is me going to get back to the castle?" the stable master asked glumly. Ki'ara could see that he was also terribly afraid. She had noticed him making signs to ward off evil all day. Why could it not be as easy as that?

"I will take first watch. Try to get some sleep. I will wake you if anything happens. Hugo, I will do my very best to get us all safely down to the harbor, that I promise. Mathus said that this thing has a limited lifespan, and we will just have to avoid it until it fades. In just a few days, it should be safe enough for you to go home," Ki'ara told her friend reassuringly.

Hugo searched her face for a moment, his eyes bright in the almost dark. He could hear the resolve in her voice. Finally, the stablemaster nodded and headed over to his own bed. He knew that he needed the rest. The long trip was getting more difficult and tiring for him every year.

The young woman hoped that she had managed to calm the old man enough to keep a cool head. Having two panicked companions on her hands would make their situation so much more dangerous. Fear paralyzed the mind and could get them all killed.

Would it really be possible for their guide to return home in a few days? What if that thing managed to feed? How much would that extend out its life? The sorceress sighed. How could she send Hugo back up the mountains unless she knew it was safe?

She might as well face it. It looked like she could not avoid dealing with that terrifying specter.

⚜

Ki'ara had set magical alarms on the incline, the rock shelf above, as well as in several locations in the natural tunnel, which led into the next valley. She had placed protective shields around the camp. No one would be able to sneak up on them without her knowing, not even that nasty apparition.

A dragon wraith. Did that mean that someone had enslaved the spirit of some poor deceased dragon? Turned it to evil and was commanding it? Who would do such a terrible thing? What kind of a sick mind would conceive such an abhorrent enchantment?

The sorceress could not help but wonder if this was one of the failed spells Hugo had told her about, the ones

Argulf kept hidden down in the cellar. Had Mathus, on one of his snooping expeditions, accidentally set something free he could not control? Was he responsible for allowing this nightmare to emerge into the world? She had so many questions and no good answers.

Ki'ara sat down close to the edge of their shelter. Here, there was just enough moonlight that she could keep an eye on the mountainside below them. Her position would also allow her to detect any approach from above. Taryn laid down close beside her. He placed his head in her lap. She absently started to stroke the catamount's soft head and ears, and he began to purr.

In the hope of gaining new insights that might help them survive, Ki'ara thought back to her time at the castle. The old magician had sent his apprentice down to the deep cellars on several occasions to fetch things.

The girl had always dreaded those tasks, but Argulf had insisted. Had she refused, the wizard would have been beyond furious, and she would have had to deal with her brother. It had been easier to just do it and get it over with.

The dungeons, on the lowest floor of the subterranean complex, had been carved far into the rock of the mountain itself. They were located several levels below the kitchen. A lengthy, pitch-black, and very narrow staircase, securely sealed off with a heavy wood door, led into this dark space from one of the man-made caves filled with supplies.

No natural light ever reached these caverns, and the young woman had to carry a lantern so that she could see where she was putting her feet on that extensive set of dangerous steps. Every time she had descended, strange sounds had echoed around the vast spaces, and the wind had moaned eerily through cracks in the rocks.

Heading down below was so terrifying that the servants refused to venture beyond the storerooms. Argulf had to go himself or had sent Ki'ara if he needed one of the ingredients he kept in the deep cellars.

❧✦❧

Being a sensitive person and empathetic, the place had given Ki'ara the creeps. It had literally set her teeth on edge and had made her hair stand up. She was usually pretty brave, but even she had found these ghastly dungeons frightening.

They had such an aura of doom, of misery, of desperation that the sorceress had always done her errands as fast as she could and had left as quickly as possible. She regretted now that she had never stayed long enough to take a look around.

Ki'ara had attributed her feelings to the illustrious history of the castle and the atrocities which had been performed in those rooms. She had been able to sense the anguish and agony which still permeated those walls.

So many unfortunate men and women had been tortured in these chambers. Being a gifted empath, the traces of those emotions had been so overwhelming that they had sent her fleeing each time.

Maybe she should have spent some time down there exploring after all. How could Argulf have been so careless? He should have known better!

❧✦❧

A hiding place like that for failed experiments was not the greatest of choices. Any magical being or item subjected to that type of an atmosphere for very long would end up twisted and dark. Possibly even downright evil.

Could that have happened to the imprisoned soul of the dragon? Poor creature! She had always admired the great beasts. The mere idea that a thinking, feeling being had experienced such a terrible fate filled her heart with pity and great sadness.

Was there a chance to set it free? She would have to think about that. There had to be some way to save herself and her companions as well as this poor bespelled dragon!

Chapter 19

A Nightmare Revealed

The night seemed to go on forever. Ki'ara and Hugo took turns keeping watch. Even up here in the mountains, the darkness was filled with sound. The wind was softly whistling among the peaks, sleepy birds were uttering an occasional chirp, and insects were singing their songs. Every so often, a distant rumbling told of rock cascades crashing down the slopes.

Ki'ara figured that the heavy rains had destabilized some of the outcrops. Good thing she had chosen this shelter! Even if the entire front side caved in, they could still leave out the back. Considering the situation, they were as safe as they could be and to the young woman's immense relief, hour after long hour ticked by without incident or any cause for alarm.

Hugo had been a little more cheerful when Ki'ara took over the last watch. She had decided that she would let the old man sleep for the rest of the night since she would need his help in keeping a close eye on Mathus for all of their sake. The tutor was so terrified he was utterly beyond reason.

⁘

Finally, the first signs of the returning day started to appear. Slowly the blackness began to turn into gray. Every minute Ki'ara could make out more of her immediate surroundings. Fingers of light emerged in the east, and the sky took on a soft shade of pink. Soon, inquisitive sunbeams playfully made their way over the tall peaks and crept down into the deep valleys, illuminating the fog hanging therein.

It was a truly glorious morning with just a few clouds in the sky and no visible sign of trouble anywhere near. The usual sounds continued around them, letting Ki'ara know that all was well. For a moment longer, she cherished the peaceful scenery. Taryn was yawning beside her and rolled on his back. He was inviting her to rub his soft underbelly. It quickly put him in ecstasy, and he began to purr rather loudly.

After one last wistful look around, Ki'ara went to wake up Hugo. As quietly and quickly as possible, they packed up their camp and got ready to ride. Carefully, they led their mounts down the steep incline and tethered them there. Only when everything else had been taken care of did the young sorceress finally wake up the still sleeping Mathus.

Ki'ara's tutor was a bit disoriented at first. Thanks to her spell, he had slept very deeply for the first time in many a day. Hugo led him down to his horse, helped him into the saddle, and handed him a thick slice of bread with ham and the delicious mountain cheese of the region. Before the anxious man was even fully awake, they were on their way back to the path.

⁘

All went well until around mid-morning. Neither Ki'ara nor her companions had seen any sign of the wraith. Their ride had been peaceful. Suddenly, Taryn's ears perked up, and the big cat's relaxed stance turned into one of instant alertness. Then, the hair along his back started to stand up like a brush. There was no doubt now, some sort of trouble lay ahead on the path.

This trail was the only way down to the town and the harbor. Whatever was ahead, they would have to face it. Ki'ara promptly reined in her horse and strengthened the shields surrounding their group even further. She assumed that anything attacking them would be instantly repelled. The resulting moment of surprise would give her an advantage and a better chance of dealing with the threat.

Ki'ara was glad that neither Hugo but especially not Mathus had noticed the catamount's alarming reaction or her sudden stop. They had continued to proceed obliviously down the path.

⁖⸙⸙⸙⸙⸙⸙⸙⸙⸙⸙⸙

Taryn was staying right next to Ki'ara's mount as they rode on. His tail was twitching anxiously. The horses were used to her constant companion, but him getting this close was upsetting her steed. To make matters worse, the animal had also picked up on the danger ahead. It took the girl sending it some calming energy to keep it moving and from shying away from her protective friend.

A short time later, the young woman and her fellow travelers became aware of a commotion ahead. As they got closer, they could make out a lot of screaming and yelling going on interspersed by an occasional roar. To Ki'ara, it sounded like people fighting for their lives. Could someone else have run afoul of the monster they had so far successfully evaded?

⁖⸙⸙⸙⸙⸙⸙⸙⸙⸙⸙⸙

Hugo and Mathus had come to a dead stop. Their horses were spooking, and both men saw themselves forced to dismount. They were looking back at the young woman for reassurance. The tutor had gone white as a sheet and looked like he was about to faint or throw up. He was shaking so badly he could barely stand and finally collapsed to the ground.

Sending her mind ahead, Ki'ara located the source of the disturbance. Several men were desperately trying to hold off the dragon wraith! They were not faring too well either. The sorceress was convinced that without magic, they would not be able to succeed against the powerful being. If they were to have any chance at all, she needed to help and soon!

Ki'ara quickly slid out of her saddle and ran a few feet ahead. She separated herself and the cat from most of the shields before firmly anchoring them around Hugo, Mathus, and the horses. "Stay here!" she mouthed before sprinting off down the path, Taryn at her side.

The girl had never been so glad that she had defied her tutor yet once again. A skirt would have prevented Ki'ara from moving this quickly and safely. For the ride down the mountains, she had put on pants instead of the elegant riding dress he had tried to insist on.

Running as fast as she possibly could, it did not take long for the young woman to get close to the clash. As she got near, Ki'ara slowed her pace and proceeded more cautiously. This might be her only opportunity to help the captive dragon, and she needed to rescue the victims. The sorceress hoped that the wraith was sufficiently distracted. If at all possible, she intended to save the poor beast as well as the people.

After rounding a curve in the trail, Ki'ara finally laid eyes on the scene of the battle. Of a group of around 20 men, only 11 were still fighting. There was no time to lose. If the dragon wraith got the chance to feed on the dead, it would become much harder to set free or to kill.

Also, she had no idea how much this would extend out its lifespan.

Feeling that she needed to be higher, the young woman searched for a good vantage point. It did not take her long to find just the right spot on the mountainside. Up there, she would be above the combatants. A large flat boulder formed a kind of shelf. It was surrounded by bigger rocks that would offer some protection.

The boulders would provide Ki'ara with some shelter to start with, and the ledge would make a good base to stand her ground on once she had been discovered. Silently she climbed up to her chosen location and crouched down behind one of the stones.

<hr/>

The dragon wraith was enormous and terrifying beyond anything she had ever encountered or imagined. It looked like something out of a nightmare. Not being completely solid, it easily evaded the weapons of the desperate men but did terrible damage whenever it connected with them. No ordinary person could possibly stand a chance against this monster. Only magic might be able to defeat it. Ki'ara hoped that she was powerful enough to do so.

The young sorceress used her senses to carefully examine the preoccupied creature. She closed her eyes so that she could concentrate better. Carefully she studied the web of energy she perceived in her mind. It was shaped like a dragon but was predominantly made up of golden strands of iridescent light.

Ki'ara knew she had to hurry, but this could not be rushed. There were too many different types of fibers interwoven with each other to dive in carelessly. It would be reckless to sever a few here and there in the hope that they were the right ones. She needed to subdue the creature, and to achieve this, she had to look for those elements standing out from the rest.

To her surprise, Ki'ara recognized the taste of the magic. So, the master of De'Aire Chateau was involved after all! Argulf must have enslaved the spirit in one of those experiments Hugo had told her about. The atmosphere in the dungeons had perverted this incantation and had turned it evil. Did it never occur to that ignorant wizard that he needed a better place to store his failed spells?

The sorceress hoped that she was powerful enough to break the enchantment. Following along the glowing filaments, she finally located what she was looking for. A net of dark, angry energy pulsing around the mythical beast's heart.

From this locus, some fine black threads spread out encircling the form, keeping the dragon's soul chained to the incantation. Patiently, Ki'ara started to severe one strand after the other until only one fiber and the dark center remained.

The sorceress gingerly cut the last filament. Now, she had the full attention of this living nightmare! The wraith stopped in its tracks and looked around. It left off its attack on the remaining men, backed up, and turned to face this new opponent. Ki'ara's eyes flew open. It was time to do battle!

The young woman took in the full spectacle of the immense spirit. Fear formed a knot in the pit of her stomach. Now that the being was this close to her, she could make out all the terrifying details of this enormous creature. She could not remember an occasion when she had been this scared.

❧

The eyes staring up at Ki'ara were the most unsettling she had ever seen. The crazed looking orbs glowed a fiery crimson and reminded her of red-hot coals. Their depth roiled with malice and madness as well as an inhuman intelligence. The girl fervently hoped that she would never face their likes again.

The wraith's face was so contorted with hatred and fury that it looked more like a demon's than that of a dragon. The teeth in the vaporous maw were enormous and sharp as needles. They were dripping with blood. Each scale, all along the body, gave off an eerie red light, and the emanation of evil was so powerful that it was about to overwhelm her.

Ki'ara was plain terrified. No wonder Mathus had been so afraid! She was sure that he must have gotten a glimpse of this monster. Was he the one who was responsible for its presence? Once this was over, she intended to find out!

Taryn was hissing and growling beside her when the being approached. He did not back up or flee like most other animals would have done in his place. Instead, the catamount pushed closer against the young woman. He was determined to face this evil right along with her.

Facing this nightmarish creature by herself would have been even worse. The sorceress was immensely grateful for Taryn's continued presence. The ghost cat would not be able to help her, but just having him next to her while confronting this fearsome apparition gave the young woman some comfort.

Now that she had been noticed, there was no sense in hiding any longer. Ki'ara rose up and bravely stepped up on the boulder. Once again, she closed her eyes. She needed to fully concentrate on the task at hand.

⚜

Ki'ara stood her ground, tall and proud. She was outlined by the rays of the sun, making her appear like some ethereal being of light. The sorceress was sending love and compassion to the captive dragon, all the while continuing to search for a method to free it from the black spell holding it prisoner. She was looking for a way, any way, to unravel the wicked fabrication which had been so haphazardly woven around its great heart.

Finally, Ki'ara found it. The enchantment the arrogant Argulf had created was such a chaotic muddle that it had taken her a while to locate its weakness. It was typical of her mentor, effective but incredibly messy. He had left a tail that she now used to undo the atrocity he had made. Piece by piece, she proceeded to dismantle the construct.

The dragon stopped. By now, it was right in front of the sorceress' perch, ready to attack. Ki'ara opened her eyes. She was level with the huge reptiles terrifying head. The young woman courageously met the wraith's crazed gaze. She watched with awe as the eyes turned from bright red, swirling with insanity and rage, to a soft blue filled with so much sadness it constricted her heart.

With a final gesture, the young woman dissipated the last of the evil compulsion and set the creature free. The dragon raised its head and roared with triumph as well as relief. Slowly, the angry shadow of the once magnificent being started to fade into pure whiteness then turned clear as glass. Within moments, it had entirely disappeared.

Ki'ara felt a ghostly touch of scaly lips on her cheek. "Thank you, child. If you ever need me, call on me. I will send help. I am Brianna, the great golden dragon. I am forever grateful for what you have done. You have set me free from an existence in torment and pain. Farewell, brave maiden, and may your life be filled with love, and your path lead you to the things you desire. I so will it, and therefore it is. Live well, little one, and fare thee well," an echoing voice reverberated in her head.

She had felt the contact, and the voice had filled her entire mind. It had been almost too much to contain. For a moment, Ki'ara remained stunned. She sensed a distinct shift and realized that her future had just been altered. The benevolence of the dragon had a magic all of its own!

A few moments later, the pressure of that immense presence was gone, but a small part of it remained within the young sorceress. Ki'ara felt like she was floating.

The entire world was brighter, more brilliant, more detailed than ever before, and, for the first time, she could clearly read the mind of her faithful companion.

It seemed Brianna had left her a most precious gift. The dragon had further awoken the young woman's senses!

Chapter 20

Unlikely Allies

Taryn's hiss shook Ki'ara out of the euphoria she was still feeling from her contact with Brianna, the great dragon. The low growl which followed was vibrating his entire body, and he had moved in front of his mistress. Because of their new connection, the cat could sense how much the recent confrontation with the wraith had drained the young lady, and he was determined to protect her.

Ki'ara quickly spotted the perceived threat and began to evaluate the situation. The survivors of the battle had somewhat recovered by now. They were gradually making their way towards her. The men's stances were guarded, but they were displaying no weapons. Why then was Taryn responding this way?

As the group moved closer, the sorceress realized that these guys were not your average mountain wanderers. This explained the catamount's reaction! Ki'ara instantly took action. She drew additional shields around herself and Taryn but remained where she was.

Being up high would give her the advantage should they decide to attack.

From their dress and demeanor, the young woman gathered that these men were not travelers but bandits. The outlaws were known to have a hideout somewhere in these mountains but usually left people on the isolated paths alone. Pickings were much richer down by the sea, so why provoke the wrath of the only persons able to lead the law to their doorstep?

The men stopped a safe distance away and bowed respectfully. After a brief discussion, one stepped forward. Fearing that their appearance might disconcert the powerful young woman, he held up a placating hand and smiled pleasantly.

❦

The robber appeared to be in his mid-twenties, and Ki'ara could see that he was rather handsome under all the blood and grime from his recent encounter. His clothes were fashionably cut, his hair had been well-groomed, and he was clean-shaven. Not at all what she would have expected from a bandit in these desolate parts!

"We mean you no harm, Lady," he addressed Ki'ara. "I am Jacques Des Montagnes, leader of this group. We owe you our lives. Had you not come along when you did, that thing would have killed us all. We are deeply indebted to you. Is there anything you require? We are at your service from this day onward," Jacques continued with a low bow.

Ki'ara's instincts told her that the man meant every word he said. She remembered hearing about the strange code of ethics these brigands lived by. Honor among thieves, who would have thought it? Many were younger sons of noble lords who did not see a future among their people and tried to eke out an existence outside the law. The bandit addressing her was apparently one of these.

How should she respond? What was the best way to deal with these men? The young woman figured that rebuking the outlaws' perceived debt would not be a good idea. It might insult them. That was the last thing Ki'ara wanted to do at this moment. She always preferred to resolve matters peacefully, if at all possible.

Not being familiar with their ways, she felt it was best to tread carefully to start with and to share as little information as she could while remaining honest. Once she had established their true motivations, she would reevaluate that stance. They already knew that she was a sorceress, so there was no sense in hiding her origins.

"I am Ki'ara of the Mystic Highlands. My companions and I were on our way down to the harbor when we heard the commotion. I came to see if I could help. I am happy that I could be of assistance and well met, Jacques of the Mountains," she responded, thinking that it was best not to mention the magician at De'Aire Chateau unless she was asked.

Some of the men had gasped and had involuntarily taken a step back when they heard that they were dealing with one of those devils from the far north. Their leader, however, had stood his ground. Either he was better informed than the rest, or he had iron control over his reactions.

"We will make sure that no harm befalls you on your travels, Lady Ki'ara. You being such an accomplished sorceress, you might not need our aid, but you never know. These mountains are a wild and untamed place full of perils of all kinds," the bandit stated with a deep bow to show his respect and gratitude.

"If I may ask, do you know what kind of monster it was we were fighting? Our weapons were useless against it! We thought we were done for until you came along. Some of us have lived among these peaks for generations and have never seen anything like it!" Jacques politely inquired.

Ki'ara realized that she would have to tread very carefully here. If she revealed the creature's origins, it could place her friends up at the castle in danger. The young woman loved them and felt very protective of them. The idea of an irate mob storming the fortress was not to her liking.

The old magician had imprisoned the dragon's soul. In Ki'ara's mind, that was an unforgivable crime against an intelligent being. To make things even worse, Argulf's carelessness with his unwanted spell had made it malicious. He deserved any punishment these bandits could give him but not so the servants. They were innocent in all this!

Of the manner the wraith had managed to get out of the dungeon, Ki'ara had only a hunch. She would not accuse anyone without proof. How much could she reveal of this without putting her friends in peril?

"What you were fighting was a dragon wraith. We first encountered it a bit higher up in the mountains and have been trying to evade it ever since. Had its attention not been on you, I am not sure I would have been able to defeat it, it was that powerful. The specter is gone now, and the trail is safe once more," Ki'ara replied carefully, hoping that she was not giving away too much information.

"Do you know where it came from and if there are any more?" the bandit asked Ki'ara respectfully, but she could detect the insistence behind his words. How could she answer this honestly? She had only suspicions at this point and no intent nor the time to return to the castle to investigate further.

"I am not absolutely certain where it came from but do seem to recall from my studies that this was a very rare creature. I do not believe that there are others of its kind on the lose here in the mountains, but I do not know for sure," Ki'ara responded thoughtfully.

Could there be more of these specters or similar beings? Maybe even something worse than the dragon? Could her friends at the castle be in danger? Ki'ara was resolved to find out from Mathus, and this time he was going to answer her questions whether he wanted to or not! After seeing the wraith and what it could do, she was determined to make sure that no more lives were lost to such monsters.

"Lady, I am grateful that you saved us, but you are very careful with your answers. You know more than you are telling me. Please, we have a deal with the people living here. Their silence in return for our protection. You came from the castle up near the top of the mountain, did you not? An old magician lives there. Is he responsible for this?" Jacques asked pointedly.

So much for keeping that bit of information hidden from the bandits! This guy was no fool. Jacques had evaluated her answers and drawn his own conclusions. Ki'ara felt no loyalty regarding the wizard but plenty towards her friends up at the old fortress. Then again, maybe this young man was just what they needed to keep them safe and make their lives a bit better!

After talking to him, Ki'ara's heart told her that this outlaw was genuinely concerned with the well-being of the folk dwelling among these peaks. Not only to keep them quiet as to the location of the robbers' den but also because he cared. Maybe she could make a deal with him and get him to come to the aid of the kind servants at De'Aire Chateau if they were ever in trouble.

"I was apprenticed to the master of De'Aire Chateau for almost two years. He is not the most pleasant of men, but his servants were kind to me. I regard them as friends. After your words, I am concerned for their safety. I want no harm to befall them!"

"Now I understand! You are also protecting those you care about! We could all be in danger, Lady, and I have a responsibility to a fair number of people! I need to know everything!" Jacques replied.

Ki'ara sighed. The man was right, there was more at stake here than just her adopted family. Many lives could be lost if other evil creatures like the dragon wraith were loose in these mountains.

"Please, give me your word that you will not hurt my friends!" the sorceress insisted.

"Lady, you have my solemn sworn word that no harm will befall your friends at my hands or those of my men! Please help me protect them and everyone else!" came the bandit's response.

The young woman searched Jacques' eyes for a moment and could find not a hint of deceit. She made up her mind to join forces with him.

"If you want answers, come with me. I know someone who might just have them," Ki'ara therefore responded.

Mathus was going to tell the truth for once, and it might just help to have some muscle along. After her battle with the dark enchantment imprisoning the poor dragon's soul, Ki'ara felt drained. Using more magic on the obstinate tutor would further exhaust her. Let Jacques get the answers out of him! She was sure that the bandit had ways of dealing with stubborn people like that!

It seemed that these outlaws had a strict code of honor they adhered to. Ki'ara could respect that. Having such allies was never a bad thing. Ki'ara sensed that these men were very much like the people of the Highlands, rough but honest and loyal to a fault. She liked that about them.

Who knew what kind of spells Argulf was hoarding up there? It was always possible that she might have to return to deal with this mess, and it would be a bonus to have more friends here in the mountains.

Ki'ara realized that she might just need Jacques help someday, or he hers if more monsters appeared.

Chapter 21

Another Disaster

The sorceress, together with some of the outlaws, returned to her companions further up the mountains. Jacques had ordered a few of his men to remain behind to protect and see to the dead and injured. He had decided that the bodies were to be wrapped in blankets and loaded on the horses. Since leaving them behind went against everything the bandits believed in, the deceased were to be taken back to the hideout for burial.

Right after the young woman had dashed off to render aid, Mathus had curled into a fetal position. He had just known that death was coming for him. When Ki'ara and her escorts arrived, he was still on the ground with his arms in front of his face and his knees drawn in as far as he could.

The tutor was shivering and sweating profusely. His terror seemed to know no bounds. Hugo stood next to him, wringing his hands and sighing with frustration. He was greatly relieved to see Ki'ara. The old man had felt utterly helpless in the face of this kind of angst. He had been trying to get through to the terrified man but in vain. Finally, he had just covered him up with a blanket and had stayed near him.

Ki'ara almost felt sorry for Mathus, but she needed to find out what was going on and if her friends up at the castle were in danger. In the girl's mind, that took priority over this cad's feelings. Had this incompetent conjurer released any more of the old wizard's spells? What had the tutor been doing down there in the dungeons? She needed to know!

Crouching down beside the shuddering man, Ki'ara told him sharply. "Mathus! Pull yourself together! The dragon's soul has been set free, and there is no more danger!"

Together with Jacques, Ki'ara pulled the tutor into a sitting position. She was determined to see his reaction, to watch his face when this welcome news sank in. It would tell her much about what was actually going on.

"It is gone? Are you sure? Really sure? The wraith is gone?" came the stuttering query. Mathus' teeth were chattering, his eyes were enormous, and the pupils hugely dilated so great was his fear.

"Yes, I am absolutely certain. You can stop being afraid. Now get up and get a hold of yourself!" the young sorceress commanded. She was observing the man carefully, and he was nowhere near as relieved as he should have been.

❦

Jacques had been right, after all. From the tutor's reaction, Ki'ara surmised that there were more bespelled creatures loose in the mountains. Mathus seemed to be not as afraid as he had been, so she figured that whatever was out there might not be quite as dangerous as the dragon wraith had been. It was, however, most likely still deadly to any who had the misfortune to cross its path.

Ki'ara exchanged a worried glance with the outlaw and gave him an affirmative nod. None too gentle, the bandit and one of his men pulled Mathus to his feet and supported him between them.

To the brigands' disgust as well as amusement, a dark stain started to spread down the tutor's pantlegs. Her brother's lackey had wet himself.

Ki'ara sighed in exasperation. How had she ever let such a contemptible cad terrorize her? Like all bullies, he was nothing but a weakling who made himself feel better by treading on others and elevating himself above them.

Amazing that he had managed to fool Ragnald so thoroughly! Or had he? Her gut told her that this was a question that would benefit from further examination but now was not the right time.

The tired sorceress stepped in front of the still quaking man. Firmly but gently, she raised up his chin. As much as she disliked Mathus, she could not bring herself to treat even him in a rude or cruel manner. Ki'ara had too much respect for all living beings.

"We have some questions to ask you! And, I will have the truth this time! People's lives may be in danger! You will answer me, and you will do so with all honesty!" she ordered.

Ki'ara had added just a tiny bit of compulsion to her words to get Mathus to obey her commands. Even this small amount of magic felt like a significant feat, and for a moment, she swayed on her feet. Jacques was watching her with concern.

✦⋆⋆✦

The young woman's store of power was almost completely exhausted, and she was barely able to stand. She needed help. This was not her home, but the land might still be willing to lend her some strength. Ki'ara directed her thoughts deep into the earth and sent out a plea. She figured that if there was no response, she could always search for a nearby ley line and draw some energy from it.

It did not take long, however, for her query to be answered. The magic of the mountains reached out to her, and power flowed back into her body. She was filled with the song of high peaks, falling water, lively streams, green grass, and swaying trees. Ki'ara relished every moment of the contact. To her amazement, it left her almost completely restored. The enchantress sent back a wave of love and sincere gratitude.

Standing up straighter and with renewed vigor, Ki'ara turned her attention back to her tutor who had not missed the change and noticed the iron determination in her eyes. He visibly cringed. Over the years, the man had become well familiar with that look and knew that it did not bode well for him. Mathus had felt the compulsion and knew that he had to fight it and hard. Good thing the lord had given him a charm for just such circumstances!

"I did not mean any harm, believe me, please! I was just curious about the spells. There are so many of them, just sitting there! Shelf after shelf! I was down there only once, just once!" The tutor could not meet Ki'ara's eyes, and he could feel the amulet around his neck heating up. It was almost hot enough to burn him, but that was still better than blabbing out all that he knew!

Mathus was blatantly lying to hide his indiscretions, hoping that the girl would assume that he was telling the truth and that her enchantment was doing its job. He had every intention to protect himself and weasel out of anyone finding out about the crimes he had committed. That this might get people killed was unimportant to him.

It was not to be, however. Mathus' heart almost missed a beat when he dared to glance at his interrogators. Seeing the look of disbelief on both Ki'ara and Jacques' faces, his stomach sank. He quickly continued. "Alright! So maybe twice! And not for very long! Please, believe me! I am telling the truth!" he stammered. He was afraid of what would happen if he revealed the real purpose behind his visits to that dark cellar.

The tutor was willing to tell any untruth in an attempt to appease Ki'ara and to get her to leave him alone. Ragnald would be furious if anyone found out what they had been up to, and his punishment of Mathus would be cruel and prolonged. At this point, the desperate lackey was still more scared of the lord than the sorceress before him. He was very relieved that the talisman allowing him to lie was doing its job.

Hugo, who had been listening, snorted in disgust. Ki'ara was not surprised by Mathus' words. Her tutor would do anything to cover his tracts if he thought that he would get in trouble if the truth came out. Of one thing she was sure, the deceitful rogue was still lying to her! Despite her incantation! Enough was enough!

<hr/>

A minor enchantment to bring out the better part of someone's personality was one thing, but having to completely override another's will was another. It just felt wrong to Ki'ara. She usually avoided casting that kind of a spell and was loath to do so now. The young sorceress had hoped to avoid using such magic on Mathus.

Having respect and compassion for others had always prevented the lady from abusing her powers, very unlike her oldest brother. Therefore, shaping such enchantments was something that Ki'ara reserved for absolute emergencies. This time, however, people's lives were at stake. She needed more information, but her tutor continued to be evasive. To her regret, it was the best option.

Reaching out, Ki'ara touched the man's forehead. Mathus turned white as he realized what she was about to do. Before he could even utter a word of protest, the spell was done. All defiance and emotions drained from the tutor's face in an instance.

"Mathus, what were you doing down there in the dungeons?" she inquired.

"I was searching for spells for my lord, just like he ordered. Something that could not be traced back to him since it was not tied to the land," the tutor answered in a monotone voice.

Ki'ara was stunned. Ragnald was using her and his lackey to find illegal enchantments! This could explain the quality of teachers she had been sent to! A competent and organized wizard would know very quickly when something went missing, while Argulf might never even discover the theft!

The possession of such spells was strictly forbidden by Highland law. If Ragnald was acquiring such illicit incantations, he was looking to place himself in a position where he had the advantage over his clan as well as the other Zidarians. Was her brother still trying to become the overlord of the Highlands? By any means possible? This was a thought which truly scared the young woman, but somehow, it felt right.

Using the power of the land against any of his own people or the other lords would have dire consequences for Ragnald. The magic would be traced straight back to him. The Zidhe would know and would not tolerate such a crime. Consequently, her brother was looking for a way to do harm while avoiding punishment for such actions!

"Have you ever done this before?" Ki'ara asked curiously. She needed to find out if there had been an added motive for her training all along. Knowing Ragnald, she would not put that past him. He was opportunistic at best, and evil at worst. It would also explain why her brother would choose such a corrupt individual like Mathus to accompany her!

"The lord was looking for any kind of spell I could transport, and yes, I did find some for him before," Mathus responded.

Ki'ara could only assume that Ragnald had amassed a fair amount of enchantments by now. In the last few years, she had studied with multiple teachers. Both her brother and Mathus were greedy and would try to collect as many incantations as possible. The tutor most likely had even kept a few for himself.

By taking possession of such spells, the lord of the MacClair Clan had violated the laws of the Zidhe, of the council, as well as of the land. Ki'ara realized that she would have to tread very carefully when she returned home to the Highlands. Who knew what kind of stolen magic Ragnald had acquired by now!

<hr>

Pulling her thoughts back to the present, Ki'ara asked her next question. "How did the dragon wraith escape? And, more important, is there anything else you might have released?"

"I had stashed six spells in a crevasse outside the castle along the path down the mountains. All I had to do was grab the bag as I rode past. I did not realize until later that it was open. One vial must have fallen out and rolled down the cliff," Mathus divulged instantly.

"When I checked the containers and realized what had gotten lose, I was terrified. My hands started shaking, and I ended up dropping another. I am so sorry! I never meant to hurt anyone! Your brother made me do it! It is all his fault!" the wretch sobbed, feeling extremely sorry for himself.

Mathus was sure that the outlaws would have no mercy on him and would make him pay for the deaths of their friends.

Ki'ara exchanged an exasperated look with Jacques. Leave it to Mathus to cause yet another disaster! What had this bumbling fool released in his ineptness? What was the other specter she needed to deal with? The girl was glad that there was only one and was determined to get every bit of information the tutor possessed about the spells he had stolen.

By the time Ki'ara and Jacques were done interrogating Mathus, the man was blubbering incoherently. The tutor figured that his life was forfeit since he was indirectly responsible for the demise of several of the bandits. He was in luck, however, since everyone agreed that there had been enough killing for one day.

Ki'ara took possession of the four remaining enchantments. She was trying to decide on the most prudent way to handle them. Sending the spells back up to the castle did not appeal to her since it was possible that other unfortunate souls were imprisoned within the incantations.

To effectively and kindly deal with this kind of magic was difficult and time-consuming. It also needed a safe place far from people. Maybe this was best left to the Zidhe.

Taking the incantations back to the Highlands was out of the question. Anyone carrying such magic would be severely punished. The lords might not believe that Ki'ara was bringing these spells back as evidence against her oldest brother.

Ragnald would claim that it was she all along, and he could be very convincing. It would give him the perfect opportunity to blame the entire crime on her. If more spells were found in her room at the castle, her fate would be sealed.

As much as Ki'ara disliked leaving the enchantments in another's hands, she saw no option. She only hoped that her new friend would agree.

Taking Jacques aside, Ki'ara explained her predicament. Being well familiar with court intrigue, he immediately grasped her situation. The bandit knew the perfect place to hide the items, and he gave her detailed directions on how to get there. On the way back to the lair, he would stash the spells in the cave for safekeeping. It was the best he could do since taking them back to his hideout was also not a viable option.

To keep the enchantments from perverting further and the creatures within from taking more harm, Ki'ara placed a protective bubble of pure love around the containers. Her magic would also keep anyone from unwittingly releasing the beings within. The sorceress constructed the spell in such fashion that not even her death would break the orb and release its dangerous contents. Only the proper command would do so.

In a show of trust, the young lady shared the words required to lift her incantation with Jacques. Someone besides herself needed to know them just in case something unexpected should happen to her. Both she and the bandit agreed that magic such as this, touched by the lingering emanations of the evil committed in those dungeons, did not need to be set free in the mountains.

Ki'ara and Jacques made a pact to keep the world safe from the specters imprisoned in those innocent looking vials. Both, however, were also committed to doing their best to set the suffering beings free one day, just as the sorceress had done with the dragon.

Another concern was all those spells at the castle. According to Mathus, there were a large number of them, shelf upon shelf. The new friends agreed that they would have to be dealt with as well.

To ensure that this would happen even if she were unable to return, Ki'ara sent a magical missive off to her uncle as well as the Zidhe.

Chapter 22

The Ghost of a Cat

Just as Ki'ara had feared, the dragon wraith was not the only entity the careless tutor had released. According to Mathus, one of the spells he had stolen was still on the loose somewhere up here in these mountains. The young woman's careful questioning had yielded vital clues on how to attract and capture this creature.

After the man had finally calmed down, the sorceress had enlisted Mathus' help in setting up the trap. With this accomplished, Ki'ara fashioned a spell that could be triggered to form a zone of protection. As soon as all was in readiness, the young woman sent the outlaws, along with Hugo and the tutor, to a place of safety a little further down the mountains.

Knowing the area like the back of his hand, Jacques had decided on a spot on a neighboring peak. This would allow them to keep an eye on Ki'ara. The group would set up camp there for the night and wait for the sorceress to join them when her task was complete.

Once Mathus set off Ki'ara's protective enchantment around them, they would be sheltered from harm as long as they remained inside the barrier. There was no way to leave and reenter. None of them would be able to assist the young woman without placing themselves in grave danger.

Taryn, as usual, insisted on remaining beside his mistress. His presence was welcome and a tremendous comfort to Ki'ara. According to the tutor, the spirit she would be facing was nothing like the dragon wraith. Mathus was not exactly sure what she would be confronting, but he was reasonably confident that it was some sort of animal.

Down in the dungeons, in a small room Ki'ara had never entered, the snooping tutor had discovered hundreds of abandoned incantations. The ones he had grabbed had been some of the most recent. Mathus had suspected that the old magician had worked his way up gradually to his final experiment of that type on the unfortunate soul of the dragon. This did not bode well since it meant that a number of these evil spells were still down in those caverns.

Since Argulf tended to be careless with things, this put her friends at De'Aire Chateau as well as all the other inhabitants in the area in danger. Here was a disaster just waiting to happen. The situation needed to be addressed quickly and with the least amount of harm to the imprisoned beings. Dealing with so many unstable enchantments, however, was not something the sorceress wanted to tackle all by herself.

The elves were the only ones Ki'ara could think of who could safely accomplish such a feat. Therefore, she had given Jacques her word that in addition to sending her message, she would petition the Zidhe to send someone back to Frankonia to help. The sorceress intended to accompany the Le'aanan if possible, and she shared the outlaw leader's urgency in getting the issue resolved.

With so many spells left in that dungeon, Jacques rightfully feared for the people he had promised to look after. The outlaw wanted to make sure that nothing like the dragon wraith haunted this area ever again. Keeping the mountains safe was his job, and he took it quite seriously.

Forced to divulge the truth, the tutor had shared what he could recall of the instructions on the broken vial. It was a complicated ritual that needed to be followed down to the letter. Ki'ara hoped that Mathus had remembered it all and correctly.

Once her friends were safely away, and the tutor had deployed their protection, Ki'ara started a fire. She added some of her magic to the flames. Soon they flared brightly. The brilliant green color reflected in an almost rainbow-like hue on the rocks around her. Step one was done, and the stage was set.

The sorceress began the chant of enticement designed to draw in the creature. Amplified by her powers, her sweet voice rose above the whistling wind and echoed among the peaks around her. Wherever the being was, the sound would reach it. Now all she had to do was wait and keep singing.

With every minute, Taryn, who was sitting next to Ki'ara, was getting more and more agitated. He was projecting hope, loss, and anxiousness. His mind was in such turmoil that it was impossible for the girl to communicate with him.

Ki'ara had never seen him like this. He was alternately mewling and purring. Finally, he began adding his voice to her song. The sorceress was stunned.

Was this a cat she was calling? One her friend was familiar with?

Taryn had been around De'Aire Chateau when had she arrived. He had moved into the old edifice at the first opportune time. For a wild animal, the cougar had behaved rather tame. Could he have been around humans before? Or, had he remained because he was looking for something? Someone?

It dawned on Ki'ara that there may have been more to the catamount's avid interest in the dungeons than mere curiosity or a desire to hunt! She usually had to call him several times before he had reluctantly followed her back up the stairs. Had something in there been beckoning to him?

Suddenly, Ki'ara could feel a presence nearby. Out of thin air, the specter of a ghost cat appeared on the rock above them. Taryn was almost beside himself with excitement. The young woman could feel the love radiating off him at the sight of the creature.

Taryn's enthusiastic greeting, however, was answered by angry hisses and growls. There was no sign of recognition from the approaching apparition. It had lost all memory and its sense of self due to the invocation it had been placed under. The poor beast had no recollection of what it had once been, it only knew that it must feed to survive.

Ki'ara's companion had not expected this kind of a response. He cowered down, unhappy, and feeling utterly rejected. His behavior confirmed what the sorceress had only suspected until then. This was a female, and she had been her Taryn's mate! She had been one of the reasons the cat had been hanging about De'Aire Chateau all that time!

Her companion had been searching for his love when the newly apprenticed Ki'ara had met him outside the castle! He had felt the young woman's own sense of loss and loneliness but also her closeness to nature. Initially, this had drawn him to her. Before long, however, this attraction had led to a bond between these two kindred spirits. The catamount and the girl had become friends, and Taryn had taken to following her around.

The sorceress' heart contracted with pity as she watched the pair. It was beyond her understanding how anyone could cast such an evil spell. This was a living soul that had been imprisoned and altered beyond recognition. How could anyone be so malicious to inflict such pain on an innocent creature?

The experiments Argulf had conducted were beyond malicious. You bet she would come back! With the Zidhe, if possible, if not, by herself! Ki'ara was angry enough to almost consider rushing up to the fortress that very moment and dealing with the arrogant man. Him, she could handle. The spells, however, she might need help with.

⊱✶⊰

The ghostly mountain cat continued to snarl and hiss at Ki'ara and Taryn. Its glowing red eyes, filled with pure fury, glared at the pair. The specter emanated nothing but hatred. The evil in the dungeon had affected it just as it had the unfortunate dragon. The enchantress hoped that she would be able to save Taryn's mate as well since she had managed to release Brianna from that horrid enchantment.

Ki'ara was observing the cat closely. She could tell by a minute change in the animal's stance when it prepared to jump. She was ready. When the puma sailed off the rock to attack them, the girl sprung her trap. The apparition was held in suspension in mid-air.

Now, it was time to get to work. The sorceress was determined to find a way to set the female free. Carefully, Ki'ara examined the construct. This web of enchantments was even sloppier than the one binding the dragon wraith had been but, having done this once, she had a better idea where to begin.

Ever so gently, Ki'ara teased apart the threads radiating out from the catamount's heart. She could feel Taryn watching her anxiously. When the last fibers had been cut, the sorceress unraveled the center of the spell. She banished it deep into the ground where it would be purified and absorbed. Never again would it harm another innocent being.

As the effects of the incantation faded, the red orbs of the puma slowly changed back to the crystal blue of clear mountain water. Its entire appearance lightened perceptibly, and the female hung there in her full glory. How beautiful she had once been, the sorceress thought with great sadness.

Had Argulf killed this magnificent creature to try his dark magic out on her? Ki'ara sure hoped not.

Having watched the dragon vanish into the ether, Ki'ara decided that she would do what she could to reunite her friend with his mate. Adding her own spell, she made the specter more solid. She could not create a new body but fashioned an impression thereof. It was beyond her powers to bring the catamount back from the dead, but at least its soul now had a semblance of life.

Gently, Ki'ara lowered the spirit of the cat to the ground. She released it from its confinement. The female was disoriented for a moment and stood there, shaking her head. Suddenly, she took notice of Taryn. With a loud purr, she pounced on her mate. The big guy was ecstatic. This was much more like the response he had been hoping for now that he had finally found her!

After a rambunctious greeting that went on for several minutes, the two animals turned their attention to Ki'ara. This slender girl was the reason they were together again! They owed her so much! Happy as can be, Taryn bounced to the sorceress' side while his love approached carefully. How could they thank this kind person who had reunited them against all odds?

After rubbing his head against Ki'ara's side for a moment, Taryn joined his mate who sat facing the young woman. The female had been watching their affectionate interactions intently. Never before had the cat seen her mate express this kind of affection towards anyone else, and it surprised her and made her curious at the same time.

Asking permission, the enchantress placed a hand on each of the catamounts' heads. Touching them made communications, one of her gifts from Brianna, a great bit easier. It would still take some of her power, just not as much. The young woman was beyond tired by now. She could barely stay upright and had almost completely drained the last of her reserves yet again.

The female, who called herself Mikka, relayed that she had slipped on a ledge. The sorcerer had found her as she lay there close to death. She had been taken to the castle and had hoped, at first, that the magician would heal her. Her injuries had been severe, but she felt that it had been well within his power to treat them.

Instead, Argulf had set up the room to work his magic. He had stood there and watched Mikka die, ignoring her pleading looks for help. The magician never rendered aid or comfort but had gleefully imprisoned her soul in that awful incantation. Then, when the results of the spell did not please him, he had banished her into that bottle, which he placed down in the dungeons.

The catamount was most grateful for having been set free from the evil which had taken over her soul. She also thanked Ki'ara for looking after her mate and being his friend. Mikka paused for a moment and just looked at the young woman. Then came her plaintive request.

'Would the lady mind very much if Taryn stayed in the mountains with her? At least for a while? Or could they both go along?'

Ki'ara smiled gently at the pair, but there also was a hint of sadness in her eyes. She knew what it felt like to be parted from someone you loved. She would have never even considered separating the two. Mikka was visibly relieved when she heard this.

The sorceress explained that she would be returning with help to deal with the master of De'Aire Chateau and all his perverted enchantments. If the cats stayed in the area, Ki'ara would be able to find them and, if they wanted to, they could then both come back to the Highlands with her. Now was not the best time.

Since their connection had deepened over the last day, Taryn instantly sensed Ki'ara's apprehensions about returning home. Being male and loving the young woman, he immediately wanted to go with the girl to protect her. He felt that she needed him. Who better to have by her side than two large cats even if one was somewhat insubstantial?

Ki'ara had to assure him several times that she would be just fine before the cougar finally relented and, with rather bad grace, agreed to stay behind. Taryn was not happy that his friend was heading into danger alone. He was rubbing all over the girl and letting her know how much he would miss her.

After one last goodbye, the pair set off into the mountains. Ki'ara watched them slink up the slope. Taryn turned one last time, and their eyes locked for a moment.

The young woman thought her heart would break. The sadness he felt at their parting was clearly visible in the big male's gaze. Then he moved on.

One minute they were right there amongst the rocks, the next they were gone. No wonder they were often referred to as ghost cats!

⸎

After extinguishing the flames, Ki'ara slowly made her way down the path to join her companions. By the time she got near their camp, she was staggering and could barely put one foot in front of the other. Jacques sprinted towards her and caught her just as she was about to collapse. Carefully, he carried her the rest of the way.

Hugo was ready. He had been around his master long enough to know how to deal with this kind of a situation. He immediately pushed a couple of thick slices of bread loaded with ham and cheese into the exhausted sorceress' hands.

Once Ki'ara had eaten a few bites, the stablemaster handed her a cup of ale. She usually did not care for the stuff, but right now, it helped to restore her.

When the sorceress had consumed enough food to please Hugo, Jacques gently carried Ki'ara to her bedroll. He tucked her in and covered her up carefully with extra blankets. It did not take long for the tired girl to fall soundly asleep. Almost immediately, she started to dream.

⸎

Ki'ara found herself high up in the mountains. A figure of light was walking towards her. The being was so bright that all the girl could make out was a shape, and she had to avert her eyes to keep from being blinded.

"Come! Please sit!" a soft voice addressed her. When Ki'ara looked up, she met the serene gaze of the greenest eyes she had ever seen. Those amazing orbs belonged to a beautiful woman. Everything about her was ethereal and light. Noticing that the goddess was pointing to a bench with bright pillows, the sorceress complied.

Once they were both seated, Ki'ara's companion reached for her hand. "I am Amara, and these are my mountains. I wanted to thank you for what you did this day. You could have destroyed both of my children. It would have been easier and far less draining for you."

Smiling, the lady continued. "Instead, you choose to restore them as much as you could. You set them free. At great expense to yourself, as it was. You totally exhausted your powers. You knew that it would take time to renew your magic and what you will be facing at home. Still, you let compassion rule your heart."

"What you did," the goddess continued. "Was selfless and brave. I commend you for your actions. As a reward, you will wake up in the morning, fully restored. Since you saved two of my children, I will also grant you something very special. This gift will come to you in a time of great need, and from this day forward, you have mine and my sisters' protection," the beautiful deity went on.

"I will know you the moment you set foot on these lands, and no one will harm you. Thank you for intending to return to deal with that man! Goodbye, dear one, and fare you well!" With those final words, Amara faded away, and Ki'ara dropped into a deep, healing sleep.

When she awoke the next morning, the young lady felt alert and refreshed. The terrible exhaustion of the previous day was gone. The sorceress could feel her magic humming happily inside her body and soul. With a quick prayer, she sent a warm thank you to the kind goddess.

As soon as Hugo realized that Ki'ara was awake, he brought her some hot tea as well as more food. Jacques sat down next to her. He was watching her eat, his forehead wrinkling with concern. After talking to the stablemaster, he expected her to be too weak to ride for several days.

Ki'ara finally had enough of his scrutiny. "I am fine, Jacques! We should be able to continue down to the harbor today!" The bandit stared at her in disbelief. How could this be possible? The question was clearly written on the incredulous man's face.

"As a thank you for saving her children, your goddess has completely recharged my powers," Ki'ara explained. "I am as good as new, really!"

The relief on the bandit's face was almost comical. It was still cold in the mountains, but temperatures were not low enough to keep his dead comrades from decomposing. Jacques wanted to get them back to the hideout for burial before the stench became too much to bear.

"I need to take my fallen friends back to our home, but I have sworn to protect you. I will not break my word to you, but to send them home without me is not a good option," he began, all the while watching Ki'ara's face.

"Staying in control of this bunch is not easy, believe me. We have something which resembles a democracy, and my primary loyalty has to be to my people. Also, I am no good to you if I am no longer in charge. Lady, I do not know how to proceed. What are your wishes?" Jacques queried.

Ki'ara smiled at the man. "Jacques, your first priority must be to your people. I am capable of protecting Hugo and Mathus. I am sure we can make it safely down to the harbor, but if it makes you feel any better, three of your men could accompany us to the city."

"Lady, you have no idea how relieved I am by your words. Thank you for your kindness. Have you any idea when you will return to deal with the wizard and his stash of spells?" the bandit asked next. He was watching the young woman intently.

"For now, I need to go back to the Highlands. I will talk to my uncle and send a request for help to the Zidhe. I will return to deal with Argulf, with or without them, of that, I assure you," Ki'ara told him sincerely. Her eyes had narrowed dangerously with her words. Jacques was glad that he would not be at the receiving end of that anger.

"I fear for my friends up at the castle. Their master has little concern for their safety or wellbeing. May I please place their lives into your capable hands? Many are too old to find employment elsewhere or are afraid to leave there. I have not yet established a home of my own, or I would have taken them all!" the sorceress stated, her eyes dark with concern.

Jacques smiled. He liked this lady. She was not like most of the highborn he had met in his days. Here was a real person, someone who cared about others, honest and steadfast. Even if he had not promised to help her, he would have gladly looked after the servants. They were after all part of his flock.

"I promise to take care of them, my Lady. Anything I can possibly do to make their lives a bit easier, consider it done," the outlaw assured a very relieved Ki'ara.

"Three of my men will go with you to the outskirts of the city. They will shadow you until you are aboard your ship. Thank you for understanding and working with me. Many in your place would have insisted on all of us coming along! With your permission, Lady, I will get my people ready to ride and well met."

After receiving Ki'ara's affirmative nod, the brigand quickly rose to his feet. He bowed deeply to the young woman before heading over to his men. A few quick orders resulted in a host of activities. The bandits assisted Hugo and managed to pack up the camp in record time. It was not long before they were prepared to set out.

Jacques introduced Ki'ara to the three men who would accompany her. Their orders were very explicit. Guard the lady at all costs, even from her companions, if necessary, especially Mathus. Make sure she gets on board of the ship unharmed. Protect Hugo on his way back to the mountains.

From the tutor's dour expression, the young woman surmised that he had heard the commands. She had to compose herself to keep from laughing out loud but could not help exchanging a secretive grin with a very amused Jacques. Several of the outlaws were also trying hard to keep straight faces.

The bandit's leader had given his orders so loud that everyone had heard him. Ki'ara was confident that he had done so on purpose. Jacques wanted to make sure that Mathus knew to behave.

None of them cared for the tutor. The brigands held him responsible for the deaths of their friends. It said a lot for Jacques' control over his people that a knife had not found its way into Mathus' heart in the dark of the night.

For a while, the two groups traveled together, but eventually, it was time to part ways. With one final wave, Jacques led his men onto the trail to their refuge. They would arrive the next morning. The bandits were a close-knit group. Everyone knew each other. Bringing home this many dead would affect most of his people.

Seeing the lady again was one thing the outlaw was looking forward to. She had been very honest and had made sure that he understood that it would not be anytime soon. Ki'ara had not said much, but the clever bandit had figured out from talking to Hugo that trouble was waiting for her at her own home.

As she was riding along, Ki'ara thought back on the events of the last couple of days. How much had happened and how lucky she had been! The girl was thrilled that she had managed to save the dragon, reunite Taryn with his mate, and she felt blessed for the gifts she had received.

Now that they were getting close to the harbor, Ki'ara was looking forward to being home soon.

Part 2

The

Highlands

Chapter 23

Memories of Home

The rest of the journey down from the mountains had been uneventful. Ki'ara, Hugo, and Mathus had safely made it to the harbor, all the while shadowed and protected by the three outlaws. The sorceress did not even have to use her magic to deter the one thief who had eyed their group. The pickpocket had suddenly felt a prick in his back and a deep voice advising him to move on. The man had done so with alacrity.

At the docks, the young lady had said goodbye to Hugo. He had happily agreed to meet her when she returned to deal with Argulf's stash of illicit spells and had promised to give her greetings to the rest of her adopted family. Ki'ara would miss the old man and the others. Her friends' welfare was an additional incentive for her to sort out her situation at home in the Highlands.

Until then, her friends at De'Aire Chateau were in good hands. Jacques had promised to look after them, and Ki'ara was confident that he would do a fabulous job. The leader of the bandits was even willing to take the group of elderly people back to his hideout and give them a home until the sorceress had a place of her own. If that meant Argulf would have to take care of himself, so be it.

Hugo had set out on his way back to the castle in the company of the trio of brigands. The stablemaster had forged a tight bond with these men and had agreed to be their liaison with the other servants. What he carried back to them was hope, something they had not had in a while. For the first time since the wizard had taken over the fortress, these unfortunate folks had options.

The *Sea Witch* had set sail the next day and had started on its long way north. Three weeks on the water were a bit much for many people, but not so for Ki'ara. She loved being on the ocean and was learning more about her vessel every day.

The ship was a clipper. It had three masts and was 211 feet long. Its square sails covered every possible area on these masts. True to form, it was narrow compared to many other merchant vessels its size, which did not allow it to transport quite as much cargo as some of the wider crafts could. Due to its large sail area and the length to beam ratio, however, the ship was faster than most and more stable.

Ki'ara had always enjoyed the way the *Sea Witch* cut through the waves. She might not be able to carry as much freight, but she could make deliveries quicker than most, especially with Marcus O'Rourke at the helm. The very competent sailor had been the clipper's captain for many years now and had the ship running like clockwork.

Under his supervision, the sailors were teaching Ki'ara about the magnificent boat. As long as she stayed out of the way in an emergency, the captain was only too happy to encourage her interest. He felt that the more she knew about the running of her ship, the better.

O'Rourke had been thrilled to hear that Ki'ara was the new owner. He had always liked the girl and was looking forward to a long, profitable partnership with the young lady. They had agreed that for now, her uncle, Lord Iain Elvinstone of Ravenshire, would continue to handle the business until the sorceress was in a position to take over from him.

⤝❋⤞

Much of Ki'ara's time was spent on deck working or just taking in the beauty around her. She could spend hours mesmerized by the sun sparkling like diamonds on the waves. At night, she loved to admire the cool twinkling of the moonlight on the sea.

Now that the Mystic Isles were in sight, Ki'ara was standing at the rail, watching the coast slowly slip past. It was cold, but the thick woolen cape she was wearing was keeping her warm.

As long as the captain would allow it, the young sorceress intended to stay where she was. She did not want to miss a moment of the view she had so longed for. Ki'ara could watch for hours as the distant landscape passed by on their way towards home.

⤝❋⤞

Earlier that day, their ship had sailed across the boundary maintained by the Zidhe. Even from out here, the death zone, separating the Highlands from their neighbors to the south, was so obvious that it was impossible to miss. The impenetrable fog bank extended a long way out into the sea. Had it not been for the protection the elves had placed on the ship, the *Sea Witch* would not have been able to navigate these waters.

The further north they traveled, the more rugged and wild the landscape became. The tree-covered rolling hills of the far southern reaches of the StCloud lands gave way to more barren mountains with their predominately moss-coated slopes. To Ki'ara, it was the most beautiful place in the world.

The young woman could barely contain her excitement. In just a few days, she would finally be back at Seamuir Castle, the place she had spent most of her childhood. She could barely believe that it had been two long years since Ragnald had sent her away.

Ki'ara had learned some new magic from Argulf, but some part of her had continued to pull her back home, no matter how busy the wizard had kept her. She always missed the Highlands and its people. Her stay had felt like forever, and she had been desperately homesick on many occasions.

⁂

The last time Ragnald had allowed her to return home had been her most extended stay in a while. She had loved it. Every day Ki'ara had been able to remain, a deep-down part of her seemed to be becoming more vibrant, more alive. She always tried to make the best of any situation, but she had not been that contented and peaceful in many a month.

On that visit, unlike on some of her previous stays, her guardian had let Ki'ara attend a few of the clan's social functions with the rest of the family. It had been the first time in years that the young woman had been able to see her uncle, Lord Iain, and other members of the clans. She had been absolutely elated.

After a while, when things had continued to go comparatively well, Ki'ara had begun to hope that her legal guardian would allow her to remain in the Highlands. She had been 22, after all, an adult by human standards just not by Zidarian law. Had her life gone according to plan, she would have already been married. The girl had not yet forgiven her brother for annulling the agreement her parents had forged.

Having to submit to such an unfair and cruel man's whim had been difficult for Ki'ara, but it had become an essential survival strategy. The young woman had stayed out of Ragnald's way as much as possible. The last thing she had wanted to do had been to annoy him any more than the mere sight of her had already done. He was the lord of the clan, and his authority over her, until recently, had been absolute.

❧

Being practically immortal was a great gift, but it did have one drawback. Most of the Zidarian children grew physically at a rate similar to their human counterparts but, due to their elven ancestry, matured slower emotionally. Therefore, their parents tended to regard them as too young and inexperienced to make any significant decisions until they were at least 30 years old.

All Zidarians were at least 50% Zidhe, whose offspring did not take an adult name until their 100th birthday. Humans, on the other hand, were considered fully mature at eighteen, sometimes even before then, depending on circumstances, while the mix-breeds could claim adulthood anywhere between the age of 30 and 50.

Ki'ara had often wondered why she was so different and had been from birth. Her own physical development had been on par with everyone else's, but her intellectual and emotional growth would have stunned her peers had they known.

❧

The ancestral lands of the MacClair Clan were called Eastmuir. Ki'ara loved her home and thought that it was the most beautiful place in the entire world. The longer Ragnald had allowed Ki'ara to remain, and the more freedom he had granted her during her last visit, the more the hope had grown in her heart that she would finally be allowed to stay.

Ki'ara had started to think that maybe her days of being shipped off to the corners of this earth had finally come to an end. For many years now, her guardian had been sending her to one faraway place after another under the guise of furthering her education in magic, but the young lady knew better. Ragnald did not want her around.

All the girl had really desired was to learn the magic of her own land from one of the brilliant teachers right there in the Highlands. Whenever Ki'ara had suggested that her brother send her to one of the powerful local enchanters, she had been ignored. The girl would have preferred to study under them than the inept conjurers the MacClair had chosen.

Time after time, Ragnald had arranged for her to be apprenticed in far off places. Just like with Argulf, Ki'ara had assimilated these sorcerers' knowledge very quickly, often in only a few months. None of them had been a real challenge for the brilliant young woman, and most of the knowledge she acquired the gleaned from the libraries of these second-rate wizards.

His sister's wishes had been of no real importance to Ragnald, and now she understood why. She had been used as a cover to allow Mathus to steal illicit spells for her brother. That her sibling would stoop so low filled her heart with great sadness.

⊱✦⊰

Ki'ara was so glad to be finally going back. The Highlands were the only place where she felt truly connected to the earth. There, the magic sang in her blood. It filled her with exhilaration, grounded, and calmed her, all at the same time. Walking across this land that she so loved gave her peace like nothing else could.

Even as a small child, she had spent many an hour exploring the moors and glades around Seamuir Castle. Ki'ara had felt perfectly safe, and her parents had never worried. The wild animals had been her friends, and no matter how far she wandered, she had always known which way led back to her home.

Ki'ara loved to travel but hated it when Ragnald sent her away to be apprenticed. No matter where she ended up and regardless of how beautiful or amazing the place, it just had not been the same. She always had the sense that she did not belong and missed the connection she felt to the very earth of the Highlands. The girl was convinced that this had something to do with her heritage and the magic of her people.

The MacClairs, one of the immortal families, dated back to the battle with Ulric. Once, they had ruled the clan as kings and queens, but, through their own fault, this had since then come to an end. In Ki'ara's grandfather's time, King Richard McCulloch of Cambria had acted as overlord, as had his father before him. While this circumspect man had held power, peace had reigned across all the realms of the Highlands.

Unfortunately, the wise king had not named an heir. Richard had just been getting into his prime, he had still been a very young man by Zidarian standards. He had figured that he had many years left to sire sons to succeed him. One stormy spring morning, his ship had been caught in a sudden squall and had sunk with all hands.

Upon the McCulloch's death, the fight to succeed him had begun. Several of the Highland kings had their hearts set on becoming the new overlord. Each had thought that he was the best choice for the job. What had started with mere squabbles, had ended in full out war. The land and its people suffered, and none of the battling rulers were prepared to relent.

One of the worst aggressors had been Ki'ara's own family. The battles between the MacClairs and the StClouds, the two most prominent families at that time, had been the bloodiest and most ferocious. The animosity, which had started with a border dispute many years ago, had run deep.

Both clan leaders had been stubborn and arrogant men, convinced of their own grandeur. Each had believed that he was the only one qualified to rule over the realms. They had craved this additional power, had almost been able to taste it already. The bloody clashes between these two and other clans had continued until, at last, the Zidhe had intervened.

The elves usually did not interfere in their neighbors' affairs unless it impacted them. This war had been doing just that. The Le'aanan had finally had enough. The battles had started to spread death and disease into their sacred territories.

The fairies had used their powers to force the kingdoms to submit. The lords had to sign an agreement which ended the senseless fighting between the clans.

One of the reasons things had gotten so out of hand in the first place had been that the MacClairs and some of the other Zidarians had grown arrogant over the years they had spent as the ultimate rulers over their realms. They had forgotten that the elves had granted them this enormous privilege, had made them kings and queens, to begin with.

The intervention of the Zidhe and the mix-breeds forced abdications had been a powerful reminder to the lords that they were only tolerated guests in these lands, which they had begun to think of as their own. It had been a rude awakening for many.

With the signing of the covenant, the nine Zidarian families relinquished their titles. To prevent further wars, the Zidhe established a committee, the Council of Lords. It would handle all major problems affecting one clan or more and would act as the primary governing body of the Highlands.

Minor problems, affecting no more than three neighboring clans, could be discussed and handled at the 'Gathering of Lords' which were to be held before weddings, christenings, funerals, and such.

The Le'aanan had further decreed that the deposed rulers would be allowed to continue handling the everyday business of their clans. All decisions involving the other regions, however, no matter how small, had to be brought before one of the councils.

Ki'ara had two main issues she needed to present to the lords. One was the problem with Argulf and his hoard of spells, the other her brother's amassing of illegal enchantments. Having to accuse a member of her family of such a crime was not something she was looking forward to. She had no idea what his punishment would be.

Even as a young girl, Ki'ara had been introduced to the stories. The Zidarians wanted to make sure that their children would never forget the price that had been paid for the peace they were now privileged to enjoy.

Knowing her people as well as she did, Ki'ara understood what it had cost them. It must have been terribly hard for the once proud kings and queens to become clan leaders only. Some of the pomp went by the wayside, much to the disgust of most of the ladies and even some of the men.

Ki'ara had heard rumors that several of the warring lords received a frosty welcome from their angry spouses and families. The wives had demanded that amends were made to the elves. As far as they were concerned, this unacceptable fate had to be changed.

In short order, the women set off with their husbands to beg the Le'aanan for a pardon. The Zidarians had done a lot of pleading and complaining as well as blaming each other, but the Zidhe had remained firm. They had enough of their guests' unruly behavior.

⟡

Any further opposition to the new order of things died very quickly when the elves informed the mix-breed lords that they were lucky that they had been permitted to remain in power at all. The whole lot of them could have been ordered into exile. Most of the rulers had not even considered this possibility.

The lords had been advised that even the slightest breach of the covenant in any way, shape, or form, and any violence between the clans would lead to the immediate termination of the involved leaders. No quarter would be given. It would happen when they least expected it, and no amount of protection would be able to save them.

Before the Zidhe withdrew into their own realm, they left the chiefs with a stern warning. "Get along or pay the price." Their words were drilled into every Zidarian child from a young age on, with no exceptions.

Ki'ara's father, Mikael MacClair, had made sure all his offspring were aware of the stories as well as the rules. He had hoped to instill the severity of the punishment they could be facing into the youngster's head in the hope of keeping them from harm. It seemed to have worked with the younger ones but not so with Ragnald.

⟡

The only form of violence the Zidhe allowed between the families was in the way of jousts. On their lighter side, these competitions turned into festive occasions with fairs, rousting dinners, and even dances. Those parts Ki'ara had always genuinely enjoyed.

The dark underside of the games, however, the girl found abhorrent. The matches were also an outlet for some of the seething resentments harbored by a few of the fighters. They often ended with injuries to one combatant or both.

Seeing Ki'ara's deathly pale face after her uncle had been wounded had been enough for her mother and father. They had not realized just how much the violence affected their sensitive child. Never again had Mikael and Ali'ana subjected their daughter to watching people she loved hurting each other for the sake of their pride or sport.

Her parents would bring Ki'ara along for the other events but had allowed her to avoid the tournaments. The girl had been most grateful to them for this reprieve.

Not all the families participated in the jousts. The Blair and Macgillmott Clans had already been tired of the bloody battles before the treaty took place. Neither lord wanted anything to do with that kind of violence, and Ki'ara completely agreed with them. These rulers would, on occasions, attend the councils held before the games but only if they had no other option.

Every once in a while, the two clan leaders would show up at the festivities to show off a daughter or son eligible for marriage, but even then, they never took part in the contests. They did allow their people to participate, but the lords and their children would not. That kind of sport was not to their liking.

The two amiable rulers had been only too happy to comply with the treaty. They had been greatly relieved that all the fighting was over and had little understanding of their belligerent neighbors.

To cement their alliance against the rest of the clans, the families had intermarried. Keeping the peace this way was something Ki'ara full heartedly approved of. She only wished Ragnald could see the benefits of such a maneuver.

Ki'ara was glad that the Zidhe had outlawed war, as well as all squabbles. She had always detested such violence.

The young woman found it regrettable that not even such a severe warning as had been issued by the elves had been enough to keep her people in line for very long. They were Zidarians, warriors, and fighting was in their blood.

They did learn, however, and most of the lords ruling at present were upstanding men who did their best for their people. Ragnald was, unfortunately, one of the rare exceptions.

Chapter 24

The Highlands

It was early the next morning, and Ki'ara was watching her beloved Highlands slide past as the ship forged its way north. She had gotten up at the crack of dawn. The tutor, she had left sleeping below. The man never did well while they were out at sea, and she wanted time to herself without listening to him complain.

The bitterly cold wind tugged at her hair and brought a glow to her delicate features. Her startling green eyes were lit up with pleasure. Ki'ara's feet were freezing, but no amount of discomfort could have made her want to return to her cabin below. Instead, she pulled the thick, oiled cloak tighter around herself.

The sun was just starting to illuminate the mountainous terrain of the coast. Its rays were playing over the hills, adding vibrant color to the yellow-green of the moss and the darker tones of the areas of bushes and trees. The interspersed white cliffs faces, reaching hundreds of feet down to the water, provided a stark contrast to the greens of the peaks. It never ceased to amaze Ki'ara how such a beautiful place could have such a violent past.

Once there had been fierce fighting here in those fields above the sea. Her own family and the StClouds had tried their best to gain victory over each other. The young woman was genuinely grateful that those times had passed, and she really hoped that Conall would continue to ignore Ragnald's incessant provocations.

The treaty imposed by the elves forced the ruling Highland families to work together amicably no matter what. No Zidarian ever wanted the Zidhe to have to interfere again. Every man, woman, and child were only too aware of what the consequences of such actions could be.

The peace, which now reigned across the lands, had not gotten off without a hitch. One last stern warning had been needed to make it last. A few years after the covenant, two of the clan leaders had paid the price for their disregard of the laws. One of these had been Ki'ara's own grandfather.

Watching the sunlight slowly work its way up onto the peaks and into the valleys reminded the young woman of some of the stories her father had told her. How glad she was that things had calmed down a lot since those tumultuous days! Ki'ara loved this land and hoped that war would never again darken these stunning slopes.

The tales were meant as a warning to all the subsequent generations. They reinforced the fact that it was vital to maintain peace or face the wrath of the Zidhe. The Zidarians might be powerful, but their gifts paled in comparison to the magic of the elves.

Ki'ara only wished that her brother Ragnald, as the present lord of the clan, would take the treaty a bit more to heart. It was beyond her understanding how the reigning MacClair could behave so imprudently when their own ancestor had paid for his defiance of the rules with his life.

⸙

The only major incident since the warning by the Zidhe took place long before Ki'ara was born. It had involved two of the clans. Naturally, one had been the MacClairs. The offender had been her grandfather, as a matter of fact. The other had been a StCloud.

The two lords got into an angry disagreement during a council meeting. It started because of a few sheep. The animals in question had strayed north into the MacClair territory and mixed with those herds. The StCloud wanted his property back plus all their offspring. Before long, this led to a bloody fight between the two rulers as well as their assembled kinsmen.

Both chiefs left in a fury. They went to their camps which, as a prudent precaution, had in the meantime been moved to opposite sides of the meeting house. Because of the squabble, everyone was on high alert, ready for anything. Sneak attacks were, after all, a specialty of the crafty Highlanders.

The two lords entered their prospective tents. They got undressed with the help of their servants and went to their cots. For extra security, they had several of their fighters make their beds up around them. Before long, all went to sleep, knowing that the guards would alert them to danger.

By morning, both rulers had disappeared into thin air. Not one of the men near them, not one of the many sentries around the tent, nor anyone in the camp had seen or heard them or noticed anything out of the ordinary.

Being warriors, the clan members' response to finding their lords gone was immediate aggression. They armed themselves and rushed off to confront the assailants, which they naturally assumed to be the other party involved in the argument. To the two groups' surprise, they meet in the middle between the tent sites.

The men had been prepared to attack the camp of the sneaky invaders, but running into each other like this, gave them pause. A lot of shouting ensued. Each accused the other of kidnapping their ruler, after all, who else could it have been?

Suspicions ran rampant. Tempers flared. The insults being exchanged were getting more grievous and colorful with each passing minute. As the mood of the crowd darkened, another fight was about to break out.

༄༅‧

Ki'ara had always thought it too convenient that just at the right moment, one of the servants cleaning the council chamber found an unrolled scroll containing a message. She could feel it in her gut that the Zidhe had something to do with this timely discovery.

The note had quickly dispelled all uncertainties. Both clans had retreated, feeling somewhat sheepish. They had muttered apologies to each other and had slunk back to their tents.

There, on the table in the very room where it had all started, had been a letter pinned with two fairy arrows. It had been short, but down to the point.

The four words this message had contained were now engraved right there on a plaque as a continued reminder. The holes left by the arrowheads still showed above it. Ki'ara had seen them herself.

"You had been warned!" was all that had been written on the plain piece of paper, but to the clans, it had said everything. Every single one of them had known, right then and there, that no further transgressions would be tolerated and that they had better behave from then on.

The two chiefs were never seen again. Both had been in the prime of their lives and should have lived at least another five hundred years, maybe more. For Ki'ara, it meant that she grew up without her grandfather, but given what she had heard of the disposition of the man, that might not have been such a bad thing.

Life since the vanishing of their hard-headed ruler had been much more pleasant for the clan. Raghnall MacClair had been a harsh and unbending man who had refused to let go of the past. Ki'ara could not really find it in her heart to overly regret his disappearance.

Losing the head of the MacClair clan had forced Ki'ara's father to step up as lord. Mikael was a very different man than his sire. Peaceful and kind but also firm and unyielding when he needed to be. He had become a well-loved ruler in record time.

After the two nobles' disappearance, the leaders had governed together peacefully over the people of the nine realms. Mikael MacClair, along with his friend, the then Lord StCloud, had made sure that it remained so. Now that Ki'ara's father had passed on the reign to Ragnald, it had fallen to the next Lord StCloud, Conall, to keep things in check. Not an easy job since he had to continually prevent the other lords from taking on her obstinate brother.

As set down by the treaty, the chiefs met twice a year to handle any situations that had arisen since their last get-together. All major decisions were discussed, and a compromise hammered out which was agreeable to most. The present MacClair only attended when he had no other option. He felt that those proceedings were beneath him and resented the other rulers' authority over him.

The lords, therefore, made their decisions without him and, once the issues had been sanctioned by a majority vote, the measures would be instituted. So far, this system had worked well, and a tentative peace had taken hold in the Highlands once more. The only threat now was Ragnald, Ki'ara's very own brother.

✦

Watching color spread to the high moors as the sun rose towards the zenith, Ki'ara's thoughts turned to Mikael and Ali'ana. She missed them dearly and had done so every day since they had left. They had made sure that she had a wonderful childhood right up to the day when they departed.

In many ways, Ki'ara had grown up like a princess. She had been spoiled and coddled, but her parents had also made sure that she understood that she had obligations that they expected her to take care of. From a very young age on, she had been taught to step up and be there for her people. This was one of the reasons she was still so reluctant to risk exile by directly confronting her brother.

✦

The clan leaders might have lost their titles, but their responsibilities had remained the same. Just like in the times before the peace treaty, the nine ruling families were expected to continue performing their duties to their people to the best of their abilities.

Representatives of the families were required to make an appearance at weddings and other festive occasions in and around their realms. Ki'ara had always thought of most of these gatherings as great fun. The funerals, however, she had liked far less, and only attended out of respect for the grieving family members.

As directed by the Zidhe, any occasions were the clans assembled were used to hold a brief council session. These meetings gave the lords an opportunity to discuss and settle minor current affairs. Even as a very young girl, Ki'ara had found the discussions most fascinating. She had quite often managed to locate an out of the way corner and had sat there enthralled and listened for hours.

Ki'ara had been good at reading the subtle undercurrents present in the room. She had realized that, since her grandfather Raghnall's disappearance, a lot of the animosity between the old families had died down, but not all. In any case, it was much better hidden. From what the girl had been told by her father, she gathered that the lords were so much more polite now. They tried hard not to offend each other and went out of their way to avoid a possible fight.

Ki'ara had truly loved these get-togethers and had always enjoyed herself to the fullest. She grew up regarding all the Zidarians as one big, happy family, and her attitude had warmed the hearts of the lords and their spouses. The sunny little girl had been thoroughly spoiled at the meetings, and the rulers had indulged her by allowing her presence during the councils.

In the Zidarians' view, she was just a small child, unable to comprehend what was being discussed. Little did they know that this was far from the truth. Ki'ara understood much of what was being said and picked up on subtle signals that a less keen observer might have easily missed. If she had questions, she saved them for her parents and the StCloud.

Mikael and Ali'ana, as well as Conall, had encouraged her interest in current events as well as Ki'ara treating the other lords and ladies as her favorite uncles and aunts. Anything which brought people closer together was good for the peace.

⚜

Maybe one day soon, she would see her extended family again. Ki'ara sure hoped so. For now, it was time to go have some breakfast and to get on with the day. Mathus needed looking after since he was not feeling well, and then there was more to learn about this magnificent ship.

After one last look at the beauty of her Highland home, the young woman headed below deck to check on the tutor.

Chapter 25

Old Resentments

As had become her habit, the next morning found Ki'ara back up on deck. With every hour, they were getting closer to Deansport, the only harbor for this size ship near the castle. She should have been ecstatic, but for some reason, her anxiety kept growing. What would it be like this time? Why was she feeling so apprehensive?

Staring blindly out across the churning sea, Ki'ara thought back upon the last few years of her life. So much had changed and not for the better! The fog hanging over the water and the dark, racing clouds overhead suited her somber mood. Being this close to home was bringing up all kinds of emotions.

The young woman had no more delusions. She might as well face it, it was better for her to be away from Seamuir Castle, no matter how much she disliked leaving the Highlands.

At least that way, she was not around Ragnald, the brother who had been left in charge of her life. Why he and Lyall, the middle son, despised her so much was beyond her understanding.

⤜⤛⤜⤛

Ki'ara's thoughts went back to her youth. She had always known that her two older brothers had resented her mother. Even though they had been adults by the time Ali'ana had come along and away from home a good part of the time, they had been spiteful and mean to their father's new wife. In their self-centered view, no one was supposed to take the place of their deceased parent.

Morena, Mikael's first wife and the boys' mother, had never fully recovered from the birth of their last son, Gawain. She had died when her youngest child was eighteen years old. Her husband had mourned her passing profoundly and for many years.

It had been another eighteen years before the lord had decided to marry again. It had been a huge surprise when he had shown up with a new wife. The clan had been overjoyed but not so his oldest sons. They had seen the beautiful bride as an unwelcome replacement for their dead mother and had hated their father for bringing the 'invader' into their lives.

The rift within the family had grown even wider when their sister had come along. Ki'ara had been born twenty-five years after the wedding. The couple had come to believe that they would never have a child of their own, and they had been ecstatic. Ragnald had detested his half-sibling from day one, and Lyall, as always, had followed suit.

⤜⤛⤜⤛

Due to all the friction within the family, the baby girl had not been born at Seamuir Castle. Being aware of the animosity his older sons felt towards his new wife, Mikael had decided shortly after the wedding that when his spouse conceived, she would have the child among her own kin. Therefore, as soon as the couple had realized that they were expecting, the excited father-to-be had accompanied Ali'ana back to her people. Ki'ara had been born seven months later.

The lord and lady had raised their little one with much love and affection. They had gone out of their way to make Ki'ara feel cherished, especially since her two oldest brothers had been nothing but mean to the small child. The only one of the three siblings who had always treated her nice was Gawain, the youngest of the boys.

It had not taken long for the proud parents to realize just how special their baby really was. Ki'ara had been given schooling most of the other children her age did not even dream of. Highly intelligent, with an unquenchable thirst for information, she had asked in-depth questions and had observed all that was around her. Her rather extensive education had begun at a very young age.

The little girl had learned incredibly fast. She had loved to accumulate knowledge of all kinds, had soaked it up like a sponge. Mikael had always been looking for the next tutor even as he was hiring a new one. Ki'ara had absorbed all that they had to teach her that quickly, just as she had done with the wizards her brother had sent her to study with.

Her father, always prudent and not wanting to increase the discord in the family further, had decided that each instructor had to be sworn to secrecy. No one besides himself, Ali'ana, and Conall were to be aware of just how advanced the child was.

Her two oldest brothers had already hated the affection showered upon their young sister. They had complained that her parents treated Ki'ara more like a fairytale princess than a real girl. Mikael had laughed at this but not so Ali'ana. She had sensed the resentment the boys had felt towards their young sibling and had tried her best to smooth things over.

Then, one day, out of the blue, Mikael and Ali'ana had disclosed their plans to depart in a week. It had taken everyone by surprise. Hurried plans had been made to install Ragnald as chief and to transfer the ruling of the realm to him. A whirlwind of activity had resulted. The passing of power ceremony had to be prepared, and the other lords invited.

Ki'ara had been hurt as well as aghast that her folks intended to leave without her. Even worse, however, had been the fact that she was to remain under the guardianship of Ragnald. This had terrified her enough to mention her concerns to her mother. The lady had reassured her absentmindedly that all would be well.

The teenager had begged her usually so loving and understanding parents to take her with them. For once, her pleas had fallen on deaf ears. The couple had been unwilling to listen. There had been an urgency to their departure, one their daughter had not been able to understand. What had they been hiding, and why did they have to leave so quickly?

Ali'ana had tried to explain that it was necessary for them to go. She had told her daughter that Ragnald could not really be lord with his father looking over his shoulder. The young man would have felt too self-conscious, and that would not have been a good way for him to start his new reign. For the clan's sake, one lord had to be clearly in charge.

When that had not overly impressed the girl, her mother had pointed out to Ki'ara that Mikael had been tied to the land their entire married life and that the couple was looking forward to their journey. Ali'ana had stated that they needed some time for themselves and that they would miss her. She asked Ki'ara not to be selfish.

Both Ali'ana and Mikael had assured Ki'ara that there was nothing to worry about. They had told her that they had made arrangements for her future, that they had gone out of their way to ensure that all would go well and as planned. The girl, however, had not been able to shake the feeling that something terrible would happen just as soon as they left.

Seeing how anxious she was, Mikael had finally taken his daughter aside. He had promised Ki'ara that she would be safe and well taken care of right here in the bosom of her family, among the members of her clan. Her dad had shared with her that Ragnald had sworn that he would take the very best care of his baby sister. The look he had received for his words had said everything.

Seeing that his child was still not convinced and at his wit's end, Mikael had brusquely explained to Ki'ara that she belonged here, with the MacClair clan, and not off traveling about. The usually so kind man had bluntly told her that she needed to continue her education, but he had also promised that he and Ali'ana would be back in a few years.

Until then, Mikael had assured her, she would be in good hands. Her brother would do his utmost to look after her. Before the girl had been able to say another word, her father had turned and had stalked off.

After that last talk with her dad, Ki'ara had started to see that nothing she could say or do would change her parents' minds. She had realized that the couple was already feeling guilty enough about leaving her and that this was the reason Mikael had gotten so angry. There had been no sense in adding to that. Therefore, the teenager had decided to keep her trepidations to herself from then on.

Ki'ara had smiled when she said goodbye to Mikael and Ali'ana. She had wished them pleasant travels and a wonderful time. Then, the forlorn young girl had watched the pair until they had disappeared into the hills. She had managed to hide her tears until she had reached her own room.

Once she had been alone, the feeling of impending doom had threatened to overwhelm Ki'ara. The appalling incident with Ragnald a few minutes later had confirmed her worst fears. His gleeful destruction of many of her treasured possessions had been a good indication of things to come.

⊱✿⊰

The teenager's heart had been breaking, especially since she had no idea why she had been left behind. Something had been going on with her folks, but to this day, she had no clue what it had been. Why else would they have placed her in the hands of her hateful brother?

Ki'ara had realized long ago that there was little love in Ragnald's heart. He disliked and despised most people but especially her. After her parents' departure, the MacClair lord had severely frightened her on several occasions, and once, he had even tried to kill her.

In the young woman's eyes, they were family, even after that. It made her sad to see her sibling so filled with hate, so stuck in the past, so willing to step outside the law.

⊱✿⊰

Ragnald MacClair was one of those few who had not given up on old grudges. He resented the new order of things. Ki'ara believed that the indoctrination he had received from his grandfather from a young age on had made sure of that. In her opinion, one shared by the Council of Lords, her oldest brother should have never become the new lord.

⊱✿⊰

When Mikael MacClair had chosen to retire from being head of the clan and had passed the rule on to his oldest son, Ragnald had started showing his true colors. It had started right after his father left for his travels. For the kinsmen and Ki'ara, life had changed for the worse from that moment onward.

The new lord's haughty attitude and rudeness had not gone over well with his peers. He had shown them nothing but disrespect. Therefore, it had not taken long for former animosities between the MacClairs and some of the other rulers to reawaken. Ragnald had very often ended up shunned at the meetings and had finally just stopped attending them whenever possible.

The young lady had realized quickly that her father's heir was an even more bitter and troubled man than she had ever suspected. He was filled with resentment that he was only a lord instead of a king. Raghnall MacClair had filled his grandson's head with stories of glory from long bygone days. Ki'ara feared that those tales had left Ragnald longing for a return to those times. He wanted the ultimate power to govern, not just over his own people, but over all of the clans.

The new MacClair ruler had soon shown himself to be a cruel and deceitful man. Until then, he had hidden this well from those around him. Ragnald had loved his grandfather and loathed Mikael. He saw his dad's compassion and fairness as a weakness. Perversely, he blamed them both, as well as the StClouds, for losing the crown.

Ki'ara had just turned thirteen when her dad had passed on the rule. It had been a sad day for her when the pair had disappeared in the distance. Ragnald, however, had been only too happy to see them go. He had despised them both and had been delighted that they were out of his hair. Over the years, he had grown tired of pretending to be someone he was not.

In the new lord's mind, he had been left with just one major drawback - he was stuck with their brat. The more Ragnald had thought about that, the madder he had gotten. How dare that woman leave that abomination behind!

Within hours of the couple's departure, Ki'ara had very suddenly found herself in hostile environs. Ragnald was finally the MacClair, the man in charge of the magic, the clan, the land, and the manor. The days he had to hide his true nature had come to an end. He was the lord, the law, he was in charge.

As far as the new ruler was concerned, he could do as he pleased. Now her guardian, he had unleashed his full fury upon the unfortunate teen. Ki'ara had not been overly surprised by Ragnald's behavior towards her. She had sensed long ago how her brother felt about her, but she had still been shocked by the depths of his resentment and saddened by his bitterness and hatred.

Ragnald had treated Ki'ara like she was a stranger, an unwelcome one at that. He had made the girl feel like she had been left behind to annoy him. He had accused her of spying on him, had told her she better behave, or he would throw her out of the house. Even on her last visit, whenever anyone had succeeded in getting the lord in a bad mood, his sister had been the one who had paid the price.

Within hours

After her parents' departure, it had become clear that the MacClair was utterly indifferent to his sister's needs. He couldn't have cared less if she lived or died and, if he were honest, would have preferred to have her gone from his life. Therefore, until he had started sending her off and, during her visits, Ragnald had left Ki'ara's rearing to her maid.

Leana had figured out very soon that it was not smart to bother the lord with any concerns regarding her charge, not even if the girl had outgrown her clothes or required new shoes. She had found other ways to take care of the teenager's needs.

Ki'ara had avoided Ragnald as well. She had learned quickly that no good ever came of reminding him of her existence.

Her guardian and Lyall always spent much of their time together. A few run-ins with these two, right after her parents' departure, had been very unpleasant. From then on, Ki'ara had gone out of her way to stay out of sight and mind of her two older brothers.

Regarding himself as untouchable, Ragnald continued to do as he pleased. The mask he had once worn had been discarded, and he allowed some of the evil festering in his soul to show. The promises he had made to Mikael and Ali'ana meant nothing to him. With no one to keep him in check, he was a menace to himself and his people.

Being brought to Ragnald's attention, was never a good thing, for any of them, not just for Ki'ara. He was impatient, unjust, and cruel to his kinsmen whom he had sworn to care for and protect. The other clans, especially the StClouds, he hated with a passion, and in his arrogance, he made no attempt to hide his true feelings.

Ki'ara had observed with great sadness how much the ill-will between her family and some of the other rulers had grown since her brother became the MacClairs' lord. All the efforts of Mikael and his friends to create a lasting peace between clans were being slowly but surely eroded.

When Ki'ara's father had still been in charge, he, his wife, and daughter had attended most of the festivities held by the other Zidarians. If the brothers were at the castle and not off fostered somewhere, they had always been invited to come along.

Ki'ara remembered how much fun those parties had been. Mikael had an easy camaraderie with the other rulers, and the girl had always admired his way with people. The lords had trusted and respected her dad, very unlike this latest MacClair. She only hoped that Ragnald changed his way before the elves interfered. He might be hateful, but he was still her brother.

The Zidarians had made a lot of progress towards being more peaceful by the time Ki'ara was born. Increasingly, they resembled a nation instead of an assembly of clans. Having to govern together had helped.

By now, most of the immortal families were related to each other by one degree or another. All those intermarriages over the years had aided in forming lasting ties among the different bloodlines. Coming together on frequent occasions had further cemented alliances.

Her parents had encouraged Ki'ara to play with all the other children, no matter who they belonged to. As far as they had been concerned, they had wanted all the Highlanders to grow into one large happy family, regardless of customs or heritage. To further this, Mikael and Ali'ana had always been trying to bring people closer together.

The couple had not cared much for some of the Highlands archaic customs. Instead, they had done what had felt right in their hearts. As such, they had allowed their daughter to spend a lot of time with one of their best friends, the heir of the StClouds, Conall.

The girl and the young lord had become very close. The substantial difference in age had never affected their friendship. The StCloud had adored Ki'ara even as an infant, he had fallen in love with her soul, her spirit from the first moment he had laid eyes on the baby.

Ki'ara's intelligence and understanding had been way beyond her tender years, and her curiosity had been insatiable. This had allowed the unlikely pair to share many spirited and fascinating discussions, which they both had greatly enjoyed. As far as the girl had been concerned, the gatherings were always more fun when Conall had been around.

Once Ragnald had taken over the clan, the invitations had soon decreased to a trickle. Then, they had stopped altogether. Apparently, no one really wanted that MacClair around if they could help it. If the family had attended one of the gatherings, the brothers had usually gone on their own, leaving their sister at home.

On the few occasions when Ki'ara had been allowed to attend one of the meetings, she had overheard many a snide comment made behind the haughty lord's back. She had realized that no one much liked Ragnald except maybe her brothers. Lyall was always utterly loyal to him, but she still was not so sure about Gawain.

Ragnald's offhand and insolent manners, together with his arrogance and air of superiority towards the other rulers, had a devastating effect. Ki'ara's oldest sibling had become widely despised.

Anything the MacClair had to say, even when it was valid, was bound to fall on deaf ears. Since fighting had been outlawed, this was a sort of acceptable option, as were malicious comments.

The Zidarians, being Highlanders, were an ornery lot. They were and always had been warriors at heart. The treaty forced them to keep the peace, but this did not stop them from expressing how they felt about one of their peers. Especially if that someone acted like he was so much better than they.

The lords just could not help themselves as far as Ki'ara's brother was concerned. This new MacClair was just too annoying. Carefully couched insults were often hurled Ragnald's way if he dared to show his face at an assembly or at any of the festivities.

The self-important man had ended up storming out of several meetings. Hearing his peers' satisfied snickers as he charged out the door had only added further fuel to Ragnald's simmering resentment and rage. Over the years, his desire to get even with each and every one of that lot had grown to gigantic proportions.

With Ragnald being so bad-tempered and utterly unpredictable, riling him up like that could have led to dire consequences. Once the hilarity ended and sanity reasserted itself, the offending lords usually decided to take extra precautions.

In the beginning, they had been in fear for their lives for several days but, when nothing had happened after the first couple of times they had insulted Ragnald, they had grown more brazen with each occasion.

It was usually Lord Iain, Ki'ara's uncle, or Conall, who reminded them of their manners. The two friends had taken it upon themselves to be the voice of reason in the council now that Mikael was no longer among them. To keep things from escalating, they put the fear of reprisal by the Zidhe back into the unruly lot.

For a while after, the other rulers would control their tempers and words. It was, however, getting progressively harder for them to hide how they actually felt about that particular clan leader, especially since they were only too aware of how Ragnald treated his clan and his sister.

Seamuir Castle had often become a virtual prison for Ki'ara. Usually, she was forbidden to even set foot outside the walls. Any time Ragnald had allowed Ki'ara to accompany him to a gathering, she had made sure to express her gratitude multiple times. She knew he liked that and could never hear it enough.

Just being among other people had increased the girl's feeling of being connected to a shred of her past. Very unlike the way they handled her brother, the other lords and their spouses had been respectful and kind to Ki'ara. They had treated her no different than before, but on occasions, when her fellow Zidarians had thought themselves unobserved, she had caught pity and concern reflected in their eyes.

This had upset Ki'ara a great deal as had Ragnald's rule that she had to stay right next to one of her siblings. She had never been permitted to speak with anyone by herself. The MacClair had warned her that if she misbehaved, she would be left at the castle from then on.

Not being allowed to associate with the other teenagers any longer had saddened Ki'ara, but that had not been the worst of the new guidelines. Ragnald had strictly forbidden her any contact with the StClouds, especially Conall, who was by then the lord of Cloudshire Hall.

Mikael had encouraged the connection between Conall and her. Ki'ara had often wondered about this. She had gotten her answer on the day she had secretly listened in at one of the meetings. Among other things, she had overheard it mention that an arrangement with the StCloud had been made shortly after her birth.

Further investigation had led Ki'ara to discover that her father had agreed to a betrothal as long as this coincided with the wishes of his young daughter. Mikael had granted Conall the right to get to know her and woo her. That had explained a lot since most children were not permitted to spend that much time with an adult of the opposite sex!

Her father, as well as Ki'ara, had seen the StCloud as part of the family, as her future husband. They had not been alone in that vision.

⛄

Her life had been going so well, and Ki'ara had been very happy. She had loved the StCloud and had enjoyed his devotion. After Mikael and Ali'ana had set off on their travels, however, everything had changed. It had been Ragnald, with his cruel words, who had destroyed all her and her parents' well-laid plans.

No longer being able to see Conall had hurt her the most of all the mean things her brother had done. The memory of that day brought tears to Ki'ara's eyes, even now, years later. Besides her parents, the StCloud had been her favorite person. She had loved him with all her heart for as long as she could recall. He was her soulmate, the only man she could imagine sharing her life with.

Conall had taken her seriously from a young age on. The handsome man had never treated her like a child. He had paid attention to her opinions and encouraged her explorations. He had even helped her sneak into some of the more secret council meetings since she had enjoyed listening in so very much.

Besides her parents and Leana, her maid, the StCloud had been the only one she could talk to about her thoughts and the things she sensed. He had the knowledge and understanding to guide her and had become her confidant, her very best friend. Losing this relationship, along with her parents, had left the girl feeling utterly alone and heartbroken.

⛄

The passage of years had not fully healed the wounds in Ki'ara's heart. She still missed the life she once had, but she also felt for her people. The young woman had never been able to understand how her parents could place the clan, the magic, the land, as well as their daughter, in the keeping of one such as Ragnald.

How had they missed what he was like? Both Mikael and Ali'ana had extremely astute senses. They had great instincts. How could they have been so blind? Either of Ki'ara's other brothers would have made a better lord than HIM! Why had they not seen that?

What had been so important to make her folks rush off so fast? Ki'ara hoped that one day she would get the chance to ask them. With a deep sigh, the young woman brought her attention back to the present.

⸎

Ki'ara let her eyes roam over the distant landscape. She drank in the sights. How much she loved these stark peaks, the brown-green of the high moors, the vibrant emerald color of the valleys belonging to the Zidhe. When the heather bloomed, it added its soft hues to the mix. It was gorgeous, even with the storm raging around them.

This was her home and, despite her apprehensions, she could not wait for the moment when she could plant her feet once again firmly on Highland Soil. She had been gone for too long. Not that she minded being at sea but, if she had been given a choice, she would have never left here in the first place.

If only her brother would find some love in his heart! Just the thought of Ragnald sent a cold shiver down her spine. Ki'ara pulled her warm cloak and knit scarf tighter around her. She suddenly felt cold, down to her bones, and the freezing wind seemed to blow right through her clothes.

Determinedly, Ki'ara stopped this train of negative and fearful thoughts. This was getting her nowhere. After a few moments, some of her usually sunny nature reasserted itself, but the view of the country she so loved had lost a fair bit of its magic. Her appetite was gone as well, and breakfast no longer sounded appealing.

With her head lowered against the gale, the anxious young woman fought her way back to the stairs and returned below to her cabin.

Chapter 26

Eastmuir

Early in the afternoon, the storm blew over and the skies cleared up. Within minutes, the day turned unusually bright and sunny. The waves were still huge, but what a difference to the morning! The sudden change was truly amazing, but this coast was well known for its unpredictable weather.

Ki'ara watched as the sun lit up the slopes reaching right down to the water. It chased the lingering shadows away in the valleys. Steam was rising off the rain-soaked land. Not long after, the realm of her clan, Eastmuir, started to come into sight. They were getting close to the end of their sea voyage now.

A deep fjord, cutting far into the interior, marked the border between Summerland and the lands of the MacClairs. Tall mountains bordered each side of this protected inland waterway. Over the years, many a ship had found refuge there from the powerful storms which could develop so suddenly on these changeable seas.

As the ship forged its way further to the north, Ki'ara was finally just barely able to make out Seamuir Castle in the distance, high up on its perch above the sea. The young woman's heart contracted with pain. She had been gone far too long. What was awaiting her this time? Over the last few years, the Highlands themselves had become much more her home than the manor she grew up in.

✦

As usual, the tutor was being a challenge. To get away from Mathus, Ki'ara had fled back up on deck. She sat curled up near the stern of the *Sea Witch*. Since it was bitter cold out, the girl had taken refuge from the biting wind behind several lashed down crates. From this sheltered spot, she could watch the coast slide past in relative comfort.

The waters this far north never warmed up. Even in the height of summer, it was freezing on the ships sailing these seas. No matter how warm the sun was, the gentlest gust off the frigid ocean would suck the heat out of anything living. Now, in late fall, it was positively icy, and only multiple layers of clothing would help keep one warm. Falling overboard was usually deadly.

For additional protection, the young woman had wrapped up in a blanket. Over the top of that, she had pulled a length of sailcloth. It helped to keep more of the ice-cold breeze out, but even then, her little nest was far from warm. Still, it was better than being confined to the cabin.

The sea had been rough for the past few days, but the waves had grown even more massive when a gale hit them during the night. The large ship had been tossed about like it was a toy, and the captain had ordered all hands below deck. Only he and the helmsman had stayed above to brave the storm and keep them on course.

Sleeping had been almost impossible. Ki'ara had envied the sailors, they had hanging mats suspended from the ceiling and fared much better than she in her cot. Her tutor, not much of a traveler to start with, had become so seasick he had wanted to die. She might not have much liking for the man but could not help but feel pity for him and had used her magic to soothe him.

Mathus being so preoccupied with himself and just wanting to sleep, however, had an unexpected advantage for Ki'ara. Her watchdog was not worried about the whereabouts of his companion.

This suited the young woman just fine. It gave her more time to herself. She was genuinely grateful for her sheltered hideout, which shielded her at least a little bit from the frigid draft and gave Ki'ara the chance to observe the magnificent landscape she loved so much as it slipped past.

Summerland, the realm of the StClouds, was located the farthest to the south. Being just a little bit warmer, it had some of the most productive soils in the Highlands. The clan had done well for themselves, and even from a distance, the young woman could see the large herds of sheep grazing on the green hills.

Their ship was heading due north and had been for several days. They were lucky that the wind was now blowing almost straight from the west. It allowed them to make good time.

Ki'ara could sense it the minute the vessel drew level with the border of Eastmuir. All of a sudden, her body started to vibrate gently. It seemed like the land was calling to her. It stunned her for a moment, but then she relaxed and enjoyed it. It was, after all, a rather pleasant experience.

The intensity of the sensation, however, increased and caught the young woman by surprise. Never before had reaching her home felt quite like this. A wave of warmth and love spread through her, driving away the cold and leaving her panting and sweating. It left her in awe. What had just happened?

When the magic retreated, Ki'ara's entire being seemed to be drawn to that rugged coast. It was almost overwhelming. Her longing to finally set foot on Eastmuir's beloved soil again became almost unbearable, and she had to fight the impulse to jump overboard and head for the shore. The sorceress just knew that she could have made it with all that heat she had been given but was not overly fond of the idea of swimming in these frigid waters.

From their present location, it was not that much longer before they would reach the harbor, but it seemed to the girl that the landscape slipped past ever so slowly. Ki'ara could not wait to get to Deansport! Taking a deep breath, she managed to relax and enjoy the incredible view.

The coastline was so wild and beautiful, it astonished Ki'ara anew each time she saw it. Mossy slopes ending in pure white beaches were interspersed here and there with stark rock faces and deep fjords. How much she had missed this!

In places, massive limestone cliffs rose up to fields of purple heather and bright green moss, which blended in with the borders of the scattered dark-brown moors. The vibrant forests of the Zidhe filled the fertile valleys in the distance with their rich colors.

When they had sailed past the elves' clearly visible barrier two days ago, Ki'ara had once again been amazed at the difference between the Lower and Upper Mystic Isles. She could really perceive it from out here at sea.

The colors of her beloved Highlands were so much more vivid and brilliant, so much more diverse due to the magic which now imbued these stunning lands. To her, the Lower Lands looked drab in comparison with their expanses of forests and fields. No place she had ever seen paralleled the rugged and vibrant beauty of her treasured home.

Now that the sun was out, Ki'ara could clearly make out Cloudshire Hall, the ancestral seat of the StClouds, in the distance. The fortress kept a watch over the fjord between the realms and the adjacent bay. No ship could slip past here without being noticed.

The young woman could not help herself. In an instant, her thoughts went to the lord of the castle. Ki'ara felt like a teenager in love. Was Conall there? It had been so long that she had seen him. Had Ragnald any intention of ever allowing her to speak to him again? Most likely not.

Conall and she had shared a deep connection even though he was many years her senior. Ki'ara had been different from the other Zidarian offspring. Had that been known, it would have isolated her. She had liked the other children and had played with them often but had sometimes grown bored with their simplistic games.

As Ki'ara grew older and even smarter, she had to be very careful to hide her true nature. Her intellect would have scared some of the more timid kids. She did not want them to avoid her, it would have hurt her terribly to be seen as a threat. As it was, a couple of times, one of the little ones had hidden behind their parents when they saw her. She had always wondered about that. What would cause a child to fear her?

As Ki'ara well knew, small ones were much more perceptive, closer still to their innate instincts. She was well-loved by most of their parents and had no problems with the other youngsters her age. In an attempt to figure it out, the girl had searched her own soul. She had been unable to sense anything inside herself that should give anyone pause. She had concluded that there was no cruelness, no evil inside her.

What then had caused such a reaction? Her stunning, bright green eyes which looked like they could see right into someone's heart? Or, her name? It was also uncommon among the Zidarians. Or, had they somehow picked up on her ability to read all their emotions? She still had no clue.

The next time she saw her parents, Ki'ara had every intention of getting an answer out of them. They had been very evasive the one and only time she had brought up the subject. Maybe they could shed some light on this mystery.

Chapter 27

A Timely Warning

It took the *Sea Witch* another two long days to reach Deansport. The waters were much less turbulent now, and Ki'ara had been enjoying more time watching the landscape slide past from her little nest on the deck. Mathus was still under the weather and asleep most of the time, something which suited her just fine. The less she had to deal with the obnoxious man, the better she liked it.

On the last afternoon before their arrival at the harbor, the clipper passed near Seamuir Castle. Ki'ara had just come up from below, and she quickly slid into her shelter. With all her mixed emotions, she preferred to be unobserved for this first closer look at the place which had once been such a happy home for her as well as the clan.

The stark, towering edifice loomed high up on its lofty perch overlooking the sea. Ki'ara was taken aback. Was the fortress even more brooding than usual? Something felt different about the entire complex and the land around it, almost as if it was slowly being poisoned. The light seemed to reflect oddly of the walls as well. Were her eyes playing tricks?

Was it Ki'ara's imagination, or was the very air around the stronghold affected? To her, it appeared that a profound sense of gloominess was hanging over the ancient structure like a miasma. What had Ragnald been up to? Had her brother further descended into darkness? She sure hoped not!

Using her powers, the sorceress checked closer. There was no mistaking it; the old building gave off a definite air of menace. Sensing this saddened Ki'ara but it also provided her with a timely warning. She would have to watch her brother very carefully. Until she knew more about the situation, she would have to be on high alert and protect herself at all times.

To think that Seamuir had once resounded with laughter! It had been a home and not just a house then. Pity for the people residing within, as well as the melancholy edifice, filled the young woman's heart. To her, buildings had souls and deserved to be cared for and loved.

All the castles had been built for defense. They served in this capacity until this very day. No invaders would land on these shores if the Highlanders could help it. Unless you were far, far out at sea or passed on a dark and stormy night, no ship could sail past any of the coastal fortresses without being seen.

A watch over the adjacent waters was kept 24 hours a day, and the Zidarians' powers could be used with devastating results. O'Rourke had sent the required signal to grant them safe passage.

It had been acknowledged. By now, Ki'ara's brother should have been notified of her imminent arrival. She assumed that the family's carriage had been dispatched that morning to fetch her.

Even with all her well-founded apprehensions, Ki'ara could barely contain her excitement when the harbor finally came into view. She was almost home! The young woman did not expect an exceptionally warm welcome at Seamuir Castle, especially not after what she had seen, but at least she would be back in the Highlands!

Ki'ara loved being at sea. She cherished the feel of the brisk wind on her face and being rocked to sleep by the waves. The girl did not mind the long voyage, but her heart was intimately tied to the land. Also, she was tired of looking after the tutor. He would be most relieved to get off this ship. Mathus was still seasick and would not feel better until he set foot back on solid ground.

As they approached the port, the *Sea Witch* had the ocean all to herself, but the previous day, the sailors had spotted a magnificent clipper heading due south. Ki'ara had watched the vessel as it sailed past. Somehow the sight of that ship had churned up feelings inside her that she had a hard time defining.

It had been a beautiful craft, richly attired, and very well kept. The sailboat had been flying a Highland flag but had been too far away for Ki'ara to make out which one. The young woman knew a fair bit about ships and could tell that this one was exceptionally well cared for and, it was fast!

Who of the lords owned this beauty, and where was she heading? Ki'ara had idly contemplated this question but had managed to come to no conclusion. The ship could be heading anywhere to the south and could have come from as far away as Larinia or beyond. Reaching out with her mind to gather the desired information would have been plain disrespectful and most likely unwelcome. Besides, if she had time and really wanted to know, she could always ask in the harbor.

In any case, Ki'ara was confident that she had never laid eyes on the vessel before, but it was such a stunning craft that she would have no problem recognizing it the next time she saw it.

It was late afternoon when they reached Deansport. O'Rourke anchored the ship in its usual spot. From what he and Ki'ara could see, the carriage had not yet arrived. When morning dawned, and no coach was in sight, they decided to make other plans. There was no sense in waiting. They would just have to work around this minor inconvenience.

The captain himself went to the town to hire a carriage to drive down to Seamuir Castle. Once he returned, the young woman's and Mathus' belongings were brought on deck and were ferried over to the dock. A couple of the sailors helped to load the items on the vehicle and remained behind to guard them while the passengers prepared to disembark.

After saying her goodbyes to the crew, Ki'ara gracefully climbed down the ladder. She managed to make it look effortless, even in her long dress. Mathus, on the other hand, had to be lowered down in a sling. He was unable to get on or off the ship any other way.

Then, it was time to say farewell to Marcus O'Rourke. Ki'ara thanked the jovial man for all his help and for allowing her to remain on deck most days, even in inclement weather. She might be the owner, but the captain was always in charge. The old salt winked at her. He felt that no one deserved to be stuck with that tutor, especially not this lovely young woman.

Once Ki'ara and Mathus were comfortably seated in the carriage, O'Rourke proceeded to give the driver some last-minute instructions. A few moments later, the vehicle was on its way south towards Seamuir Castle.

※※※

The coach trip gave Ki'ara an opportunity to mull over a variety of possible reasons for the absence of a ride for her and the tutor. In the past, the family carriage had always been sent to pick her up. Why not this time? She was sure that the *Sea Witch* had been seen passing by the day before.

The signals sent to the castle were specific to each ship, and the receipt of theirs had been acknowledged. That had been yesterday, so there had been plenty of time to dispatch the carriage while their vessel sailed around the spit of land sheltering Deansport.

The young woman was a bit disturbed that the coach had not shown up but was not completely surprised. Ragnald, after all, had not been happy about her coming home. The lack of regard, however, along with her impressions of the castle the day before caused Ki'ara to experience a deep sense of foreboding. She feared that this was just an indication of things to come.

Her oldest brother had become progressively more distant and unfriendly on each of the intervals between teachers. Seeing no other option, he had allowed Ki'ara to visit while he had hunted for the next place to send her. Two years ago, things had gone pretty well for a bit but, towards the end of her stay, Ragnald had been more hostile than ever.

The young woman had been trying to figure out the MacClair's reasons for behaving this way for years now. So far, she had no clue why he hated her.

※※※

This time, however, things would be different. For one, Ragnald was no longer Ki'ara's legal guardian. In addition, she had been made a lord. Instead of nine Highland rulers, there were now ten. Did her brother find out somehow? As far as she knew, the council had honored her request to keep this a secret until she arrived at her own home.

She had her parents and uncle to thank for the change in her situation. Ki'ara had been pleasantly surprised when a representative of the council brought presents for her on her birthday! He had come all the way to De'Aire Chateau! THAT had never happened before!

The envoy had insisted on delivering the gifts in person. He had been shown to her rooms by Pierre, the sort of butler at the dilapidated castle. The tutor had been following hot on their heels. He had no liking for this state of affairs since it had been out of his immediate control.

Mathus had unsuccessfully attempted to intercept the gifts as well as the envoy and had been trying to salvage the situation. He had been only too aware that his lord would be more than displeased if Ragnald's sister received items her guardian had not approved.

⁕⁂⁕

The messenger had known that Mathus reported directly to the girl's brother. Therefore, he had impatiently ordered the tutor out of the room. Turning towards the sorceress, the young Zidarian, Airon, had introduced himself. He had respectfully bowed to Ki'ara and had handed her an artfully wrapped parcel.

The paper alone had been beautiful, and an enchantment had been added to make the bow give off little stars when she touched it. The young woman had been absolutely delighted.

Ragnald's minion had completely ignored the command to depart. Seeing this elaborate present, he had once again tried to object. He had known that his master would be livid when he found out about his sister receiving a gift. The lackey's failure to keep Ki'ara isolated from all Highlanders would be punished severely.

In spite of his fear of Ragnald, however, Mathus had started to retreat rather quickly when the envoy had drawn his sword to emphasize the seriousness of his desire to have the tutor gone from the chamber.

The gangly man had been furious and had protested vociferously on his way towards the door. When none of his threats had gained him any ground, he had stalked off in a huff. Once again, he had reminded Ki'ara of an ill-tempered stork.

Chapter 28

A Welcome Surprise

Ki'ara had been only too happy to see Mathus put in his place. She, however, had not been the only one who had enjoyed the show. Pierre, De'Aire Chateau's butler, had just known something interesting would happen as soon as he had opened the gate. That someone would knock had been out of the ordinary to start with but to have a stranger miraculously appear on their doorstep and asked for the Lady Ki'ara? Unheard of! How had he gotten up the mountain all by himself?

The man had been determined to witness every second of this event and had lingered so that he could report these fascinating news to his friends down in the kitchen. The servant had not been disappointed. What a show this had turned out to be! It had most certainly broken up the monotony here at the castle!

When the door had slammed with a loud boom behind the disgruntled tutor, hitting him in the rear, Pierre had started grinning from ear to ear. It had done so all by itself! 'Magic!' he had thought to himself. 'Served that one right! Finally, he got what's coming to him. The lady is much too nice to him, anyhow!'

The butler had enjoyed himself tremendously watching Mathus being run from the room. He and the rest of the staff despised the uppity tutor. Pierre had wanted to share the news that very moment and, therefore, had bowed and made his own exit. The man had been looking forward with glee to telling the others about the dressing down the unpleasant scoundrel had received.

Pierre had been just about to close the door behind himself and rush to the kitchen when he was called back. Airon had need of a guard. The envoy had explicit instructions to keep Mathus from overhearing and figured that the sneaky foreigner would creep back to listen at the door. This had to be prevented at all costs.

The servant had so anticipated apprising his friends that he had been clearly disappointed to be asked to remain. To appease him, the messenger had sweetened his request with a couple of gold coins. With a glint in his eyes, the old man had happily agreed to take up his post in the hall. He had felt very important. He, Pierre, had been chosen to make sure that the young lady and her guest were not overheard!

⁕

Ki'ara had watched as the envoy set wards. This had to be very important for the Zidarian to go through all this trouble to make certain that no one could eavesdrop on them. She had been really curious by then, and her stomach had been doing flipflops due to all the excitement. The young woman had just known that something wonderful was about to happen to her.

After relaying greetings from her uncle and the council, the messenger had asked Ki'ara to please open the parcel. Along with some small gifts, it had included a missive. Airon had stated that the lords had requested that she open it right here in his presence.

To Ki'ara's surprise, the package had contained a gift-wrapped bundle of papers along with a small box. Her fingers had been trembling with anticipation. After carefully untying the ribbon, she had cautiously unpacked the documents.

The top piece of paper had been a letter from her parents. To hear from them after all this time had been an enormous shock for the girl. Ki'ara had been glad she was sitting down. Her hands had begun to shake so badly that she had barely been able to hold on to the note.

Airon had seen how affected the young woman was by this unexpected turn of events. With Ki'ara's permission, the envoy had laid out the documents for her. After reading the communications, she had looked up at the man in disbelief.

From that moment on, she had the power to decide her own fate! This was the best present since the engagement ring from Conall StCloud on her eleventh birthday!

⟡⟡⟡

The gist of all the documents had been simple but had changed her entire world. Not only was Ragnald no longer her guardian, but from that day forward, she would never again have to rely on the charity of her brothers. Nor did she have to tolerate their abuse.

She now had a significant amount of money of her own, as well as a home and a ship. Ki'ara had cried with relief when she read these words. The letter from her parents had been apologetic and sad at the same time. They had genuinely hoped that things would turn out different.

Ki'ara was so grateful that Mikael had been such a prudent man. Her father had always examined a situation from all angles and had been ready for all eventualities, this time as well. He had hoped that Ragnald would turn out to be a good lord but had taken steps in case he did not.

Airon had divulged to the young woman that, before he had departed, Mikael had deposited several letters for Ki'ara with her uncle. Her situation on her last birthday had determined which one was to be sent. The messenger had felt that Lord Iain had chosen wisely. Ki'ara had fullheartedly agreed.

⚜

Mikael had loved all his children. He had hoped that this specific letter would not be the one to find its way to his daughter on her 24th birthday. But, just in case things went wrong, her parents had taken steps to prepare. Ki'ara had been glad to see that they had planned for such a contingency after all.

Her father's strategy had been set in motion months ago by her uncle. Lord Iain had made sure that everything went along smoothly and with the full approval of the other lords. Most of them were close to loathing Ragnald anyhow, so that part had been easy. The rulers had also all happily agreed to keep the entire affair a well-guarded secret.

According to the provisions her father had made for Ki'ara, she was to be declared of legal age on the day of her 24th birthday. Normally, she would still be considered a child by the immortal families' standards, but thanks to Mikael, she had become the exception.

⚜

For the first time in years, Ki'ara had the option to come or go as she pleased. Taking a stand against the MacClair, however, would have grave consequences. Lifelong banishment from the realm was the least of the punishments she could be facing. None of her people would ever be allowed to speak to her again, and she would be shunned by all in the clan.

Mikael, however, had made sure to anticipate such a possibility. He had not forgotten the cruelty he had once seen in his oldest son. Her dad had hoped that Ragnald had outgrown this, but just in case he had not, the prudent man figured that his daughter would need a place to call home as well as protection.

Therefore, besides being declared an adult that day, Ki'ara had also become the proud owner of the small but delightfully playful and airy Fairholme Castle. She had loved the quaint residence as a child, and it was a truly generous gift, one that had been long in the making.

The young lady's new home was located half a day's ride further south from Seamuir Castle along the fjord, which separated the MacClairs' region from the StClouds. Conall had been looking after the manor and grounds ever since her father's departure.

Ki'ara had been granted sole possession of the fortress along with all the lands surrounding it. This area had been declared a new realm and stretched all the way down to the sea. The young woman was now responsible for the people living there, and she had access to a sheltered deep-water harbor if she so desired.

Her father had separated the land out from the MacClair jurisdiction long ago under the pretext that he wanted a place to return to after his travels. It had never belonged into Ragnald's domain and now never would.

The biggest surprise for the young woman, however, had been the next sheet of paper. This document, signed by the ruler of the elves as well as every lord of the council except Ragnald, had made her Lord Ki'ara of Fairholme. Where there had been nine lords since the birth of the Highland Kingdoms, there were now ten!

To make it official, the Zidarian messenger had bidden the young woman to rise and to raise her left hand. He had regarded her gravely and had then asked her if she was ready to serve her new clan. Ki'ara had only been able to nod, no sound had wanted to come out of her tear-chocked throat.

Once the ceremony was over, the newly made Lord had stood there for a few long moments. Ki'ara had been speechless. This sudden turn of events had been overwhelming. She had stared at Airon in wonder. It had taken a while for the true meaning of all this change to sink in.

Not only did she now have the right to take her place at the council, but her brother would face the wrath of the other lords as well as of the magic of the Highlands if he ever tried to harm her again! She was finally safe!

As a sign of her new position, the envoy had presented Ki'ara with her very own seal strung on a fine-looking ribbon. Lord Mikael had chosen her symbol of power, and it had been incorporated into the crest. Airon had very ceremoniously placed it around her neck. This way, the ring would be kept well out of sight of any prying eyes.

Next, the Zidarian had solemnly reached for the young woman's left hand and had slid a stunning aquamarine ring on her finger. This was a gift from the Zidhe. Long ago, when all the other clans had come into existence, the then kings had received theirs. Now it was her turn!

The band was formed from the purest silver with the emblem of her clan on each side, reaching around the stone to help hold it. Ki'ara had loved it the moment she saw it. Her father had chosen the animal for the insignia, a phoenix, the mystical bird reborn from the ashes.

Ki'ara had been thrilled. This and her engagement ring were now her most treasured possessions. To her delight, Airon had stated that it should be safe for her to wear this stunning gift. Only the council members loyal to her were aware of its meaning.

Until her new clan had been officially proclaimed and her crest added to the others, most people would just see it as a gorgeous ring. Knowing, however, how curious this piece of jewelry would make Mathus and not wanting to lie, the sorceress had added a spell to the band to keep it invisible right there on her finger.

⊱•⊰

To the young woman's surprise, that had not been the end of the bounty. To top it all off, there had been one more present. Ki'ara had been granted the full ownership of her very own clipper! The *Sea Witch* was hers! She loved that vessel, and it held fond memories of traveling together with her parents and Conall. Ki'ara had to admit that this came very close to her other favorite belongings.

The young woman had thanked the messenger with tears in her eyes. Her heart had been filled with immense gratefulness to her parents, her uncle, the Zidhe, and the council for the bounty she had received. Ki'ara had asked Airon to convey her sincerest gratitude to Lord Iain as well as the other rulers. What a wonderful birthday! She had been truly blessed!

⊱•⊰

As was customary and befitting her new station, Ki'ara had desired to send her thanks in writing as well. The envoy had waited patiently for her to pen her replies. This had taken a fair while since she had to compose a note for each of the lords as well as the Zidhe.

The new ruler had felt that it was vitally important to do this correctly and to get things off to a good start. If Ragnald, once he found out, reacted the way she feared, there was trouble coming her way. Ki'ara had been only too aware at that moment that she might soon need all the allies she could possibly get.

The sorceress would have loved nothing better than to resolve the differences between herself and her oldest brother. She was willing to keep trying, even with the odds stacked against her. Ki'ara thought that coming from a position of strength might help. After all, she was now his equal and no longer his charge, something he would have to be told very carefully.

The young woman really wished that Ragnald would finally accept her and that they could coexist peacefully. Ki'ara was a realist, however. She was conscious that there was little chance of this. The hatred her sibling felt for her seemed to go too deep to allow for friendly relations.

The new lord made up her mind that this time, when Ragnald mistreated her, she would take a stand. He was the ruler of the MacClair clan, but she no longer had to stay there. Ki'ara had her own place she could go to, but she would have preferred to move there with his blessings.

The reception awaiting her at Seamuir Castle would tell her a lot. If not sending the carriage was any indication of what was to come, Ki'ara might be best off making immediate preparations to secretly move her things to her own place. The girl knew that she could rely on her maid to take care of the details.

The young sorceress felt that it would be a good idea to have a plan should the situation get out of hand. After some contemplation, she decided that in case of an emergency, she would send Leana to contact her uncle for help. She had full trust in her maid and knew she would not fail her.

As long as her brother stuck to his usual punishments, Ki'ara believed that she would be able to get away quite easily. Ragnald had a tendency to lock her in her rooms whenever he was displeased for some reason, which was often. He did not know it, but that had never worked too well before. Ki'ara was confident that she could find a way to sneak out and ride over to Fairholme.

The council would make Ragnald hand over the few possessions she had left at the castle. The only items she really cared about she would keep with her to start with. The rest could always be replaced if, in a fit of temper, her brother destroyed her belongings.

Never again would she allow him to send her away from the Highlands. It was her home, and that was where she intended to stay. Ragnald could accept that or not, but that was the way it was going to be!

Withdrawing allegiance from one's lord was almost unheard of and was very seldom an issue. From childhood on, obedience and reverence to the ruler, as well as the laws of each clan, are instilled in its members. The chief's authority over his people is almost absolute to this day, or as close to that as it can get in the Highlands.

Just contemplating such an act filled Ki'ara with dread. She was only too aware that her two oldest brothers would never forgive her. It made her heart hurt to even think of breaking the family ties. She loved all her siblings but especially Gawain. She would miss him. The young woman was sure that Ragnald would forbid him to speak to her ever again.

For her, such a radical action was the very last option. Ki'ara was a peaceful person, and conflict was not to her liking, but she did believe in being prepared. Nothing like an extended ride in a carriage to gather ideas! The young woman was glad she had this time. It allowed her to weigh her choices and, as long as she was silent, Mathus might keep his mouth shut as well.

Thinking of her tutor, Ki'ara gave him a curious look. She noticed that he was still looking slightly green. He seemed disinclined to talk and only moaned on occasions. The young woman figured that the man had not fully recovered from the sea voyage, and the motion of the coach was making him sick once again. At least he was not complaining!

Being a wizard, he should be able to take care of his own malaise. Why then was he so sick? Was he even weaker than she had thought? Or had he exhausted his magic on something else before they had left the castle back in Frankonia? Maybe she would offer to heal him when they got closer to Seamuir, but for now, she was glad to have the time to explore possible options.

Suddenly, another thought occurred to Ki'ara, and she brightened visibly. Once she had broken her allegiance to Ragnald, she would be able to do as she pleased. No longer would she have to shun the StCloud! She would be free to choose who she wanted to speak to. This filled her heart with incredible pleasure and offset the negative consequences she had been considering by a fair bit.

<hr/>

The last letter in the bundle the sorceress had been presented on her birthday had been from the Lord of Ravenshire. Morena, her father's first wife, had been his sister. He was her brothers' relative, not hers, but he loved the girl like his own child. Iain was her uncle as far as the two of them were concerned, and that was that. The lord had always been there for Ki'ara and had tried as much as he could to protect her from Ragnald.

Knowing her well, Lord Iain had figured that the young lady would try a peaceful approach. He had little hope of her succeeding since he had found Ragnald so filled with hatred the last time they had conversed that he felt his nephew was beyond reach.

The MacClair seemed to have lost all perspective as well as his moral compass and was a danger to anyone who garnered his displeasure.

The old gent was genuinely concerned about his niece's safety. He had assured Ki'ara that, if things got out of control at Seamuir Castle, he and the other lords were more than prepared to come to her aid. Even though Ragnald was his beloved sister's son, the lord felt strongly that he could not support the man's actions any longer.

Lord Iain had finished his message by stating that he would be keeping a close eye on the situation at the castle just in case her brother decided to cross the line yet again. He informed Ki'ara that her trusted maid would know how to reach him if an emergency arose and not to hesitate to call on him at any time.

The young woman had been intensely pleased by his offer. She loved her uncle dearly and had always relied on him for advice. Causing even more of a rift in the family, however, did not appeal to Ki'ara. Lord Iain was her brother's blood relative! She would do what she could to resolve the situation as peacefully as possible.

Ki'ara felt that this was her fight and that she should keep everyone else out of it unless there were no other options.

⚬⚬⚬

The gifts Ki'ara had received for her birthday had changed her entire life. For the first time in all the years since her parents' departure, the young woman had felt a sense of independence and hope. She still could barely believe it. What an amazing day that had been. Things were sure looking up!

Never again would she allow Ragnald to treat her like a prisoner in the family's home or abuse her in any way, shape, or form. She would face the future bravely, no matter what happened.

Taking such a drastic step as renouncing her allegiance to the lord of the clan did scare her. It was huge for a Highlander, and the young lady still hoped against hope to avoid it.

Ki'ara had made up her mind, however, that in case it had to be done, she would not hesitate to declare herself free.

Chapter 29

A Chilly Greeting

Ki'ara was only too aware of what the situation at the castle would be like for her once Ragnald found out that he was no longer in charge of her life. As far as the young woman knew, her improved status was still a secret, so not bothering to send one of the family carriages to retrieve her might be a good indication of her brother's feelings towards her.

Was this Ragnald's way to send her a message? Ki'ara was wondering about that. Her oldest brother did tend to take pleasure in making her feel unwelcome. He barely tolerated her as a member of the clan as it was. Near the end of the last visit, he had even stopped hiding the dislike he felt for her.

Since then, Ki'ara had gained an inkling of the depth of Ragnald's aversion towards her. Had the MacClair been able to have his way, he would have banished her to a far corner of the earth. Anything to get and keep her out of his sight. Only the council's disapproval and warning had prevented such an action. The young woman had no clue why her brother felt such animosity towards her.

The time Ragnald had crossed the line and had tried to kill Ki'ara, he had received a stern rebuke. He had been given guidelines for future behavior. The consequences of noncompliance had been clearly laid out. It had forced the lord to treat his sister with some civility despite his hatred.

Ki'ara and her oldest sibling had never been close, but he was still her brother, and she did love him. If he had wanted her to dislike him, however, he had most certainly succeeded.

⁕

Ragnald was the MacClair, the ruler of the clan. Ki'ara was now a lord in her own rights. Once he was informed of this fact, would her sibling allow her to remain a member of the MacClairs? Somehow, she doubted this.

Disobeying her brother in any way or disrespecting him meant that he had the right to ask her to leave his lands. He would find some reason, and she would no longer be welcome. The young woman loved her childhood home and found that prospect heartbreaking.

Banishment, however, no longer carried quite the same threat since Ki'ara had a place of her own now and a clan to take care of. She had always loved Fairholme. As a lord in her own right, she needed to break free of Ragnald's rules regardless of what this would cost her. She intended to do right by her people as well as herself.

Thanks to her father, she was a legal adult and had been given the power to stand up for herself. Maybe it was time to evaluate all the constraints Ragnald had laid on her over the years.

By abiding by her brother's wishes, Ki'ara had been able to keep confrontations to a minimum. Now, however, she feared that a conflict would erupt rather sooner than later. Ragnald had allowed her to return, but that had been something she had intended to do with or without his permission.

Ki'ara's thoughts drifted back to Frankonia and her journey through Mercede down to the harbor. The *Sea Witch* had been diverted there to pick her up and carry her home since Ragnald had not wanted to send one of his own ships.

The small town of Mercede had its very own flair. The buildings had been painted in bright, happy colors. Flowers and garlands had decorated most of the houses. Ki'ara had found it all very flamboyant and very unlike the seaports back home, which tended to be much more subdued and more to her liking.

The narrow streets had been full of people and merchants, and the noise had been almost deafening. After having been away from crowds for so long, the hustle and bustle of all this humanity had been something the young woman had no longer been used to. It had quickly become overwhelming for her, and she had been relieved to get on board the ship.

The large clipper had been in the port when Ki'ara and Mathus had arrived. The harbor was too small to allow a vessel of this size to dock. Therefore, the *Sea Witch* had anchored out in the bay. As luck would have it, the ship had been delivering a cargo of wool not far down the Frankic Coast. After picking up a load of wood, something that was rare in the Highlands, the captain had set a course for Mercede to pick up the passengers.

The young woman had eyed the magnificent craft with pride. She had always loved this ship and even more now that she was hers!

Marcus O'Rourke had been the captain of the vessel since her very first day. He was a competent but jovial man with whom she had always gotten along well. His men loved and trusted him. Under his guidance, the *Sea Witch* ran efficiently as well as profitably.

The skipper had been only too happy to pick up the youngest MacClair. The girl loved being on the water and never got seasick. She had a sunny disposition and was always a pleasure to have along, very different from her sourpuss tutor.

Like most, the captain could not stand Mathus. Being an intuitive person, he was sure that Ragnald's lackey did not have Ki'ara's best interest at heart. Whenever he picked up the pair, Marcus watched the man like a hawk. He had decided if that creep even thought about hurting the lady, he would go swimming in the blink of an eye.

The captain had transported all of the family members at one time or another. Lord Mikael, his wife and daughter, and at times the Lord of the StClouds, had been frequent guests on the *Sea Witch*. Marcus would have never said so out loud, but he really preferred having the young lady on the ship to ferrying any of her brothers.

Gawain was not too bad, but the older two were arrogant and unpleasant. They made a strange pair, always together, whispering and carrying on. Marcus had seen his men make the sign to ward off evil whenever Ragnald and Lyall were on board.

The old sailor had been fiercely loyal to Mikael MacClair, but he had never liked Ragnald. Marcus had been extremely relieved when he was informed that his lord had kept ownership of the ship when he passed on the rule. The captain would not have worked for the new lord and would have hated giving up command of such a fine vessel.

To keep Ragnald entirely out of the loop, Mikael had assigned Iain Elvinstone as his agent. Under the shrewd lord's guidance, the shipping business had gone very well these last few years. The *Sea Witch* had made good profit, and O'Rourke, as directed, had used some of the money to keep her in excellent repair.

Ki'ara was kind and treated the sailors with respect, very unlike the oldest MacClair. She never complained and, if there were a need, would even lend a hand in bad weather. No matter how rough the passage became, the young woman did great. Her cast iron stomach had earned her the admiration of all of the men.

The captain had been angry as well as concerned when the family carriage was not at the pier to pick up the girl and her tutor. He had made sure that the coachman was someone he could trust to deliver her safely. He had ordered the man to keep his eyes and ears open and to do a bit of snooping if it was safe.

Marcus expected a full report on the situation up at the castle. He did not like the rumors he had picked up while looking for a ride for Ki'ara.

The MacClair was having an affair with a female riverboat captain who was not only mean to the bone, but she was also accident-prone. So far, she had wrecked several barges, but her association with the lord kept her employed.

One of O'Rourke's friends had overheard the woman talking about how much Ragnald hated his sister and that he wished she was dead. When she had been really drunk a few days ago, she had mumbled something about a plan to get rid of Ki'ara.

The captain had felt concerned enough to dispatch a falcon with a note to Lord Iain. O'Rourke could not shake the feeling that by helping Ki'ara get a ride to the castle, he had sent the girl into danger.

The hired coach was much slower than the family's carriage would have been. Even with the use of the gate, it was several hours later before Ki'ara finally caught her first glimpse of Seamuir Castle. There it sat, giving off an air of doom and gloom. The stronghold's towers stood out starkly against the threatening sky, like broken off teeth.

The place had once resounded with laughter, but no more. To the young woman, it was upsetting that the fortress' aura had gotten so much darker since her last visit. Her heart contracted in pity for her people who suffered under Ragnald's rule and for the magic of the land. Neither they nor it deserved to be abused in such fashion.

Seamuir Castle was perched far above the sea with a good view up and down the coast. This allowed the inhabitants to keep watch over the waters. They would alert their neighbors as well as the Zidhe by magic mirror if any dared to invade. To warn the population, the signal fires further up in the mountains were always kept at the ready.

A village and a small fishing port were located down the slope from the stronghold. Sheep and a few cows grazed on the hills around it. The scene looked peaceful and serene, but Ki'ara could sense a dark undercurrent. Things were not right in this place.

The harbor here was shallow, and a ship as large as the *Sea Witch* could not enter or get close enough to safely send in a boat. Ki'ara and Mathus could have gone to Seamuir in one of the smaller ships, but it would have added several days to their voyage. Going by coach had been the fastest way for them to get home.

A boat from Deansport had to go all the way around the spit protecting the bay. Then, it had to work its way south along the coast. Usually, this turned out to be an uncomfortable trip since the waters close to shore were rough, and storms blew up without warning.

Anyhow, the young lady preferred the feeling of having her beloved Highlands under her feet or at least the wheels of the carriage. She never tired of watching the landscape as they were rolling along. In addition, this was easier on Mathus. The one time they had taken one of the small boats to Seamuir Castle, her tutor had wanted to die.

The road from Deansport first headed inland to avoid the wetlands bordering the shore. Once those were passed, it curved and headed up the coast. It wound its way between the heather-covered hills and the deep brown moors. To bypass this long and winding road, they had traveled by gate. It had cut a day of their journey and avoided the bogs.

❧❀❧

The abundance of moors made peat the primary heating source for the area. Wood was too rare and way too expensive for most to use for such a purpose. On their way, Ki'ara had seen several men cutting the prized turf.

It was dirty labor, but the Lord of Seamuir Castle paid well for a good product. Ragnald was rather fond of his comforts, and when it came to his own wellbeing, he spared no expense. Where others were concerned, however, he couldn't have cared less.

Not that the young woman blamed him for liking good blazes in the multiple fireplaces. The castle could be very cold and drafty in inclement weather. She just wished that Ragnald would care to make life better for all of the clan like their dad had.

❧❀❧

Now that they were nearing Seamuir, Ki'ara was so excited that she was hanging out the window of the carriage. She wanted to watch the castle come closer. The icy wind was tugging at her hair and had soon pulled much of it out of its neat coiffure. Before long, the waist long red strands were happily blowing in the cold breeze. For the first time in many months, the young sorceress felt truly alive.

Finally, the coach pulled up in front of the castle, and Ki'ara swiftly braided her hair into a semblance of neatness. She had a duty to appear at least somewhat orderly upon her arrival. To the young woman's utter astonishment, however, the courtyard was totally empty. Not even the watch was to be seen.

What was going on here? Why was the place virtually deserted? No one was there to greet them. Ki'ara's hopes sank even lower. She had not expected this kind of frosty reception. This was not a good omen of things to come, but she decided to reserve judgment until she had more information.

The driver, a middle-aged man named York, helped the young lady out of the carriage. He walked up to the door with her and knocked. Never before had he seen a castle this lifeless and abandoned. It was almost as if no one lived here at all. It would have been genuinely frightening had they arrived after dark.

Ki'ara was filled with apprehension. Not sending a coach was one thing, but no one being here to receive them was another. So far, this welcome was far worse than it had ever been before. What was going on in this place? Where were all the people? Why was no one on guard?

The coachman had to knock for some time before the door was finally answered. An irritated looking servant opened the door just wide enough to stick her head out. "Who are you, and what do you want?" the woman asked so rudely that both York and the young lady involuntarily took a step back. Who was this horrible person?

Ki'ara had never met this individual, but such conduct could not be tolerated, especially not from a retainer. Not only was Ki'ara a MacClair but also a lord in her very own right. It was time to put this impudent being firmly in her place.

"I am Ki'ara MacClair, Lord MacClair's sister, and this is my home. Who are you to address me in such an insolent manner? Now, get out of my way!" the young woman replied calmly, taking a step forward.

"I don't care who you say you are! And who I am is none of your business! I am the housekeeper here, and my word is law! No one told me to expect a visitor! How do I know you are who you say you are, anyhows? You wait right there while I go ask the lord!" came the brash answer before the woman tried slamming the door.

The driver seemed to have anticipated her intention. His foot firmly held the door open. York's quick reaction irritated the servant further, and she tried kicking at his shin. The coachman nimbly avoided her boot. He grinned smugly when the housekeeper's shoe connected hard with the door. The woman let out a loud howl of pain.

At this point, Ki'ara had enough. "Just who do you think you are talking to? I will wait in the den while you get my brother and prepare my rooms. Now step out of my way!" she ordered, using her magic to enforce the command and to push open the door.

Once she had stepped into the entry hall, the young lady turned to the driver. She softened her voice. "Would you please bring my luggage in and help Mathus?" she asked him politely. "And thank you kindly for your timely assistance!" she continued, giving the man a mischievous smile.

"No way! If you must come in, so be it! But the luggage stays out! He can wait!" shrieked the irate housekeeper. It seemed that her self-importance was stronger than her sound judgment. No one in their right mind would ever dare to speak to any Zidarian in such a fashion!

The moment those words left the argumentative servant's mouth, she realized her mistake. Next thing she knew, the young woman before her was towering over her. Berta shrank back, suddenly very, very afraid.

Those intense green eyes, which were suddenly boring into the depth of her being, seemed to peek down into her very soul. The housekeeper felt as if all her secrets were being uncovered and pulled into the light. She could tell that she was found wanting.

If there had been any doubts in the housekeeper's mind of who she was dealing with, they were now gone. She involuntarily gasped and cowered back further as she sensed the immense power coming of this youngest MacClair. Not even the lord was this scary, and he had the magic of the land!

Who could have expected such a gift to be hidden in such a slip of a girl! Crossing this innocent appearing young lady had been a colossal mistake! Berta hoped that Ki'ara would have mercy and that her insolence would only cost her this job. That, she was actually good with, the castle was not really such a pleasant place to work in the first place.

"Please forgive me, your Ladyship! I am Berta, begging your pardons! I will inform your brothers of your arrival immediately!" the housekeeper stammered in fear for her life. She had seen how the MacClair dealt with those who displeased him, and this was his sister, after all.

The woman's mind was trying to find a way out of this dire situation. How could she best smooth over her faux pas, appease the young lady? Should she tell the lord about his sister? How powerful she was? No, Berta decided. She had seen how Ragnald rewarded unwanted news. Let him find out for himself!

"Please, why don't you have a seat in the den? Would you like some refreshments? I will have them brought to you immediately!" the housekeeper continued, deferentially. Gone were all the arrogance and the bravado, which had gotten her into trouble in the first place.

Berta was hiding her hands behind her back. She did not want the lady nor the coachman to notice just how badly they were shaking. The woman had never been so afraid in her life. Regardless of who was in charge of this castle, the housekeeper knew that she would rather go up against the lord than cross his young sister.

"Could your driver please put the luggage right over there by the stairs? I will have it taken up just as soon as your chambers are ready!" the now utterly cowed servant stuttered before rushing off to find the lord and give orders to prepare the young lady's rooms.

The coachman and Ki'ara exchanged a glance. Both shook their heads in disbelief. That had to be the worst mannered servant either of them had ever seen in their lives. How could Ragnald tolerate such behavior? What was going on in this castle?

Seeing the determined set of Ki'ara's mouth, York almost felt sorry for the rude housekeeper. She should have known better than to treat the mistress of Seamuir Castle this way! What had that woman been thinking? And, why was she not better trained?

York had genuinely enjoyed watching Berta being put in her place. He had been awed by the display of such immense power. It had radiated off Ki'ara in waves. Did this young woman have any idea how strong she really was? Somehow, the man did not think so.

How much his passenger had changed in just a few hours! The coachman could tell the difference. When Ki'ara first boarded his carriage, she had an air of power about her, but now, she seemed to glow. The magic of the Highlands suffused her entire being. York suddenly got the powerful feeling that he needed to tell her.

"Lady, please, it is not my place to say, but can ya hide that power? His lordship, he ... he ... he," York broke of stuttering. Ki'ara looked at him in surprise then went inward. A feeling of awe crossed her face when she realized just how much stronger she had become since setting foot on the soil of her homeland.

Quickly, Ki'ara drew most of her power within. She created shields to hide all that had become hers since returning back to the Highlands. She only left the amount of magic showing Ragnald would expect her to have but no more. No good would come from tipping her hand to her brother!

The sorceress was incredibly grateful for the timely warning. Had Ragnald seen her like that, it would have been bad. Who knew how he would have reacted! What puzzled Ki'ara, however, was how she could possibly have acquired this amount of power in such a short time.

"Thank you, York, for your warning! It took a lot of courage for you to tell me, and I am most grateful! How could you tell?" Ki'ara asked quietly.

"My dad is one of you, so I got some sight, and you glowed, lady! You glowed!" the very impressed coachman responded. "Best keep it a secret for now, eh?" he continued, giving her a conspiratorial wink.

'Captain Marcus will love this!' York thought to himself. 'Maybe hearing what the lady is capable of will ease some of his worries!'

The driver quickly unloaded the luggage. He could not wait to get back to Deansport! York relished the thought of sharing with his friends down at the pub the juicy news of how Ragnald MacClair allowed his servants to treat his very own sister. Not that anyone expected much better from that cad!

'What a great tale this will make down at the Black Bull!' York could not help thinking. 'The others will love hearing what goes on in this castle!' The lady's amplified power, however, he would keep a secret. Let the MacClair find out for himself when he crossed her!

The Lord of Seamuir Castle was widely despised, especially by most members of his own clan. None of them could understand how this petty, mean-spirited, foul man could possibly be the son of the kind and fair Lord Mikael! He was nothing like his father at all.

Once York arrived back in Deansport, and before he could head to the pub, he had one last errand to do. This was something he was now looking forward to. As requested, the coachman would report back to the captain who had hired him.

What a tale he had to tell that old salt! 'Lord Iain and the council are sure to hear of this shortly,' York thought to himself rather gleefully.

Marcus had charged him with looking out for the Lady MacClair. The O'Rourke had made no bones about how furious he was about the slight done to the young woman. He had felt that not sending a carriage was more than just rude but typical of her nasty brother.

The old mariner had been ferrying Ki'ara back and forth from her home to the places she was sent to for many a year now. The captain liked her company, she was bright and eager to learn, but he had not missed the sadness in his passenger's eyes every time she was forced to leave the Highlands.

It was beyond O'Rourke's comprehension why she was being treated like that. Marcus was a loyal and faithful man but had less liking for the present lord all the time. He thanked the gods every day that Lord Iain oversaw his ship and not the MacClair.

⊱⋅⊱⋅⊰⋅⊰

Marcus O'Rourke would do anything for the Lady Ki'ara, even ride up to rescue her from that gloomy old castle. If York were to report that she was in danger, he and his men would be on their way in a few minutes. Just in case, the captain had already organized horses and had secured the backing of the StCloud.

As a respected member of the secret clan council, created after their ruler started to abuse his position, O'Rourke did have some clout. On numerous occasions, he had spoken out against the MacClair. If the situation at Seamuir continued to deteriorate, something would have to be done about that tyrannical man.

The captain was hoping that no further disrespect had been done to Ki'ara, but he doubted that very much. His experience told him to expect the worst, especially when it came to that malicious and dastardly lord.

The seasoned sailor was so angry he wanted to hit something, preferably that underhanded villain up at the fortress. Just the thought filled him with relish. Marcus O'Rourke was well known for his explosive temper, and Ragnald was really getting under his skin.

⊱⋅⊱⋅⊰⋅⊰

Knowing the captain well, the coachman figured that delivering the news of the incident at the castle would upset the volatile man. He would tell O'Rourke of the lady's power, but only him. York felt that it was important that his reporting was done with a wee bit of extra caution. You just never knew who was listening in around here these days!

⋆⋆⋆

While the driver was speeding back towards Deansport, Ki'ara was waiting more or less patiently in the den. She was enjoying the tea and crumpets she had been hastily provided. A servant had brought the treats almost before she had taken a seat. Now, this was service!

Berta had returned rather quickly. "My Lady, I have informed your brothers of your arrival. They will be with you shortly. My apologies for not having your room ready, but no one told me about your upcoming visit," the housekeeper stammered nervously, curtsying respectfully.

"Your chambers are being prepared at this very moment and should be done in just a few minutes. Is there anything else you have need of? May I fetch you some more refreshments while you wait?" the woman inquired anxiously.

Ki'ara was secretly amused at the sudden politeness and reverence of the previously so cocky and rude servant. She had not yet decided how she would deal with the woman's transgression, but something would have to be done.

Was this the way all guests were and had been greeted at this castle since her father's departure? This would explain partly why the other lords despised Ragnald so much! Was it possible that he had been showing them this kind of disrespect all along?

⋆⋆⋆

Staying at Seamuir Castle looked less like an option with each passing moment. This place certainly had changed and not for the better. The young woman decided that she would have to speak to Leana about getting her belongings out of here and soon.

Her maid was very resourceful and most certainly had allies among the clan. She would take things in hand with her usual efficiency. Not that Ki'ara owned much anymore, only the possessions Leana had been hiding, her bed, and what was contained in the trunks of her luggage.

After this chilly welcome, Ki'ara thought that it was best if she was safely moved into Fairholme before Ragnald found out that she was now head of her own clan and him no longer her guardian!

Chapter 30

The Brothers

After the reception she had received so far, it did not surprise Ki'ara that her brothers took their time in coming to greet her. All the while, she started to feel more and more like a stranger in what had once been her home. Even most of the servants she had known since childhood seemed to be gone.

Much of the happiness and pleasure of finally returning to the Highlands and the house she grew up in were swept away as the minutes ticked by, and no one appeared. Ki'ara had figured that at least Gawain would be happy to see her and maybe even Lyall.

Never had she felt so unwelcome, not even the day Ragnald had tried to kill her. Then, her other brothers and some of the servants had stood by her. So many things had changed since her parents' departure! It was most definitely time to leave this unfriendly place!

Waiting did give Ki'ara some time to put up additional shields. There was no sense in exposing herself to all the negative emotions she could sense all around her, she had her own thoughts and feelings to deal with.

After what seemed like forever, Gawain, her youngest brother, was the first to arrive. He bounded into the room with his usual flair. Of the other two, there was still no sign.

Just before his appearance, Ki'ara had been seriously contemplating leaving for Fairholme right then. She had considered catching a ride with one of the farmers heading that way. Now, she was glad that she had waited.

The youngest of the MacClair men was also the most handsome. His hair was a beautiful dark red color, almost mahogany, not too unlike his sister's copper-colored curls. It was wavy, and he usually allowed it to fall into his face and cover one eye, giving him a rakish air. His features were open and pleasant and beautifully set of his stunning brilliant blue eyes.

The siblings embraced warmly. Ki'ara had always been closest to Gawain, and she was genuinely delighted to see him. How often she had wished that her other brothers were more like him!

"Welcome home, beautiful! How long have you been here? How was your voyage? What a pleasant surprise! I had no idea you were arriving home today! Ragnald has not said a thing!" her brother shouted excitedly, crushing her to his barrel chest.

Holding his sister at arm's length, he continued. "Let me look at you! You are even more gorgeous than the last time you were home! It is so good to see you!"

Once again, the high-spirited young lord hugged his sibling. Cheerfulness and exuberance seemed to come off him in waves. Here at least was someone pleased to see her! Ki'ara beamed up at him happily. "Come, sit down and tell me what you have been up to!" her brother went on while guiding her over to the settee.

Suddenly, however, he grew very still. A frown crept onto his handsome face. "Why are you waiting here, like a stranger, in the den? And, are you still wearing the clothes you have traveled in?" he inquired quietly.

"It is all good, brother dear. I have dealt with the situation. The new housekeeper had no idea who I was and took her job of guarding the door a little too seriously," Ki'ara explained with a laugh. She had decided to keep the rest of the unpleasant scene to herself.

"And, she had no idea that I was arriving today. It seems Ragnald did not bother to mention it to anyone. My rooms are being made ready as we speak," Ki'ara calmed him, smiling.

Just then, their oldest brother, Ragnald, finally strolled into the room. Ki'ara rose to greet him, prepared to let bygones be bygones, and give him a hug. The haughty young lord took one look at his sister and then shook his head in disgust.

"Haven't changed much, have you? Wild child, as always. We don't need the likes of you, here in this castle! When will you ever grow up and make this family proud?" the lord snarled at his sister.

Ragnald gave Ki'ara a look so filled with contempt and revulsion, she cringed and stepped back. She bumped into the sofa and involuntarily sat down. Just for a second, some of her shields dropped, and her oldest sibling's emotions washed over her like a wave. They left nausea in their wake. How could he hate her this much? And why?

The oldest MacClair's hair was raven black and always immaculately cut and combed. His features were even and clean cut. He would have been rather handsome if not for the perpetual scowl, which marred his visage.

Giving Ki'ara one last look, Ragnald's face contorted into a grimace of pure loathing. His black eyes sparkled with malice. How much he detested this woman! His half-sibling or not, he would get rid of her and soon!

Without saying another word, the MacClair stalked off back to his office. Gawain stared after him in barely repressed fury. This was their sister, a part of their family! How could this insufferable tyrant treat her like this!

Ragnald had not bid Ki'ara welcome of any sort, and there had been not a smidgen of happiness to see her, just the opposite. It seemed the mean-spirited lord was not even hiding his distaste anymore.

Gawain had a bad feeling all of a sudden and decided that he would keep a close eye on things from now on. No one was going to hurt his little sister if he could help it!

Ki'ara felt like someone had twisted a knife in her heart. She had long since forgiven Ragnald for all the awful things he had done. Why was he so cold and cruel when they had not seen each other in two years? What had she ever done to him?

She had been expecting some rudeness, but this was an absolute confirmation that she was indeed not welcome in her family's home. It hit Ki'ara hard. The MacClair had made sure that she understood his feelings once and for all. The young woman watched his departing figure with great sadness and a complete lack of comprehension. Why did her oldest brother despise her so?

Just then, their middle brother, Lyall, came in from the stables. With one glance, he took in his sister's unhappy face and his oldest brother's departing back. Ki'ara rose and took a step towards him, but he held out his hand to stop her.

The second MacClair's loyalty had always been clear. As his mud-colored eyes met his sister's, he gave her a brief, disinterested nod. So, she was back, what did he care. All her presence would do is make life more unpleasant.

Lyall had never taken the time, nor had he felt the inclination to get to know the 'brat,' as he and Ragnald called Ki'ara. To him, she was no different from a stranger, except that maybe he disliked her more.

Since Ragnald loathed her, he was always in a bad mood whenever Ki'ara was around. Life was much more peaceful when she was not at home.

After a curt nod to his youngest brother, whom he actually liked only marginally better, and without further acknowledging his sister, Lyall followed after Ragnald. He could not wait to get out of the room.

⊱ ❦ ⊰

Ki'ara watched his retreating back. She had always felt pity for this man. His shoulders were slumped, and he moved without the pride in his step, which set apart his brothers. Lyall usually sported a downtrodden air, and it did not surprise her. Being around their oldest sibling so much would suck the life out of anybody.

Lyall was entirely Ragnald's puppet. He had never developed much of a character, had no distinct personality traits. This MacClair's plain disposition was very much reflected in his drab looks.

Beside his siblings, Lyall was strangely colorless with his mousy hair, dull eyes, and pasty face. What further set him apart was his almost complete lack of magic, which caused him to have very little if any connection to the land.

Ki'ara had always thought that the absence of powers could be responsible for his lackluster appearance.

⚬⚬⚬

Gawain saw the tears in his sister's eyes at the frosty welcome she was receiving. His heart contracted in pity for a moment, but then his anger flared. None of this was Ki'ara's fault. Why could his brothers not be civil to this delightful young woman? She had not done one single thing to harm them!

The compassionate man had never been able to understand how Mikael had been able to just walk away from his daughter. He had been a wonderful father when Gawain was growing up. The child had needed her parents, and they had failed her, had left her in the hands of a monster! What was going on with them that they had just abandoned her like that?

Their father should have known that life for Ki'ara would not be pleasant with Ragnald as her guardian. Their oldest sibling had been the one who dug up the prophesy and brought it to the family's attention. And he had been the one insisting that it was their sister the vague forecasting was talking about!

It was not the girl's fault that the MacClair believed that Ki'ara was the person spoken of in those ambiguous words! That oracle was hundreds of years old and could have long since been fulfilled. No one really knew much about it, and there was no proof that it was talking about their sister to start with!

Also, there was a minor fact his older brothers conveniently kept on ignoring. They kept insisting that it was not relevant, but Mikael had disagreed, and Gawain shared his opinion.

Most of the other prophecies in that same book had never come true as far as anyone was aware of. Why then should this one? Because Ragnald believed it so? Or because he wanted it to be true?

✦⁖✧⁖✦

Gawain gently brushed a strand of unruly hair back from the young woman's face. He could not help thinking that she was truly beautiful with that red hair and those piercing green eyes. Ki'ara's skin was clear and unblemished. It glowed with magic and health.

"Ki'ara! Never mind them!" Gawain told her gently. He put a comforting arm around her slim shoulders. "They don't even like themselves. I am delighted that you are home! Now tell me about all that has happened since the last time I saw you!"

The empathetic man started asking his much younger sibling about her life over the last two years and about her voyage home as he guided her back to the table.

He had always been able to distract her after such unpleasant incidents and had every intention of succeeding this time as well. Gawain was all smiles and cheer on the outside, but inside, he was fuming.

✦⁖✧⁖✦

Once he got Ki'ara talking again, he asked her about her journey down the mountains. Gawain was amazed at her story. He could barely believe it when she told him about the dragon wraith and how she had set the creature free. That had to have taken some serious power!

Pouring them each another cup of tea, he kept inquiring about De'Aire Chateau, Taryn, and that eventful trip to the harbor. Gawain was absolutely fascinated by her account.

How much she had grown! With a feeling of intense relief, he realized that Ki'ara might be able to hold her own against Ragnald, but just in case, it would not hurt to keep a very close eye on things.

The young man had his sister smiling before long. Gawain was good at cheering Ki'ara up, and at this moment, she needed his light-hearted banter to take her mind off the way she had been greeted by their hateful older brothers.

Chapter 31

Gawain

Gawain was very unlike the mean-spirited Ragnald and the submissive Lyall. The youngest brother's friendly and outgoing temperament was more like Ki'ara's sunny disposition. This made him a favorite among the staff of the castle as well as a darling of all the ladies in any tavern he entered.

The contrast between the eldest and their younger siblings was almost like night and day. Gawain believed that the significant difference in personalities had a lot to do with their age and upbringing. By the time he entered the world, their father had grown to be a much kinder and more peaceful man. Also, Raghnall, their infamous grandfather, was long gone by then.

Mikael had lovingly looked after his ailing wife and his third son. Due to his lady being too sick and exhausted to spend much time with the boy, the MacClair had taken a more than usual interest in the care and raising of their infant son. They had grown very close.

Ragnald had already been 73, a full adult, and Lyall 43 years old when their youngest brother had been born. They had both resented the attention the child had been getting and, in their hearts, had blamed Gawain for the illness of their beloved mother.

The slow decline and eventual death of Morena MacClair had left the family in deep mourning and their ruler heartbroken. The couple had waited until Mikael had been almost 400 years old before having their first child. Neither had ever expected that such a natural thing as childbirth would end up costing the lady her life!

This last baby had been somewhat of a surprise. The couple had not conceived in so many years that they had assumed that their childrearing years were over. They had both accepted this long since, and Mikael and Morena had genuinely enjoyed the time they got to spend with just each other.

The pregnancy had gone better than the other two for most of its duration. It had not been until the very end that problems had appeared. Sudden weight gain and the onset of an overwhelming lethargy had been the forbearers of worse to come.

When labor had finally begun, it had been long and more painful than it should have been. It had seemed to drag on without end. The midwife had started to fear for mother and child. The competent Zidarian witch had realized that her skills and her magic were not enough to save mother and child.

Being a wise and prudent woman with lots of experience as a healer, she had been aware of her limitations. She had recognized that this situation was beyond her abilities. If the lady was going to survive this difficult birth, the midwife needed help from someone much stronger. No one near was more powerful than the Lord of the MacClairs.

There had always been rumors that Mikael had more Zidhe blood than most of the other Zidarians and that this allowed him to have a closer connection to the land and greater powers. The healer had hoped this was true, for she had feared that the lady would need all the help she could get. She had sent an urgent request for the lord to attend them. The anxious nurse had felt that if anyone could save Morena and her unborn child, it was he.

The situation had been dire for many hours. It had taken both the woman's and Mikael's magic and all the midwife's skills to finally bring the boy into the world. To them both, it had seemed as if some unknown power was trying to prevent the baby from leaving the womb. Gawain had been barely alive by the time he was finally born.

"Save our son!" had come Morena's urgent whispered command before the lady had lapsed into deep unconsciousness. The determined nurse had almost completely used up her magic. Lord Mikael had been fairly exhausted as well. He had been torn between healing his wife and saving his infant son.

Realizing that his lady would never forgive him if he let the baby die, the skilled sorcerer had used most of his remaining power on his child. His own gift had not been enough, and the lord had needed to draw heavily on the magic of the land. It had been more than willing and had shored up his flagging strength. Once the boy had been out of imminent danger, Mikael had felt it was safe to desist. Only then had he tend to his dying spouse.

The nurse, in the meantime, had done what she could for Morena. Between them, the lord and the healer had eventually managed to pull her back from the brink of death, but they were unable to fully restore her.

After the traumatic birth, it had been touch and go for both mother and child for a few more days. Mikael had refused to leave them for more than just a few minutes during this time. The lady had been too weak to nurse the infant, and a wet nurse had to be brought in to feed him.

Eventually, the tiny boy had started growing stronger. Morena, however, had never entirely recovered. Only her iron will and determination to stay with her son for at least a little while had kept her alive as long as it did.

⁘

The couple had expected to spend the rest of their long lives together and watch their children have children of their own. They should have had at least another few hundred years together. Now, this was not to be.

The lady's last request, when she realized that she could hold on no longer, had been for her husband to take special care of their beloved youngest child. She had also insisted that Mikael should marry again.

⁘

Morena had made sure that her older sons heard her last wishes. She had not missed the resentment they felt towards their younger brother and had been very unhappy with the way the two had been behaving. The perceptive lady had known only too well that she had their grandfather to thank for the darkness invading their souls.

How could Raghnall have had so little regard for the wellbeing of his grandchild? He had filled Ragnald's head with all kinds of tales and resentments of old. The boy had seen him as this great hero and not as a man only concerned with his own agenda as Morena had. She had never been able to understand why the old curmudgeon could not leave all that hatred in the past where it belonged.

After his wife's death, Mikael had done what he could to comfort his then 18-year-old son. The boy was, in many ways, an only child due to the significant age gap between him and his brothers. The compassionate youngster had spent a lot of time with his dying mother, and they had been very close. Her passing had left a hole in his life.

Gawain had read to her, brought her flowers, and described the world outside for Morena when she grew too weak to sit by the window. Being so long-lived, 18 was no age at all, the boy was still a child in so many ways.

The bond between father and son had grown even tighter during this time of grief. The existing love and deep affection had further intensified, and their relationship had become very different from the one Mikael shared with his other two sons.

Seeing how much more their father seemed to love his youngest offspring had sparked additional severe jealousy in the older ones. Gawain did not believe that Mikael had ever realized how deep that resentment ran or how bitter and angry Ragnald had in fact become. That young man had grown very adept at hiding his real emotions.

Having been imbued with so much magic from the land during his birth, Gawain was very perceptive. He had come to see early on that Ragnald not only blamed him for their mother's death, he also hated him for stealing their father away from him. The anger inside the oldest MacClair burned red-hot and had been and still was threatening to consume him at times.

To Gawain, it seemed that their father had never really known his eldest son, for if he had, Mikael would have never put him in charge. The signs had been there. All their dad had needed to do was look under the surface of Ragnald's smooth outer facade. Instead, he had ignored all warnings, had put his head in the sand.

Their father's blindness had resulted in detrimental consequences for his younger children, the clan, the land, and its magic. They had been paying the price for their lord's inability to see what was right under his nose. Mikael was off somewhere enjoying his life while the people he had once sworn to protect suffered. Somehow, that just did not seem right.

To be fair, Gawain had to admit that Ragnald had taken great pains to hide his true feelings, but he had slipped up from time to time. Their father had been intimately connected to the magic of the land. He should have been able to peer through this deception! Had he refused to see what was right in front of his nose because of a sense of guilt?

Ragnald had waited until after their dad had abdicated the rule to him and had left for his travels before dropping his mask. Once he had known Mikael was gone and not coming back, he had shown his true colors. Life for all the clan's people had changed drastically from that day on and not for the better.

As the youngest son, Gawain had always been much closer to his parents than his siblings. The two older MacClairs shared a tight bond with each other and spent most of their time together. They had treated their young brother as an intruder into their lives. This distance had only further increased once Mikael went on his way.

The only one of his siblings he had ever been close to was his sister. Gawain had been overjoyed when his father brought home a new bride. He had known how lonely Mikael had been and how much he had missed his late wife's companionship even after so many years. Their dad deserved to be happy again, and it was about time! Gawain had liked his new stepmother and had gotten along with her famously.

The Lady Ali'ana had been a kind and gentle soul full of love and compassion. She had regarded Mikael's sons as her own. Gawain had enjoyed having a functional family again, but despite all the lady's best efforts, Ragnald and Lyall had continued to resent her. They had treated her with just enough respect not to appear overly insolent.

By the time their father had remarried, the two older MacClairs had been well into adulthood. They had been spending a lot of time with their uncle, who had been teaching them the ins and outs of the shipping business. Lord Iain had also been instructing them in the most beneficent ways of governing their people.

It was customary for the young Zidarians to be fostered by the other clans in an attempt to widen their education and to further goodwill and peace among the families. Each lord had a different style of ruling, and the more the youngsters learned, the better sovereigns they would make in the end.

Ragnald and Lyall had returned home rarely during those years. Whenever they had come to visit, however, things had grown tense very quickly. The pair had started fights with their father and brother and insulted the Lady Ali'ana. They had been rude and harsh to the staff, who were mostly clan members. Usually, everyone had been happy to see them depart once again. Soon, they had only visited on the most important occasions.

Gawain, Mikael, and his new wife had gotten along well without them. The youngest MacClair thought that

Ali'ana was sweet and a pleasure to be around and had grown to love her. Life had been very peaceful without the older two present, and the clan and the land had prospered under the gentle rule of the family.

For 25 more years, it had been predominately the newlyweds and Gawain residing at the castle. No one had ever expected this to change. When the couple had not conceived for many years, they had given up. They had been loving life and had not really intended to have a child at that point. It seemed that the magic of the land, however, had other ideas. In spite of their precautions, Ki'ara had been conceived.

The Lady Ali'ana had the habit of traveling back to her family for a visit every few years. She had usually remained for several weeks. It had been right before one of these stays that the lady had discovered, to her immense surprise, that she was pregnant.

Lord Mikael had been overjoyed, and the clan had been delighted, but it had not taken long for the memories of the birth of his last child and the terrible consequences to rise to the surface. Also, there had been Ragnald and Lyall, who had been nothing short of disagreeable at best, as well as the promise he had made to himself.

The father-to-be had believed that the last thing Ali'ana needed in her delicate condition was to be exposed to that resentful pair, to their negative energy. Mikael had been resolved to do anything he could to make things as pleasant and comfortable as possible for his wife during her pregnancy.

Even though he had been overjoyed with this unexpected turn of events, Mikael had not been able to help himself. Before long, fear had gripped the MacClair's heart like an iron fist. He had lost one wife due to complications during childbirth and was not going to allow that to happen again. This had made him determined that he would proceed as he had planned so long ago.

The anxious lord had consulted with a healer and the midwife. They had agreed with him that Ali'ana was better off giving birth among her own people. That way, if things went wrong, there would be others present as powerful as the MacClair, who would be able to save mother and child.

Mikael had immediately made preparations to accompany his wife back to her folk. Leaving his trusted chancellor in charge, the pair had departed just a few days later. Gawain, a full adult by then, the lord had charged with helping to run things in his absence. Exactly where they had gone or who Ali'ana's kin was, nobody knew to this day.

The couple had returned several months later with their tiny baby girl. The child had been beautiful with her light copper curls and rosy cheeks. She had an air about her that was both sweet and ethereal. Ki'ara's bright green eyes had watched everything around her with intense interest. Gawain had been instantly smitten.

Unfortunately, his older brothers had been less than pleased. Mikael had called them home to share in the happy occasion of the new family member's arrival. They had come, but grudgingly so and had no intention from the outset to give this new intruder a chance.

Just as they had done with their younger brother, the two had resented the small girl from the very first moment they saw her, maybe even before then. They had been furious when they had been informed that Ali'ana was expecting. Neither had wanted another sibling and especially not one from 'that woman' as they had taken to referring to their father's new wife.

Seeing Mikael's protectiveness and love for his baby daughter and fearing his wrath, they had tried to hide their feelings but still had acted distant and cold. Both had realized that their sire might be less than pleased with a more antagonistic reaction and had feared that he might cut them off if they behaved hatefully towards the child. How his brothers had been able to resist someone so cute had been beyond Gawain's understanding.

Claiming they still had much to learn and were at a critical point in their studies, Ragnald and Lyall had returned to their foster lord as quickly as they prudently could. Their father had been saddened by their response and had watched them leave with some apprehension.

Try as he might, Gawain could not understand why Mikael had left his beloved daughter in the hands of one who so obviously disliked her. Ragnald had been the one to uncover the prophecy. He had found it in the library of his then foster father, Lord Macgillmott.

Gawain was confident that if this convenient piece of information had not come along, his brother would have kept digging until he had found something, anything to justify how he felt about his new baby sister.

In a conversation over evening drinks, the old lord had mentioned that he remembered reading something about a female MacClair and a warning. Those words had been enough to send the spiteful Ragnald on a desperate hunt.

The embittered man had scoured the extensive library at his foster father's castle for weeks. He had finally managed to get Lyall placed there as well so that he could help him. They had systematically looked through each and every book on the many, many shelves. This task had consumed every free moment they had for several months.

The oldest MacClair had just about given up hope when they finally found his holy grail. The long searched for reference was in an old, obscure little book that had not been opened for many a year. It had been covered in dust and well-hidden and was in danger of falling apart.

Ragnald had located this prized volume in a back part of the vast library on a very high shelf. It had been stashed away behind some other old tomes by the same author. Leaving Lyall behind to take care of his duties, he had immediately set out for Seamuir Castle. How could his father not see reason and send his daughter and wife back to her people once he saw this?

When the excited young man had shown the ancient prophecy of a female MacClair being the catalyst for great change or possibly even doom to his father, Mikael had scrutinized it carefully. He had studied the book and some of the other predictions it offered. The lord had consulted with several of his friends as well as a Zidhe visiting the council.

After finding several other ambiguous references, the MacClair, as well as all those he had discussed the foretelling with, had come to the conclusion that the book was complete rubbish. Mikael had decided it was time to confront his son. He had hoped that he could get Ragnald to understand that the author had not been much of a prophet.

Gently, their father had tried to get his oldest to see that the tome was full of other oracles, which were either slightly off or had utterly missed the mark. He mentioned that he and his friends felt that the reference was unreliable at best. This did not please Ragnald, who had harbored such high hopes of getting rid of Ali'ana and her offensive offspring. From the angry set of his son's mouth, Mikael could tell that there was no way to reach him.

The MacClair had further alienated Ragnald by telling him that there was no proof that this ancient text, even if it was not total fiction, was referring to his little sister in the first place. And, the lord had continued, the wording was so cryptic that it was entirely open to interpretation.

Ragnald had blanched at his father's words. The little love and respect he had held for his sire died at this very moment. He had left the castle in a fury and ridden back towards Caithyll. This was the last time anyone saw him at Seamuir for several years.

⸙

The rift in the family had never truly healed. For a long time, the only one who had made an effort to re-establish relations had been Ali'ana. The lady had been most unhappy with this state of affairs. She had wished for peace among the family but had been only too aware that neither Ragnald nor Lyall cared much for her. Her goal had been that the two would at least get along with their father.

Mikael seemed to have been oblivious to what was going on in his family. The lord had been easy going, kind, fair, and happy. He had been in love with his beautiful wife and had adored his small daughter as well as his youngest son. Such darkness as had taken root in his older boys' souls had been alien to him and appeared to have been beyond his comprehension.

To this day, Gawain was made to suffer by his brothers for his closeness with his sister and dad. He was thankful, however, to have had that time with Mikael as well as Ki'ara and Ali'ana. He, for one, felt blessed to have been part of that second and very happy family.

Now that his father and his wife were off to who knows where, no family cohesion remained. They were really two sets of siblings. Due to the age difference, they had grown up worlds and ages apart and did not even share the same values.

⋙⋘

Ragnald had been the leader of the clan for a good while now. Life had been miserable for the kinsmen under his rule. He was in complete charge of their well-being but cared little for how they fared. The heartless lord only did what he had to in order to avoid running afoul of the council.

Due to his behavior, the rift between the MacClair and the lords had widened with each passing year. Most of the other chiefs had little patience for the rude and resentful man. They had heard the rumors of his conduct towards his people and felt helpless and angry that any Highlander should be treated with such disrespect.

Some had hoped that getting older and a bit wiser might help to mellow Ragnald and Lyall a bit. But, if anything, the coldness and resentment of the two brothers had grown over time. Both, Gawain but especially Ki'ara, were made to pay for perceived crimes they had never even committed.

Gawain had often wondered about the dissimilarity between himself and his brothers. He had noticed two significant differences. By the time he was born, things had changed in the Highlands as well as at home.

⋙⋘

The age gap between Gawain and his brothers was huge and not just in years. Ragnald was 159 and Lyall 129 years old to Gawain's 86, and when they had been children, life had been much harsher and more violent. Ragnald was born right after the covenant when the Highland clans were still going through some significant adjustments.

For one, their grandfather, Raghnall MacClair, had been the clan head then. He had just been dethroned. The ruler had been furious and severely bitter about the loss of his crown. He had enjoyed being king and blamed all others except himself for the loss of his status.

When a brief time after that momentous event Raghnall's first grandchild, Ragnald, had been born, the old man had seen him as a means to get vindication. His resentment had known no bounds, and he had vowed that one day the MacClairs would not only be kings again but overlords over all the Highlands as well.

The small boy had not just adored his grandfather, Ragnald had utterly idolized him. Like a sponge, he had soaked up all the embellished stories of the glory of times long past. To top it all off, Raghnall had carefully filled the child's head with feelings of acrimony against the new order.

Ragnald had spent as much time as he could with his hero. His granddad had gone out of his way to feed an overinflated sense of self-importance in the innocent youngster. He had wanted him to grow up feeling like a future king or maybe an emperor even.

Stealthily, Raghnall had skillfully molded his grandson into a small version of his old self. He had encouraged the child to keep secrets, to lie to his parents. Mikael had never suspected a thing. He had been happy to see how well the two were getting along. One day, it had all changed.

⁕⁕⁕

Raghnall MacClair had a hard time forgetting old grudges. He and the head of the StClouds, Daron, had remained bitter enemies despite the treaty. For as long as the two could remember, they had barely been able to stand the sight of each other. Both had been furious that the covenant forced them to keep the uneasy peace.

Ragnald had been 22, still a mere babe in Zidarian eyes, when his grandfather, along with Daron StCloud, had vanished. The adversarial lords had come to blows over an issue during the council. They had allowed this to escalate into a bloody fight between the two clans. Both had been punished by the Zidhe for this indiscretion.

⚜

Over the years, Ragnald's adoration for the ornery old ruler had grown into absolute worship. Raghnall could do no wrong in his eyes. The loss of his idol had hit the young Zidarian hard. He had always blamed the uppity StClouds for his beloved ancestor's sudden disappearance.

When Lyall was born eight years later, his older brother had entertained him with stories of the exploits of their grandfather. With each retelling, their beloved idol had grown more heroic until both boys fairly deified him. With time, the old rogue had morphed into a figure larger than life, a true god among men.

Unbeknownst to his parents and just as his grandfather had done, Ragnald had filled Lyall's head with tales of kings and heroic deeds. He had made the child believe that they should be living like that instead of being the sons of a mere chief. He had told him of all the injustices done to the clan and that one day, together, they would set things right once again.

Over time, Ragnald had poured all the hatred, resentment, and bitterness growing in his own soul into his impressionable brother. He had nurtured the seeds of discontent and loathing carefully. Slowly but surely, he had formed the boy into a younger version of himself.

Lyall became the unwitting keeper of Ragnald's deepest and darkest secrets, his confidante, his only friend. The poison his brother had sown found fertile ground in the young man's innocent heart.

After their sister was born, the older MacClair siblings had come up with a course of action to achieve their desires. As part of their plot, they had hidden their true feelings and agenda from their father as well as the clan. They had started acting more respectful to Ali'ana and her daughter, at least for a while. Once Mikael had dismissed the foretelling, however, his older sons had stayed away most of the time.

***

Gawain, they had always considered a mama's boy, of no consequence to their lives and desires. Ragnald had decided early on that the kid was useless to him and his ambitions. He and Lyall had figured that they could easily keep their sibling in line with a few well-placed threats.

The two older brothers had been so arrogant and full of self-importance that they had never realized that the small boy they had so summarily dismissed had actually been spying on them. Gawain had gathered a wealth of information he had no idea what to do with.

It had taken several years for the youngster to make sense of all he had overheard, but once he did, he had been completely appalled. Gawain had tried to talk to their father, but Mikael had never taken it seriously. Their dad had believed that the plans his adult sons were making were just a flight of fancy, wishful thinking, nothing more.

***

Once he had realized what was really going on with his brothers, Gawain had been immensely grateful that Ragnald already had Lyall as well as other interests by the time he was born. The youngest MacClair had shuddered at the thought of sharing the fate of his older sibling. He had come to understand that the young man had no real mind of his own, that he had been robbed of the chance to become an autonomous person.

Gawain had been able to clearly see what their father had not. Lyall did whatever his older brother expected of him or ordered him to, and his only allegiance was to Ragnald. The rest of his family meant little to him.

***

For a time after this insight, Gawain had done what he could to reach out to his brothers. It was against his nature to just give up on them altogether. He had felt that somebody needed to make an effort since Mikael continued to ignore the situation.

The young man had tried to find some way to bring Ragnald and Lyall back into the family fold, to bridge the gap between his siblings and father.

All his well-meant advances had been coldly rejected. After many years of unsuccessful attempts, Gawain had finally given up. There was no reaching either one of his brothers. Now, they shared the same house, but relations they were only in name.

In his heart, Gawain longed for the family they could have been. He would have loved to have a real relationship with Ragnald and Lyall and knew that Ki'ara felt the same.

The compassionate man could not help but regret that he had failed in reestablishing friendly relations. Had there ever been a means of bringing the older boys back into the family? If there had been, he had not found it.

What would it have taken to prevent Ragnald from turning into such a bitter, cruel, and evil man? Could they have undone the damage Raghnall had caused? Or, had it already been too late by the time Gawain came along? Somehow, he thought so.

Chapter 32

The Decision

It had taken a few more minutes, but then Ki'ara's room was finally ready. Gawain extended his hand to help her rise. When he pulled her in close for a hug, he could feel his sister's sadness. This welcome home had been far worse than she had expected, and he felt pity for her. He was also quite angry with both of his brothers. How dare they treat his favorite sibling like that!

The young lord gently released Ki'ara to arm's length. "Just look at you! I can't get over how much you have changed! You are getting more lovely with each passing year! It seems all that traveling agrees with you!" he told her admiringly.

Tears began to shimmer in the young woman's eyes. They started to slowly roll down her face. Once more, Gawain pulled Ki'ara close. With his thumb, he gingerly wiped away the moisture from her soft cheeks. "Never mind them, I am happy you are home! Those two don't like anyone, not even themselves!"

Keeping one arm wrapped around his sister's waist, Gawain turned to the nervously hoovering housekeeper. "Have my sister's things taken to her rooms this instant!" he ordered. He gave the woman a withering look, and she rushed to obey.

"Come along, beautiful, I will walk you to your chambers," Gawain said chivalrously. He was beaming down on his youngest sibling, and after a moment, Ki'ara gave him a weak smile in return, but the unhappiness still showed in her eyes.

Inwardly, the young lord was furious. Ragnald, he could not do much about but not so this servant. He decided that he would have a word with the housekeeper right after he took Ki'ara up to her apartment.

If that woman ever treated his beloved sister disrespectful again in any way, shape, or form, she could find work elsewhere and preferably south of the Highlands!

⚜

Ki'ara was looking around her attractive chamber. Her mother had lovingly furnished it years ago. Ali'ana had replaced the dark curtains and wallpaper with bright colors. She had chosen a rose and flower pattern for the walls and bedding. Even the carpet sported a matching design. The entire room had a cheerful and soothing atmosphere.

Ragnald had known that she was coming home this very day, but nothing had been prepared in advance. This had never happened before. At least there had been a pretense of a welcome the previous times. That the relations between them had deteriorated to this point filled the young lady with great sorrow.

Was her brother trying to drive home the point that this was no longer her father's house? That she was not and never had been welcome? Ki'ara had no idea what motivated Ragnald to act as he did. Why would he fail to inform Gawain and Lyall that she was arriving?

It had taken a little while, but there was a nice warm fire burning in the fireplace. The room had been dusted and cleaned, the bed made and turned down for Ki'ara. A bowl of fruit, as well as some bread and cheese, had been placed on the table.

An out of breath servant had hastily brought up her luggage and had piled it by the bed. There, it still sat. The young woman was starting to think that maybe she should not even bother to unpack. She doubted very much that she would be here for more than a few days.

Her homecomings had always been a bit tense, but this time, it had been far worse than she had anticipated. Ki'ara's heart was heavy. There was little chance of remaining at the castle and among the clan for much longer.

She could have gone to Fairholme to start with but had wanted to give the relationship between herself and her oldest brother one more chance. She feared that this was the last occasion she would get. He would find out soon enough that Ki'ara was now his equal, and with that, any opportunity for a reconsolidation might completely disappear.

The young woman missed her parents, missed having a family. Her heart kept drawing her back here to Seamuir Castle and its land. Was this house really her home, or did she just yearn for the way things used to be?

Ki'ara loved the manor house in spite of its hostile airs. Seamuir Castle was a dark and foreboding fortress, a leftover from the days when the clans were at war. It was easily defensible, and its position high up in the hills made it difficult to approach unseen. It actually was a castle only by name.

When Ali'ana, Ki'ara's mother, moved into the stronghold, she had decided that change was in order. The lady had gone out of her way to refurbish some of the rooms in the mansion in a more welcoming, up-to-date, and bright fashion.

This had not been an easy task and had met with some resistance from the males in the family. A compromise had been struck. The men's rooms and halls had retained the dark and brooding furniture of their ancestors while some of the rest of the house had been redone to create a more pleasant living environment.

The new decorations had done a lot to lighten the mood in the castle. Having a mistress again had helped further. Mikael had been happier and much more relaxed, and laughter had started to ring out more often among the austere walls. The servants had even felt cheerful enough to sing as they worked.

By the time Ali'ana had conceived, the atmosphere in the fortress had significantly improved. The kinsmen had been content and well-fed, the clan had prospered and gained status as well as wealth. The land itself had been humming with pleasure, and the farms had grown more productive with each passing year.

Only Ragnald and Lyall had been like a dark cloud on the horizon. Each time they had come to visit, the whole keep had seemed to hold its breath until they had left once again.

During their stays, any clansmen working in the castle had made sure to be extra well behaved or out of sight if at all possible. No one had wanted to reap the displeasure of those two young lords. Any who could absent themselves had disappeared on some errand or another just as soon as news of the pair's imminent arrival had spread through the fort.

Mikael had been honorable and fair, Ali'ana kind and sweet, Gawain easy to get along with but not so the other two sons.

Ki'ara's relationship with her two oldest brothers had always been distant. She had tried in vain to get to know them and had no idea what possible reason they had to remain so standoffish. They were a family, after all!

For years she had attempted to bridge the gap between them, but her efforts had been rudely rebuked and more cruelly now that their father was no longer the lord.

Her parents had been the ones Ki'ara had been closest to, especially her mother. The young woman missed her deeply. How comforting it would have been to be wrapped into Ali'ana's arms right about now! She wished with all her heart that her father had stayed chief just a while longer.

Ｔhe magic in the Zidarian families' blood made them extraordinarily long-lived, almost immortal. Most clan leaders, therefore, remained head of the family for about 150 to 350 years before passing the position on to one of their children.

The retired lords' time then was their own. By law, they always had a place in the castle, but most preferred to stay in one of the other manor houses in the realms. It would only create conflict to have two rulers under one roof even if one was no longer in charge!

The castles the ex-lords decided to inhabit were divided out from the rest of the lands. These areas would remain under the rule of the former sovereigns until their death. Then, these regions were once again integrated into the rest of the realm.

In the not so distant past, it had been rare for one of the lords to live to a ripe old age. War, squabbles, and later jousting had made sure of that. Only a very few had ever reached their full potential of a thousand years or more.

Ki'ara's parents had made plans for their leisure time together long before Mikael had retired. They had wanted to travel and explore more of the Mystic Isles. The last the young lady had heard, they had intended to visit Islandia and then head for Larinia, but that had been many years ago. When they had left so abruptly, no mentioning of a destination had been made. Where were they now?

One day, everything had been fine, the next day, the couple had spoken of leaving and had rushed to do so. It had been a huge surprise to everyone. Mikael and Ali'ana had even abandoned their training of their talented young daughter.

Ki'ara still felt that there had been so much left for her to learn from them both!

As was the custom in the Highlands, Ki'ara had been instructed in magic as well as in the use of weaponry from early childhood on. She was quite proficient in both and could hold her own with a sword against any of her brothers. Her mother had been teaching her how to run a household and her father how to best govern a clan.

During her training, Ki'ara had shown a kinship with horses that had surprised even Ali'ana. The girl had been able to ride many of the feral, shaggy beasts roaming the realms.

Whenever she had been out wandering the land as a girl, the ponies had soon found her. They still did, and they had been Ki'ara's frequent companions on some of her solitary walks across the desolate moors.

The young woman was not afraid to be out in nature on her own and never had been. She had been allowed to explore the environs around the fortress from very young on. After her parents had left, there had been times when she had felt safer out there among the wild things than at home in the castle.

The realm had called to her, insistently and powerfully. Ki'ara had often wondered if she did not have a stronger connection to the family's lands than her siblings. She had been able to sense any changes long before her brothers took notice but, on her mother's advice, had taken great pains to hide this.

Ali'ana had been convinced that if Ragnald had known, he would have hated them both even more than he already did.

⸎

Ki'ara loved all the realms and had always felt that life here was close to ideal. Conventions were much different than in the places she had been sent to.

In the Highlands, she could be the perfect lady one moment, and no one would raise an eyebrow if she donned britches the next and went out to hunt, fight, or compete with the men.

The first time Ki'ara's brother had sent her away had come as a profound shock. Her ties to her home ran so deep that living anywhere besides in the Highlands just felt wrong. Being away from the land, she had lost part of her grounding, had felt disconnected.

Ragnald had been clan leader for just a few weeks when Ki'ara had been forced to depart. After her parents had left for their travels, life around the castle had been drastically changing. Much of the laughter, which had filled its halls for so many years, had died in this short time.

No amount of pleading had been able to change the lord's mind. Ragnald had stated that it was time for his sister to learn different types of conjuring. To serve the clan best, she needed to expand her magical vocabulary.

A few days later, Ki'ara and her newly hired tutor had been sent off to the plains of Espania far to the south to study with the first of a number of teachers.

Since then, the MacClair had only allowed her to come back for brief periods whenever she had completed her training in one place. Usually, she had been shipped off again very quickly to continue her education with a new instructor at some other location.

There had been a fair number of them over the years and little time spent in the Highlands.

·····❀··❀··

Ki'ara was upset over being more unwelcome here at the castle than ever before. It no longer even felt like her home. What would she be facing next? A confrontation of some sort was sure to come soon. At least Ragnald no longer had the authority to send her away.

The Highlands were the one spot where Ki'ara knew that she truly belonged. Her heart had ached, longed for her connection to the land whenever she had been away. Somehow, she had felt uprooted and lost when she had been elsewhere as if part of herself had gone missing.

At times, she had grown so homesick that it had made her physically ill. Having even a small memento of the Highlands with her had helped. Ki'ara had started to carry some rocks and a bit of soil from the moors to remind her of home. It was sad that now that she was finally here, things were going so poorly.

·····❀··❀··

Standing at the window, Ki'ara looked out with blind eyes over fields of heather and moss interspersed here and there by the brown of the moors. The beauty she was viewing, and which usually kept her enthralled, did not even register this day.

Ki'ara's thoughts kept coming back to the same old questions. Why did Ragnald hate her this much? Why had he tried to kill her and continued sending her away? As far as she knew, she had never done anything to him to deserve this kind of treatment.

The other lords' daughters were taught at home if they so wished. The teachers came to them instead of the girls being shipped off to faraway places. As far as Ki'ara could see, there never had been a reason to send her away except that Ragnald had preferred it this way. She only wished that she could discover some clues to his motives.

Ragnald and Lyall were inseparable and had been for most of their lives. As long as their mother had been well, they had a fairly decent relationship with their parents, especially their mom, whom they idolized. With their dad, the interactions had been more distant even then.

From what Ki'ara had heard, however, Mikael had been much less approachable then. Raghnall had not tolerated weakness of any kind and was hard on their father. By the time the youngest son was born, the old tyrant had been gone for many years, and their dad had changed. He and Gawain ended up being very close.

Ki'ara had often sensed that she was barely tolerated by her oldest siblings. She had started being aware of their feelings as a very small child. Their dislike had grown worse as she got older, and, since their parents' departure, Ragnald and Lyall had gone out of their way to make sure that their sister understood that they had never seen her as part of the family.

They were her relatives, but if the young woman was honest, she missed the Highlands themselves much more than her two oldest brothers. She had always wondered why they could not be as close as the other clan families were. Most of them got along pretty well. Why were things so different at Seamuir? And, why did her parents have to leave when they did?

Ki'ara was grateful that at least she had Gawain. He tried hard to be there for her whenever she needed him, but his power to help her was limited. He was part of the clan, and, unfortunately, Ragnald was the lord.

A sudden knock interrupted Ki'ara's downhearted thoughts. "Come in," she shouted towards the door. Her maid Leana entered the room. She was smiling from ear to ear. It was evident that she was genuinely pleased to have her mistress to look after once again.

"My lady, I am so happy to see you! It has been way too long since you were home!" the middle-aged woman greeted her, making a deep curtsy.

"Leana! It is so wonderful to see your friendly face in this inhospitable place!" the girl cried with delight.

Not caring about her station, Ki'ara rushed to embrace her one and only true friend among the staff of the castle. Leana was much more than a maid to the girl; she was her ally and confidante. Soon, the two women were hugging each other, overjoyed to be reunited.

Ragnald expected his sister to do for herself whenever she traveled. Therefore, he had not allowed her servant to accompany her. Ki'ara felt lucky to be permitted her maid's services at the castle and had been afraid every time she had left that she would never see Leana again. Should her brother ever get an inkling of how close the two were, the maid would be instantly fired. The MacClair might even go as far as banning her from the clan!

She and Leana were not just mistress and servant. The matronly woman was more like a second mother and teacher to her. She had been there to comfort and advise the girl after her parents had left and had taken care of her injuries after the incident with her brother.

The maid had ways of finding things out, and she had traveled extensively when she was young. Leana had given Ki'ara valuable tips about the customs and climates of the places she had been shipped off to every time Ragnald had sent her away.

Without Leana as an ally and for support, Ki'ara's visits to the castle would have been even more difficult. She was just thankful that so far, the two of them had managed to hide their friendship from the disapproving eyes of the family and retainers but especially from Ragnald.

"Dinner will not be for a little while yet. I thought you could use a nice hot bath after all that traveling you have done," Leana declared with a motherly smile. A whack on the door announced the arrival of the tub. The servants put it down on the tile in front of the fire.

Next, more retainers arrived carrying pitchers. Soon the bathtub was full. The maid helped her lady undress once the door was firmly barred, and Ki'ara gratefully slid into the steaming hot water. She lay back and closed her eyes. This was pure bliss after all the months of doing without such heavenly pleasures!

The young woman luxuriously soaked in the pleasantly warm liquid. As she relaxed, her thoughts drifted to one of her favorite subjects, Conall StCloud. He was never far from her mind, especially now that she was back in the Highlands. How much she missed that man! Why, of all the lords, did her brother have to especially hate this one?

It had been a while since she had seen Conall, but he haunted her dreams as well as her waking hours. There were times Ki'ara could feel him around her. He was part of her soul, the love of her life. How many nights had she run into his arms? Had passionately kissed him only to wake up in her cold, lonely bed?

As she contemplated what it would feel like to be held close to him, Ki'ara's insides contracted pleasantly. It seemed thinking of him had that kind of effect on her every time. If it could only be for real! She idly wondered where he might be and if he was here in the Highlands.

Maybe Leana would know, she was always a wellspring of information! She would ask in a bit, but for now, the young woman gave herself over to the pleasure of the sensations.

⁂

While her mistress was enjoying her daydream, her maid had started to empty out some of the luggage. She had begun to put away the young lady's meager possessions. Sensing Ki'ara watching her, she looked up. Her mistress was signaling to her to stop the unpacking.

Puzzled, Leana stepped up to the tub. Ki'ara had her finger over her mouth and made the sign they had always used for ears listening in. Now the maid was sure that there was more going on than she was aware of. She had expected as much after the message she had received from the young woman's uncle.

Lord Iain had indicated that something was afoot but had refused to go into details. He had charged her with watching out for Ki'ara and had sent her an amulet imbued with extra power so that she could contact him in case there was trouble.

Leana had been very touched by the lord's concern for his niece. She had intended to keep him informed as it was. She did not really need the charm, however, but appreciated the gesture.

⁂

The young woman's uncle had no way of knowing how powerful Leana was, something she had kept hidden even from her cherished mistress. The servant had her own well-concealed magic mirror, one of the few found outside the realm of the Zidhe.

Only the lords, the council, and the gates were equipped with this kind of communication device. This looking glass was a rare and precious thing that allowed her to connect with her people and to contact Lord Iain and the other rulers if the need ever arose.

The talisman, however, would make it easier to stay in touch with the girl's uncle without expending her own energy. The maid understood why he feared for the young woman. Ragnald was a menace.

What she needed to fully assess the situation and to protect Ki'ara efficiently was more information. Leana was sure she would find out soon enough.

⋆˚✦˚⋆

"How about I wash all that travel dust out of your hair since the water has sufficiently cooled?" Leana inquired with a wink. Best to act as normal as possible until the time was right for that private conversation. Ki'ara was only too happy to allow her these ministrations. How good it felt to be cared for once more!

Presently, the long copper tresses were covered in a rose-scented lather, and Ki'ara's friend was energetically massaging her scalp. It felt wonderful! How much she had missed this! Having done without these kinds of indulgences for the last couple of years, the young woman could genuinely appreciate this luxury now.

While working along, Leana was catching her mistress up on some of the major and minor events which had transpired in the Highlands in her absence. It seemed that Ragnald had become more unpopular than ever, and this made Ki'ara sad for her clan.

As usual, her confidante eventually got around to 'The StCloud', since Leana knew that he was never far from Ki'ara's mind. The young woman felt the familiar tingling sensation in her stomach at the mere mentioning of that name. She still missed him so very much!

Leana had heard that the lord was off adventuring somewhere up north and was expected to be gone for several months. Ki'ara sighed.

It sure looked like that there was no chance of her accidentally running into Conall StCloud any time soon!

Ki'ara had obeyed her brother all these years. It had broken her heart to do so, but she had played by his rules. Ragnald being her lawful guardian had not given her much of a choice. His position had given him the right to confine her to the castle or punish her as he saw fit.

From the reception she had received this day, Ki'ara was convinced that her brother had every intention of sending her off again as quickly as he possibly could. This time, however, she had a choice. It was such a relief that Ragnald was no longer her guardian!

The sorceress had realized, however, that being at Seamuir Castle put her in a much more precarious spot than she had initially thought. She was starting to see that she had made a mistake. She should not have come back to Eastmuir!

Arguments were not one of the young woman's favorite things, and she feared her brother's vicious temper. Ki'ara was only too aware of how he would react if she questioned or opposed his commands. He was a tyrant with the people of the clan but even worse when it came to his sister.

It would be ugly, that was for sure. It was better to keep the peace for the moment. If at all possible, Ki'ara intended to be safely away from Seamuir Castle before Ragnald found out about her changed status or she had to defend herself from another attack on her life.

This time, however, she was much stronger than she had been all those years ago when her brother had just about killed her. Ki'ara's power and knowledge had grown much more than Ragnald could ever imagine. She was anything but helpless now!

Laying there in that bathtub, Ki'ara came to a resolution. She decided that if it became necessary, she would take a stand.

The young woman made up her mind that if a confrontation arose, she would protect herself. She would not instigate a fight nor attack him, but never again would she allow Ragnald to harm her.

If it came to a magical duel, she would do whatever was necessary to survive and to disable her opponent. Ki'ara hoped with all her heart that it would never come to such an unpleasant confrontation. Ragnald was her brother after all.

Chapter 33

A Pleasant Enough Dinner

The bell rang downstairs in the hall calling the family to dinner. Ki'ara had finished her bath and was dressed. She had savored the luxury of being looked after. How much she had missed the simple pleasures of having her hair washed and brushed! And, having her clothes picked out and readied! Pure heaven!

While her parents were still in residency, Ki'ara had grown up surrounded by retainers. All that had changed once Ragnald took over. The new lord had commandeered most of the help for his own. He had left his sister only the one maid his parents had permanently gifted to her and then just while she was here at the castle.

If the MacClair could have taken that last servant as well, he would have. Such an act, however, would have been seen as a grave offense towards Ki'ara by his uncle and the other lords. That kind of disrespect would have given the council cause to interfere, something Ragnald wanted to avoid at all costs.

⋯✦⋯✦⋯

While Ki'ara made her way to the stairway, she was reflecting on the cherished moments of care she had received as well as the pleasurable time she had spent with her friend and confidante. How much she had missed her!

She and Leana had kept their conversation rather superficial. Being caught up on some of the current events of the Highlands made the young woman feel like she was finally home. They would talk more about personal things later after making sure that they could not be overheard.

While they had chatted, Leana had managed to tame Ki'ara's willful mass of hair. The maid had seated her charge in front of the hearth and had brushed the copper curls until they were dry and shimmered in the firelight like spun glass.

Next, Leana had arranged the shining tresses into a neat coiffure. Parts of the unruly locks were now confined in an intricate braid that hung down the young woman's back while others framed her beautiful face.

The maid had chosen a deep green dress which complemented her mistress' bright green eyes and red hair to perfection. Ki'ara truly looked like the young princess she once would have been. Very elegant, regal, and befitting her station.

⋯✦⋯✦⋯

The young lady made her way down the stairs and to the dining room. A servant opened the door for her and announced her. Ki'ara was taken aback. Was this a new tradition or one designed to make her feel even more like a stranger? When Gawain entered right behind her, and no such pomp was performed, she had her answer.

Ragnald looked her up and down. The way his eyes traveled over her body made Ki'ara's skin crawl. His gaze was cold, evaluating, and finally dismissive. He sneered at her, and she could sense his barely concealed loathing.

"Somewhat better! So, you do know how to properly conduct yourself in my house! After seeing the way you looked earlier, I was starting to doubt that! Have a seat, and don't keep us waiting!" came his snide comment.

Ki'ara just looked at Ragnald and nodded her head in acknowledgment. She was not going to take the bait and start a fight. Her brother would have loved that! Why was her presence such a problem for him? What had she done to him to dislike her so much? Would she ever get the answer to these questions?

Gawain pulled out the chair next to him, and Ki'ara gratefully slid onto the soft cushions. Ragnald's hostility had made her knees feel week for a moment, and she was glad to be able to sit.

The young lady took a moment to look around the beautiful chamber and thought of her parents and the times they had spent together in this very room.

Ki'ara had fond memories of many an entertaining hour spent here with Mikael, Ali'ana, and Gawain. The family had taken most of their meals in this dining hall and had often lingered long after they had finished eating to talk or play games. How much she missed those joyful days!

As usual, the chamber was pleasantly warm. A lively fire was burning in the large fireplace, and the room was brightly illuminated. The placement of the candelabras set of the lovely décor to perfection. This was one of the chambers Ali'ana had refurbished during her time here at the castle, and to Ki'ara's surprise, Ragnald had left it that way.

The Lady MacClair had chosen moss and rust tones for the carpets and upholstery to complement the dark, ancient furniture. The effect was simply stunning. Together with the thick, green velvet curtains, this created an impression reminiscent of the Highlands themselves.

The atmosphere now, however, was nothing like then, much less cheerful and happy. Realizing this made Ki'ara quite blue. So much had changed at this castle!

When the siblings were all seated, the servants brought in the first course. The food was excellent, and the wine imported from Frankonia. As usual, Ragnald had spared no expense when it came to his own comforts.

In the beginning, some awkwardness had remained due to the MacClair's hostile reaction to his sister's presence. The conversation had been a bit halting but had eventually picked up speed.

Gawain, as usual, had managed to finally put everyone at ease. He had them all laughing before long, and the mood in the room became noticeably lighter.

In spite of the rough start, the siblings managed to keep the dialog agreeable and friendly. The expensive wine flowed freely, helping to further relax the tension around the well-laden table.

Ki'ara sipped her wine very slowly. She had long since discovered that any kind of spirits affected her link to the magic of the land. The power singing in her blood was too delicious for her to want to dampen it in any way, shape, or form. She had done without this wonderful feeling for too long as it was.

Fearing that her days at Seamuir Castle were numbered, Ki'ara had every intention of savoring each second of that welcome connection. What would her linking to the Fairholme lands feel like? Would it be as powerful as this?

Deep down, Ki'ara was curious to find out, but for now, she needed to focus on the present. Inattention was another thing Ragnald just hated.

After the MacClair's rude comment when she had entered the room, Ki'ara decided that it was best not to disrupt the fragile peace of the moment. She did not want to irritate Ragnald further or be the cause of a disagreement during their dinner.

From long experience, Ki'ara knew it was best if she stayed as quiet as possible. Therefore, she spoke only when one of her brothers addressed her. Otherwise, she remained silent but listened intently.

The young woman had figured out years ago that this was the best way to avoid needless conflict. There was nothing to be gained by allowing herself to be pulled into one of her brothers' longstanding arguments. Each always assumed that he was in the right and would vehemently defend his position.

The debates tended to get rather heated. All three of Ki'ara's siblings had an opinion on most subjects and, usually, a rather strong one. Their points of view were often radically different, but each felt that his was the only proper outlook on the subject. Even the usually so submissive Lyall would get involved in these discussions.

Having three people at one table who felt that their belief was the only valid one often led to shouting. No one wanted to give any quarter and admit that he might be wrong. One or the other of the brothers storming off angrily was often the result of such disputes.

If Ki'ara voiced her own opinions or tried to smooth her siblings' ruffled feathers, the three warring parties were not beyond uniting against her. In the heat of battle, even Gawain had turned on her a time or two. She had realized long ago that here, there was no winning. It was best to avoid drawing their attention in the first place and to give them no opportunity to attack her to start with.

⁘✿⁘

Since the departure of Kiara's parents, family meals had, on occasion, turned downright ugly. Some arguments had continued on for several days or had resulted in fistfights between the brothers. That was most certainly not something she missed while she was away!

This evening, however, the conversation remained pleasant. Gawain made sure to include her and to steer the dialog away from any uncomfortable subjects. He kept asking her questions about her voyages, and, with his encouragement, she finally began to open up a little.

To Ki'ara's surprise, her anecdotes of some of the things she had seen and experienced on her travels were a big hit with all three of her brothers. They had always loved her stories, and she soon had them spellbound, hanging on her every word. Even Ragnald seemed to enjoy himself.

Ki'ara purposely kept her tales light and funny. She knew from bitter experience how quickly the mood around the table could change and turn against her. Ragnald's temper was extremely mercurial. He could fly into a rage at the slightest provocation. If she wanted to experience a few more hours of relative peace at Seamuir Castle, it was best to avoid angering him.

Ragnald and Lyall could get extremely cruel when they felt provoked and were not beyond dressing her down right then and there. Gawain trying to intervene on her behalf had seldom helped much. Instead, it had usually made things worse.

The two older MacClairs not only resented his interference, having their little brother take their despised sister's side against them seemed to infuriate them enormously. Ki'ara knew that Gawain meant well, but his allying himself with her had often made the situation even uglier than it would have been otherwise.

Ki'ara was determined to keep relations as peaceful as possible for as long as possible. Strive with anyone upset her, and she felt that her situation at the castle was precarious enough and did not need to deteriorate further.

By the time the servants brought in the after-dinner port, the young woman was very tired. She was still weary from all the traveling she had done and was longing for her bed. Therefore, Ki'ara rose gracefully and asked to be excused.

Ragnald condescendingly waved her towards the door. As was polite and expected, Ki'ara thanked him for dinner. She then wished each of her brothers' goodnight. After making a final respectful curtsy to the lord of the manor, the young lady headed for her chambers.

Being in the same room with the three of them had always drained Ki'ara. The barely suppressed hostility among them, all that harsh energy emanating from Ragnald and Lyall, as well as having to be constantly on guard, was extremely fatiguing for a sensitive person like her.

The long coach ride and the events of the day had added to exhausting the young woman emotionally. With drinks being served, her excusing herself was acceptable, and Ragnald could not find fault with her actions. After everything which had happened, Ki'ara desperately needed time to herself as well as a good night's sleep.

Leana was already waiting for her. Ki'ara gratefully accepted her help in getting out of the dress and into her nightgown. The maid undid her mistress' braid and brushed the copper-colored curls until they surrounded the young woman like a shimmering curtain.

All the while, Leana kept up a soothing stream of conversation, intended to relax and put Ki'ara at ease. The maid had become instantly aware of the tension in her charge's neck and shoulders when the girl entered the room.

The familiar anger towards the lady's brothers had risen up in Leana's heart. Why did they treat their baby sister like that? What was wrong with that lot?

<hr/>

When her mistress yawned yet once again, Leana lovingly tucked her into bed like a small child. She even gave Ki'ara an affectionate kiss goodnight and bade her sweet dreams before extinguishing the light and making her way to her adjoining chamber.

Ki'ara sleepily thought how nice it was to be loved by someone in this unfriendly place, to have one true friend she could rely on. Leana had always been there for her. Her maid had done what she could and then some. The young woman was sure that her confidante would be able to come up with a clever idea to get them to their new home. Maybe her youngest brother would be willing to come?

Gawain and Ki'ara got along pretty well, and he did try to take his sister's side as often as possible. Of all her siblings, he had always been her favorite. He had been the only one of the brothers to play with her when she was little.

Very unlike the older two, Gawain was an open, honest, and friendly young man. He was cheerful and affectionate. Ki'ara, however, could sense that even he was more reserved around her at times than he should have been. Almost as if he was afraid to love her as much as he wanted to.

Why Gawain would feel this way was beyond Ki'ara's comprehension. Was there some deep, dark secret she had no knowledge of which kept her siblings from loving and trusting her? Maybe it was time to believe her instincts and find out!

If only the StCloud were around! If she could get him on his own somewhere, he would give her the answers! Conall had always been truthful with her. The lord made it his business to be well apprised of everything going on in the Highlands.

Ki'ara was sure that he knew all about her brothers' reasons for behaving so strangely towards her. She was also convinced that the StCloud would share them with her.

⁕⁕⁕

Ki'ara was determined to find a way to arrange a meeting with Conall just as soon as he returned to the Highlands, regardless of how Ragnald felt about it. It would be so wonderful to be able to talk to him again, spend time with him. It had been too many years since she had been able to do so!

If she and Leana had managed to retreat to Fairholme Castle by then, it would be no problem. If they were still under Ragnald's roof, however, the situation would be vastly different.

She and the StCloud would have to get together in secret unless Ki'ara was prepared to openly defy her brother and clan lord right then and there, something she was more ready to do with each passing moment.

⁕⁕⁕

Before Ki'ara and her intended had been so cruelly separated and forbidden to speak by Ragnald, Conall had not only been her future husband but also her ally and best friend. He had been one of the very few people who had known about her intense interest in the world around her, as well as her advanced mental and magical development.

The StCloud had always been a welcome source of information for Ki'ara. The lord was widely respected, trusted, and able and willing to keep a secret if necessary. He tended to be aware of almost everything that was going on in the Highlands. Often, long before the council, and in more detail. The young girl had been endlessly fascinated by Conall's stories and the depth of his knowledge.

Ki'ara was sure that the StCloud would be able to shed light on the mystery of her brothers' behavior. She was resolved to find out and would not take 'no' for an answer.

Chapter 34

Becoming

It had been a day full of upsets. Laying warm and safe in her comfortable bed, Ki'ara was still trying to make sense of all that had happened. One thing was undeniable, and she had to face the bitter truth. Seamuir Castle was no longer her home.

Ragnald had made sure that she understood very clearly that she was only a barely tolerated guest in his house. He had been friendly enough at dinner but had otherwise gone out of his way to maintain the distance between them and to make her feel unwelcome.

Unbeknownst to her brother, Ki'ara was now the Lord of Fairholme. Therefore, it was her right to be treated with the same civility due to a fellow ruler. She could have spoken up and demanded more respect but saw no advantage in such a rash course of action.

If anything, it would make her position more perilous, and, from what the young woman had seen, Ragnald did not treat the other lords much better.

Ki'ara was not sure how her brother would react once he found out about her new status. She was convinced that Ragnald would be furious. He might even become irate enough to fly into one of the rages he was so famous for. Even the bravest of her kinsmen feared their lord when he was in such a state.

If at all possible, Ki'ara wanted to avoid facing Ragnald like that. Her brother lost complete control during those fits and was a danger to all who had the misfortune to come into his presence. Sometimes Lyall would manage to calm him, but he was not always around or cared to intervene on another's behalf.

Ragnald had almost killed his sister during one of those frenzies. Once had been enough as far as Ki'ara was concerned. She did not care to give him another opportunity to harm her, he had done plenty of damage already.

⟡

The oldest MacClair had managed Ki'ara's life with an iron fist these last few years. Whenever she had visited the castle, he had tried to control almost every moment of her day. Ragnald had decided where she went, who she spoke to, and what she did. Any infraction or questioning of his orders had led to dire consequences for the young woman.

Just as the lord had misused his authority over the clan and the land, he had abused his hold over his dependent sibling. Once, the infuriated tyrant had punished his sister by confining her to her room for an entire month. It had been for a very minor offense - he had not liked the look on her face while he was talking to her.

The only person allowed to see Ki'ara during that time had been the cook. The gruff elderly woman had been fiercely loyal to Ragnald. Since her lord hated the girl, so did she. She would unlock the door and hand in the food and drink without so much as a word.

⊱•⊰

Had Leana not had another key and been able to come and go as she pleased without anyone knowing, this time of imprisonment would have been far worse. As it was, the maid had smuggled in a new book every morning and had kept Ki'ara up to date on the events in the castle.

The two spent many enjoyable hours together during that month. They played games, practiced magic, had long conversations, and slipped out onto the moors late at night when everyone else was sleeping.

In this manner, the time passed quickly and very pleasantly. The young woman had been immensely grateful and thought that she would have gone crazy all alone in her room had it not been for Leana. Of Ragnald, she had been even more wary from then on.

⊱•⊰

From watching him closely, Ki'ara knew that her brother loved being in charge and having the ultimate authority over the lives of all others. He craved power, unlike anyone she had ever seen. To Ragnald, it was as important as the very air he breathed, and he hated relinquishing even the tiniest bit of control.

Perversely, the MacClair had also resented being responsible for Ki'ara. He had never let her forget that their father had dumped her on him and had often told his sister that he was stuck with her because Mikael did not love his daughter enough to take her along. Ragnald had made absolutely sure that his defenseless sibling understood just how bothersome he found her.

Still, Ki'ara feared that the lord would see losing the guardianship over his bothersome sister as a slap in the face. He saw her as his property to do with as he pleased. The MacClair enjoyed tormenting Ki'ara and making her life as miserable as he possibly could. Having the power to send her away from her beloved Highlands gave him immense pleasure each and every time.

Ragnald was a bully, and giving up this enjoyable sport anytime soon was not on his agenda. In addition, as long as Ki'ara was under his thumb, he could keep her from the one person she truly loved and whom he hated the most, the StCloud. Just knowing that he was hurting them both filled the cruel lord with a deep sense of satisfaction, something he had been unable to hide from his sister.

From past experience, the young woman was sure that a clash was on the horizon. All the signs were there already. Ki'ara only hoped that she and Leana could manage to leave soon and such avoid a major confrontation.

The MacClair would find something she did or said offensive. In the past, he had screamed at her over trivial things such as a strand of hair escaping from her hairdo after a walk on the moors or a wrinkle in her dress after she had been out riding. It was not very often that he had allowed her such freedoms to start with.

On one occasion, Ragnald had even yelled at Ki'ara for the way her eyes appeared when the light hit them. On a bright, sunny day, the siblings had been walking to the stables together when the girl had noticed a ship on the horizon. Her stare had reminded the lord of the fierce mountain cats who lived high up among the peaks of the Highlands.

Suddenly furious, the MacClair had ordered Ki'ara to stop her eyes from appearing like that. He had called her gaze soulless and her an abomination. Ragnald had screamed at her to stop looking like that at once. How dare she let this happen? What if anyone else had seen her?

Ki'ara had regarded her brother with a sense of shock and incomprehension. How could she guard herself against such an unprovoked attack? What control did she have over how her eyes looked to others? And, how could he call her an abomination? What had she done to deserve this?

When his sister had been too stunned to immediately respond, Ragnald had almost hit her. Had his yelling not attracted an audience, he most likely would have. Ki'ara had been dumbfounded. She had not been able to think of anything to say and had finally stammered an apology and had fled to her room.

From then on, Ki'ara had gone out of her way to avoid Ragnald. She had realized that he would find fault with her no matter what. The only recourse she had was to stay away from him as much as she possibly could. She even started taking her meals in her room whenever her brother would let her.

Every time the young woman had been allowed to come home, no matter how careful she had been, the MacClair had found an opportunity to unleash his anger on her. As much as she had missed the Highlands, being away from Seamuir Castle and her brother had started to feel like a reprieve.

The way this visit had started, Ki'ara was sure it would not take long for Ragnald to find some reason to scream at her or punish her. The thought filled her with apprehension. All she wanted was to live in peace with all of her brothers, to be a family again. Why was that so very difficult?

Putting those unhappy thoughts aside, Ki'ara snuggled down under the covers. She loved the scent of lavender Leana had added to her pillows. It always helped calm her and to find sleep even with all the turmoil going on in her heart.

It was nice to be in her own soft bed after the voyage. Despite all the unpleasantness, Ki'ara found some comfort in being in the home she had grown up in. So much here was familiar, and so many good memories were attached to this ancient place and her chambers.

The large, intricately carved sleigh bed had been a gift from her parents on her 10th birthday. They had intended it to be part of her dowry and to go with Ki'ara to her future husband's home. Her brother had made sure that did not happen by breaking her engagement to Conall, but at least so far, he had left the bed alone.

Would Ragnald allow her to take the things which belonged to her? Out of all the furniture in the room, this bed meant the most to her. The headboard was decorated with the carving of a huge tree surrounded by elves. The footboard showed a ship on the sea. Mikael had it especially made for her. It was beautiful and one of the young woman's prized possessions.

Could it be sneaked out of the castle? Ki'ara decided to consult the wily Leana about that. She had confidence in her maid and was sure that her loyal friend would find a way to take along this treasured piece of her past.

꧁༒꧂

Burrowing down further among the soft blankets, the young lady made herself more comfortable. She started to consciously relax her body and to release all the tension which had built up this day. Ki'ara let go of all the hurt she felt and forgave Ragnald for his ill-treatment. This did not make his actions right but unburdened her soul. There was no sense in dragging all that garbage around with her for one moment longer.

After all, carrying a grudge would hurt her and not her malicious brother. Ki'ara did not want that kind of negativity in her life. She only had to look at Ragnald to see what holding on to past resentments did to a person, and she did not want that for herself.

⚜

It took her a little while, but finally, she was more at peace. Ki'ara let her awareness wander. Soon, she entered into a pleasant contemplative state. This usually helped her center herself. The young lady wanted to put the events of the last few hours out of her mind. Very quickly, her thoughts were drawn to the beauty of the countryside around her.

Using her imagination, Ki'ara visited all those places she loved best. She stood on the cliffs close to the castle and looked out over the sea. She ran laughing along the familiar trails leading across the moors and climbed the hills towering above Seamuir. What bliss it was to be back home in the Highlands!

⚜

After this relaxing meditation, it did not take long for the exhausted young woman to fall deeply asleep. Almost immediately, she began to dream. Ki'ara felt herself rise up out of her body. This surprised her at first. She hovered next to her sleeping form for a few long moments and watched herself take deep, regular breaths.

After adjusting to being in spirit form, curiosity got the better of Ki'ara. She was not sure why this was happening but had every intention of enjoying this new sensation. After a bit of experimentation, she discovered that all she had to do was to want to go somewhere, and she started walking that way. Delightedly, she headed for the door. Something was drawing her outside.

Ki'ara's insubstantial hand reached for the door handle but passed right through it. Instant panic arose and threatened to swallow her whole. This had happened every time she had found herself locked in somewhere since the day Ragnald had trapped and sealed her in one of the castle's old cupboards.

Leana had found her many hours later. Being unable to free Ki'ara without using some very elaborate magic, she had gone for help. The woodsman had finally used his saw to carefully cut open the wardrobe to free the traumatized girl. She had nightmares about the incident for many days after and had woken up screaming each time.

Thanks to her varied magical education and strong connection to the power of the land, that kind of abuse was one thing she would not have to endure from Ragnald ever again. As far as Ki'ara was concerned, her brother had done enough, and she would tolerate little more.

The young woman firmly brought her mind back to the problem at hand. How was she going to get out of this room if she could not push down the handle? Just the idea was enough to allow the terror to rise up again to overwhelming proportions. For a moment, Ki'ara lost all ability to form a rational thought. All she wanted was to rip open the door and escape.

Taking some deep breaths, she centered herself. She had learned a new technique of late, which helped her deal with pain and unpleasant emotions of all kinds. It had been part of the knowledge which had been given to her by Brianna, the golden dragon she had set free. As far as Ki'ara was concerned, it had been a truly precious gift, and she was most grateful. Maybe this method would work in this case as well.

Instead of fighting against the rising panic, Ki'ara embraced it. She accepted it as part of herself and forgave herself for this momentary weakness. As she incorporated the emotions into her very being, her heart stopped racing, and her breathing slowed. It was working!

Once Ki'ara had calmed down enough to be able to think rationally again, it suddenly dawned on her. She did not need to open the door! If her hand could pass through the handle, she could walk right through it! The young lady laughed with relief and felt a bit sheepish for the briefest of moments.

With a sense of wonder, Ki'ara phased right through the wood. It did not take her long to realize that she did not even need to walk but could will her body to glide along the hallway towards the stairs. Soon, she serenely floated down to the ground floor and then out the front door. In just a few moments, she stood in the fields outside of the castle.

It was as if the magic had been waiting for the young sorceress and was welcoming her home. The sentient power was playfully rising up out of the ground like a phosphorescent mist. It started to form a circle around her and rose higher and higher. Ki'ara stood there entranced, watching the incredible display.

The luminescent wall began to swirl around Ki'ara. First slowly, but as its height increased, it spun faster and faster. It reminded the girl of a sparkling tornado of iridescent fireflies. The young woman laughed with delight. She felt no fear, was utterly at ease. Being at the center of all this magic just seemed right. What a beautiful sight!

Carefully, she extended her hand towards the whirling power. Shyly, almost like a wild animal, a tendril of the magic reached out and sniffed Ki'ara's outstretched fingers. It touched the tips of her digits for a fleeting moment before it withdrew back into itself.

The magic seemed to like the feel of her, however, because after that brief contact, the colors of the spinning curtain brightened and intensified further. It moved closer. The young woman now found herself in the contracting center of a swirling mass of pure, vibrating power.

This time, the magic approached her. A small part of this incredible wall of energy detached itself and formed a ball that landed gently on Ki'ara's upraised palm. Here it spun in place for a moment. It felt warm and rather pleasant where it touched her bare hand.

The young lady watched in amazement. She was smiling happily at this unexpected interaction. Instinctively, she sent her love out towards it.

※※※

Ki'ara was thrilled beyond words. Never in her life had she experienced anything comparable to this! What must it be like to enjoy the full connection to the land the nine lords had! The girl could not wait to find out. Would it feel like that for her at Fairholme? She sure hoped so!

Suddenly, the curtain of pure energy sent out a shoot towards the orb. Once it touched the sphere, the two parts connected. The tendril grew thicker as the glowing mass of the wall began to flow over and into the globe. Unexpectedly, the power started to stream into Ki'ara. She gasped in surprise.

Vibrant and alive energy suffused every fiber of the young sorceress' spirit being. She spread out her arms and threw her head back with the pure ecstasy of the feeling. Ki'ara lost herself in the incredible sensation of being one with the very magic of the land she so treasured.

※※※

Infused by this remarkable power, Ki'ara took wing. She soon found herself flying over the realms, embracing the feeling of the wind, the smell of the moors, the view of the rugged coast, and the magnificent mountains. How she loved this place and how fun it was to explore from above!

Ki'ara was so grateful to her father. Due to his forethought, she could now remain here in her beloved Highlands! She was severely tired of living in distant places where she felt alienated and alone, out of touch with her powers.

Even worse, Mathus had done his best to keep her isolated and off-balance. Ki'ara was sure this had been done on the orders of her brother, whom the tutor feared. Never again would she have to suffer through that!

Even thinking about the past few years upset Ki'ara, but the reawakened turmoil in her heart and soul was chased away by the sights of the land she loved so very much. This was where she belonged! The young woman could sense her bond to the earth, to the soil, the rocks, and all things which grew and lived here deepening as she floated along.

Now that she was back in the Highlands, that her feet had been planted on her native soil again, she could feel herself coming fully alive once more. She was home where she belonged! The magic called to her and sang in her blood. It felt wonderful, and Ki'ara happily basked in its glow.

Her spirit began to explore her homeland on a level the young woman had never known before. With a twirling motion, she sank deep into the earth, into the very rock. She moved along veins of silver, crystal, and gold and uncovered the secrets hidden far beneath the soil. She trailed along submerged rivers and marveled at the caves that she found.

Ki'ara raced high into the clouds and wove her way among the towering peaks. She discovered that, if she looked just right, she could see the luminous ley lines spreading all across her beloved Highlands. By the difference in energy, she could make out the borders of each of the realms.

The domain of the Zidhe was clearly discernible from the rest. Here the magic was the strongest and the lines more abundant and significantly brighter, especially near their population centers. The elven city showed up as a collection of blinking lights from this height, which reminded her of a shining five-pointed star.

Pure joy filled her, unlike any she had ever known before. Ki'ara flew even faster. It did not take her long to reach the rugged western coast and the sea. For a moment, she rested in midair and drank in the sight of the beautiful landscape bathed in silvery moonlight. How much she loved this place! How much she had missed it!

An insistent tugging drew Ki'ara further to the south until she got to the border with the Lowlands. The Zone of Death was clearly visible, even from this high up. The sentient fog roiled with bright flashes of power, which increased as she drew near. It was as stunning as it was frightening.

Just to the north of the mist, a strip of ground appeared dark and lifeless. Ki'ara noticed that the ley lines here were a very different color. She realized that their magic had been altered to allow them to do their job of protecting the realms. Instead of the pure white of the rest of the Highlands, the power here had a reddish tint to it interspersed with black flickers. Not a very welcoming place!

After watching the barrier for just a moment longer, she started flying back towards the east. She was moving unbelievably fast, and before long, Ki'ara reached the lands of the StClouds. The magic here was well cared for and looked amazingly healthy and vibrant, more so than it had in many of the other realms.

The clan's prosperity started to make sense. No wonder their herds did so well and multiplied in such vast numbers! Conall's close and carefully nurtured connection to the power must be the reason for this incredible abundance! He had learned to properly care for his realm, very unlike her own brother!

She could not help herself. After a moment's hesitation, Ki'ara dove down towards Cloudshire Hall. The fortress looked imposing and serene in the pale light of the moon. It gave off a far more pleasant air than her own home. Too bad Conall was not here, or she would have been tempted to stop in for a visit!

After circling Cloudshire Hall and admiring its beauty, Ki'ara turned north towards Seamuir. Her path brought her to the fortress her father had gifted her, Fairholme Castle. The lands here were fertile and well cared for. It showed that the StCloud had been looking after the area since her parents' departure.

Ki'ara could see a distinct difference between that region and the rest of Eastmuir where Ragnald had been the one responsible for its health. Anywhere her brother's influence had spread, the magic was dull and lifeless compared to the parts under Conall's skilled ministrations.

The young woman could feel the power's unhappiness, its wariness, and mistrust. It gave off an air reminiscent of an abused child. What had her brother been doing to affect the land in such a damaging fashion? And what could she do to make it right?

⚜

After sensing the wretchedness emanating from Eastmuir, Ki'ara decided to head inland instead of towards Seamuir Castle. She was not yet ready to return to her body, and curiosity was getting the better of her. She wanted a closer look at the center of the Highlands, at the mysterious home of the elves.

The young woman had always been interested in her legendary ancestors and wanted to learn more about them. Ki'ara had heard so many rumors about the wonders which could be found in their section. How much was true, and how much had been an exaggeration?

When she reached the area, she was not disappointed. How stunning this realm was to behold! Now that she was flying lower, Ki'ara got a better picture of the real beauty of this region.

The home of the Zidhe shone with a web of power that incorporated the ley lines feeding the land, all spreading out from one point. That had to be Elvenhorst, their central city!

What a marvel it was to behold! The magic congregating there was beyond anything she could have imagined.

What a gift she was receiving this night! All this knowledge and the opportunity to see things others could only dream of! Profound gratefulness filled Ki'ara's heart. She was confident that she would never forget this momentous adventure.

Some instinct told her to take a closer look at the ley lines. Ki'ara followed one of the main ones extending out from the city and leading towards Eastmuir. When she reached the border, she noticed a large lake of magic just inside the realm of the Zidhe. On the MacClair side, the shining line dimmed and thinned noticeably. Was something blocking the flow, or was the power reluctant to enter her brother's environs?

Ki'ara decided to investigate. Gliding lower, she hovered over the spot. She could see nothing out of the ordinary and no reason for the magic to pond. By all appearances, it should have been flowing freely. What was going on here?

Suddenly, she felt a strong compulsion to land. As soon as her feet touched the ground, the ley line leading into Eastmuir brightened visibly. To Ki'ara's astonishment, she started to hear a humming which kept increasing in volume. Looking around for the source, she realized that it came from the magic pooling in the realm of the Zidhe.

The sound reached deafening proportions, and Ki'ara had to cover her ears. Then, as if a dam had burst, all that power flooded towards the unsuspecting young woman and engulfed her. She was swept up in its torrent and spun around a few times before being pushed to the surface. Here she found herself being gently cradled as she was being carried along with the flow.

Once Ki'ara was able to reorient herself, she realized that they were heading towards the coast along the main trunk of the ley line. They were moving at breakneck speed, and the landscape was flashing past in a blur. Magic was spreading out into the realm as they passed, leaving the land visibly brighter. The young woman observed with great pleasure that the healing of her home had begun.

⚜

The power, however, was not just rejuvenating the realm. As Ki'ara was being carried along with the wave of energy, more and more magic infused her. It was burning through her, taking possession, making her its new host.

Before long, the young woman's spirit could feel every single ley line crossing through the MacClair lands, every creature, every plant, the soil, the rocks, all that made up Eastmuir.

When the wild ride finally came to an end somewhere near the family's castle, Ki'ara decided to continue to explore. Maybe there was more she could do.

Using her new powers, the sorceress looked for areas where the magic had been stagnating or had been perverted by the unlawful acts of her brother. She found many.

One after another, she healed them and restored the land back to a semblance of what it had been.

Chapter 35

Leana

While Ki'ara lay sleeping and her spirit roamed free, her knowledge and link to the land grew with every second. For the first time in her life, her connection expanded to the point where it was far beyond that of an ordinary Zidarian. The magic had examined her, had washed through her, and had liked what it found. That night, she became 'The MacClair,' the true power behind the rule of Eastmuir.

Unbeknownst to the dreaming Ki'ara, Leana, a powerful enchantress and skilled herbalist, had slipped back into the room as soon as she had felt the young woman link with the power. The maid was going to watch over and protect her mistress as she had done for many years now, especially while the girl was in such a vulnerable state.

Leana had come to the castle with Ki'ara's parents after the baby had been born among Ali'ana's people. She was much more than she seemed and was fiercely loyal to those whom she loved. She had been looking after the girl from the moment she entered into the world and was determined that no harm would ever befall her.

Leana was certain that Ki'ara had no idea where she was born or who her mother really was. Her parents had made sure that it remained a well-kept secret. The dislike the child would have been subjected to would have been even greater had her older brothers known her real heritage.

To ensure that the destination of their trip remained a mystery, the lady and her husband had decided to bring only a couple of the most loyal kinsmen along on the way to her folk. This pair of guards had been prepared to die rather than to break their lord's trust. They had gone everywhere he did and had usually been enough to keep their master safe on his travels.

Once they had the child, however, Mikael had felt that a bit of extra protection could not hurt. Some of Ali'ana's family and loyal friends had happily volunteered to accompany the new parents. They had disguised themselves as Zidarians to avoid arousing suspicion. Leana had been one of those who had made that journey.

In actuality, the maid was Ali'ana's own sister and Ki'ara's aunt. She was a powerful enchantress and gifted clairvoyant. Right after the baby was born, Leana had a compelling and unsettling vision, which had made her realize that the girl would need surreptitious protection in the years to come.

Therefore, when the others had returned home, Leana had stayed behind to help look after her niece.

⁕⁕⁕

Ali'ana had been leery of Ragnald and Lyall almost from the start. She had tried hard to befriend them but to no avail. The lady had sensed the violence hiding in the oldest MacClair and had been very upset when Mikael did not fully believe her. Her husband was a good man, but when it came to his sons, he tended to be just a bit shortsighted.

The concerned mother had felt that she was perfectly able to protect herself and the baby but had realized that she could not be with her child all the time. That, and her sister's vision, had been enough to convince her that something had to be done to ensure Ki'ara's safety at the castle.

Therefore, before they had even left their home to travel to Seamuir, she and Leana had come up with a plan. From past observations, the lady had concluded that the best way to move about the castle almost unnoticed was as one of the servants. So Ali'ana's sister took on the appearance of a middle-aged woman and became the infant's nurse and protector.

A well-placed spell had made Leana appear familiar to the clan and its people. Everyone had believed that the maid had always been there and was returning to Seamuir with the lord and his wife. It had worked so well that not even Ragnald had any idea to this day.

Hiding in plain sight had been the perfect way for Leana to look after Ki'ara without anyone knowing or growing suspicious. She had been especially on the alert every time the older boys had come to visit and would not leave the small child out of her sight while they were in residence. Her vigilance had paid off several times.

Years later, when Ki'ara had no longer needed a nurse, Ali'ana had changed Leana's position into that of a chambermaid for the young girl. The aunt had remained in the small room adjacent to her niece's spacious apartment. Mikael had made sure that nothing could ever change that, not even the new lord of Eastmuir.

Ki'ara and Leana had formed a tight bond, had become friends. A glamour had kept the girl from looking more closely at her trusted retainer. Instead, she had accepted the maid just as she appeared and had confided all her problems to the matronly woman who was always there for her with help and advice.

Before Ali'ana had left, she had made sure that her daughter understood that she could fully rely on Leana. She had assured Ki'ara that the maid would have her back, no matter what. The lady trusted her sister more than almost anyone else.

At the time, Ali'ana had felt this vague feeling of unease. She had been unable to ascertain what was so insistently setting off her sense of alarm. She had been sure that something was about to go terribly wrong, but she had been unable to determine the exact source of this inkling.

Ali'ana did, however, suspect that it had to do with her distrust of Ragnald. She had to depart, had no option, and leaving her sibling to protect the girl had been the best she had been able to do for Ki'ara under the circumstances.

The worried mom had assured her unhappy child that the servant's loyalty would be to Ki'ara, and to her alone, not to the new lord of the castle. She had told the girl that she could trust her maid with her very life.

Leana and her sister had believed that they had things under control. The two ladies, however, had not counted on Ragnald sending Ki'ara away.

⚜

Being the girl's maid had allowed Leana easy access to the child, and it had made her invisible in a way nothing else could have. Who, after all, paid attention to the servants, especially a middle-aged, dumpy, unattractive appearing woman? Except, possibly the castle's new ruler.

Once Ali'ana and Mikael had left, conditions at Seamuir had gone downhill fast. Leana had been extremely alarmed. To ensure that she could continue to guard Ki'ara, the aunt had taken some further precautions.

Using her powerful magic, she had surrounded herself with a spell which made all others except Ki'ara forget her existence or ignore her completely. Their eyes would glide right over Leana like she was not even there, seeing her without ever becoming aware of her presence unless she wanted them to.

The maid had rapidly figured out that not coming to the new lord's attention was best. As vindictive and mean as Ragnald had quickly shown himself to be, he would send anyone away who was close to his sister just to hurt her. Leana preferred to avoid a confrontation with that despicable man since it would have revealed her actual powers.

To keep an eye on Ki'ara, Leana took up watch by her bed. After barring the door, the enchantress had moved one of the chairs to where she could see the sleeping young woman without turning her head.

This allowed the concerned aunt to observe her niece in some comfort. She had promised the child's parents that no harm would come to this girl if she could possibly help it. The shrewd lady had every intention of keeping her word.

Here she now sat, hour after hour, guarding and shielding the sleeping Ki'ara. To keep the situation from getting out of hand, Leana had also had a chat with the magic. She had stopped it from making its intention known to Ragnald before they were ready and safe.

It would not do for the present lord to discover that his power was being usurped.

Usually, a Zidarian lord worked in full collaboration with the magic of his realm. The connection was deep and absolute. Not so with the present MacClair. Ragnald's link to the land was not all that strong, and he had to fight to maintain it. Force was never a good way to gain a sentient power's willing cooperation.

Leana had no illusions about the master of the castle. The MacClair was a hateful, evil man, greedy for power and control. His kinsmen had suffered greatly under his rule these last few years. He would not take losing his title and position kindly and would fight to the death to maintain them.

Ki'ara, on the other hand, was a gentle and kind soul who tried hard not to do harm. Taking her brother's place had never been the young sorceress' intention, but the magic had a mind of its own. It had enough of being abused. Leana doubted that the girl was even aware of what was happening to her at this very moment.

⚜

The observant Leana had felt the power growing in her niece and friend over the years. She had warned the girl long ago to shield herself well at all times. The exact extent of her abilities had to remain secret from her brothers and kinsmen until it was safe for her to reveal just how strong she really was.

Under normal conditions, Ki'ara was able and skilled enough to maintain her protection even when deeply unconscious. When the earth powers came calling with this kind of intensity during the makings of a lord, however, all bets were off. The magic had a tendency to blow all shields to bits. Even the most skilled of the Zidhe would have been laid bare under those circumstances.

It would not do for Ragnald to realize that his sister was far more in touch with the powers, that she was now the chief and not him.

⚜

After the vile man had taken over the clan, Leana had quickly discovered that the lord had to force the magic into submission each and every time he needed to use it. It had never helped him out of choice and was rebellious and unhappy at best.

Coercing anything or anyone usually only gained the oppressor limited cooperation. Ragnald was going against the natural flow of things by trying to impose his will on the land. The magic had withdrawn from Eastmuir as much as it could and would assist the present lord only grudgingly and when it absolutely had to.

To Ki'ara, the power came willingly and with ease. It always had, even when she was just a small child. Leana, Mikael, and Ali'ana had gone to great length to hide this from his sons and the clan. Ragnald had been resentful enough already.

The child had displayed an intimate connection to the magic and an incredible understanding of her surroundings, starting at a very young age. Her capabilities had gone well beyond her tender years. Her parents and the StCloud had observed and nurtured her gifts with delight but had also taught Ki'ara from very early on how to hide her true nature.

Now, the magic was claiming the young woman as the new lord. Ragnald hated Ki'ara already as it was. Giving the volatile man yet one more reason to harm his sister was just not wise. Leana decided that they would have to play this very, very carefully.

Coming up with a workable plan did not take long for the cunning enchantress. The protection and welfare of Ki'ara were her utmost priorities. She had no loyalty to the clan nor its people, she was not really a member to start with. She would, however, do anything to keep her niece safe.

Once again, Leana reached out to the magic. Since having been abused by the present lord, the power had grown petulant and suspicious. It took the enchantress a bit to convince it to listen. After laying out her strategy as well as pointing out the possible consequences of any rash moves, she managed to persuade it to go along with her plot.

The power had harbored some ideas of its own, motivated by a deep sense of resentment. It had taken some serious persuasion to keep the magic from just killing Ragnald in his sleep as it had intended to do. The death of her brother would have terribly upset the kind-hearted Ki'ara and would not have been a good way for the young woman to start her reign as the new lord.

Leana was sure that Ragnald would do anything to maintain control over the realm, the clan, and the family, including killing his sister. Now, with the magic to protect her, his chances of success had been significantly reduced, and the girl was a bit safer even if he did try something untoward.

The way Ki'ara had been treated when she had arrived made Leana believe that the conniving lord had ulterior motives for allowing his sister's return. What was Ragnald up to this time?

That afternoon, when she had first sensed Ki'ara's presence and had realized that the girl was home from Frankonia, Leana had made herself perceptible again. She had volunteered to supervise the cleaning of the young woman's chambers. The flustered housekeeper had been only too happy to have that chore taken off her hands so that she could continue working on making amends.

As it was, Leana had looked after the rooms in her niece's absence. She had been living in the small servants' chamber, which was part of Ki'ara's large suite.

Her spells had kept all others out, even the lord who would have liked nothing better than to snoop around among his sister's possessions.

Little had needed doing beyond putting clean linens on the bed, refreshing the lavender, a quick airing, and the lighting of the fire. The housekeeper, however, had not known that. She had assumed that it would take hours to clean the long-neglected rooms. Berta had been more than happy when it had been completed so quickly.

Leana had handled the preparations on her own since she did not want a servant to discover or upset one of her spells. Having been all alone in the chamber over the last two years had given the enchantress ample opportunity to redraw the runes of protection under her niece's bed once per month, for she knew that eventually, Ki'ara would be allowed to return home.

Since Ragnald was so unpredictable, Leana had figured that it was best to be ready for anything coming their way. To keep people out of the suite in Ki'ara's absence, she had placed a spell of aversion and forgetting on the door strong enough to deter even someone more powerful than the MacClair.

The enchantment would prevent all but Ki'ara and herself from entering the apartment unless they were invited. Leana's magic had also ensured that the rooms were well guarded against prying minds. Ragnald had never suspected a thing, and she liked it this way.

The shields protecting the suite were cleverly designed to allow no magic to bleed through to the outside and to reflect anything evil trying to get in. Leana had crafted them carefully and had fine-tuned them over the years.

What she and Ki'ara needed most at the moment was privacy. Having Ragnald barge in while her niece was in the throes of the 'Becoming' had to be avoided at all costs. The girl was defenseless in the state she was in, but the magic would not allow anyone to hurt her. It would be only too happy to unload all its bitterness and rage on the unsuspecting lord.

Leana sat watch to avoid drawing the MacClair's interest in the first place. Since all Zidarian children were taught to safeguard themselves from very young on, Ragnald expected no different from his own siblings. He knew Ki'ara had been well trained since he had overseen her education these last few years. He figured that by now, she should be an expert at shielding.

The distrustful tyrant would be instantly alerted, therefore, if he detected even a faint trickle of power emanating from his sister's rooms. This would be entirely out of character for her and could only mean that something unusual was afoot that warranted his investigation.

If Ragnald's full attention was ever drawn to the chambers, Leana knew that there would be no stopping him. A spell baring entrance would only confirm his suspicions if it did not dissipate in time. Facing an unauthorized enchantment in his own home would infuriate the hot-tempered man beyond all reason.

To prevent such problems, Leana had taken steps to keep any intruder from finding signs of her magic as well as Ki'ara's. If access were gained by force or under duress, her enchantments would immediately jump into action, and nothing remotely objectionable would be left in the chambers.

In most clans, having signs of protection in one's suite would be no problem. Witchcraft was not against Highland laws, and Ki'ara was a trained sorceress after all. She was a Zidarian, allowed to use her powers as she saw fit just as long as she harmed none.

Leana had no doubt, however, that the MacClair would seize every available opportunity and twist anything he might locate of a magical nature into something that he could use against his innocent sister. She had seen him read up on an obscure law that allowed for the elimination of imminent threats.

The maid had managed to get a hold of his notes. To start with, Ragnald had intended to accuse Ki'ara of stealing his power, which would have explained his lack of full access to the magic of the land.

Then, the MacClair would have claimed that his sister had been illegally blocking him all this time, also a crime punishable by banishment or death.

To prevent the council from getting involved and to achieve his goal as fast as possible, the callous lord had added an additional step. He had planned to plant an item which he then could misrepresent as malevolent and designed to do harm. This would have allowed Ragnald to declare Ki'ara a danger to the clan, which would have given him the right to take her life right then and there.

The worldly and well-traveled Leana had been appalled by what she had read on that paper. To coldly plot the murder of his own sister was vile, even for one such as Ragnald.

A well-placed enchantment had made him forget all about that evil scheme.

Given the circumstances at the castle, Leana was grateful to have been born with the ability to outthink most people as well as the capability to plan for many possible contingencies. She could see a number of possible futures and block the ones she did not like. She regarded this as an incredible gift and had sworn to use it only for good.

The experienced enchantress had learned much during her long life, but her time in this castle had taught even her a thing or two, and none of it pleasant. Ragnald was by far the most disagreeable Zidarian Leana had met since dealing with his namesake, Raghnall, so many years ago now.

That one had not gotten the better of her, and neither would his detestable grandson.

❧

By now, Leana was well prepared for numerous possible outcomes. There had been plenty of time during Ki'ara's absences to come up with all kinds of scenarios and take steps to foil them. She had put safeguards in place all over the suite and created a way for them to exit the chambers unseen.

The maid had a couple of good friends in the castle who would help her and Ki'ara escape undetected once they got down to the stables. If they had to flee, Ragnald would never figure out how his sister had gotten away.

In an emergency, they could escape into the hidden passage in the walls. Leana could then trigger the spell she had placed on the door, and it would become visible once more. The aversion enchantment would disappear altogether the moment it was confronted with the lord's fury, or someone tried to force entry. The backlash of energy would wipe out the runes under the bed and sent all magical items into a well-hidden space. It would also alert herself and Ki'ara.

To prevent Ragnald from planting false evidence against his sister, any magical item carried over the threshold would turn into ash but not before burning the culprit. The door itself would behave as if it had been stuck, and no bar would be anywhere near it.

As an extra precaution, however, Leana had placed an incantation on the threshold, which would wipe out all memory of there ever having been some kind of a problem. It would calm tempers and make the whole incident appear like it had just been a misunderstanding on their part.

This way, she and Ki'ara would not have to come up with a convincing explanation for the irrational lord should they have the misfortune to get caught while trying to flee.

Leana was powerful but also quite prudent. She felt it was best to avoid trouble to start with. Knowing Ragnald, however, and being only too conscious of the depth of that cruel man's perversion and hatred, she had tried to take all possible actions to ensure both Ki'ara's and her own safety.

Chapter 36

The Awakening

Hour after hour during that long night, the faithful Leana sat beside her niece's bed. She kept reinforcing Ki'ara's protection as well as the shields surrounding the room. The land's magic had decided to cooperate and was assisting the powerful enchantress in this task. It was also feeding her energy, which was helping her to stay awake.

When the first light of dawn started to work its way between the panels of the heavy velvet curtains, Leana briefly slipped into the kitchen. Since she was now perceivable and once again one of the servants, the maid needed to make sure that she would not be missed by the always suspicious housekeeper.

Acting as if she had just gotten up and was not fully awake yet was easy. Leana was actually glad that she did not have to suppress most of her yawns. After downing a quick cup of coffee and eating a small breakfast, she returned to Ki'ara's apartment.

Her relief that the protection had held in her absence was heartfelt. Quietly, Leana got things ready for the day. She kept checking on her niece every few minutes. The enchantress was a little concerned by the young woman's complete stillness. Ki'ara was deeply unconscious, but her breathing was even and strong.

The land's magic kept assuring Leana that the girl was just fine and that there was nothing to worry about. She would wake up when her journey was completed. Until then, Ki'ara had much to experience, much to learn, and the bond had to be strengthened.

The maid could feel the power emanating from the young woman growing with each passing minute. She once more reinforced the shielding of the room. At this point, there was no telling how long Ki'ara would dreamwalk, how long the magic of the land would keep her within.

Ki'ara would never be the same, of that Leana was certain. Until the time was right, this had to be hidden at all costs from her family, especially Ragnald. It was a good thing that the brothers did not know their sibling that well. This sad fact would now work in the girl's favor.

The only one who may notice that Ki'ara was different might be Gawain. Leana was sure, however, that he would not betray his sister. He loved her too much to ever do her harm, very unlike the oldest MacClair.

After watching Gawain carefully over the years, Leana was confident that he did not care much for Ragnald nor for Lyall. Being the youngest and barely tolerated by those two, he had tried hard to keep the peace while still helping the people of the clan as much as he could.

As far as Leana was concerned, Gawain was the only decent one of the three brothers. The youngest MacClair had always treated her with kindness and respect despite her appearing as just a nurse or a maid. He had a caring heart and was a good man, just like his father.

The sorceress was glad that Gawain was so dissimilar to his brothers. This gave Ki'ara at least one sibling she could trust and connect to. Leana hoped that their relationship would grow closer over time.

It was past noon when Ki'ara finally woke up. She felt fabulous, more alive than ever before in her life. The young woman stretched luxuriously, yawned expansively, and then scooted up to lean against the headboard. For a moment, she rejoiced in the feeling of wholeness, of completeness. How wonderful it was to be back in the Highlands!

What a night this had been! She remembered having the most amazing adventure. At first, Ki'ara was not entirely sure if it had been a dream or if all these marvelous things had actually happened. She wanted it to be real, but the rational part of her brain was not yet convinced.

When she checked closer, Ki'ara thought that she could sense a remnant of the astounding connection to the magic of the land sing in her blood. To her, it sure felt like she had been one with that incredible power! How was that possible?

As Ki'ara slowly became more awake, the impressions of that dream started to appear too fantastic to be real. In the bright light of the new day, the entire venture was beginning to seem increasingly more imaginary with each passing minute. Why then did her instincts tell her that something momentous had happened?

During those hours while she lay sleeping, the astounding closeness and knowledge of the realm had felt more tangible to Ki'ara than anything she had ever experienced before. Could it have actually happened?

The young woman thought she had fallen asleep the night before. She had been exhausted from traveling and all the upheaval. She remembered a moment of floating very much like when one first starts to dream. It had been a welcome relief from the tension she had felt all day.

Then, everything had changed. Ki'ara recalled suddenly feeling wide-awake and vibrantly alive. Now that she reflected on the entire incident, it started to make more sense. The girl realized that she had left her body behind! It had been her spirit that had joined with the immense soul of the land.

More details came back to her. Ki'ara recollected that she had flown across the countryside from coast to coast in what had seemed like the blink of an eye. She had explored the rest of the Highlands and the realm of the Zidhe. She had found a pool of magic and had been instrumental in restoring its flow into Eastmuir.

Upon her return to Seamuir on the flood of pure energy, Ki'ara had felt compelled to get to know each nook and cranny of the MacClair realm. Initially, she had explored Eastmuir from the air. Then, she had landed and had traveled along on the ground.

The young sorceress had been greatly surprised to be introduced to an entirely new and different facet of the land she loved so much. For the first time, she was privy to the secret life of her home. Even as in tune with the realm as she had been, much had been concealed from her until that moment.

Ki'ara had discovered strange plants she had never known to exist. She had examined each and every one with great pleasure. How amazing and intricate some of them were and how unusual! The young sorceress had been filled with sincere gratitude that she had been granted a glimpse into this world unseen by most people.

The hidden inhabitants of the cliffs, woods, and moors had also come forth to meet her. She had greeted them all with delight as well as respect. Ki'ara had known of their existence from childhood on, had been told the old stories, but had never met or even seen some of them.

The young sorceress had been aware of how shy the fey could be and truly appreciated being able to visit with these elusive beings. Most did not trust humans nor Zidarians and preferred to remain concealed at all times.

As a girl, Ki'ara had encountered some of these mysterious beings but never in such numbers. She had made contact with several dryads when she had set out to cut a wand for herself one spring day many years ago. She had been nine at the time. As was required, she had asked permission from the tree and its resident before even thinking of setting a blade to the branch.

After some initial reluctance, not just that one, but several of the nymphs had allowed Ki'ara to perceive them. Once they had overcome their wariness, they had many questions for her. These women of the woods had much they had wanted to know. They had ended up inviting their new acquaintance to sit among the trees with them, and they had talked merrily for many hours.

The afternoon had passed pleasantly but rather too quickly for the new friends. All too soon, the time had come when the girl had to return to her home. The moors and lands adjoining Seamuir Castle were no place for anyone to be wandering around in after dark, not even for Ki'ara, who knew the area better than most. Also, her parents would have been worried if she had stayed gone too much longer.

Ki'ara had enjoyed herself so much she had completely forgotten about the reason she had set out in the first place. To her delight, she had discovered the branch she had wanted on her windowsill the next morning. Her father had helped her fashion it into a beautiful wand. She still had it but kept it well hidden. It was powerful, and her brother would have taken it from her given a chance.

The girl and the beautiful dryads had become good friends. She had gone back to visit with them as often as she could after that day. They had taught Ki'ara much about the woods and had introduced her to others of their kind. Mikael and Ali'ana had encouraged her exploits. How much she had loved those carefree years!

⚜

Once Ragnald had been made Ki'ara's guardian, everything had changed. She had been under his complete control and had to look for a way to sneak out to visit with the nymphs or walk on the moors. After her parents had left, it had taken the girl several days before she had managed to finally slip away unnoticed.

Her friends had been excited as well as relieved to see her. Once they had all settled in so that they could talk comfortably, the girl had explained her altered situation. The dryads, in turn, had shared their own misgivings. They had sensed the difference in the magic of the land the moment the new lord took over. Many of them had been afraid. After talking to Ki'ara, they had realized that their apprehensions had not been without cause.

While she and her companions had sat there chatting, the girl had suddenly been overcome by a horrifying vision. It had been sent as a warning. What she had seen in that foretelling, had filled Ki'ara with revulsion and terror. It had shaken her badly. There was, however, a way to prevent this nightmare from coming true, and she saw this in an instant. Ragnald had to be kept from ever finding out that she cared for the nymphs!

The image of trees being cut down and the dryads dying had been burned into Ki'ara's mind. It had almost broken her heart when she understood at that moment that her brother would do anything just to hurt her. The girl had become aware right then and there that she would have to be much more careful to prevent bringing harm unto others.

With great sadness, Ki'ara had realized that the best thing she could do to protect her friends was to stay away and only visit on very rare occasions. When she had explained this to them, the fairies had been sad, but in the end, they had to agree that this was the only viable option.

There had been one thing she had been able to do, however, before she departed. She had aided the dryads in making their area safer. Working together, they had created a spell to protect the grove. From then on, anyone nearing these trees would be deterred and go elsewhere, leaving the woods and their inhabitants alone and unharmed.

As reticent as these beings usually were, the nymphs and other fey had come out in large numbers to visit with the young lady during her journey the previous night. They had all wanted to meet her. Her old friends had been thrilled to see Ki'ara again and had happily introduced her to some of the other inhabitants of the land.

Ki'ara had listened patiently to the elementals concerns for the realm. She had realized that much more than she had thought possible had been going awry since Ragnald took over. To avoid enslavement by the cruel lord, many beings had gone into hiding or had fled to the safety of the domain of the Zidhe.

That the magic had worked with them, had protected the fairies from the clan leader, said a lot in itself. It had made Ki'ara sad for her brother, the land, and its peoples. Did Ragnald not grasp what a privilege it was to care for all this, to have the connection to the realm, the power to do so much good? Did he not understand what an incredible gift he had received?

The MacClair's actions had violated the basic terms of the covenant with the Zidhe. He had mistreated and abused the magic, the fey, and the clan. How had he gotten away with this for so long? It was beyond Ki'ara's comprehension that no one had stopped him from committing such offenses.

The young sorceress had come to the decision that very moment that she would do everything possible to undo the damage her brother had done. She had realized that she would have to outsmart him. A notion had taken shape in her mind. To carry it out, she would need allies as well as the council behind her.

⁕⁕⁕

Ki'ara had assured each of the groups she had met that night that she would do what she could. She had told them that she had a plan and had asked them to please be patient just a little while longer. The sorceress had promised the elementals that she would work as fast as she could to remedy this dreadful situation.

Patiently, Ki'ara had explained that a direct confrontation or challenge could have dire consequences for her. There was the possibility of being punished by the Zidhe as well as the council if she broke the rules and attacked the reigning lord. Only in self-defense was she allowed to oppose him.

For now, her brother Ragnald would have to remain the official ruler, but the girl was sure that his days were numbered. Ki'ara had promised that she would, with the magic's help, remedy a few of the immediate problems to make life a little better for those in the realm.

Again and again, Ki'ara had stopped to talk to new groups of the fey. As she had traveled across Eastmuir, the young woman had restored the land wherever she could. Her voice had risen in the healing songs of old that had been part of her heritage for hundreds of years. Some she had not been aware of until the moment they had poured forth from her lips.

The ley lines had visibly started to brighten, and the magic had sung along with Ki'ara. It had been much happier once some of the effects of her brother's evil deeds had been undone. It had kept guiding her to places which had desperately required her attention, to folk which had needed reassuring. Finally, it had led her down to the sea.

The merpeople had been waiting for her. Ki'ara had glimpsed mermaids and mermen before from the shore or from aboard of a ship but had never actually spoken to them. After she had reinforced the neglected and failing protective net running along the coast, the young woman had met some of the guardian monsters of the seashore. Their handlers, the merfolk, had been proud to introduce her to their beloved pets.

⁕⁕⁕

The entire experience had been so new and wonderful, but it had felt so right. All those strange beings Ki'ara had encountered had been a little wary in the beginning but had also been very deferential towards her. She had been treated like she was royalty. The sorceress had assumed at the time that this was due to her being a MacClair and the sister of the present ruler.

The more Ki'ara thought about it, however, the more puzzled she became. What was she overlooking? The magical inhabitants of Eastmuir had, in a way, treated her as their queen, their lord. But she wasn't, was she?

Ki'ara recalled that many of the fey who had been withholding their allegiance and loyalty to Ragnald had given it freely to her. They had placed their trust in her, had become her people. How could this be if she was not the lord? The magic should not have allowed this!

The young lady could sense that she was missing something. Her brow wrinkled in concentration as she went over the facts one more time. Ki'ara was determined to figure out exactly what had happened to her during her nighttime adventure.

Piece by piece, she examined the situation. Her oldest brother was the MacClair. The magic, as well as the connection, were his or should have been his. Ki'ara was grateful to have gotten a taste of what it must feel like for him. Did his bond go even deeper? Would it be like that for her at her own home of Fairholme?

After exploring the realm's surface, her spirit had been prompted to descend into the earth itself. Ki'ara had discovered the riches resting below the land, had come across the cities of the dwarves hidden deep inside the mountains. Until that moment, she had no idea that any members of this secretive race even lived within their realm!

Towards the end of her underground journey, she had stopped and had become very still. Deep peace had washed over her. Slowly at first, but then more rapidly, her being had expanded. Ki'ara had become one with the very soil, with the vegetation, with the rocks, with the rivers. She had felt the pulse of the sea beating against the bluffs below the keep and the sleepy burbling of the high moors.

The profound sense of belonging, of being home had filled her with awe. This must be what it felt like to be the lord of the realm! Ki'ara had loved the intimate connection with her surroundings. She would miss it.

With a pang of sadness, the young sorceress thought how lucky Ragnald was to be part of this wonder every day!

⊱•✦•⊰

For a moment, resting comfortably in the bed from her childhood, the sense of loss almost overwhelmed Ki'ara. Soon she would have to leave here, to make her way to Fairholme. Staying at Seamuir Castle was just too unpleasant and dangerous for her and Leana. Also, it would be easier and safer to help Eastmuir from a distance.

Somehow, however, this did not feel right. Why did her instincts tell her that she still belonged here at Seamuir Castle? Suddenly, it dawned on Ki'ara. What she had experienced the night before must be what it actually felt like to be the MacClair! She had been granted the real thing!

With a sudden shock, Ki'ara realized who she had become. She WAS the new lord! Did Ragnald know? If he did, her life was in imminent danger! What could she do to protect herself and Leana?

⊱•✦•⊰

The young woman gently reached out to the magic. It came to her eagerly. Upon sensing her fear, a deep sense of calm and reassurance flowed into her. Everything was fine for now, and Ragnald had been kept in the dark, but the situation had to be handled with ultimate care!

From listening in on the council, she knew that her brother should have instantly detected what went on with the magic! How had he managed to remain the lord without that close a connection? Ki'ara was amazed by the depth of his deception. He should have sensed it the moment the power touched her!

A certain sense of glee from the magic told Ki'ara all she needed to know. It had been working against her sibling all along! The young woman concluded that much had been hidden from Ragnald as a result of his trying to bend the power to his will, to force it into compliance with his harmful desires.

Instead of acting with the magic by establishing cooperation, her brother had attempted to subjugate the power, to make it do what he wanted. It had fought him every step of the way, had taken his commands literal, had done anything it could to get back at its callous oppressor.

To Ki'ara, on the other hand, it had come willingly and happily. She realized that the magic had shown her many of the secrets it had withheld from Ragnald. The young woman felt honored as well as grateful for the trust she had been granted, and she was determined to prove herself worthy.

If her people ever needed resources, from this day forward, Ki'ara knew where to find them. She had been presented with the information necessary to lead her clan into prosperity.

Without the young sorceress even being aware of it or asking for it, her life, her soul, her very being had been intimately tied to the land.

Ki'ara no longer had any doubts. She, the despised younger sister, had become 'The MacClair,' the actual lord of the keep! This was as exhilarating as it was terrifying! The magic would protect her in a direct confrontation, but the young woman preferred to find a diplomatic way to take over the rule.

What would her brothers do when they found out? Ragnald had made it abundantly clear that he cared little for her. The other two? Lyall would most likely stand against her, Gawain possibly with her, but at what cost to himself?

Just then, Leana entered the room. One look at Ki'ara told her everything she needed to know. She rushed over and pulled the young woman into a comforting embrace. "You know, don't you?" she asked in a low voice.

The new lord nodded. For a moment longer, her eyes were wide with wonder as well as a slight sense of panic. That the magic had chosen a different ruler while one was still in place had never happened before in all the time the clans had existed! This was unchartered territory, without precedence and would need careful handling.

Ragnald could not really harm her anymore now that she was under the protection of the land, but a direct clash might still lead to trouble with the Zidhe. Her grandfather had not fared so well when he went against their rules. The young woman had no desire to share his mysterious fate.

The events of the night before had changed her situation considerably, but still, Ki'ara decided that it would be best to stick with her plan. She needed to find allies, file an appeal with the council and the elves. This was the only legal way to remove her brother as lord and the least dangerous to her person as well as her friends.

⁂

Leana had arrived at a similar conclusion. She had just dispatched an urgent magical message to the girl's uncle. The enchantress had bespelled the missive for Lord Iain's eyes only just in case it should fall into the wrong hands. The note would find the ruler wherever he was at the moment. If things went wrong here at Seamuir Castle, they would need all the help they could get.

How far this child had come! The matronly woman solemnly regarded Ki'ara and smiled at her proudly. This young woman was a treasure to both of her people. Leana had the feeling that the time was close at hand for the girl to find out who her mother and servant really were.

But first, they had to get through the next few days with minimal drama.

"We have to be careful. Ragnald will not like giving up his position! Do not worry, love, you will be able to keep this from your brothers until the time is right. Shield yourself well, and for now, do not use this new-found power of yours no matter what happens!" Leana advised her.

Ki'ara buried her face in the wise woman's shoulder and nodded. She could do this! After all, it would not be the first time she had hidden things from her siblings. Her brothers had no clue what she was actually able to do.

To stay safe, the young woman had been keeping much from those around her over the years, had become a master of obscuring her emotions, of sneaking off. Now, she had a considerable advantage. She had ample magic at her disposal to protect herself in an emergency.

Seeing the look on her niece's face, Leana decided that it was time to divert her attention. There was no sense in allowing Ki'ara to continue to stress about the current situation. "Are you hungry?" she asked the contemplative young woman.

"Now that you mention it, I am ravenous! I don't think I have ever been this hungry before," Ki'ara replied with a laugh.

"I figured as much! You stay right there in that bed, love! Let me dash down to the kitchen and fetch some food for you! I will be back before you know it!"

It did not take long for Leana to return with a tray full of sumptuous edibles for her niece and mistress. On the maid's orders, things had been kept ready for when Ki'ara woke up. Magic adventures burned a lot of calories, which needed to be replenished and soon.

Ki'ara devoured the meal. It all tasted so much more intense than she could remember, just as if her taste buds had been asleep and had now come to life! This was definitely something new and a most welcome treat!

Looking around, Ki'ara realized that her vision was also sharper than it had been the previous day. She began to notice things that had escaped her until that moment. The texture of the walls, the play of the light across her bed, and the furniture, the gleam of the polished wood floor. It all took on a beauty she had never perceived until then. The colors appeared so much brighter, more vibrant, more alive than ever before.

Her hearing had become more astute as well. When she listened closely, she could tune into conversations and sounds she had formerly been unable to make out. She discovered that she could direct her attention to specific areas of the keep and overhear what was being said. This might really prove useful in figuring out what Ragnald had planned!

When the newness of her now highly developed senses wore off just a little, Ki'ara realized that with these new powers also came responsibilities. Just because one could do something did not mean one should. It was not polite to listen in on private conversations unless there was a good reason to do so, like protecting oneself. Ki'ara turned her hearing outward, beyond the walls of the castle.

Soon, she was enthralled by the birdsong surrounding the keep. Never before had she perceived anything this beautiful! To Ki'ara, it seemed that the birds were singing just for her, a tune of love and welcoming, a greeting to their new lord.

Now that Ki'ara had become aware of it, she grasped that all her senses had become more refined, including her touch. The bedspread felt so much more textured, her silk sheets so much smoother, slicker. She could distinguish every single thread on her blanket, feel each little hair on her arms.

"Leana, what has happened to me? My vision, hearing, and touch are so much sharper! Oh, and I can smell more as well," she laughed. "I can sense the land! It almost seems to be breathing, alive! I can feel the rivers dancing over the rocks as they work their way towards the sea, the lakes, the moors," Ki'ara continued after a minute.

Once again, the young woman paused before going on. "I can even feel the plants push their roots further into the earth and spread their leaves up into the sky. I am one with the very soil and everything in and on it. How did I get so blessed to receive this amazing connection?" she asked in wonder.

The maid regarded Ki'ara for a long moment. "The realm chooses its own ruler. Ragnald is the present lord, designated by your father. Most of the time, the oldest child becomes one with the land but not always. Sometimes, the prospective leader is rejected by the magic. Your brother managed to hide this," Leana explained.

"Ragnald will not be happy to hand over the reins. You will need allies if you want to survive this. Be very careful not to reveal what you have become," Leana cautioned yet once again. Ki'ara nodded her understanding and smiled at her friend.

⚜

The longer Ragnald had been in power, the worse things had become at the castle. The girl's aunt had been furious at the disrespect her niece had been subjected to when she had arrived home the previous day.

Leana feared for Ki'ara's safety for an excellent reason. Ragnald did not play fair, ever. He never had, and he never would. He had all kinds of vicious tricks up his sleeve and would kill his sister without a second's hesitation. The young woman was strong but much too gentle and kind and not devious enough to deal with the likes of the oldest MacClair.

'If only the StCloud were home!' Leana caught herself thinking. Unlike Ragnald, he was an honest and upstanding man. Conall would stand with Ki'ara in a heartbeat and help her take what was now rightfully hers. The sorceress was sure that the lord would protect the girl with his life if needed.

The land had spoken, the youngest sibling was the new Lord MacClair. Now it was just a matter of keeping Ki'ara alive long enough to assume the rule of the clan. Leana could not help it. She let out a sigh.

Chapter 37

A Torturous Evening

Ki'ara had remained in her room until it was time for dinner with her brothers. She had spent the afternoon meditating and exploring her new gifts. With the help of Leana, she had tried to develop an effective way to protect herself from the onslaught of intense sensations. Before long, the sorceress had come to the realization that it would take a while for her to adjust to her heightened senses.

Once the bell announced that it was time for the evening meal, Ki'ara went to join her siblings. When the young lady entered the dining room, she interrupted an angry discussion. The men were arguing over who would represent the family at a wedding in Deansport the next day.

By law, a member of the MacClairs had to attend. The bride and groom belonged to the clan, and it was part of the ruler's responsibility to appear at such functions. Now, her brothers were trying to decide which one of them would get stuck with this 'unwelcome' chore.

All the lords had been invited and, due to the high status of the happy couple, several of the chiefs would be there to share in the joyful occasion. There would be feasting, drinking, and dancing far into the night. Most of the Highlanders and Zidarians saw such a gathering as an excellent opportunity to strengthen relations and have a fun time.

Not so Ki'ara's two oldest siblings. Especially since, as it was customary, a council of lords would be held before the start of the festivities. Any problems needing the assembled rulers' attention would be addressed and dealt with.

Ragnald had been pushing the limits of what a chief could get away with and knew that it would not do to completely absent himself from these functions much longer. In this instance, however, he felt that sending a representative was perfectly legal.

Both the MacClair and Lyall resented having to follow the rules. They detested all gatherings of this kind as well as any others. They despised their fellow Zidarians and knew that the feeling was mutual. Therefore, the pair avoided getting around the other lords as much as they possibly could.

As it was, Ragnald was confident that nobody would miss them. He knew that the majority of their peers were only too happy not to have to deal with him and his younger brother.

As part of the duties assigned to the chiefs by the Zidhe, the lords or their legal representatives had to appear at such functions. Ragnald did not want to supply the Zidhe with an excuse to replace him as ruler, something which was bound to happen if he continued to ignore the elves' laws. Consequently, to avoid getting into trouble, one of his siblings had to attend.

Since they had no intention of going to this event, Ragnald and Lyall, therefore, were trying to apply progressively more pressure on their youngest brother. As usual, they had expected him to represent the MacClairs at the meeting, but so far, he was flat out refusing to comply with their wishes.

⚜

Unbeknownst to his siblings, Gawain had made other plans. He was loath to give up his date with a particular young lady down at the pub. Sure, he could attend the council and still make his rendezvous, but he just did not want to.

Gawain had enough and was feeling downright rebellious. He was balking for once. He realized that one of the family would have to go, but why did it always have to be him?

As lord, it was really Ragnald's duty to go to the council meetings and to keep apprised of current affairs in the Highlands. Gawain thought that it was high time that the laggard looked after his own responsibilities!

"I am not going to this one! I have attended all the other meetings you sent me to, but for once, I have other plans! Why don't you do your job for a change!" Gawain hissed at his oldest brother furiously just as Ki'ara entered the room.

⚜

Those angry words surprised even Gawain. Where had that come from? An abrupt hush had fallen over the place, and the servants had stopped in the midst of setting the table. The silence in the room was suddenly deafening.

All eyes turned to Gawain, and he squirmed uncomfortably in his seat. Usually, he was much more diplomatic and careful than this and never openly challenged his lord. As it was, Ragnald was staring at him like he had just spotted something he wanted to kill. The young man could see the fury building in those stone-cold orbs.

His bravado and rebelliousness deserted him, and Gawain shivered. His fear rose as he took in Ragnald's reaction to his brash words. 'Maybe I have pushed it too far! How can I best diffuse this and quickly?' he thought desperately. He needed to come up with an idea to divert this building wrath away from himself.

⁕⁕⁕

The youngest MacClair looked around frantically. He needed a diversion and fast. Gawain's gaze lit upon his sister. "Let Ki'ara go instead of me! She has been missing out on all the fun while she was away studying! Why can't she take a turn?" he proposed flippantly.

Gawain hated putting this off on his sister, but at the moment, she was all he could think of. He could not help feeling guilty and intended to apologize later. He knew that Ki'ara did her utmost to avoid Ragnald's notice as well as his ire, and he had just focused the full force of his attention on her.

"Great suggestion, brother! Now, why did I not think of this? And, you can go with her to make sure that none of the lads get any dumb ideas and that we are well represented! That should do perfectly to appease the council and avoid bringing trouble down on this clan," came Ragnald's sarcastic reply. The lord was so furious he spat the words out through clenched teeth. His hate-filled glare dared his younger siblings to voice an objection.

Gawain made a face but did not protest. He was only too happy for the reprieve and loath to push his luck any further. He would have to change his plans, but he was sure that the lady would understand and allow him to reschedule their date.

Ragnald's response had greatly surprised him. Ki'ara attend a council meeting and the wedding? This outcome was completely unexpected. Gawain had been grasping at straws and had never anticipated that the MacClair would actually agree to his proposition.

✦

Within seconds of his offhand comment, Gawain had seriously regretted not keeping his mouth shut. He had been so angry that the words had just slipped out. What had possessed him to openly challenge his oldest brother and lord? No good ever came of such confrontations! Ragnald had almost killed Ki'ara for less!

Not that Gawain's resentment was without cause. He had been attending the majority of the mandatory events since Ragnald became ruler. Against his will, he had become the official family representative and had been forced to make most of the choices for the realm.

To top it all off, the MacClair had punished Gawain severely every time one of the decisions his youngest brother had agreed to displeased him.

✦

The haughty Ragnald had nothing but contempt for the council and his fellow rulers. Since he had taken charge, he had only attended the functions if his presence was explicitly demanded by the other lords or the elves. Even then, he had only shown up half of the time.

In a couple of those instances, when the MacClair had been forced to appear, the arrogant ruler had been severely chastised for the treatment of his sister or his people. He had been advised that his disregard of the laws laid down by the Zidhe would not be tolerated much longer.

On each of those occasions, the MacClair had returned home fuming. It was beyond his understanding why the council would interfere in the governing of HIS clan and HIS lands when all he had done was bring back the laws his grandfather had instituted. In Ragnald's view, a return to the old ways had been long overdue.

As far as the defiant lord was concerned, Raghnall MacClair had known how to reign better than any of the present rulers. Ragnald had nothing but veneration for his ancestor. No one had dared to question him or disobey him! His idol had stood up to the council and all those who dared to challenge him whenever he felt like it!

His grandfather had done pretty much as he pleased right up to the day he and that despicable StCloud disappeared. His son had taken over as chief. Ragnald could not comprehend how such a strong man like Raghnall could have sired a pushover like Mikael but figured that sometimes family traits just skipped a generation.

In Ragnald's opinion, his father had been weak and much too tolerant. He had coddled his subordinates and made their life much too easy. The MacClair felt incredibly blessed to have inherited Raghnall's admirable qualities instead of his dad's. He had no intention of repeating Mikael's mistakes.

The proud lord preferred the old ways. Ragnald saw himself as the absolute ruler of his realm with power over the lives and deaths of all those under his control. He felt that what he did in his own domain was up to him and that neither the council nor the Zidhe had any rights or business to tell him how to conduct his affairs.

The MacClair, therefore, had ignored all the well-meant warnings he had received over the years. Ragnald saw himself above the other chiefs and even the elves. He was determined to one day take his rightful place as their overlord. As far as he was concerned, the council was all talk and no actions anyhow.

One day he would make them all pay for their insolence, starting with the traitor to their family, his uncle, Lord Elvinstone.

Making his youngest brother attend the council meetings was the MacClair's not so subtle way to snub the other chiefs. They had soon realized that Ragnald ignored most of the agreements the young man worked out with the other rulers, which made Gawain's position at the assemblies even more uncomfortable, something which immensely pleased the cruel lord.

A couple of times, when he had needed Gawain to take care of problems elsewhere, the MacClair had made Lyall go in his place. His favorite brother had complained about this imposition bitterly for weeks after and only stopped when Ragnald promised to never send him again.

As far as the lord and Lyall were concerned, matters for the upcoming wedding were all settled. Gawain, however, looked around the table in helpless fury.

Once again, he was the one forced to stand in for the family. The young man resented Ragnald for pushing his responsibilities off on him while allowing their brother to shirk all public appearances.

Everybody knew that the mousy Lyall was incredibly uncomfortable around strangers. Had it been anyone else, the MacClair would have told them to get over it, but he indulged his favorite sibling most of the time. Ragnald even went as far as to cover for him if he had to.

Gawain knew how much his older brother had hated attending the meetings on those occasions when he had been sent elsewhere and had been unavailable to act as the family representative. He could not help but feel a perverse sense of glee at the thought that Ragnald had to deal with the council himself for a change.

That small satisfaction, however, did not make up for having to be present at the upcoming wedding. Gawain was not about to say so right then, but he saw no good reason why his sister could not go by herself.

※

Ki'ara was well-liked by the other lords, she was courteous and socially more adept than any of her brothers, including himself. Gawain had no illusions about that. She had a grace and poise that he could only admire and love, especially since it really irritated their older siblings.

Why did anyone have to go along to babysit such a beautiful and confident young woman? She did not need a chaperone nor someone to guard her. Gawain was certain Ragnald had just ordered him to go because he had dared to defy his authority and because the lord was now aware that he had something else he had wanted to do.

Their sister was perfectly capable of protecting herself as well as handling any unruly kinsmen. Ki'ara had studied magic for years. She was a skilled sorceress. Gawain figured that her life was more in peril here at the castle than elsewhere. Most people loved the vivacious young woman. The reason he was being sent was as punishment, nothing else.

Then, a sudden thought occurred to the young man, and he felt like he had just been doused with ice water. What was their brother up to? There had to be an ulterior motive for this sudden change of attitude towards Ki'ara, with Ragnald there always was.

The MacClair never did anything out of the goodness of his heart, he ALWAYS had a hidden agenda.

※

Gawain had been mortified when he had blurted out the suggestion. It had been the first thing that had come to his mind. He deeply regretted those words now and had never expected Ragnald to agree to it since it was truly unprecedented. He had usually kept the young woman a virtual prisoner whenever she was home.

Over the years, the controlling lord had not allowed their sister to go anywhere if he could help it, especially not to an occasion where she could speak unsupervised to the other Zidarians. Their brother was always afraid that Ki'ara could divulge the true extent of the cruel treatment she was being subjected to by her own family.

For a moment, Gawain considered the possibility that Ragnald felt that it was safe for Ki'ara to attend the ceremony since the only other perceived threat to the paranoid lord, the StCloud, was far away at the moment. He quickly discarded this notion. Somehow, it did not feel right. There was more going on here.

This wedding would be attended by a fair number of Zidarians. Ragnald would not want their sister talking to them if he could possibly help it.

The troubled Gawain suddenly had an awful feeling. He had learned to trust his gut and was convinced that Ragnald was up to something. The MacClair saw Ki'ara as a risk to his grandiose plans. Just because she was their sister would not stop him from doing her harm.

What did their brother have planned? Gawain decided that he would keep a very close eye on the situation and do a bit of snooping about. Maybe he could uncover the plot and prevent its execution. He was resolved to keep Ragnald from hurting Ki'ara. It was deplorable that she would not be out of danger until they reached the wedding.

Maybe it was time he talked to their uncle again, Lord Iain. Gawain decided to send him a message. He was determined to make sure his sister came to no harm. His instincts told him that every day Ki'ara spent at Seamuir

Castle, her life was in peril. It would be best if she went to live elsewhere and soon.

⁘

The wedding would be a weekend affair, and they were not expected to return for several days. Gawain felt that he needed to act. He loved Ki'ara. She was the only one of his siblings he really cared about. Maybe it was time for both of them to find another place to reside. Seamuir Castle was most certainly no longer much of a home.

He made up his mind to talk to his sister's maid about the situation. Gawain would put the packing and smuggling out of their things into her capable hands. He trusted the woman, always had.

Leana was fiercely loyal to Ki'ara and a master of accomplishing the impossible. Good thing Ragnald was not aware of the servant's talents, or he would have done away with her long ago!

Gawain figured that a couple extra suitcases could be hidden in the carriage without arousing suspicion. The rest could be concealed in outgoing wagons. Since he and Ki'ara would be representing the clan, Ragnald would expect them to look their best at all times.

His sister, therefore, would need her maid and a fair amount of luggage to accomplish this properly and to meet their brother's high expectations of her.

'It is too bad the StCloud is off traveling somewhere! He would have been only too happy to assist Ki'ara and me in our escape! I am sure he would have given us shelter,' Gawain could not help thinking.

He actually liked the lord, especially since he knew how much his oldest brother hated the personable ruler. That man would do anything for Ki'ara, that was for sure!

⁘

Ragnald loathed Conall with a passion, one that went beyond all reason. As far as Gawain was concerned, the

Lord of Cloudshire Hall had never done anything to their family to deserve such feelings. Their grandfather had more than earned his fate, he had it coming!

The StCloud loved their sister with all his heart. He had been invited to come for a visit shortly after the baby had arrived at Seamuir with her proud parents. Conall had adored Ki'ara from the very first moment he had laid eyes on her. Just like her youngest brother, the man had been instantly smitten.

Gawain was convinced that if the lord were aware that the young woman was in danger, he would do everything possible to come to her aid. He still loved her after all these years. Maybe their uncle could reach him somehow?

Ragnald had mentioned that he was hoping that the man had finally given up on marrying their sister and was off somewhere else looking for a suitable wife. After all, there were plenty of women who would jump at the chance to become Lady StCloud.

Who could have blamed Conall for taking another bride? Ragnald had broken the arrangement their father had made and had cut all ties between the two clans. The MacClair had even threatened the other lord with death if he dared to go near Ki'ara.

As far as Gawain was concerned, no sane Zidarian would willingly marry into this crazy family!

※※※

Now that he had made the decision not to return to Seamuir Castle, Gawain intended to keep his date after all. The young man was tired of being terrorized and treated like his brothers' lackey. Being clanless was better than the life he had been leading these last few years! His only regret was that this would make things worse for their people.

'I am done doing as I am told!' the fuming Gawain thought to himself. He saw no reason why he should accompany Ki'ara to the council or the wedding. She would be safe among the other lords. He intended to drop by later that day to plead for sanctuary with their uncle, something he was sure would be granted and sanctioned by the other rulers at the breakfast meeting the following morning.

Ki'ara was perfectly capable of handling all the political aspects of the meeting preceding the festivities, the StCloud and Mikael had made sure of that. She had been oppressed long enough by their brother. It was time she remembered who she truly was and took her place among the other Zidarians!

All the women in the other families had equal status with the men and were accepted as representatives of the clan. Gawain knew that Ki'ara had always conducted herself with honor and obeyed Ragnald's commands. She had stayed away from the StCloud as ordered even if doing so had just about broken her heart.

Gawain had realized that the only way to maintain a semblance of peace and to keep her life in the castle bearable had been for Ki'ara to do as she was told. Some of the orders issued by Ragnald had been downright bizarre. They were meant to make her life as miserable and lonely as possible. Still, the girl had heeded them most of the time.

There was only one thing she had secretly defied the MacClair on. Gawain had always known that Ki'ara seized any available opportunity to sneak out onto the moors. She had done so all her life and had continued to go for her hikes in spite of Ragnald strictly forbidding her to leave the castle without his permission.

꧁ꕥ꧂

Since he found some of the rules Ki'ara had been subjected to rather ridiculous, Gawain had never told on her. He had no understanding of the way Ragnald treated the girl. Why keep her a near-prisoner in the family's home? Their sister was a kind and very beautiful person who was well versed in how to conduct herself properly.

In the first place, what was wrong with her going for a walk all alone? Her parents had never had a problem with that! The way Gawain saw it, Ragnald had done everything he could to make Ki'ara's life as wretched as possible. Not that his existence, as the youngest and unwanted brother, had been much easier, but he, at least, had retained some freedom.

Gawain was tired of being treated like a servant and of carrying a lot of the responsibilities. He was sick of walking on eggshells around his volatile brothers, of being the scapegoat, of being abused. All he wanted was to live in peace and without fear.

None of the other Zidarian lords governed or behaved like the MacClair. He ignored the council and had broken the laws laid down by the Zidhe on multiple occasions. His idol, their grandfather, had paid the price for his disregard of the rules. How was it possible that Ragnald had gotten away with this for so long?

Regardless of the way he had been treated, Gawain still loved his brother. He just did not like him very much and suspected that Ki'ara felt the same way. Nevertheless, they were family. The young man hoped that someone could talk some sense into Ragnald before he shared the deadly fate of their arrogant ancestor.

Putting these morbid thoughts aside, Gawain shot his brother a furtive look. Ragnald seemed unusually pleased with himself. He was definitely up to no good!

The MacClair, as usual, was not interested in Gawain's feelings. He had decided, and that was that. Ragnald couldn't have cared less if his two youngest siblings liked his decisions or not. He was the lord, and they would do as they were told.

Secretly, Ragnald was filled with glee. He had a hard time keeping a straight face and hiding his elation. Gawain had just provided him with the perfect opportunity to carry out his latest plan to get rid of the hated abomination.

⚜

Dinner turned out to be a reasonably peaceful affair once things settled down. Ragnald seemed to be in an uncharacteristically good mood. The brothers talked, but Ki'ara remained quiet.

She listened to the banter between her siblings but did not allow herself to be drawn into the conversation. It was best to just pay attention and observe.

Gawain was a great source of information. He loved the local gossip, the juicier, the better, and had a knack for finding things out. He now regaled Ki'ara with some of the events that had taken place while she had been away. Just like his sister, the young man was a talented storyteller and knew how to spin a yarn in such a way that his audience never lost interest.

Ki'ara paid close attention. She appreciated getting caught up on more of the local news. Gawain was giving her vital insights that would keep her from committing possible faux pas at the wedding. It would be much easier to move among the other Zidarians with confidence if she was aware of the latest developments.

⚜

The young lady had not missed the flash of defiance in Gawain's eyes when he thought himself unobserved. Ki'ara had the feeling that she would be attending the wedding alone. She figured that her brother had other plans for the next day and that they did not include accompanying her.

It seemed her favorite sibling had just about had enough of their tyrannical brother. Ki'ara could not blame him, he had a right to a life of his own. Ragnald would never know that Gawain had gone off unless he decided to check on them with his magic mirror.

The sorceress assumed that she would find out about his plans soon enough. Gawain was purposely imparting very valuable knowledge to her disguised as entertaining stories. She smiled at him gratefully.

The last thing she wanted to do was to give offense in her ignorance of current affairs. She needed allies, not enemies.

As the evening wore on, the conversation around the table covered many different subjects. It touched on a multitude of people. The one person her brothers never spoke of, however, was Ragnald's archenemy and her once best friend, the StCloud. It was almost as if they feared that mentioning the hated name would draw his very presence into their midst.

In a way, Conall seemed to hang like a ghostly apparition over their heads. Ki'ara was secretly amused at the length her siblings went to in order to avoid acknowledging the StCloud. Talk about giving something you do not want power!

The hidden animosity made Ki'ara sad. Why could her brother not leave the past where it belonged? What possible sense was there in carrying on these ancient grudges? Some went back hundreds of years!

Their father had never felt this way, so why did Ragnald?

Finally, the meal drew to a close. When her brothers prepared to retire to the library for their customary after-dinner drinks, Ki'ara got up and made her excuses. She felt immensely relieved that the ordeal was over.

It took every ounce of her willpower not to rush from the room. Instead, she bid them goodnight one by one. Gawain was the only one who reached out to hug her.

Ragnald avoided touching her entirely and even shrunk back when she came near him.

Once the MacClair had granted her permission to leave, the young woman quickly headed back towards her chambers. When she reached the stairs, she stopped for a moment. For the first time since entering the dining room, she felt like she could breathe freely.

Ki'ara felt drained after spending this time with her siblings. Their emotions had washed over her like waves, and, at times, it had been hard to concentrate on the conversation. The usually surly Ragnald seemed to have been very pleased about something. That alone was enough to make her suspicious.

What was he up to? Ki'ara decided that she would have to be extra careful and watch out for the unexpected every single minute from now on. Having to be so on guard filled her with great sorrow. She missed the days when she had felt safe and protected in this house.

Ki'ara took several deep breaths to calm herself. She managed to let some of the anxiety she was feeling flow away but could not shake the feeling that she was in imminent danger. Maybe Leana could help her figure out what was coming her way.

⁘⁂⁘

The dinner had been taxing, and she was glad that it was over. For Ki'ara, it had been worse than usual. She had sensed her siblings' feelings even more intense than before. Ragnald's profound resentment of her tinged with stark hatred, Lyall's indifference, and Gawain's unhappiness, anger, and sadness had deeply affected her.

On the surface, everything had appeared to be fine, but the underlying tension had been so thick it had been palpable to everyone in the room. The servants had felt it and had been so on edge that they had continued to drop things.

Ki'ara had noticed that Ragnald had watched her closely the entire evening. She had felt his calculating gaze on her every few minutes while they had been listening to Gawain's stories. It had given her the creeps. She had felt like some sort of specimen ready to be dissected at any moment. It had taken all her will not to start fidgeting under that merciless glare.

Ragnald's hidden hostility and aggression had affected Ki'ara almost physically. She had also picked up on his barely suppressed glee, and it had filled her with a sense of foreboding she had been unable to shake.

What had outwardly been a reasonably pleasant dinner, had been a torturous evening for her. At times, she had wanted to rush from the room just to escape the onslaught of antagonistic emotions.

The meal with her family had left Ki'ara with a throbbing headache and a nagging sense of unease.

Chapter 38

Increased Sensitivity

Her dreamlike encounter with the magic of the land the night before seemed to have affected Ki'ara more than she had first assumed. She had grown much more sensitive to people's emotions than ever before. Her shielding protected her from harm but not from the influx of feelings assaulting her senses.

It had been almost unbearable for Ki'ara to be in the same room with her siblings. The scene she had walked in on had been bristling with hostility. The MacClair and Lyall had apparently been bullying Gawain, who had finally snapped. She had been so proud of him, but the blast of fury coming from Ragnald would have been enough to cow even the bravest of souls.

The incident had given Ki'ara an entirely new insight into what Gawain's situation was like here at Seamuir Castle. She had been gone so much and preoccupied with her own problems when she was present that it had not dawned on her how difficult life was for her favorite brother. He had never complained, had never said a word about the treatment he was receiving.

Gawain had always been there to help her, had even protected her from Ragnald on several occasions. This must have made his already unpleasant circumstances here even worse. He had nowhere to escape to. Having been sent off suddenly did not seem so bad anymore.

As far as Ki'ara was concerned, the MacClair was acting like a vindictive tyrant. Did he have love or compassion for anyone? Maybe for Lyall but apparently not for the rest of his family nor for the people of his clan or the magic of the land.

Having his little brother stand up to him had really infuriated Ragnald. Ki'ara was sure that the lord had seen it as the worst kind of betrayal, something he would never forgive. It had required some serious courage for Gawain to take her side all those times, and she deeply admired him for that.

⚜

The barely contained aggression between her siblings during the dinner had set Ki'ara's teeth on edge. Each one of her brothers had been hiding his true feelings. It had been difficult for her to deal with the simmering fury interspersed with strange flashes of glee coming from Ragnald, the anger and annoyance from Lyall, and the resentment tinged with anxiety from Gawain.

Her experience with the magic had knocked her off balance. It had left her feeling as wide open and defenseless as she had been as a very young child. Ki'ara had been very vulnerable to people's moods then. Negative emotions had even affected her physically and had caused nausea and headaches. It had taken some time, but with the help of her parents and the StCloud, Ki'ara had learned to cope. All this had changed in one night.

None of the techniques Ki'ara had learned over the years were enough anymore. Since her interaction with the magic, her sensitivity had risen to an entirely new level. If not for the iron control she had over her body, she would have gotten sick on several occasions during the meal.

The young woman intensely disliked being so vulnerable. She regarded it as a weakness to be overcome. Ki'ara made up her mind. She would find a way to avoid letting the feelings of other's pain her this much. She realized that she would have to come up with a creative method to make all those incoming sensations flow around her. Maybe some of the techniques she had learned over the years could be adapted to serve her needs now.

All the power which had coursed through Ki'ara during her interaction with the realm's magic had left her senses raw. Knowing her own capabilities and resilience, the young lady was confident that she would figure out how to feel more centered within a few days.

For now, however, Ki'ara decided that she would have to be prudent and not expose herself to her oldest siblings any more than she had to. It was with great relief that she entered the welcoming sanctuary of her candlelit chambers.

Leana had made the room as pleasant and as soothing as possible. She was waiting for Ki'ara. The attentive woman knew the MacClair brothers' habits quite well and had been confident that their sister would not join them for drinks. She never did.

The maid feared that after the young woman's experience with the magic of the land, it would be even more difficult than before for Ki'ara to be in the company of the three of them for any length of time.

To be around the two oldest MacClairs was a challenge for just about everyone. The clan leader and his cohort Lyall treated most people with an arrogance and indifference, which had not been seen since the Zidarians' time as kings. To make things worse, any judgments Ragnald made were arbitrary and often unfair.

It had not taken the members of the clan long to figure out that no good ever came from seeking help from their lord. They had stopped bringing their problems to their ruler and avoided dealings with him, if at all possible. Leana had watched this with incredulity. How had Ragnald managed to fool his father so completely?

Most lords looked after the realm and lands for a few hundred years. They were usually happy to retire at that point and reclaim their own lives. During the passing of power ceremony, the 'Choosing,' the magic was relinquished by the reigning lord. If the successor was acceptable, he or she became the next ruler.

Most of the Zidarian lords were honest, some to a fault. They would not expect one of their own to lie to them like the MacClair had. Leana had always suspected that Ragnald's connection to the magic had been gained by force and was not what it should be. Somehow, he had managed to successfully deceive his father as well as the council.

So far, Ragnald had gotten away with the sham and the abuse of the power granted to him. When no one came to the aid of the land and the clan, the magic had selected its own champion. It seemed that it had finally had enough.

The choosing of a new lord in this fashion and the power's willingness to assist with the dethroning of the sitting leader was unheard of. As far as Leana knew, this had never happened before since the founding of the Zidarian clans.

Leana had been stunned when she had realized the magic's intentions. She was convinced that Ki'ara would need all the help she could get to navigate these unchartered waters. Typically, a new lord was given several days to adjust to his or her heightened senses. The ruler would withdraw for a time until he or she once again felt emotionally stable. For Ki'ara, such an option was not possible while she lived here at Seamuir Castle. To survive, she had to hide who she had become.

The enchantress had suspected that this evening would be especially challenging for her niece. Therefore, she had prepared a soothing pot of tea and sweetened it with a couple teaspoons of local honey. Leana had also added a spell that would help to calm the girl's nerves. The steaming cup was now sitting on the hearth, ready for Ki'ara.

From the look of the young woman when she came into the room, it was evident that she needed some comforting rather badly. Ki'ara's face was pale, and her cheeks flushed. Her shoulders slumped as she closed the door behind herself, and she let out a sigh of relief.

The maid had known this girl from a babe on and could tell that she had a headache. Without saying a word, Leana opened her arms. Ki'ara gladly rushed into her loving embrace. The young woman's nerves were so badly frayed that her entire body felt cold, and she was shaking. She clung to her friend for a long moment before composing herself and stepping back.

Leana gently guided Ki'ara to a chair by the fire. She wrapped a blanket around her and made sure that her niece was warm and comfortable before handing her the cup of tea. The youngest MacClair gratefully accepted the hot drink and took a sip. Tasting the calming herbs, she smiled up at her confidante, who was expertly rubbing the girl's tensed up neck and shoulders.

"Thank you, Leana. You always know just what I need. What would I do without you?" Ki'ara exclaimed softly. "Being around them is never easy. I am so exhausted, but for some reason, all my senses are tingling with alarm. Ragnald is up to no good, I am sure of it!"

"You should have felt the glee coming off him! I thought I was going to get sick every time I sensed that! I have no idea what he is planning, but I am certain that he thinks that he has found a new way to get away with doing me harm. I can feel it in my gut!" she continued, looking up at her friend with eyes filled with anxiety.

With a resigned sigh, Ki'ara placed the side of her face against her friend's hand. The gesture reminded Leana vividly of how the girl had acted when she was tired or weary as a child. It showed her the real depth of worry in her young niece.

"What happened during dinner? What exactly did you pick up from him?" the enchantress asked urgently. She was stroking Ki'ara's hair, giving her what comfort she could. To safeguard the girl effectively, however, Leana needed all the information she could get. They had to talk.

If Ki'ara was that alarmed, there was a good reason for it; of this, Leana was certain. She kept asking questions until she was sure that she had a thorough comprehension of the situation. It did not take the enchantress long to understand the young woman's concerns.

Ragnald was capable of anything and did not play by the rules. He was not a happy man, very seldom smiled, and almost never laughed. Without fail, if he was delighted about something, it bode ill for someone else.

"Ki'ara, you will need to be extra careful. Please, my sweet, be prepared for anything from now on. We are both only too aware what Ragnald is like. I fear for you, child. Make sure you shield yourself at all times and never, not even for a second, let your guard down!" Leana cautioned.

"We need to add some more defenses to this chamber, my love. I know you are tired, but this has to be done. Adding your power to mine will make the enchantments harder to break no matter what unearthly magic that brother of yours brings into play!" the maid continued.

For more than an hour, Leana and Ki'ara worked together to increase the protection around the suite and to modify the existing enchantments. The situation had changed, and it no longer mattered if the MacClair detected their spells. Safety came first.

The two ladies placed a spell of warding on the door that was strong enough to keep Ragnald at bay for a good while, even if he did use some of the illegal incantations he had acquired. They were determined that no one would set foot into these rooms uninvited.

The magic would also alert the ladies the moment someone got near the door. This way, they would not be caught unawares. Having at least a little bit of warning would give them enough time to grab the few necessities they had packed and flee into the secret passage if needed. They would be long gone by the time Ragnald would finally manage to make his way into the chamber.

When she had first arrived at Seamuir all those years ago, Leana, together with her sister Ali'ana, had used her magic to create the escape route. They had made sure that it was well protected and isolated from the warren of passages running behind the thick walls of the fortress.

For additional security, the ladies had created two exits. One ended in a tunnel leading into the moors, the other near the stables, close to a hidden door through the walls. No one except Ki'ara had been told, not even Mikael had known about this secret precaution.

For the moment, Ki'ara was as safe as she could possibly be within the walls of Seamuir Castle. Still, Leana was not satisfied. Her niece's life was at stake. Not only was the girl her own flesh and blood, but she loved her like a daughter. She would never forgive herself if something happened to the young woman that she could have prevented.

Therefore, on Leana's suggestion, she and Ki'ara turned to the magic of the land for help. It appeared to have been waiting for the contact and flowed into them both with such an overwhelming sense of joy that it filled the two sorceresses with a giddy sense of delight.

Once they explained the situation, the exuberant power was willing and eager to further reinforce the defenses of the apartment. It excitedly wove itself around Ki'ara and sung with happiness and pure contentment. Here was a real lord, someone it could love and work with, not like that nasty man ruling the clan for the moment.

⸎

Dealing with the magic of the realm was almost like dealing with a small and very stubborn child. You had to win its cooperation by explaining the situation in such a way that it could grasp it. Still, it very much had a mind of its own, and it was determined to protect its new champion at all costs even if that meant killing the official ruler.

It had taken Leana a while to dissuade the impatient power from taking action. It had wanted to oust Ragnald immediately instead of waiting. Such a move could have turned ugly real fast for all those involved.

The maid had not wanted to put the girl in more danger, so she and the entity had worked out a compromise. The magic could protect Ki'ara but not give the change away while the new lord was this vulnerable. With poor grace, the petulant power promised to be patient for the moment but not for much longer and only as long as nothing else untoward happened.

Finally, Leana was convinced that everything that could possibly be done to keep the chambers safe had been accomplished. The enchantress pulled another chair over to the fire. She poured a steaming hot cup of tea for herself and Ki'ara and then sank into her seat with a relieved sigh. They could relax, at last!

The two women sat in companionable silence, sipping their hot beverage for several minutes. Each was lost in her own contemplations. The magic had settled down as well and was curled around them like a contented cat.

Ki'ara could not get their plans for the next day out of her mind. She was really looking forward to getting away from the castle. The young woman was only too aware that she would have to be on guard until she reached the wedding. How sad to be in more danger in one's own home than anywhere out there!

Her thoughts kept coming back to Ragnald. What was her brother up to? Ki'ara had no intention of giving him more opportunity to harm her than necessary. She would eat breakfast in her room and wait to go down until it was time to leave. This should significantly reduce the window of time for him to try something.

What was he planning? Ki'ara finally concluded that she was too tired to attempt to figure it out. Ragnald was so devious that there was no telling what he had come up with. Most people's minds would not go to the places her brother's did. It was comforting to have more power than he now, but still, it was always best to be prepared.

Ki'ara could not stop yawning. She decided that she would put off her contemplations of the danger she had sensed until morning. For the moment, all she wanted to do was relax in the safety of her room in the company of her friend and confidante. It was pleasant to be surrounded by the power of the land as well.

What was that sound? Ki'ara could have sworn she had just heard the magic purr with contentment. The idea made her smile and filled her with love.

Her aunt's thoughts, on the other hand, were of a very different nature. The wise Leana did not trust the lord and master of the castle. She had seen through his masquerade from the first day she had met the young man. Ali'ana had been suspicious of him as well but had tried to get along with the impossible cad for his father's sake.

Leana had heard that Ragnald had been a cruel and spiteful boy, even as a very young child. She could well believe it. Age and maturity had not improved him. The oldest MacClair had just gotten better at hiding his real self as he grew into adulthood, but compassion or niceness were not part of his makeup.

Ragnald had most certainly fooled his good-natured father. Mikael had been utterly blind to his oldest son's true disposition. Ali'ana had tried to warn him, but for once, the lord had not listened. Leaving their daughter in the present MacClair's hands had been his decision and against the wishes of the child's mother.

The pensive Leana feared for Ki'ara's life. Yes, the young woman had incredible capabilities, and the magic of the land was behind her, but Ragnald was sneaky and prone to fight dirty. He would stoop to methods his sister and most people would never even consider.

'I wished the StCloud were near to help me look out for my girl! That man knows a trick or two Ki'ara has never even heard off, and he loves her. I am sure Conall would take on Ragnald if he even thought that she was in danger!' Leana could not help thinking yet once again.

Both she and her niece were skilled sorceresses, but sometimes, ability alone was not enough. Who knew what spells Ragnald had amassed! Having Conall as an ally would have made them both feel just a bit better, and he would have been a stout supporter of Ki'ara's cause in the council!

Being so dishonest and without any scruples at all made the MacClair a danger to anyone who garnered his displeasure. Leana had watched him use incantations which were not of the land to accomplish his dirty deeds. This was strictly against the rules set down by the Zidhe, but so far, somehow, he had gotten away with it.

For a while now, the powerful enchantress, as well as the other rulers, had had their suspicions where Ragnald had gotten his illegal spells. Ki'ara had just confirmed this. With Mathus being back, it would not be hard to get the proof the council wanted. Getting that slimy wiesel of a man to talk would be easy. One simple, little spell should do it.

Leana had been keeping a close eye on the MacClair on Lord Iain's request. The reports she had secretly sent him had included all the details the maid could gather along with who had been harmed, how, and when. There was a long list of transgressions by now.

All those misdeeds should make it easier for Ki'ara to get the council on her side. With the other rulers' help, she could oust her brother more peacefully. Ragnald would not stand a chance. He would have to step down or else face the elves.

Not only the magic felt that it was past time that something was done about this rogue lord. The clan and the land deserved to be governed by someone other than him.

Once they had finished their tea, it did not take Leana long to get Ki'ara ready for bed. While brushing out the young woman's long red hair, the experienced enchantress explained to her niece what to expect for the next few days. She gave the girl some valuable tips on how best to deal with her new abilities.

Despite having slept for half the day, Ki'ara was tired again. Being so raw and unguarded after the experience of the previous night made being around people and their emotions plain exhausting for her. The young woman was looking forward to the welcome oblivion of Morpheus' arms.

Leana watched Ki'ara with love and concern. She was only too conscious that the young woman's new powers would take some adjusting to. Until the girl had a chance to fully explore and grow into her new abilities and get used to being so sensitive, her devoted aunt was prepared to do all she could to make it easier for her.

Chapter 39

The Gaining of Knowledge

As was her habit, Ki'ara snuggled down under the covers. She had pulled them as tightly around herself as she possibly could. The young woman was cozy and warm, but the blankets yielded no protection for her otherwise. Her senses were still being bombarded by a constant barrage of sounds, emotions, and thoughts.

Now that she was trying to relax, Ki'ara could sense what every single person in the entire castle was feeling and all at the same time. It was overwhelming, like a waterfall of constant uproar. Anything from happiness to despair was flooding in on her. Her shields would protect her from danger but not from this kind of assault.

After trying different grounding and protective techniques without success, Ki'ara could take it no longer. She turned to the magic of the land for help. It seemed to have been waiting for her request and responded almost instantly. A feeling of warmth enveloped her like a cocoon and shut out all but her own feelings. She sighed with relief.

Since assisting her had been so easy for the power, why had it not done this before? It appeared to be very eager to please. Ki'ara was puzzled for a moment but then remembered free will. That was it! The young woman realized that, if she wanted to receive aid, she had to ask for it. She could not help but laugh at herself.

How could she have forgotten something so fundamental? It had been her own fault that she had suffered all that intrusion! Ki'ara sent a silent thank you and her love out in return. As an answer, she perceived a wave of utter happiness and elation.

The magical entity of the land was beyond delighted. Finally, a lord who showed it some respect! An almost imperceptible purr filled the room, and the very air seemed to sparkle.

From the comfort of her bed, Ki'ara could look back upon the day with more detachment. She had shielded herself during the entire meal, but it had not been enough. Her senses were oversensitive right now, they had picked up even the slightest discord. She had known exactly what her brothers had been feeling, and it had hurt her, as always.

Why did her two older siblings resent her? As far as Ki'ara was aware, she had never done anything to them, which justified those emotions. Was it due to jealousy of all the attention Mikael had lavished on his youngest child? Or was there another reason? Even as a girl, she had felt that something was being hidden from her. Maybe, it was time she found out.

There were such turmoil and so much unhappiness here at the castle. Being subjected to all those feelings in addition to those of her family had made it even harder for the sorceress to maintain her composure.

Ki'ara was grateful to the magic for the shelter and protection from the storm of sentiments around her. It was wonderful to just deal with her own emotions once again. She would have to learn to handle this new ability before it drove her to distraction.

The picture of a ship's bow came to Ki'ara's mind. Then of a large rock with water streaming around it. Could she let the influx of sensations flow around her just like that? Could it be that easy? Would that keep the bombardment of emotions from touching her and affecting her so much? Somehow that seemed right. She would try it in the morning. For now, she needed some rest.

⊱⋆⊰

Before long, the young woman fell into a restless sleep. Time after time, she would wake only to sink back into slumber again. At first, her dreams were chaotic. She found herself in a dimly lit, seemingly endless space filled with a fog, both cold and cloying. A never-ending parade of strange and familiar faces kept swirling around her, but whenever she focused on one, it disappeared into the mist.

After several attempts to connect with the disembodied visitors only to have them vanish, Ki'ara became frustrated. Realizing that she was getting upset, the young woman decided to change the rules. This was her dream, after all.

Instead of reaching out, she stepped back. She began to observe without paying attention to any of the countenances in particular. Now, the specters were trying to engage with her, becoming more and more insistent the longer she ignored them. Soon, they had her completely surrounded. The faces were pushing right up against hers, and the young woman started to feel somewhat claustrophobic.

When Ki'ara refused to react despite getting more and more uncomfortable, the scene changed. Suddenly, she found herself in a pleasant garden full of the most enchanting flowers. Vibrant sunshine lit up well-kept paths meandering through a charming landscape. What a difference to the place she had been but a moment before!

Ki'ara looked around herself with delight. This was such a beautiful place! She had seen grounds like this but only far to the south and never ones as large as this. Best of all, she appeared to have them all to herself, something she cherished tremendously after the first part of her dream.

As she grew more peaceful, her breathing deepened, and her mind and body became calm. Ki'ara decided to explore her surroundings. There were groves with giant, ancient sequoia trees. Babbling brooks ran through some of these, and benches had been placed near the banks. Ki'ara could not resist. She sat for a moment and watched the sunlight play on the water. It was mesmerizing!

Realizing that she was drifting into a trancelike state, Ki'ara shook herself back to full awareness. What would have happened if she had remained here much longer? Maybe nothing but her instincts told her to be careful all the same. It was possible that this place was not without dangers of its own.

Stepping out from under the trees, Ki'ara headed for a more open section of this incredible park. She wandered around among the beds full of flowers. There was a profusion of colorful blooms everywhere she looked. The plants were all exceedingly healthy, and the young lady was stunned by the variety of shapes, forms, and sizes.

The flowers smelled heavenly! Every few steps, a different aroma wafted across to her. Ki'ara was enjoying herself immensely as she was walking along. Some of the plants she knew, but others she had never seen before in her life. Her curiosity was quickly getting the best of her.

As she was bumbling along, she spotted a huge flower off all by itself. It was exquisite and had been planted in a round bed bordered by decorative stones. A broad swath of grass separated it from all the other vegetation. The girl's interest was instantly piqued.

Ki'ara left the path to examine the object of her fascination. In the beginning, she perceived the odor only faintly, but it grew stronger with every inch she moved closer. The aroma was subtle yet powerful and seemed to stimulate all her senses.

Suddenly, Ki'ara came to a stop. Now that she was just a few feet away from the unusual plant, the scent in the air was heady. Surprisingly, it was also very familiar. She was sure that she had smelled this before, but where? Something told her that it had been a long time ago.

Finally, it came to her. The odor reminded her of the perfume she had been given by Conall on her 10th birthday! How much she had loved that incredible fragrance! She had used it only on special occasions and then only sparingly. How could she have forgotten something so precious to her?

⁘⸱🙠⸱⁘

Maybe the memory had been so painful, and her mind had blanked it out. After Mikael and Ali'ana had left, Ragnald had searched Ki'ara's room. She had managed to hide many of her prized possessions, but not all. The small bottle of perfume had caught her oldest brother's attention. With a wicked laugh, he had snatched up the ornate glass vessel.

From Ki'ara's anxious reaction, the MacClair had known instantly how much the item meant to his little sister. He had also remembered who had given it to her, that contemptible StCloud. Ragnald was determined that nothing that man had touched would remain in his house.

Giving the girl a look filled with pure malice, the cruel lord had walked over to the windows, all the while watching his sister. Sensing his intentions, Ki'ara had turned deathly white. Her eyes had been brimming with tears.

With a laugh as hateful as any the young lady had ever heard, Ragnald had leaned casually against the sill. Ever so slowly, he had extended his arm. Using only two fingers, he had held the perfume out into thin air. He had kept it there for several long minutes, all the while taunting his sibling. When he had grown bored with his wicked game, he had just dropped it.

The glass vial had shattered into a thousand pieces on the jagged rocks below. The precious liquid had seeped into the cracks among the moss-covered stones and had been lost to Ki'ara forever.

The girl had been heartbroken. The destruction of many of her other possessions had seemed trivial compared to this despicable act. This incident had been a good indication of things to come. The MacClair had turned out to be anything but the loving guardian he had promised to be.

From that day on, Ki'ara had hidden all those belongings which had special meaning to her. Ragnald never did find any of the clever places she had used for concealment.

Shaking off that gloomy recollection, Ki'ara once again inhaled the heavenly fragrance. Now that she could place the aroma, she realized that the flower did smell just like the perfume. How well she remembered it all of a sudden! This incident with Ragnald had been so hurtful that she had suppressed all recollection associated with it until now!

For a moment, the young woman stood there with her eyes closed, taking in the scent. Memories of Conall flooded her mind, and tears started to run down her cheeks. She vividly recalled the day he had presented her with that little bottle. Such a special present, just for her! Ki'ara had been overjoyed!

The perfume had been created by the StCloud with the help of the magic of his realm. It had been one of a kind. How much she wished that she still had that precious gift! The fragrance had been so unique that she had never even tried to replace it.

In some ways, her brother might have done her a favor. The scent would have always reminded Ki'ara of Conall. She would have never been able to wear it without feeling the pain of his loss. As it was, she still thought of him almost every day, even after all these years. Being able to reunite with him was one of her dearest wishes.

Ki'ara stood there for a few minutes longer, lost in visions of times long past. Her childhood had been happy, close to ideal. Her parents had loved her deeply, and they had spoiled her in countless ways. She had shared fascinating times with the StCloud. Why did it all have to end?

<hr/>

The sound of a chime finally startled the young woman out of her reverie. Curiously, she looked around. Something seemed to have changed while she had been preoccupied with her thoughts. Ki'ara could not detect an immediate threat, but she remained on high alert.

The hair started rising on her neck when she began to feel like she was being spied on. Ki'ara opened her senses but could not locate anything which presented an imminent peril. All that she could see were the magnificent plants with their remarkable blooms.

Suddenly, Ki'ara noticed eyes among the flowers. They were brown with long, dark lashes and hovered in mid-air. First, there was only one pair, then more and more. They were observing her intently and followed each move she made.

Ki'ara was no longer alarmed. The way those floating orbs watched her put her mind at ease. It had been a long time that she had been regarded with such gentleness, with so much emotion. That gaze made her feel warm all over and filled her with a strange sense of longing.

When she examined the eyes closer, Ki'ara realized that they all looked identical. Every one of them had the same color and tender expression, almost like they all belonged to just one person. How could this be? There were so many of them!

A stunning notion flashed into her mind. Somehow, these beautiful brown eyes seemed very familiar! They reminded her of someone, but who? They watched her with such love, it left her in awe. What must it be liked to be cherished this much? It had been so long that she had almost forgotten.

Her entire being started to vibrate with deep yearning. Ki'ara realized that she knew those eyes, but for the life of her, she could not recall to whom they belonged. It almost appeared as if something was keeping her from remembering. That could not be tolerated!

She noticed that one pair seemed more prominent than the rest. Ki'ara determinedly stepped closer, but then she hesitated for a moment. She suddenly felt unexplainably shy, and her stomach started to tighten. When the young woman finally found the courage to raise her eyes and meet that affectionate stare, she felt like she was drowning.

It had been years since she had felt anything like this. Just the memory made Ki'ara's mouth curve into a gentle smile. How wonderful a sensation! The young woman decided to give herself over completely to the moment.

Deeper and deeper, Ki'ara sank into that mesmerizing gaze. Everything around her faded away except those kind brown eyes and the love she saw in their dreamy depths.

If only this could last forever! It felt so good, like coming home, like reuniting with a lost part of herself. There was a sense of belonging, of peace here that she had missed for so many years.

For several minutes Ki'ara rested in this cloud of tender emotions. She felt sheltered and safe, a feeling she had not known since her parents' departure. A haunting tune came to her mind, and she began to hum the song in her sleep. When the magic joined in, everything around her turned bright and full of light.

Ki'ara drifted in that all-consuming whiteness for what seemed like an eternity. Her being had become part of the whole. She was one with all that was, had been, and ever would be. Knowledge which had been hidden from her until then took root in her brain.

When she had learned all that she could assimilate for the time being, Ki'ara started to wake. What an amazing experience this had been! The information she had gained was priceless. It supplied her with an edge when dealing with Ragnald. She could hide her abilities, survive his attacks.

Right before the young woman reached full consciousness, those remarkable eyes appeared to her yet once again. This time, Ki'ara met their gaze without any hesitation. They were smiling at her and so full of love that it made her heart skip a beat for an instant.

Having felt that connection one last time infused the young woman with happiness but also with a sense of profound loss. For her taste, the moment had been all too brief. She would have gladly spent an eternity drowning in those gentle brown orbs.

Sleepily, Ki'ara reflected on the dream. She was so very relaxed and filled with a sense that everything was going to turn out just fine. How, she was not sure. The means did not seem to matter, were not very important right now. Powers greater than herself were at work here.

Of one thing Ki'ara was certain. She would recognize those eyes the next time she saw them. How could she ever forget them? They were burned into her memory. Those warm brown orbs promised safety and unconditional love, they felt like home.

All she could do for the time being was trust and believe. Her instincts told her that this was precisely what was being asked of her. Ki'ara was under the protection of the magic of the land. Whatsoever was to come, she would survive, would thrive. Of this, she no longer had any doubt.

⚬

Ki'ara understood, however, that it was prudent to play it smart. Her instincts told her that before much longer, the Zidhe would have gotten involved in the MacClair Clan's situation. This never did bode well for the offender. She now had the ability to smooth things over, all she needed was the official sanction of the other lords.

The sorceress was determined to do anything in her power to make sure that her brother did not end up sharing the fate of his beloved idol, their grandfather. Ragnald had treated her cruelly and had never been much of a brother to her, but they were still family.

⚬

Feeling at peace, Ki'ara started to slide back into slumber. Her thoughts wandered back to those incredible eyes. All of a sudden, she was wide awake. She sat up in bed with a gasp, and instinctively, her hand covered her heart. A thought had flashed through her mind. Did those gentle, kind eyes belong to the StCloud?

Why had this not occurred to her before? After all, she thought of him all the time! Strange! It had been a long time since Ki'ara had seen Conall, but would she not recognize that gaze as his? Or, did she just want it to be his? Was this a case of wishful thinking?

Calming herself, Ki'ara looked inward. She emptied her mind, put aside all hopes and fears. From this place of detachment, she could evaluate her dream more objectively. Yes, those eyes had been the StClouds. She was convinced of that now.

Ki'ara had never stopped missing or loving Conall. He had haunted her waking hours as well as her dreams, and on occasions, the loss had felt almost unbearable. She was not sure she would ever be able to fully forgive Ragnald for what he had done.

✦⋇✦

Now that she was the lord of Fairholme Castle, Ki'ara could take charge of her own life. She could marry any available Zidarian noble she wanted, the choice would be hers and hers alone. For so long, her heart had belonged to one man. It still did, even if she had not seen or spoken to him in years.

She had made up her mind when she was very young. There was only one person she wanted to spend the rest of her life with, and he was Conall StCloud. Ki'ara was incredibly thankful that once again, this was a possibility. She just had to safely get away from Seamuir Castle, and that would happen the very next day! A blissful smile spread across the young woman's face, and her entire body relaxed.

With this new hope for the future, a deep sense of serenity and contentment filled Ki'ara. She laid back down and made herself comfortable. It was not long before, at last, the young woman slid into a peaceful sleep.

Chapter 40

A Gracious Gift

The next morning, Ki'ara was awake shortly before the sun crested the horizon. She headed over to her east window and curled up in the alcove created by the thick walls of the tower. She always kept pillows and a blanket in this space, which allowed her to watch the world around her in comfort.

Slowly, the dawn's soft light infused the realm and chased away the shadows. Ki'ara looked on as color spread across the highlands and gave definition to the landscape surrounding the castle. She never grew tired of witnessing this miracle. The Highlands were her home, and, as far as she was concerned, there was no place more beautiful.

The young woman loved these early hours. It did not matter if she was on the ocean or on land, Ki'ara did not believe that she would ever get sick of viewing the dawn. Seeing the sea change from dark grey to a vibrant deep blue as the brightness of the day increased or the land take on the first soft hues of green never failed to fill her with wonder.

This was her time, and it was precious to her. Ki'ara enjoyed the moment and meditated. She thought of all the things she had to be thankful for, and her mood lightened perceptively. There was nothing like gratefulness to help set the stage for a new day. No matter how bad things seemed, listing her blessings infused her heart with joy and peacefulness.

⁜

Ki'ara's chambers were in the south tower. Her parents' apartment had been right below hers. Ali'ana had preferred those bright and airy rooms to the dark and overstuffed master suite in the center of the keep. Those rooms had been furnished long ago by Raghnall MacClair and were a direct reflection of his pretentious taste and cruel personality.

Ki'ara's father had grown up with all the dark and heavy furnishings, and they did not bother him like they did his new wife. Mikael had shared these quarters with his first wife, Morena. He had seen no reason to redecorate the main apartment and was only too aware of how much this would have offended his oldest son Ragnald.

Until Ali'ana came along, the lord had never even considered the effect the place might have on a lady. At first, he had balked at moving, but Ki'ara's mother had explained to him that all the latent memories in those chambers were disturbing for her.

In the end, Mikael had been only too happy to start their new life in brighter environs. They had remodeled the entire south tower. Ali'ana had been allowed free reign in the decorations as well as the furniture. She had created an atmosphere of light and peacefulness, which suited her temperament much better.

When their daughter had gotten too old for the nursery, she had been permitted to move into the quarters above the couple. Ki'ara had loved the apartment since it gave her a bit more privacy, and she had a fantastic view. One of her windows looked out over the sea, another over the inland moors, and the one from her bath over the castle yard. Her rooms had always been her favorite place in the entire fortress.

⁂

This morning, fog billowing up from the sea was hanging over the rugged landscape. At brief moments, the sun managed to send a few wavering beams through the thick whiteness. The details of the land surrounding the castle appeared blurry and mysterious and reminiscent of a dreamscape.

Ki'ara adored days like this. She had always envisioned all kinds of creatures hiding in the mist. The reality had been even more amazing than she could have ever imagined. The young woman felt incredibly blessed to have been allowed to meet the unseen residents of Eastmuir.

A deep love for her home and all its inhabitants filled her heart to overflowing. As Ki'ara sent those feelings out towards the realm, they were returned many folds by the very magic of the land itself. She could sense its happiness at the contact with her and for being acknowledged. It seemed this had not happened in a long time.

How could Ragnald have neglected the power so thoroughly? He had been taught to respect the magic, to cherish it, and to treat it as the sentient being it was. Ki'ara herself had sat in on those lessons. Their father had wanted to make sure that all his children understood the connection with the realm and knew how to value it.

What had happened to her brother to make him so callous, so uncaring? He had been loved by his parents and siblings, and, from what she had been told, his grandfather had just adored him. Where did this meanness of spirit come from? Certainly not from Mikael nor from Morena who had been gentle and kind.

⁜

After getting dressed with Leana's help, the young woman sneaked out for her usual morning walk. She had gotten very good at moving about the castle while evading detection in the last few years. Not being seen or running into her siblings was always best as far as Ki'ara was concerned.

As much as she avoided the human inhabitants of Seamuir, she appreciated the many animals residing within. She loved having their company on her hikes across the land. Soon, several of the castle's dogs were exuberantly racing along beside her. They followed Ki'ara across the moor and into the uplands. For a little while, even one of the cats had tagged along.

The hounds were racing around the young sorceress, happy to be out of the yard and with someone who loved them. Many had welts on their backs and sides. They were much skinnier than they used to be, and it was evident that they were being abused and neglected.

Their handlers had not been treating them well, yet another thing Ki'ara intended to change immediately once she took over as lord. She had sneaked the poor animals some food before they had set out. The hounds had been so hungry that it had broken her heart to see them like that. Now, fed and feeling much improved, the dogs enjoyed nothing better than an outing with their kindhearted friend.

⁜

Ki'ara found herself heading towards one of the places of old, located not far from the castle, further up in the hills. It was one of the sacred spots of the Highlands, well hidden in one of the valleys. The ancient ring of stones seemed to have an irresistible draw for her this morning. Realizing that there must be a good reason for that feeling, she stopped fighting the urge.

Ki'ara had found the site by chance as a young girl. It had intrigued her from the very first moment, and curiosity kept bringing her back. Whenever she could, she had spent many hours sitting among the stones meditating or examining the rocks carefully. What secrets did these huge boulders hold? Who had placed them there? She had so wanted to know.

Now that she was more aware, more in touch with the land, all the circle's mysteries were laid bare for her. Nothing about it was concealed from her any longer. For the first time, Ki'ara sensed the power hidden here, and she was awed. There was a presence here, an ancient one, predating the Zidhe, and it had called her, demanded her attendance.

As soon as the young woman neared the circle, her excited companions stopped their running about. They had been here before with her, but this time felt different. They could sense that something had changed.

As Ki'ara stepped within, they whined unhappily and attempted to follow. No matter how hard they tried, none of them could cross within. In fear, they retreated a few steps and milled about, very clearly full of anxiety.

Suddenly, the hounds' ears perked up. As if they had been given a silent command, they spread out around the outer perimeter of the ancient ring of stones. The dogs took up guard positions. Gone was all hesitancy, fear, and insecurity. Their stance was one of confidence and alertness, and they seemed to have grown, filled out. No playfulness remained; they were all business. None would be able to approach while their mistress was busy within.

The girl immediately felt the increase in energy as she stepped between the massive boulders. It amazed her that she had never sensed this before as much time as she had spent here. Ki'ara felt an intense pull from the largest of the stones. With deep reverence for the magic gathered in this sacred space, she knelt before it and lowered her head in respect.

For a while, there was only silence, but then, a gust of wind rustled her hair, and a gentle voice suddenly appeared in her mind. "Greetings, young one, and well met. We have found you worthy and offer you the gift of power. Do you accept?"

Ki'ara was so stunned that she was speechless for several moments. This had to be about the magic of the land. What else could it be? She had believed that she was already lord. Had she been wrong? Did she have a conscious choice after all? Should she decline for Ragnald's sake?

✦

Thinking that it was up to her to accept or refuse the rule of the clan, the young lady decided to weigh the options. Ki'ara believed that there had to be some good in her brother. She felt that he would have been a better lord had he let go of his obsession with turning back time and his hatred of the StClouds. Was that enough, however, to allow him to continue on as he had?

The oldest MacClair had made the conscious choice to treat the members of their clan and the magic of the land without respect. He had failed to honor his obligations. Every time Ki'ara had been home, she had witnessed the clansmen's increased avoidance of their lord. They rather dealt with things by themselves than come to him for justice of any kind. It had upset her that their people no longer had a ruler they could trust. Was it fair to let this continue?

Then, there was the realm. Ragnald had not been keeping things up. The roads were in terrible shape, the harbor overdue for dredging, bridges needed to be repaired, emergency shelters restocked and cleaned. It seemed her brother had neglected to see to these duties completely.

Another consideration was the magic. From her contact with the power, Ki'ara knew how much it had been abused and neglected. It was sentient and had feelings, not unlike a small child. How much had it suffered to see itself forced to take action against the MacClair?

Also, Ragnald would not listen to reason. His behavior and misdeeds had come to the attention of the council. He had been advised several times to improve his performance and see to his responsibilities. This had only infuriated her arrogant sibling. He had grumbled for weeks. How dare those nitwits try to tell him what to do? To interfere in the running of his realm?

Feeling that he had been wronged by the other rulers, Ragnald had snubbed them. He had dropped all pretense of civility and had disregarded the lords' well-meant recommendations. His attitude of superiority had resulted in the MacClair being intensely disliked.

Most of the residents of the Highlands wanted to maintain peace. They saw her volatile brother as a threat to their way of life. His unpredictability and loathing for some of the other Zidarian leaders, including his own uncle, as well as the Zidhe, had been observed with concern. Nobody wanted the vindictive and spiteful man to start another war among the clans.

Even with the limited amount of time Ki'ara had spent at home these last few years and the little contact she had been allowed to have with others when she was here, she had noticed the changes. More and more, the opposition to Ragnald's rule had grown. Few of his own clan had any love for him, something that was unheard of in the history of the Highlands.

The concern and objections to her brother's conduct had spread well outside of his own realm by now. Ki'ara had come to the sad realization that many, and not just the lords, felt that Ragnald's disrespect of their laws and customs made him a danger to their way of life. His cruelty in dealing with the people he was supposed to care for had garnered him hatred.

In addition, the lords were not blind to the MacClair's ambitions to govern them all nor of his opinions of the rest of the rulers. Ragnald had long since stopped hiding his true feelings and treated them all with contempt. His behavior and angry outbursts had very effectively managed to alienate even those he had once called his friends.

After evaluating the situation at Seamuir as objectively as possible, Ki'ara saw only one course of action. For her clan's sake, as well as her own, she could not refuse this priceless gift. The realm and its inhabitants deserved better than they had been getting.

Ki'ara was only too aware that Ragnald would hate her even more than before, but she honestly did not see much of choice. She was grateful, however, to have been given a chance to make things right for her people, to make up for the damage her family had caused. She was determined to do her very best for the clan, the land, as well as the magic.

"I accept this most precious of gifts with deep gratitude. Thank you for allowing me to be the lord of the MacClair clan and lands. I will do my utmost to be the best leader I can be," she finally uttered, feeling completely overwhelmed with emotions. Tears of both joy and sadness were rolling down her face. How would her brother handle the loss of the position he so clung to? The death of his dreams?

"Child, that was an answer both gracious as well as becoming a future ruler. We are well pleased with your words, but even before you entered here, you were already the lord of the clan." The gentle voice whispered in her ear.

Ki'ara could feel the air stirring with each word but could see no one when she turned to look. She was so preoccupied with the phenomenon that it took a moment for the words to sink in. When they did, however, she was thoroughly confused. If this was not about the magic of the land, then what was it about?

"Lady, please rise and be at ease. You seem to have misunderstood us. You have been chosen by the magic of the realm to be its champion. That you freely accept that while still being concerned for your brother, says much about your character," a different voice explained.

"The power we offer is one older than that. It was here long before your ancestors came to the Highlands, as were we. We were glad to see the elves care for the land and have supported their efforts to make this land more habitable," the words flowed into Ki'ara's mind.

"All the land is calling to you, child. We wish you to keep the peace, to be the champion, the guardian, not only of your own home but of all the Highlands. We need someone to represent us. We have been hiding too long and want to become known once again," continued the wistful explanation. Ki'ara could hear the longing for recognition, of being acknowledged, and maybe even worshipped like they had been long ago in the gentle voice.

"Events have been set in motion, but until you are in the position where you can accomplish the tasks set before you, keep your power and us a secret. You will function not as an overlord but as a guiding hand. You will be the one who speaks for the magic itself and for us, the gods of these lands," the first being clarified.

"Is this why I can feel more than my home? Why I can see the difference between the realms?" Ki'ara inquired in awe. Much of what she had experienced during her dreamlike encounter started to make sense.

"Yes, little one," came the whispered response. "We ask you again. Do you accept our gift of the power?"

· · ❧ · ·

Ki'ara realized the momentous significance of the offer she was being made. The responsibilities she would be taking on were enormous, but so was the honor. She, the outcast sister, was being freely granted a power Ragnald would have killed for. In her opinion, he really did not know what was important in life.

Since she would be hiding her new status until the time was right, Ki'ara's exalted position was not something Ragnald would become aware of any time soon, which was good. The young woman felt pity for her brother. She was sure that the loss of his rule would be detrimental to him.

Having three older siblings, Ki'ara had never even imagined that one day she would govern the clan. Now she was not only a lord, but the guardianship of the entire Highlands was within her reach. Just the thought made the young woman's head spin. Having this kind of power over others had never been one of her aspirations!

Feeling wholly overcome with awe, Ki'ara sank back down on her knees and bowed her head for a moment. The gift being offered came with an obligation that was beyond anything she had ever imagined taking on. She was confident, however, that all the different methods of performing magic she had been taught would help her immensely.

Taking on this task would allow her to make up for some of the awful things Ragnald had done. How ironic that the teachings she had been privileged to would help her accomplish the proposed task. Something good had come out of the years she had spent away from her home, the times Ragnald had sent her away, after all!

Ki'ara raised her head proudly. She was not sure where to direct her answer, so she spoke to the wind swirling around her. "I gratefully accept your gift of power and thank you for your confidence in me. I will do my very best, this I do swear. I will not use my magic to harm anyone or anything unless there is absolutely no other option," she promised.

What followed were several formal and very ritualistic questions. Ki'ara assumed that they were part of an ancient ceremony that had not been performed here in the Highlands for thousands of years.

"Do you agree to become the guardian of the Highlands and all of their peoples and creatures?"

"Yes, I do," Ki'ara responded.

"Do you promise to help and heal the land and all in need wherever and whenever you can?"

"I do."

"Do you accept our gift of the magic of all the Mystic Isles and beyond?"

For a moment, Ki'ara hesitated. What was that all about? Would her powers actually extend beyond the Mystic Isles? That would be fabulous since it would allow her to help her friends in Frankonia even if the Zidhe did not want to come! She would have to ask about that later since she felt now was not the right time.

"I do," she answered.

"Do you agree to be our high priestess? To represent us and tell the people about us?"

"I do."

"Are you willing to serve all of the Highlands to the best of your abilities for as long as you live?" the voices finally asked in unison.

"I do and gladly," the young woman promised. She felt incredibly honored to have been granted the opportunity to make a difference for the benefit of the Highlands and maybe even beyond them.

"We so will it, and therefore it is," the voices replied as one, concluding the ancient rite. The contract had been sealed, and a new age of cooperation between the gods, the magic, and the people could now begin, starting with the granting of power.

A feeling of elation washed through the circle like a wave, and an enormous power flowed into Ki'ara. It raised her up and held her suspended above the ground in the very center of the ring. The magic looked like bolts of lightning as it arced into the young woman from each one of the stones.

Soon, Ki'ara was surrounded by a field of glowing, sizzling energy. She had spread her arms as wide as she could to allow it easier access to all of her being. The skin on her entire body was tingling. She felt the power enter her core and fill her up until she feared that there was more flooding in than she could contain. Still, it kept coming.

The magic took up residence in her body, heart, and soul. As it made itself at home, it ran through her blood like fire. It rummaged through her memories and thoughts. Ki'ara could feel her very chemistry changing, and the love which enveloped her was like nothing she had ever felt, all-encompassing. Tears were streaming down her cheeks from the pure ecstasy of the joining.

It took a few minutes for the power and the girl to merge completely. Ki'ara watched in awe as the magic playfully flowed out of her fingers and toes like luminescent ribbons. Never before in her life had she experienced anything like this!

When the process was complete, Ki'ara gently floated back down until her feet touched the ground. It took her a moment to adjust to this new state of being and for the occasional crackle of bright sparks playing all over her body to subside. She felt amazing, full of energy, and incredibly well and healthy. What a gift she had received!

⁂

Picking up that something enormous had just occurred, the hounds raised their heads and let out a long howl. Other dogs further away joined in the message. With Ki'ara's enhanced senses, she could follow it as it was being picked up all over the Highlands. How amazing to be able to direct her attention to a place so far away and see and hear what was happening there!

Remembering her sensitivity to human emotions, Ki'ara could not help asking. "Will you be there to guide me if I need help? This has all been a little overwhelming," she confessed with a smile. In response, knowledge started appearing in her mind, and much she had been wondering about started to finally make sense.

She felt like an immense pressure was lifted from her shoulders all of a sudden. Ki'ara could have never imagined that it could be so simple to get her powers under control. Her relief was heartfelt. Being able to shut out that influx of sensations would make it so much easier for her at the wedding and around her brothers!

The young lady relaxed for the first time since becoming a lord. She could feel her heart open up and with it, her whole being. The love which flooded into her left her breathless for a moment. Ki'ara could have hugged the entire world; she was so happy. What a welcoming! Her determination to do her absolute best grew to new heights with the realization of how much there actually was to be done.

No time like the present! There was much she could do from right here, right now. Centering herself, Ki'ara got started. Like lightning, her senses spread out to encompass the lands of her clan, then went beyond them. Sinking back to sit comfortably, she gave herself over to this marvelous task.

As she had promised, Ki'ara began to heal the land and its creatures wherever she could. It did not take her long to comprehend that not even the immense power she had been granted was enough to make more than a dent in the labor set before her. It would take time and the cooperation of all the Highlanders to undo the damage which had been caused over the years.

Not all the harm had been done out of malice. Neglect, ignorance, and thoughtlessness had contributed their fair share. Ki'ara was stunned to see so much disharmony across the lands she cherished so very much. She realized that education would play a big part in preventing further injury to their beloved home, and she was prepared to speak up to make things better for the realms as well as its people.

The young woman grasped that it would take a while to accomplish her goals, but she was determined to do her very best to not only make up for what Ragnald had done but to improve the situation all over the Highlands. Ki'ara loved her home and was incredibly honored to have been selected as its guardian. This was more than she had ever expected or even dreamed of!

Ki'ara's musings returned to her sibling. She now had the power to vanquish her brother with a mere thought, but even the idea of doing him harm was abhorrent to her. He was a living, breathing being with feelings and a soul after all. That his heart was so full of hatred, and he was willing to do anything to achieve his objectives did not mean she had to lower herself to his level.

Violence had never been to her liking. Ki'ara felt that diplomacy and patience would serve her better than raw power. Watching Ragnald had definitely reinforced that. Being high handed was not her style in the first place and only caused ill will. The challenge would be to accomplish the change of power as peacefully as possible.

It would not be easy, knowing her brother. Appealing to his better side would be useless. Ki'ara would have to be very circumspect and allow the other lords to take the lead. She hoped that the passing on of the rule of the clan could be achieved relatively painlessly. Ragnald was still family, and she loved him.

Determinedly, Ki'ara put all contemplations of the future conflict out of her mind. She noticed that her entire body had tensed up with her thoughts about Ragnald. Everything would work out, she could feel it. Her brother could no longer harm her since she was now protected by not only the magic of the MacClair lands but of the entire Highlands. Releasing a deep sigh, the girl relaxed once more.

After spending a few more minutes in deep meditation in this sacred place, Ki'ara thanked the gods of the land. She made sure to show them the proper respect. Too long had the Divine been ignored or slighted. She felt blessed to have been chosen to speak for it from now on.

The faithful animals were ecstatic to see their mistress and crowded around her as soon as she stepped out of the circle of stones. Each one wanted pettings, and Ki'ara could not help but laugh at their antics. She had not seen them this happy for a long time.

The young sorceress had always loved these hounds and decided that she would have a talk with their keepers as soon as she returned to Seamuir. Never again would her friends be neglected or abused if she had anything to say about it.

After spending a few more minutes having fun with the dogs, Ki'ara started on her way back to the castle. The hounds were bouncing around her more playful than they had been in a long time. They looked better as well, their coats were shiny once more, and they were no longer as skinny.

Just seeing the improvement in her companions' appearance filled Ki'ara with sincere gratitude, and she sent a silent thank you to the Divine. It seemed that the healing she had received had benefitted them as well and had undone some of the injuries they had suffered.

Maybe one day, with her help, her fellow Highlanders would come to understand that all beings had feelings and needed love and respect.

As Ki'ara was walking towards her home, her long, red hair was flowing around her like a copper mane. It was being blown here and there by the wind like a thing alive. The young woman loved the sensation, it made her feel happy and free. The locks had come loose during her time in the circle, and she had left them that way since she intended to slip back into the castle unseen by her brother.

Not that it was of any importance. Ki'ara had realized that her sibling would judge her regardless of how well she behaved or how proper she appeared. No matter what she did, how hard she tried, he would find fault with her. For some reason, she could never measure up in Ragnald's eyes. Now, it did not affect her as much.

The gentle young woman was no longer as hurt by the fact that her brother seemed to dislike her so much.

She had come to understand that this was all about him and actually had little to do with her person. For the first time in a very long time, Ki'ara felt complete peace in her heart. The magic of the land had helped her see that she was not responsible for her brother's emotions.

The knowledge and comprehension Ki'ara had gained would help her navigate through the events to come. Recognizing this filled her with confidence and chased away her fears. The girl was aware that the challenges ahead of her would not be easy, but she was convinced that she could handle them. She had lots of help after all, and insights few others possessed. And, she had a plan!

Once she arrived at the wedding, her first course of action would be to request sanctuary for herself as well as Gawain, if he was willing to join her. Then, she would ask for a full council of lords. Ki'ara needed the majority of the rulers to back her to take over the clan, and she had to have the Zidhe's approval. They were the final authority in the land.

One person Ki'ara knew she could count on was her uncle, Iain. She was reasonably confident that the StCloud or his representative would back her as well. That would leave six lords to convince, but she had the feeling that it would not be all that difficult. Ragnald had made sure of that with his treatment of those around him.

Once she took her rightful place as the Lord of the MacClairs as well as her own lands, she would try to heal the rift among the family. Ki'ara was determined to show her siblings kindness and respect, no matter how ugly they had behaved. She was not like Ragnald and Lyall. She would not retaliate for the way they had treated her and Gawain. It was just not her nature.

As a lord, Ki'ara would make sure that life improved for all the members of the clan. Her people had suffered enough, and so had the land and the magic intimately tied to it. Much had been let slide these last few years and would need to be addressed. Also, her father's laws would have to be reinstated, and fairness brought back into play.

Ragnald had brought his downfall on himself. He had been cautioned for years that his actions would have unpleasant consequences. Instead of paying heed to those well-meant warnings, he had put his own ambitions first and had disregarded his responsibilities.

This could not continue. It was time for a change! Still, Ki'ara felt bad for her brother. He was about to lose his whole world.

Chapter 41

A Deadly Trap

After having a light lunch in her room, Ki'ara started getting ready for the upcoming wedding. She had managed to sneak back into the castle without running into any of her brothers. She could handle them now, but what a relief it had been to avoid all confrontations just a little while longer.

Since there might not be time to change once she got to the hall, Ki'ara needed to put on her formal attire here at the castle. Leana helped her get dressed. The maid had chosen a stunning midnight blue velvet gown that was so dark that it was almost black. The color and cut set off the young sorceress' fair beauty to utter perfection.

The dress was one of Ki'ara's favorites. It was very form-fitting around the bust and clung to her small waist. It had a cowl in the rear which reached nearly to the young woman's buttocks. It left a small part of her flawless back bare, just enough for a peek. The gown had once belonged to Ali'ana and always made the girl feel beautiful and desirable as well as close to her mother.

Leana artfully made up her mistress' face. She used a salve, made from beeswax and red stains derived from berries and plants, to give the young woman's lips just a bit more color and gloss. She outlined Ki'ara's green eyes with a thin line of Kajal to emphasize them and make them appear even larger and more mysterious than they already did.

The skilled woman pinned Ki'ara's hair to one side and, with a bit of her magic, tamed it into long corkscrew curls. The locks tumbled down nearly to the shapely hips. As a finishing touch, Leana applied just a hint of a powder made of crushed pearls and rice all over the girl's face and added a bit of rouge.

The result was striking. The effect of the dark material of the gown, Ki'ara's fair face, mesmerizing eyes, and long red tresses was stunning and timeless. Shimmering diamond earrings, molded into the shape of crescent moons, complemented a necklace with the same stones. Her father had given the set to her on her tenth birthday.

A dark midnight blue cloak, trimmed with fur around the hood, cuffs, and hem, completed the ensemble. Dressed like this, the young woman looked indeed like the young queen she would have been long ago. Gone was the wild child who had returned from the hills just hours ago. In its place was a perfect lady, beautiful, confident, and ready to do whatever she must.

When it was time to leave for the wedding, Ki'ara turned to Leana. "I am glad that we have several days before we will be missed. Being able to relax and enjoy good company will be nice. I am really looking forward to this," she said with a smile.

"Since Gawain has arranged for you and his man to take another carriage so that we can take more luggage, please grab anything else you possibly can. Some of it might be best off being invisible to keep Ragnald from getting suspicious. Once you leave this room, please seal and hide the entrance just as before. It might be a while before we return," she continued, looking around her lovely room with a sense of regret.

Ki'ara reached out and hugged Leana for a long moment. "Most important of all, be careful, dear friend. As long as Ragnald is in power, this is a dangerous place for us both," she finished. Her voice held a hint of sadness but also one of resolve. The time for change was fast approaching for this keep.

Closing the door to her chambers behind her, Ki'ara made her way down the upper hall. When she reached the landing, she saw Ragnald standing in the foyer talking to Gawain. Knowing the MacClair, she was confident that he was giving their brother last-minute instructions and warnings. The lord would want to make sure that his siblings toed the line even when he was not with them.

As Ki'ara swept down the stairs, she drew her brothers' attention. Gawain gave her an approving smile full of love and admiration. The young man looked rather dashing himself, and she was sure that he would be the darling of all the single ladies as always.

Ragnald's face, on the other hand, underwent several rapid changes of expressions. First, he looked stunned, then something, it could have been fear but was quickly suppressed, crossed his visage just to be replaced with a look of extreme distaste and anger. Catching himself, the lord contorted his features into a smile that was so obviously fake that it looked comical. It did not escape Ki'ara that he had been visibly taken aback.

The moment Ragnald's eyes took in his sister as she was gliding down the stairs, a multitude of emotions hit him at once. She resembled her mother so much that, just for a second, he had thought she was Ali'ana. All he had been able to do was stare at her in disbelief.

The Ki'ara he was used to seeing was a bit of a wild thing, strands of her hair flying all over and forever escaping any attempt of confinement. The MacClair had not expected her to turn into such a gorgeous apparition full of poise and confidence as was now descending towards them.

When he noticed the air of royalty that surrounded his sister, Ragnald's eyes narrowed speculatively. Not only was Ki'ara beautiful, but she was also every inch a MacClair, much more so than Lyall or Gawain could ever be. To the harsh lord, it was as if he was seeing his youngest sibling clearly for the first time. A stab of fear went through him and shook him to his very core.

The brat or abomination, as he had always called her, might be even more of a threat than he had thought! How could he have missed this air of dignity and self-possession? Ki'ara radiated health and assurance, she was downright regal! 'Has she always been like this? Why have I never noticed this before? Was this something new?' went through his mind in rapid succession.

One thing was unquestionable, however, to the cruel lord. Ragnald concluded that the abomination would need closer watching if she managed to survive by some fluke.

Maybe all this training in sorcery he had sent Ki'ara off to had not been such a great idea after all. Good thing he had already set things in motion to deal with her once and for all!

With a sense of extreme glee, Ragnald looked forward to the events to come. 'How powerful are you really? Well, I am about to find out! I doubt you will stand a chance against me, brat! I can't wait to be rid of you,

you miserable wretch!' he thought, rubbing his hands together in anticipation.

Ki'ara stepped out of the castle doors into the courtyard all by herself. Gawain had been sent off on a last-minute errand by Ragnald. As she started to walk towards the carriage, she noticed that the usually bustling place was virtually deserted. Only a few animals and people were present. This was more than a little suspicious, and she instantly went on the alert. Something was up, she could feel it.

She would have to be very careful since she did not want to give herself away or respond in anger. Ragnald would try to confront her directly if he realized just how strong she was. Ki'ara wanted to take over the clan in the manner laid down by the law, not win it in a magical battle. Having warning made all the difference, she would be prepared for whatever was coming her way.

Determinedly, the young woman reinforced her shields. She reached out to the magic of the realm, which responded instantaneously to her touch. She could feel the power of the Highlands weave itself invisibly around her. She was as protected as she could possibly be without drawing undue attention.

Since it had rained the night before, Ragnald had ordered extra straw to be spread. That in itself was nothing out of the ordinary except that this layer was much more substantial and thicker than usual or necessary, especially along the most direct path leading to the far side of the yard. It covered the mud between the manor and the stable, and there was no way to avoid it. To reach the carriage, Ki'ara would have to cross the thickest part of it.

As the young woman set foot on the dry hay, she detected a hint of magic. Some strange spell had been used to alter the very fibers of the straw and make them readily combustible. It would only take a small spark to create an inferno. This was a trap she was walking into!

The flammable layer reached from the front stairs of the castle right up to the carriage over by the stables. Most of the courtyard was covered with the stuff creating a wide space just waiting to burn. Looking around, the sorceress realized that she was not the only one in danger.

Ki'ara could not believe it. Had her brother really lost all sense of perspective? Did he intend to set the whole place on fire? Or was this someone else's doing? As she was moving along sedately, the young woman used her senses to surreptitiously examine the enchantment more closely.

It took her a moment of searching, but finally, she found what she had been looking for. Ki'ara detected the vibrations of the person responsible for this catastrophe-in-the-making. Having her suspicions confirmed filled her with dismay. Ragnald had undoubtedly been the one who cast this incantation!

Was killing her so important to her brother that he would risk harming innocent bystanders as well as the animals? How could he be so blinded by hatred? Or was he trying to find out just how powerful she actually was? He knew her well enough to realize that she would do anything to keep others from harm!

What could she do to minimize the danger to those present without giving herself away? She figured the trap would be sprung when she neared the center of the courtyard. She was almost there now, so there was little time left to act.

Ki'ara could feel the magic respond instantaneously to her request. It was more than happy to help. To make sure that things would remain under at least some control, Ki'ara asked it to imperceptibly wet down all the straw around the edges, a little way in, and around any animal or person and to alter it back to plain hay.

Her precautions should prevent any flames from reaching the buildings or the waiting coach. Ki'ara hoped that it was enough to keep everyone else from being harmed. This way, the inferno would concentrate mainly on the area around her.

⚜

Ragnald knew that she had enough sorcery at her disposal to protect herself, but Ki'ara realized that she would have to run to keep her brother from becoming aware of the extent of her abilities. With great sorrow, she realized that the MacClair was entirely beyond reason and that there was a good possibility that he was no longer sane.

If Ragnald was willing to risk lives to achieve his goal, he might also be tempted to use their family or people as hostages. All bets were off where he was concerned, he had become too unstable, too unpredictable. She would have to play this just right for all concerned.

Having gotten almost to the middle of the field of straw, Ki'ara stopped for a moment to make a very brief fuss over her garments. First, she shook out the skirt of her dress, then she brushed of some blades of hay clinging to the hem of her cloak.

Next, she carefully gathered both in one hand. She made a great show of making sure that her clothing was well above the offending matter before continuing on her way.

⚜

Suddenly, the hay began to burn. The flames spread out from the far side of the yard with incredible speed. Ki'ara could sense that a second spell had been combined with the first. Together, the enchantments created an inferno that she would not be able to contain unnoticed without the added power of the land.

Chaos ensued, and people and animals were both screaming and panicking. All were trying to escape the raging blaze and in the process, were getting into each other's way. Something had to be done and fast!

For a second, anger rose up in Ki'ara, and she was tempted to use her powers to douse the fire and send her brother to oblivion, but then, sanity reasserted itself. She started to sprint, picking up speed with every step, but the flames were still gaining on her!

Very quickly, the young woman realized that it was not easy to run for one's life and, at the same time, use her spells to help the others in harm's way. She would need to direct the magic to do some of this for her. All it took was a thought to set things in motion.

Not a moment too soon! The coach horses were neighing in sheer terror and were trying to break loose from their handlers right into the flames. Suddenly they calmed and reversed course. Pulling the carriage along, they, together with four other steeds which had been in danger, allowed themselves to be led out of the gate in an orderly fashion.

Ki'ara was glad that they seemed mostly unharmed. She had not been able to spare them more than a glance since she was desperately sprinting for the safety of the castle steps, which still seemed a long distance away. Ragnald had really gone way too far this time!

✦⁘⁘⁘✦

A quick look over her shoulder when the fire had started had shown Ki'ara the cause of the conflagration. Ragnald's mistress, a female riverboat captain named Gina O'Malley, seemed to have 'accidentally' dropped a lamp. She was now pressing up against the wall in an unsuccessful attempt to keep herself from being burned. Her screams and pleas for help echoed around the courtyard but could barely be heard over the roar of the flames.

The attractive but none too smart woman was known as a walking disaster. Wherever she went, accidents followed, and usually, people got hurt. Since she flaunted her association with the lord to anyone who would listen, people tended to ignore her unless they needed her to gain favor with Ragnald.

Not one person in the entire keep had any understanding why the master would choose such a woman when he could have a real lady. After all, some beautiful Zidarian girls had been presented to Ragnald by their fathers when he first took over the rule. What did this wench have that could possibly entice a noble-born man?

Gina did more damage than good and had terrible manners. She was a true sailor. She cussed like a deckhand and loved to get drunk and belligerent down at the pub. It was rumored that the MacClair was not her only lover. Since she was nothing but trouble, most of the castle's inhabitants avoided her like the plague.

❧✶❧

As the fire made its way across the courtyard, people and animals continued to scatter in terror. With so much of the square ablaze, it was hard to find safety. Every look over her shoulder showed Ki'ara that the flames were still getting closer. A quick thought to the magic slowed the inferno down a bit, just enough to allow her and others to escape but not enough for her brother to notice.

Having to run for her life in a long, formal gown and fancy shoes was more than a little undignified. Especially since she was well protected by the powers of the Highlands. She had chosen, however, to keep up the appearance of being in peril for her own sake as well as her brother's.

Upon her request to the Divine, any people or animals in harm's way were also making their own getaways with mostly minor injuries. It was still flabbergasting that Ragnald would set this kind of a trap. He had really crossed the line this time!

⟡

Ki'ara could not help but feel some frustration. She knew that she was able to put the blaze out with a simple wave of her hand. She could not do so, however, without giving away who she had become. If that happened, Ragnald would attack instantly, of that she was sure. She did not want to have to kill or maim him to save her own life or to protect others.

She had done what she could to minimize the damage, but still! People and animals had been hurt! Ki'ara was tempted to confront her brother right then and there but was only too aware that no good would come of that, not for him nor for her. Unfortunately, allowing events to unfold was the most prudent but also the most infuriating option at this time.

The elves had laid down strict laws concerning magical duels. Any problems with a ruler had to be presented to the council instead of taken up with the offender. If Ki'ara did get into a battle with Ragnald, the Zidhe were well within their rights to make them both disappear. That was a chance she could not take. Too much was riding on her staying alive.

As the champion of the realms, Ki'ara had a responsibility to all the Highlands, not just to her clan. This incident actually gave her claim for taking over as lord a lot of additional power, especially since Ragnald had broken more than one law this day. He had used foreign magic, two different spells matter of fact, he had harmed his own people, and he had once again tried to kill his sister.

⟡

The young woman was still hoping against hope that the MacClair, who was watching and laughing, would see reason and intervene. He had started this conflagration, and it should be easy for him to put it out. Such an action might gain him some mercy with the council and the Zidhe. After all he had done, he would need it.

Her report would damn him, but at this point, Ki'ara saw no other course of action. Her brother was not fit to rule and, in her opinion, should have never become a lord in the first place. She felt that the gentle Gawain would have made a much better choice.

✦❦✦

The two oldest MacClairs had just entered the courtyard when the inferno erupted. Instead of helping and dousing the fire, something that would have been well within his power, Ragnald had stood there cackling at their sister's desperate run ahead of the flames.

It had taken Lyall a moment to fully comprehend what he was seeing, but once he grasped it, he was too stunned to speak. Having no doubt that Ragnald was responsible for the fire, the horrified man decided that he would have no part of this. He suddenly understood that his sibling had gone way beyond the limit this time. This was not just unacceptable, this was insane!

Lyall, who was usually on his brother's side and seldom questioned his actions, was utterly appalled by what was taking place right there in front of his eyes. He was Ragnald's best friend and confidante but had not known anything about this plan. Had he been privy to it, he would have done his best to talk him out of such foolishness!

There would be repercussions, and they would not be pleasant. The usually submissive Lyall decided that it was time to act. He was hoping to minimize the fallout from this incident for his beloved sibling by talking Ragnald into stopping this right now. Then, maybe, just maybe, they could claim that it had all been an unfortunate accident.

Having little magic himself, Lyall desperately tried to get Ragnald to put an end to the inferno before someone got seriously hurt or killed. His urgent pleas fell on deaf ears. His brother was enjoying himself too much to even hear him or pay attention.

Tears started to brim in the faithful man's eyes. He realized that Ragnald was determined to kill their sister regardless of the costs. It was all the MacClair had talked about for days! That he would go this far, however, Lyall had never suspected.

Ragnald had refused to share his plans. This had never happened before, and Lyall had been deeply hurt by this rejection. Had he not always been there for his brother, backed him up, been his confidante? Now he understood why he had been kept in the dark. Any sane person would have tried to stop this depravity!

This was crazy! Ragnald had to know that no ruler had the right to behave this way, no matter the reason! Nor could he expect to get away with something like this! Lyall realized that his brother was doomed, he was just too filled with hatred and bitterness to know it. How could he be so arrogant to think himself untouchable?

Lyall's heart was breaking. He loved Ragnald and had been his closest and only friend since he was a small child. At this moment, however, he felt like he was truly seeing his favorite sibling for the first time. He was stunned that he had been so blind.

When Ki'ara reached the two men and safety, she saw the hatred burning in her oldest brother's eyes. His plan to kill her had failed. The risk he had taken had been enormous, and he had lost. She was still alive and Ragnald was no wiser than before where her powers were concerned. Was he even aware that his actions would have serious consequences?

Lyall, on the other hand, rushed towards her and grabbed her arms. "Are you alright? Have you been hurt?" he asked her repeatedly. For the first time, Ki'ara saw true worry in his eyes, and she smiled at him sadly. "I am mostly unharmed, Lyall. Nothing a quick spell cannot fix. Thank you for your concern!"

The relief crossing her mousy brother's countenance was almost comical. He pulled her into a close hug and for a long moment, clasped her tightly. She could feel his whole body shaking. This was the first embrace from Lyall she had gotten as long as she could remember! Was he holding on for her sake or his own? He reminded her of a drowning man who had managed to grab onto a lifeline.

Ki'ara wiggled in Lyall's arms until she could study his face. He met her eyes without hesitation. She observed great sorrow in their depths, and tears were clinging to his pale lashes. The young woman reached up and ever so gently touched her brother's face.

At her loving gesture, the lids closed and hid the deep pain she had seen. When Lyall met her gaze again, something had changed. Was she wrong, or was there a new resolve shining forth, one that had never been there before? And, to her immense surprise, there was love.

She was stunned when Lyall gingerly grabbed her hand and kissed it before releasing her and stepping back. Something had happened to her usually so reticent sibling to show her such sincere affection.

Lyall had an air of lostness about him and of profound grief. Had Ragnald pushed even him too far this time?

Chapter 42

Feeling Betrayed

Standing on the landing of the castle, the MacClair was watching his siblings on the stairs below him through narrowed eyes. He was furious, and his face had turned bright red. How could Lyall do this to him? Did he truly care what happened to Ki'ara? His brother had never done so before, so why would he now? Was this all an act, or was he for real? Was he trying to save himself now that they might be in a little bit of trouble?

Turning on his heel, Ragnald stormed off. He understood that he had gambled and lost. He had never even considered the possible consequences should his plan to kill Ki'ara fail. The MacClair was absolutely stunned. He had been so certain that she would perish in the magical flames. He knew that he had so much more power than she, and, with the stolen incantations to hide his involvement, the trap had been perfect.

Not only had his sister survived, but some of the animals, as well as members of the clan, had been hurt, among them his own mistress. Not that he cared much what happened to Gina and, if he was honest, he had hoped she would also be killed in the fire. He was tired of the obnoxious woman. That had been the reason he had given her the enchanted lamp in the first place and had bespelled her to drop it on his unspoken command.

The lord suddenly realized that he could be in even more serious trouble with the other rulers as well as the Zidhe than he had anticipated. He still had no clue why his trap had not worked as designed.

At first, everything had gone exactly the way Ragnald had planned it. Ki'ara had been in the center of the courtyard with the magic-fueled inferno racing towards her. It should have engulfed her and burned her alive within seconds just as he had envisioned.

Ragnald had intended to play the hero and put the fire out as soon as his sister was beyond saving. He would have been too late to rescue his sibling and Gina, but no one else would have been injured.

At least, that was the way the MacClair had imagined the event during the days he had spent devising Ki'ara's demise. It had never even occurred to him that something could go wrong and that she could survive. With the stolen magic as well as the power of the realm behind him, he had figured that she would have no chance to escape his deadly ambush.

As it was, the inferno had almost caught up with Ki'ara and had started to surround her. Ragnald had been fully expecting to see her burn any second and had looked forward to the moment with malicious glee. As he was waiting for the inevitable to happen, all his concentration had been focused on the scene unfolding before him. He had paid no attention to anything else going on.

Somehow, however, the abomination had managed to stay ahead of the flames. She had looked so ridiculous running in that long dress that Ragnald had not been able to help himself. He had burst out into maniacal laughter, all the while anticipating Ki'ara to falter and fall. He just knew the incantation was going to trip her up at any instant now since it had been designed to keep her from escaping.

Ragnald had not been able to take his eyes off the spectacle of his sister's desperate dash. He had entirely forgotten that he had intended to put out the fire and keep his people from harm.

The homicidal lord had stood there, mesmerized, waiting for the moment when the blaze would finally engulf and incinerate Ki'ara. He had been so preoccupied that his composure had slipped.

For the first time in many, many years, he had let the true depth of his depravity show. Not until Ki'ara had safely reached the stairs did it dawn on him what had just happened. The looks of his kinsmen were a testament to his blunder.

There was no way to keep this a secret from the council; there had been too many witnesses. Word of his actions would get out and would spread like wildfire. Ragnald feared that his reputation would be tarnished forever, and it seemed that even Lyall had been taken aback by the cruelty and wickedness he had seen in his brother.

At the time, Ragnald had never even considered that his own behavior would point the finger at him as the incident's culprit. Now, it dawned on him that he had been beyond careless.

How could this have happened? It was only a second before the irate lord concluded that it had to have been

Ki'ara. That witch had put some sort of a curse on him to make him lose control!

The MacClair was totally aghast that he had been bespelled to let his guard down, had permitted his real emotions to show. This was something he had not done since he was a very young boy. He had understood long ago that displaying his true disposition would adversely affect his and Raghnall's well-laid plans.

His grandfather had spent hours drilling into Ragnald that he could never let anyone know how he actually felt, especially not his family. They would not understand. Not even Lyall, who had always been closest to him, had been privy to that dark, carefully hidden part of his soul.

The face Ragnald presented to those around him had become so much a part of him that to maintain it had become second nature. For the most part, he no longer had to think about how to act to hide the true extent of his cruel self and total lack of regard for others. The lord felt that he had done an excellent job until a few minutes ago.

It had taken him years to figure out how people expected him to behave, how others conducted themselves in certain situations. Ragnald had watched and learned but had resented having to do so in the first place. Was it his fault that he lacked the emotions needed to guide him? That society would see him as a monster?

Thinking back over the last decades, Ragnald was beyond confident that his act had been perfect. He was convinced that not one living soul had ever seen through his carefully crafted disguise, not even that Ali'ana. He had always been vigilant until just now, in the courtyard.

How could this have happened? The MacClair was sure that he would have never lost his composure like that unless there had been some sort of foul play. What had that brat done to him? A truth spell? But how? And when? Had she aimed to expose him?

All who had seen his reaction would testify against him, of that Ragnald was sure. As far as he was concerned, they were a resentful and discontent lot to start with, just waiting for their lord to screw up! None of them would pass up this chance! They would love nothing better than to replace him, those bastards!

Could they not see that he, Ragnald, was a true ruler, just like his grandfather before him? He had never coddled the members of the clan like his foolish father had done. They were his to command, their duty was to serve him! Not the other way around, what irrational thinking! How could Mikael have been so misguided?

His father had spoiled the lot. They had resented their new ruler from the very start, of that Ragnald was sure. He had always suspected that they talked behind his back. How often had he walked up only to have a conversation come to a dead stop? Did that ignorant bunch really think that he missed the glances they exchanged when they thought he was not looking?

The MacClair was convinced that none of the clan members had ever liked him. He felt that he was completely misunderstood and misjudged by all those around him. The way he had been treated had been most unfair!

His intentions, after all, had been good! All he had ever wanted was to make his clan great again, but this had been lost on that ungrateful bunch! They would be only too happy to speak out against him!

✦

He could still barely believe that his meticulously crafted plot had so utterly failed. Ragnald had been extremely cautious while setting things up. He had left nothing to chance. Only a Zidarian lord or one of the

Zidhe would have been able to detect his carefully concealed spells. Had he not been enchanted by Ki'ara to slip up, it would have been hard to prove his involvement.

What a debacle! The MacClair was still shocked that he had lost control so completely. After what his people had seen, he would not be able to claim that this had been some sort of an unfortunate accident. It was all her fault! And Mikael's for bringing that atrocity into their lives!

Even the usually oblivious Lyall seemed to have put two and two together. He had dared to beg Ragnald to stop the inferno and had been visibly upset. Had Ki'ara finally gotten to him as well? Had she bewitched him like all the others? It was beyond his understanding that they could not see her for what she truly was. Was he the only sane person around here?

The MacClair was certain that the abomination was capable of anything. After all, given her nature, how could anyone love such a creature? Ki'ara had to be using some sort of a charm. Ragnald could not understand that the people around him could not grasp the threat she represented to the Highlands and their way of life!

⚜

Just thinking of his 'sister' made the MacClair more furious. She needed to die, and he would make sure of that! He might have failed this time, but next time, he would be even better prepared. It was not murder; it was the right thing to do since she was the real monster here!

Ragnald felt strongly that someone had to act, and since all others were blind, the responsibility fell to him. Would anyone understand that he was only doing this for the good of the Highlands? Maybe, once she was dead. How was it possible that his father and all the others had not seen that it was a terrible mistake to allow Ki'ara to live?

That witch was a blight on the face of the earth, and now she had taken his last ally! It was more than unfair that he, Ragnald, would end up getting punished while that thing went free! They all loved her, and if she managed to take over the clan, they might even make her the overlord instead of him!

Was that the change she would bring to the Highlands? Not if he could possibly help it!

Ragnald's mind was racing as he made his way into the castle. He was feeling utterly abandoned. His thoughts were jumping from one subject to the next, becoming more twisted and incoherent with each passing minute. He was afraid and resentful and feeling immensely sorry for himself because of the fate he might be facing.

How could life be so unfair? Why did he end up being the victim? What would happen to him? These questions kept bouncing around in Ragnald's brain. He was getting more and more panicked. Resentment, dread, and hatred were burning away all reason.

'What will the council do to me? They have warned me before,' he kept thinking. He knew that their uncle Iain saw himself as sort of a protector of the abomination. Ragnald was sure that he would speak out against him, and this time, he would be facing the lords all by himself. Would he end up sharing his grandfather's fate?

At that moment, it hit the MacClair like lightning. Could this be the reason why Lyall had turned against him? Was his cowardly brother trying to spare himself the anger of the other rulers or maybe worse? The gravity of the crime he had just committed suddenly sank in but was just as quickly justified into oblivion.

Trying to kill another Zidarian was rated among the ultimate offenses. In Ragnald's eyes, however, he was guilty of a little faux pas, that was all. As far as he was concerned, Ki'ara was not really one of the mix-breeds to start with. He felt that he had only done what needed doing.

He was, however, not so delusional that he did not realize that he had gone against several of the elves' 'stupid' rules.

⁂

A shiver of fear ran down the lord's spine and lodged itself solidly in his gut. Ragnald had never even considered the possibility of the harsh outcome he could now be facing. The future suddenly seemed very uncertain and frightening to the oldest MacClair.

Would the Zidhe get involved in his punishment as well? Was his once favorite sibling trying to protect himself by ingratiating himself with Ki'ara?

Just the thought infuriated the lord further. They had shared everything! How could Lyall abandon him now when the MacClair needed him most! Just to save his own worthless skin? His brother was nothing without him! Had he, Ragnald, not practically raised him, comforted him, made him his second in command? What a despicable traitor!

Ragnald was beyond himself. Even the idea that the usually so loyal Lyall could be jumping ship like a rat leaving a sinking vessel incensed him beyond belief. Talk about ungrateful! How could someone who professed to love him do this to him?

Had he not given his brother as much of his heart as he was capable of? Had he not made Lyall what he was today? The MacClair could not fathom how the one person he had trusted and had allowed close to him could desert him just because he had made a tiny mistake! It should have worked! Ragnald had planned every last detail most carefully and was still incredulous that things had gone wrong.

She should have burned! They should have been rid of that abomination by now! With Ki'ara's death, her spells would have faded. Ragnald had counted on that then, finally, everyone would see the threat she had embodied. How grateful they would have been! He would have been celebrated as the hero who saved the Highlands from the evil witch!

As it was, things had not turned out like he had intended. Ki'ara's enchantments persisted, and worse, now he was truly alone. How could his one and only confidante, the brother he had showered his love on, turn his back on him after everything he had done for the miserable wretch?

The MacClair stopped in the hall. He spun around and gave his siblings one last scathing look through the wide-open doors. Then, he turned and stormed further into the house. As soon as he thought himself out of earshot, Ragnald started mumbling angrily under his breath.

"That bastard! How dare he? That witch should have burned, and he should have been glad! Lyall should be thanking me that I am working on getting rid of that abomination! I can't believe he is actually concerned about her!"

"I thought he was on my side! How can he not see her for the threat she is? He is just as weak as our father! She should have never been allowed to live in the first place! How could Lyall turn against me like this? I thought he at least would understand why I did this!"

Ragnald continued his rant while making his way to the den. He could not remember ever being this angry or feeling this deserted and betrayed.

He was all alone now, there was no one left he could turn to for help or reassurance. With a resigned sigh, the

MacClair accepted his fate. So, it was just him now, but did he really need anyone else?

His grandfather had always said that it was lonely at the top and that the average person would not be able to understand what he was trying to do. How right he had been! He should have never allowed anyone close, not even Lyall!

Ragnald figured that a large glass of that well-aged whiskey he kept hidden in his desk for special occasions was bound to make him feel at least a little bit better.

"Pox on him! I don't need his approval or his help!" the MacClair decided. "Grandfather was right, as always! He told me to keep to myself! From now on, I will trust no one! Not even my own brother! Who needs a spineless little twit like him anyhow? I don't, that's for sure!"

Reaching his destination, Ragnald angrily kicked the door open and let it slam loudly behind him.

"Doesn't he see that I am only doing what is best for the Highlands? What a fool! When I am lord of them all, I will make them pay for the way they have treated me!" he raged.

"And, I am going to start with him! Did Lyall think because he is my favorite sibling that he could get away with betraying me like this? I will deal with him right after I kill that unholy thing father brought into this house!"

Ragnald poured himself a large glass of the amber liquid and downed it in one gulp. He put the tumbler down with an air of finality. He had made his decision and woe be them all!

The livid Ragnald had not realized that he was being overheard. Ki'ara, with her enhanced senses, had not been able to shut him out. The simmering rage carrying along those angry words had speared into her with such ferocity that her knees had gone weak. She had been glad that Lyall had been there for her to hold on to.

The tirade Ki'ara was blasted with only convinced her further that her brother had lost all perspective. He was the danger to the clan as well as the Highlands and not she. What had happened to Ragnald to warp him so? Had it indeed been their grandfather like Ali'ana suspected or had he been born this hateful?

The MacClair was still steaming. He had poured himself another glass of the whiskey, and instead of making him feel better, it was like pouring fuel on the fire.

"How could Lyall do this to me? How can he just desert me like this? Have I not shared everything with him? Were we not closer than brothers? Did I not take him into my confidence? Was he not the one I told of all my plans?" he screamed into the room.

A niggling voice asserted itself at this point. It would no longer be ignored. Ragnald, even with drink starting to cloud what little was left of his judgment, had to admit to this one truth.

On that one point, he might be condemning his sibling unfairly. He had told Lyall only what he wanted him to know since he had desired his brother to see him in the best light. Not that he had needed his approval, but it had been nice to have his support and adoration.

Lyall had worshiped his big brother from a small child on, and Ragnald had basked in this admiration. It had fed his soul and allowed him to justify some of his more depraved acts. After all, if Lyall could still love him, all was right with the world and whatever vicious thing he had done, could not have been all that bad.

Thanks to Ki'ara, all that had changed. She had taken his brother from him just like she had stolen their father,

Gawain, and maybe now even the clan. She would pay for this, Ragnald vowed to himself.

Instead of quick, he would make sure she died slowly and in the most painful way he could come up with. How much he looked forward to that delightful event!

⁜

An evil smile had found its way onto the MacClair's face. Had anyone been there to witness it, they would have shuddered at the sheer viciousness and insaneness of that visage. This was one of the rare unguarded moments when Ragnald allowed his true feelings to show instead of the mask of polite indifference and disdain.

The lord was so angry as well as hurt that he no longer cared if anyone saw him. As far as he was concerned, he was now all alone in the world.

The alcohol only made Ragnald more vicious. It also contributed to him feeling more sorry for himself and heightened his sense of being the victim in the entire affair. Feeling alone and betrayed, he bitterly missed his grandfather.

⁜

Ragnald could not stop thinking about the scene on the steps. How was it possible that Lyall of all people had turned his back on him? He poured himself yet another glass of the strong spirits, his fifth he recalled vaguely. With his reasoning even further impaired, a new thought wormed itself into his befuddled brain. Maybe it was time to get rid of all of his siblings? If they were of no use to him, why keep them around?

Yes! That sounded like a perfect idea! Next time, however, he would have a much better plan, one which would not fail like this one had. That abomination should have burned in the fire! Ragnald still could not believe that she had managed to outrun the fierce flames in that floor-length dress. How had she done it? There had to be something he had missed!

He had watched Ki'ara so very closely. Ragnald had detected only the kind of magic emanating off her you would expect from any of the MacClairs. Except for Lyall, of course. He would be the easiest to do away with having almost no powers. With a drunken snicker, Ragnald decided that maybe he would start his campaign with his once-favorite sibling.

The other two would be gone for several days, and the perfect opportunity was sure to present itself in their absence. He would make Lyall hurt, oh yes, beyond anything his weakling brother had ever suffered before. Just the thought made Ragnald lick his lips in anticipation.

He could almost see the scene in his mind. Suddenly the vengeful lord was really looking forward to hearing his younger brother's pained screams.

Chapter 43

The Aftermath

Ki'ara had watched her brother storm off in a huff. She had not missed the hatred in his eyes when he had glared at her before turning around and leaving. She knew she was more powerful than he, but still, that look had filled her with trepidation. Old habits were hard to break.

Was Ragnald aware that he was no longer the lord? Thinking back over the incident and the rant she was overhearing, Ki'ara concluded that he was not. Had he even suspected that she was a threat to his rule, he would have confronted her right then while he thought that she was still off-balance from escaping the inferno. Also, he would have used an additional backhanded spell in his trap to make extra sure that the flames found their intended victim.

Her brother was devious, and he was smart. This had been a vicious attack. Had he really thought that he would succeed? Ki'ara suddenly realized that if she had not had the magic of the land on her side, she could have just as easily met her end in that blaze. This shocked her so much that she shivered. They were family, and to Ki'ara, this meant something but not so to the MacClair.

Ragnald really did want her dead. She had been stunned by the depth of his hatred and greatly surprised that her brother had lost his composure so completely. He had shown a part of himself even Ki'ara had never suspected.

The cruelty and disregard for life Ragnald had revealed, however, would help her case. He might have gotten away with this attempt on her life had it not been for his insane behavior. The incantations he had used would be untraceable in a few hours, and no proof would remain. It would have been her word against his.

But why had he used his longtime mistress if he was trying to hide his involvement? This truly puzzled Ki'ara. Gina was a direct link to him! Everything seemed to have been very well planned except that. Something was going on with Ragnald, and the young woman felt compelled to figure it out.

⚜

Ignoring the influx of Ragnald's continuing outburst, Ki'ara reevaluated the situation. She knew that her oldest brother had a terrible temper. He would have been beyond furious had he even suspected that his rule was in danger. He had intended to kill her but had not added an excessive amount of magic to make sure he succeeded. The sorceress was reasonably certain that he would have done just that had he known that she would soon take his place.

Also, the MacClair still had his enforced connection to the land. Nothing had been done which would have alerted him to a change. Ki'ara could sense the dark tendrils of this coerced bond. The magic could have easily shaken off those unwelcome restraints but was continuing to cooperate to hide her secret even after this horrific event. She was genuinely grateful for this.

It had not been easy to convince the sentient force. While running from the flames, Ki'ara had done her utmost to keep the infuriated power from turning on the murderous lord. It had finally accepted her reasons, found them compelling. For one, he was still her brother and two, some might have blamed her for Ragnald's death. That was not the way she wanted to begin her own rule. Just because he behaved in such a depraved manner did not mean she had to lower herself to his level.

To keep Ki'ara safe as well as to please its new partner, the exasperated magic had agreed to keep up the pretense. It was not happy about it, especially after what Ragnald had done, but seemed to understand the necessity for this course of action. The young lady was relieved as well as delighted to have established such pleasant relations. It would make her future rule over the realm much easier and more rewarding.

For a moment, Ki'ara reached out to the power and sent it her love and gratitude. The response was immediate. Like a happy kitten, the magic started to softly purr into her ear. Even in the midst of such dark contemplations, the young woman could not help but flash a brief smile.

Ki'ara concluded that she could have understood Ragnald's heightened resentment if he had realized what had been done. To try to kill her for no good reason at all, however, made little sense to her. What was going on in her brother's mind?

⁕

Just then, Ragnald's murderous thoughts broke through her concentration. She had managed to somewhat tune out his ravings, but the emotions behind this new barrage hit her with such power that Ki'ara almost lost her balance. She had to lean up against the castle to brace herself and could not help but react. Her entire body was now shaking like a leaf.

Lyall immediately rushed to support her. Ki'ara clung to him while the cascade of spiteful words and enraged feelings washed over her. She had gone deadly pale and felt like she was freezing. Finally, with the help of the magic, the young lady managed to resolutely push the tirade away.

Taking a relieved breath, Ki'ara looked up at Lyall who was watching her with concern. She met his gaze steadily and searched his face for a trace of deceit. Finding none and sensing only a budding love towards her, she gave him a grateful smile.

"I am fine, Lyall. I think it was just a moment of weakness after all that has happened. Now that I am safe, it has caught up with me," Ki'ara explained. She was waving her hand at the charred chaos in the courtyard. Lyall had always loved Ragnald, and it would only hurt him to find out what their brother was contemplating.

"I am a little singed, but nothing a quick spell won't fix. How are you? He will be very angry with you for showing me such affection!" she stated, all the while holding onto his arms. How could she get her sibling out of harm's way?

Lyall lowered his eyes for a moment, then met her gaze with more openness than she had ever expected. "I don't know who he is anymore, Ki'ara. There is so much hatred inside Ragnald, and it just keeps on growing. I fear that he no longer cares who he hurts! I have never been afraid of him before, but I am now! You at least have your magic to help you. I don't even have that." He confided resignedly. She could tell that his heart was breaking.

"Do you have any place to go where you can stay for a few days?" Ki'ara inquired immediately. She was more than a little alarmed. Leaving Lyall here, defenseless, after what she had just gleaned from Ragnald's thoughts, was no longer an option.

"He has been my only friend all my life. Uncle Iain's, possibly. Or maybe I could just meet you and Gawain in Deansport? If that's ok?" Lyall asked hesitantly. All the while, his eyes looked at her pleadingly. Ki'ara could tell that he was genuinely afraid and for the first time in his life, was looking to her for assistance.

"You coming with us would be fun, Lyall! We would love to have you! Why don't you go and get your things and put them in the carriage while I see to those who were injured?" she responded with an encouraging smile.

Lyall's face lit up for a second but then fell again as fear stabbed through him at the thought of Ragnald's reaction once he found out. Ki'ara had just had a similar notion. She could tell from her brother's tense expression that he was desperately trying to find a solution. She wanted him away from the castle but realized that it might be better if they did not travel together.

"I have a suggestion. Why don't you take your horse and leave before us? You can meet us there. Don't tell anyone where you are going and head in the other direction until you are out of sight. I think that might be safest for us all," Ki'ara proposed. Lyall instantly liked her idea, and his whole body relaxed.

Studying the young woman's upturned face, Lyall realized that Ragnald had never looked out for him with this much caring. Their brother was only concerned with himself and more so with each passing moon. What mattered to Ragnald the most was what others could do for him. Anyone else's needs or desires were only addressed if it benefited him somehow.

Lyall had known this but had loved his brother anyway. It was the evil he had perceived in his sibling this day that he could not ignore. He felt like he was finally seeing things clearly and could no longer understand why he had ever disliked Ki'ara at all.

Had this been due to Ragnald's influence? Gawain was right; she was gentle, sweet, and loving, and, for the first time, he felt proud to be able to call her his sister.

"Thank you, Ki'ara. You are most kind after all the mean things I have said and done to you over the years. I am truly sorry for the way I have treated you!" he uttered ashamedly.

This was so unexpected that Ki'ara was too stunned to speak. Instead, she stepped forward and put her arms around her brother, who hugged her back gladly. Once again, she could see tears in Lyall's eyes.

⁓⧽✦⧼⁓

After giving his sister a quick kiss on the cheek, something he had never done before, Lyall rushed off to his room to prepare for the journey. Ki'ara gazed after his departing back with wonder. His warmth and openness were a precious gift she had never expected but cherished deeply.

One good thing had come out of that horrible incident after all. Who would have ever thought that Lyall would show her that kind of affection? He had always been so loyal to his beloved brother.

⁓⧽✦⧼⁓

Ki'ara could not help but feel bad for Ragnald, who saw himself as betrayed and abandoned. Why could he not understand that his own actions were to blame for that state of affairs and not the world around him?

Ki'ara had never been able to fathom why her older brothers resented her the way they did. She knew in her heart that she had never done anything to justify those emotions. To have Lyall change his attitude towards her meant a lot to the young lady. At least some of the family was coming together!

Let Ragnald hate her! There was nothing she could do about that. Ki'ara had reluctantly obeyed him all those years, had respected the majority of his wishes, and had tolerated being sent off like some unwelcome relation. A lot of his commands had gone against everything she believed in, but he had been her guardian and clan lord.

No more! Never again would she allow anyone's judgment or will to override hers. Ki'ara was committed to following her own instincts. This would help her make decisions that were best for herself as well as for all others concerned.

From now on, Ki'ara would assume full responsibility for herself. She was determined to take charge of her life as well as the clan. Her people deserved to be ruled with kindness, fairness, and consideration.

After what he had just done, she no longer felt quite as much pity for Ragnald. He had proven beyond a shadow of a doubt that he was not fit to govern. Ki'ara was confirmed in her intentions to petitioning for the rule of the MacClair clan as quickly as possible. It was high time for a change, but before heading out, she needed to see to the injured.

Several people and one of the horses had suffered burns from the blaze. Among the wounded was Ragnald's mistress Gina, the unintentional starter of the inferno. When she saw Ki'ara head towards her, she broke down in tears and fell to her knees in front of the young woman.

"Lady, I's so sorrys! I's don know hows that fire spreads like thats. Its weres unnaturals, its weres! Nevers haves I's seen anything likes it!" Gina sobbed inconsolably. "No yard burns likes thats!"

Clinging to Ki'ara's legs, Gina continued to cry uncontrollably. "Whys did hes give mes that lamp? Hes knows I's drops things! I's so sorry thats peoples gots hurts! I's nevers wants to hurts anyones!"

Ki'ara gently detached the hysterical captain and raised her up. "Who gave you the lamp?" she questioned calmly. She was reasonably certain that Gina meant Ragnald but wanted to make sure.

"Him gaves its to mes, Ragnald, the lord. Gots mes burned too, sees?" the woman responded, holding out a severely scorched and blackened arm. Next, she raised what was left of her charred skirt to show off angry-looking blisters on both of her legs. Several places on her face had been singed as well.

It was evident to Ki'ara that the riverboat captain was in severe pain. It had to have been agonizing to get down on her knees, but Gina had done so. The young lady could not help but feel a growing respect for this woman whom so many intensely disliked. Her brother's mistress might be a klutz, but she was displaying a lot of backbone and forthrightness.

"When hes wants mes, it's all good, but wheres is hes when I's needs him? I's coulds have been killeds! Hes does not really cares abouts mes, does hes?" Gina mumbled unhappily.

The captain had uttered those words just loud enough for Ki'ara to hear. Not only had Gina been injured, but it seemed that she had realized that she had been used and badly so. With her accidental dropping of the lamp, she had become instrumental in an assassination attempt on the Lady MacClair.

By clan law, her life was forfeit by this act, and Gina knew it. As it was, several of the men had already drawn their swords when the riverboat captain had reached for Ki'ara. Only the lady's adamant shooing motions had kept her self-appointed protectors at bay.

Ki'ara had wanted to hear what the woman had to say. She needed to be sure of her facts when she presented her case to the council. Yes, she had detected the strange magic, but she was certain no one else had.

Ragnald might still try to claim it had all been an unfortunate accident. It was better to have a firsthand witness who could testify to his involvement. She needed Gina alive and not dead.

The MacClair had the right to pardon his mistress, but he was nowhere to be seen. It was therefore up to Ki'ara to decide her fate. "Give me your arm please," she directed the captain. Gina looked at her with horror in her eyes but obeyed instantly. She knew the lady was a powerful sorceress and could kill with just a touch if she so pleased.

The captain was prepared for her death. She felt that she deserved the punishment. She had allowed her own ambitions to get the better of her, had been using the lord to improve her standing. He was a nasty man, and she had little love for him but had genuinely enjoyed the status she had gained from being his lover.

In the end, Gina acknowledged to herself silently, she the user had been used. It seemed that Ragnald cared even less for her than she did for him. If he wanted to, he could save her, have his sister spare her life. He, however, was nowhere to be seen.

Expecting to die at any moment, Gina, therefore, was stunned when Ki'ara gingerly took her burned arm in her hands. The riverboat captain watched with disbelief as the lady she had almost inadvertently killed restored her burnt flesh first on her arm, then on her legs and face.

Gina was dumbfounded. The witch her lover had spoken so disparagingly off and had called evil beyond compare had used her magic to heal HER, the one who had accidentally started the inferno! Ki'ara had been kind and gentle with her, very unlike the lord who liked nothing better but to take her by force or beat her until she begged for his mercy.

Once again, Gina sank to her knees in front of Ki'ara. "Lady, my lifes is yours. If yous allows mes to lives, I's wills serves yous with all mes hearts. Please, I's did not means to hurts anyones!" she begged.

"You will serve me without question and do as I tell you?" Ki'ara asked, somewhat incredulous. Coming from a woman who was best known for her willfulness, this was kind of hard to believe.

Gina looked up and squarely met Ki'ara's gaze. "Yes, lady, I's will serves yous and do as yous tells mes, I's swears!" she answered fervently. The captain's eyes held no falsehood, and the young lady could only stare at the woman in wonder.

"I accept your life as mine," Ki'ara spoke the ritual words while placing her hand on Gina's head. She had uttered them loud enough for all nearby to hear.

Loud gasps could be heard around the now bustling courtyard. Not one of the members of the clan had expected the captain to receive such forgiveness.

The men who had been ready to come to their lady's rescue were more than a little surprised. They had expected to be given the order any minute now to arrest the obnoxious woman and take her down to the dungeons. The lord's plaything or not, they had figured she would be punished severely.

It had been many years that kindness had been shown to any of them. When Mikael and his wife left for places unknown, life had changed drastically for all of the clan. What Ki'ara had seen as a small act, was huge for her people. Hope was born but also the determination to rid themselves of their unwelcome lord.

The lady had brought a ray of sunshine into their miserable lives. More and more of the folk of the castle drifted near Ki'ara to see what she would do next. Would the lady really take that clumsy woman as her servant?

Some snickered behind their hands at the thought of how much patience would be required to deal with one such as Gina.

It had taken Ki'ara a moment to become aware of the effect her simple gesture had on her people. She saw hope shining in their eyes as more and more of them congregated around her. They were all pretending to be taking care of something, but as far as she could see, nothing was actually getting done.

This would not do, she decided. It was not a good idea to add fuel to the fire of Ragnald's hatred should he see this.

Therefore, Ki'ara set about organizing the lot and, in short order, the aimlessly milling around crowd had been put to work getting the courtyard cleaned up. Once they were all busy, the lady turned to her new servant.

"Your first task will be to help me with the injured. Please go fetch some clean water," Ki'ara directed.

Gina immediately rushed off to do her bidding and quickly returned not just with clean, hot water but also with washcloths and bandages. Her new mistress was duly impressed.

Gina turned out to be a capable nurse. She stayed by Ki'ara's side as one person after the other was healed. The captain, who had frequently been laughed at for her clumsiness, was steady and calm. She did not spill or drop anything. Even her speech started to improve as they were moving along.

More than one unbelieving glance was exchanged by those watching. Ki'ara observed this with amusement but did not say a word.

Only she knew that Gina's klutziness and language impairment had stemmed from a defect in the front of her brain, one the lady had healed when she had placed her hand on the contrite woman's head.

Chapter 44

The Drive to Deansport

The courtyard was a charred mess. Of the hay which had provided the fodder for the fire, little was left except black ash. In some places, even the soil had been burned, and only Ki'ara's covert intervention had saved the people and animals from the worst. She had managed, with the help of the magic, to slow down the flames just enough to allow folk to escape, but she had not been able to prevent all injuries.

That Ragnald would set a trap for her out here in the open where others could be hurt and witness the occurrence was beyond the young lady's understanding. Her oldest brother had tried to kill her before but never in public. He had taken a huge risk, and he had lost.

Had he succeeded, Ragnald could have presented the entire incident as an accident. With all the evidence destroyed, it would have been hard to prove otherwise. Without Ki'ara for support, none of the clan members would have dared to speak out against their lord. They were only too aware that retribution would be dished out very quickly. There would have been suspicions but not a smidgen of proof.

As it was, some of the men had overheard Gina's testimony against their cold-blooded lord. The anger in their faces said everything. Ragnald was already widely despised, especially by his own people, and the brazen attempt on the life of another Zidarian had just been added to the list of his offenses.

Word of such an atrocity would spread fast and would reach the council's ears within a day. If Ki'ara wanted to prevent intervention by the Zidhe, she would have to act quickly. She still believed that every person was precious, even one as murderous as her oldest brother. She did not want to see him killed.

Ki'ara suspected that the opposition to Ragnald's rule would only increase after this incident. The clan had loved their father, Mikael, a progressive and fair lord, and had resented the drastic steps backward, which had been implemented once her brother took over.

<hr/>

As the governing lord, looking after his or her people was supposed to be the ruler's first priority. Ragnald, however, was nowhere in sight. No one had expected any different. The clan had learned by now that their chief was rather uninterested in their health and well-being. Since Lyall had no powers and Gawain was still occupied elsewhere, taking care of the injured had fallen to their sister.

Healing was something that came easily to Ki'ara. It was a talent she was immensely grateful for. Since she had been very young, she had genuinely enjoyed easing the pain of any creature in need, whether human or animal. It had been the one gift she had been able to use without giving away the actual extent of her power.

Her first patient after Gina turned out to be the wounded horse. It's screaming was upsetting all of the other injured, and they were glad to wait as long as the animal was made to quiet down. Ki'ara eased its pain and the worst of the burns. She would do a full healing after she had taken care of the humans.

Going from person to person with Leana and Gina in tow, it did not take the sorceress long to restore burned flesh or heal any other harm her people had sustained while fleeing the blaze. The new tissue would need to be protected at first, and it was best to keep it covered for a few days. Her two companions expertly bandaged those their lady had healed.

After all other hurts had been seen to, Ki'ara returned to the now patiently waiting horse. The animal had panicked when the fire had started. It had tried to run for the gate through the inferno. This had earned it several deep burns.

Ki'ara checked the mount over carefully to determine how much harm had been done and to make sure she did not miss anything. It did not take her long to soothe the rest of its injuries and restore the beautiful creature to its former glory. Gina and Leana took over from there while she was petting the animal's head.

Feeling rather frisky all of a sudden, the playful beast took a nip at her hand. She quickly evaded those teeth and rewarded the culprit with a very light tap on its velvety nose.

The young lady did not want to punish it, but the large animal needed to be reined in just a bit. She understood that it had not really meant to bite but wished to express its gratitude for the help it had gotten.

She could not help but laugh at the grateful stallion's antics as he insisted on nuzzling her fingers. Much of the tension inside Ki'ara dissolved at that moment. She realized that whatever was coming her way, she could handle it. If nothing else, adversity had taught her great coping skills.

Now that the job was completed, the sorceress was glad that she had been able to assist all those who had been in harm's way. With the horse taken care of, her part of the healing was over. Leana and Gina could handle the rest.

Once they were done, they would follow with the wagon transporting the luggage she and Gawain would need for the wedding.

To make herself presentable again, the young lady used a quick spell to restore her dress to its once pristine condition. Once this was accomplished, Ki'ara retrieved her cape and gloves from where she had left them and headed for the waiting coach.

Suddenly, Ki'ara stopped in mid-stride. The dream she had back at De'Aire Chateau came back to her mind, and she gasped. She had been wearing this same dress! There had been a fire, and she had come close to dying! A deep sense of gratefulness that this had turned out better than that nightmare flooded through her.

Ki'ara realized how different today could have turned out. Had it not been for the magic of the land's help, her fate might have been sealed, and Ragnald might have actually succeeded in his attempt to murder her!

Seeing Gawain waiting by the carriage, she moved on. He looked like he had been very busy, and Ki'ara could not help but wonder what he had been up to. The look he gave her told the young lady that she would find out soon enough. Whatever he had been doing, it seemed he did not want to advertise it.

Having been too late to assist his sister, Gawain had set out to find out exactly what had happened. He had been stunned by the devastation in the courtyard and amazed that Ki'ara had managed to escape. It had not taken him long to appreciate that she almost did not.

After talking to several witnesses, he had realized that no natural fire could have possibly burnt that violent and spread that quickly. The more Gawain had heard, the angrier he had grown. What had possessed Ragnald to do this?

His outward appearance was calm, but inside, Gawain was seething. When Ki'ara met his gaze, she could see the concern as well as the fury in his eyes. She knew that he would have questions. Maybe it was just as well that Lyall had already left and would not be riding in the coach with them. It would give them the privacy to talk freely.

Keeping the coachman and the guards from overhearing would be no problem. Ki'ara would use a spell to make sure that anything they discussed did not reach hostile ears. She liked to call that particular enchantment her 'sphere of silence' and imagined it as a pink, iridescent orb reminiscent of a large soap bubble like the ones she had loved blowing as a small child.

One of the guards helped her embark. The man kept shooting curious glances at her, and Ki'ara could detect a bit of anxiety in his aura. It made her sad, but there were always those who dreaded the unfamiliar. It was human nature to fear the unknown.

As soon as Ki'ara and her brother were seated comfortably, the footman closed the door, hopped on the back, and they were on their way.

⁂

The carriage rolled out of the courtyard, picking up speed with every yard. Once the sound of the horses' hooves had stopped echoing on the thick walls leading to the gate, the siblings knew that they had almost left the castle behind.

Gawain, who had become very fidgety and anxious once they were alone, could barely restrain himself any longer. Impatiently, he waited for them to clear the drawbridge. Ki'ara quickly put her enchantment in place.

"Are you alright?" Gawain asked his sister with obvious concern. "I do not know why Ragnald keeps that woman around besides that he seems to enjoy her favors. She is a walking disaster! Associating with the likes of her is very unbecoming of a Highland Lord to start with! And that fire, it was not natural, was it?"

"No, I believe that the hay was doused with one sort of magic, the lamp with another. Once the two combined, the flames were out of control. Gina was not totally to blame. She was set up. As it was, she was badly burned. I decided to spare her life and have taken her on as my servant," Ki'ara explained.

"You did?" Gawain responded, shaking his head in disbelief. "I am sure you had your reasons, but Gina? Was that necessary? Anyhow, there was magic involved here, but it was not of the land, was it?" he inquired. His face had grown grim.

"No, I believe that it was some sort of an illegal enchantment. At least, that is what it felt like to me," Ki'ara told him without hesitation.

<hr />

Using imported magic in the Highlands without the approval of the council was considered treason. It gave the wielder an unfair advantage over his peers and could be used to commit crimes without anyone being able to trace the spells back to the Zidarian who had deployed them. It was against the law as well as morally wrong.

Ki'ara could tell that Gawain was livid. "This time, he has gone too far! Everyone in that courtyard could have been killed!" he shouted furiously. "Has he completely lost his mind? Not even he could be that stupid to think he could get away with something like this!"

The scowl on her favorite sibling's face clearly showed just how upset he was over the incident. Gawain was irate with Gina, who he felt was a menace. She had even wrecked her own boat several times! He had little understanding of why his sister would take that woman into her service instead of sending her to the dungeons.

And, he was furious with their brother. He had been just in time to see Ragnald standing there laughing while Ki'ara ran for her life. The lord had not lifted a finger to help her or anyone else. Even if he had not been responsible for setting the trap in the first place, he was most certainly guilty of gross negligence towards his people, a crime that had resulted in injuries.

Gawain was glad that he was not in his brother's shoes. Ragnald would be facing the council just as soon as they found out about this. The fool had publicly tried to kill a member of his family. Not a good thing if you wanted to remain the ruler of the clan!

"Are you sure you are alright? The heat from those flames must have been tremendous!" Gawain queried Ki'ara again. From the testimony of the eyewitnesses he had interrogated, her survival had been a close call.

"I am fine, a little smoky perhaps but otherwise unharmed. I have repaired most of the damage to my garments and hair. I can still detect just a hint of a smell, but that is nothing a quick refreshing spell will not fix. Gawain, why does he hate me so?" Ki'ara replied.

"I wished I could tell you, but I don't really understand it either. I think it has something to do with some bizarre reference he found long ago. To be honest, with the possible exception of Lyall, I don't think Ragnald likes anyone," her brother answered carefully.

If he told the young woman about the ancient prophecy, Ragnald would never forgive him. Gawain had no intention of returning to Seamuir while his brother was the lord but also did not want to be responsible for widening the rift in the family further. What good would come out of their sister knowing about it anyhow? It was garbage to start with.

Telling Ki'ara the truth would only hurt her, and that was something Gawain could not bear to do, especially right now. He felt that she had been subjected to enough turmoil for one day.

After about three hours, the town of Deansport came into view. The *Sea Witch* was gone, but a tall ship was moored far out in the harbor. The siblings eyed the vessel with interest. As they got closer, they were able to discern more of the details.

The clipper was magnificent and much larger than they had first thought. Ki'ara and Gawain took in its clean lines and well-kept sails. They eyed what they could make out of the intricate woodwork with appreciation. It was indeed a beautiful craft.

Neither of the MacClairs had a clue who it belonged to. It was not part of their fleet.

How unusual for this little town to be visited by a ship that size, one that obviously did not belong here! The *Sea Witch* and several others owned by the MacClairs were quite a bit smaller and considered this their home port. This ship had not been announced at the castle nor had it, as far as either one of them knew, requested permission to anchor.

Who could this beauty possibly belong to? Was it the same vessel she had seen a few days ago? Ki'ara could not help but wonder. It sure looked a lot like it!

Chapter 45

A Late Arrival

When the carriage neared the town hall where the wedding was to take place, Gawain looked at his sister. She had touched up her clothes after the long ride, eliminated most of the smell of the fire, and redone her hair. Ki'ara was so beautiful and vivacious that she seemed almost luminous.

The young lady was once again calm and composed. Talking about the incident had made both of them feel better. The siblings had agreed that the council needed to be informed of the event at the castle and that they would not return home to Seamuir until Ragnald was no longer in charge.

Gawain had volunteered to face the lords with her. He was more than prepared to stand with his sister. Ki'ara had thanked him but had very graciously declined. This was something she needed to do on her own. Also, she knew he had a date, and if she did require his testimony, he would not be far away.

Ki'ara had decided to place her trust in Gawain. She had told him about the present she had received on her birthday as well as her new position, and she had laid out her plans. The young lady had only withheld that she had become the guardian of all the Highlands. The time to divulge this was not yet.

Her brother had been surprised at first to hear that Ki'ara intended to take over the clan. She had always been so obedient and almost meek around Ragnald, not good attributes for a future ruler.

Right then, however, there had been nothing timid about her, just the opposite. Ki'ara had become every inch a lord. Gawain had realized that something had changed. He had searched her face for a moment and had seen a resolve and determination which had either not been there before or had been carefully hidden.

Could it be true? Could their little sister really pull this off? Free them all from this nightmare? Hope had lit up Gawain's eyes and flooded his soul. Before either of them had known it, he had been on his knees swearing allegiance to her. He was happy to follow Ki'ara, ruling the realm was not really something he had ever wanted to do.

Gawain was looking forward to his date but was even more excited about the changes to come. He was almost tempted to insist that his sister take him along.

⁕

For a moment, a ray of sunshine found its way into the carriage. It outlined Ki'ara in brilliant light and set her copper hair aglow. Gawain could not help but think that she was stunning. It truly surprised him that no one had come along to claim her as his bride. But then again, would Ragnald have allowed it? As her guardian, he could have argued that she was too young.

Still, were the men around her blind, or did his sister discourage them all? Was there someone in one of the faraway places she had been sent to, and she was just waiting for the right time to reveal this? A few of the Zidarians lived in all corners of the world. She could have met one but, somehow, this did not feel right to Gawain. She would have told him if she had a beau, of that he was certain.

A new thought occurred to him. After all this time, could Ki'ara still be in love with the StCloud? His gut told him that he was right. Mirth bubbled up inside Gawain. He could not help himself and almost laughed out loud. Ragnald was really in trouble now because that man would come calling just as soon as he realized that his beautiful ex-fiancé was no longer under their brother's control.

Conall would be a valuable ally in their upcoming battle to take over the clan. He had always looked out for Ki'ara's best interests, even after Ragnald had strictly forbidden him to speak to her or to go near her again. Gawain was confident that the StCloud would do anything in his considerable power to aid and protect her.

Not that his little sister needed someone to look out for her. Gawain had no worries about letting her go to the meeting and the wedding alone. Ki'ara exhibited enough confidence and poise that no man would dare cross her boundaries. If he did, he would most likely live to regret it.

Gawain had the suspicion that his sibling had more magic than even he was aware of. He had been able to tell that she was holding something back. She had, however, confided in him that she could have taken on Ragnald and won. If Ki'ara could defeat their brother, she would have no problem defending herself if she had to. Besides, that young lady was able to deal with people better than anyone he had ever known!

The last thing Ki'ara would want was a watchdog, especially among her fellow Zidarians. Gawain thought with a smug smile that their brother was truly no longer in charge of their lives.

When the footman opened the coach door, Gawain disembarked first. He turned to help his sister. Ki'ara took his hand and regally descended the carriage steps. He could only admire her; she was every inch a queen. How had she hidden this so well? Or, was this all new? Somehow, he did not think so.

Once she was standing beside him, Ki'ara smiled up at him sweetly. "Enjoy your date, Gawain. Please take it easy on the drink just in case," she told him with a laugh. "If I need you, I will send someone to the 'Seven Sailors' to fetch you. Have a wonderful time, and I will see you later tonight. Or, maybe not," she finished with a wink.

Gawain could not help but laugh. "I think I will join you after they get the meeting and then the wedding ceremony over with. The celebration afterward is much more my style. Arabella will understand, and I might even bring her. Good luck with the council, beautiful. I am sure you will have them all wrapped around your finger in no time at all!"

"I will do my best," Ki'ara replied, giving him a mischievous look. "I think I have a pretty good case, don't you? Have fun, and I will see you in a bit!"

Gawain kissed his sister's soft cheek and hugged her briefly before stepping back. He gave Ki'ara a formal bow and waved at the building. "Get going, little one! You are already late! I am sure the assembly has already begun," he told her. With one last encouraging smile, he turned and strode off towards the harbor.

Ki'ara entered the hall. People were milling about, but none of the lords were in sight. Gawain had been right. The council meeting was already in session.

Thanks to her enhanced senses, she could hear the voices coming from the assembly chamber.

She and Gawain had been set to leave much earlier and would have reached Deansport in plenty of time had it not been for the incident at the castle. Due to the fire and the healings Ki'ara had done, they had been significantly delayed. Her brother was late for his date, she for the council.

Ki'ara had figured that this would happen but had decided that it was more important to help those who had been injured. She had never turned her back on anyone in need before and had not been about to start. The lords would understand. All Zidarians could appreciate that duty to the clan came before anything else.

⚜

The young lady usually made it a point to arrive before the start of a function and was therefore not thrilled to be making such a late appearance. This time, however, it might just work to her advantage.

Only a small number of Zidarians should be present at the meeting, but in an emergency, others could be called in through the network of magic mirrors. Ki'ara would be making quite an entrance due to the two guards stationed at the doors of the chamber. There was no way to slip in unnoticed, especially since they would insist on announcing her. It was part of their job.

Ki'ara tended to be a bit shy at times and would have preferred to remain in the background and listen. It had been an effective way for her to gather information. Once people forgot about her being present, they would speak more freely about matters concerning the realm and the MacClairs.

Now, blending in was no longer an option. Not only due to her tardiness, but also her new station. It might actually benefit Ki'ara to interrupt the meeting. All eyes would be on her, and they would wonder why she was late. She could ask for a special council right then but thought that too dramatic.

Ki'ara intended to make her request coolly and composedly once they were assembled around the table, right before they were seated.

⋆⋅☆⋅⋆

With a silent prayer for courage, Ki'ara squared her shoulders as she moved towards the chamber. As was customary, she stopped at the altar to the left of the doors. She was most likely the last to arrive but passing by the shrine without stopping just went against everything she believed in. Since she was already late, a few more minutes would not make much of a difference at this point.

The altar was housed in an alcove that contained a shelf with flowers and several statues of the different gods. A receptacle for offerings had been placed beneath. To bring blessings to the council and smooth the waves so that their debates yielded agreements benefiting them all, each lord had put a gift to the divine in the bowl.

Standing in the recess which had been carved into the thick walls, she could hear the murmurings of the people within the hexagonal room. The assembly was in full swing, and a discussion was taking place. Every once in a while, someone raised their voice just a little, not an unusual thing among the hot-tempered lords of the Highlands.

She should have taken the time out for the usual ritual, but for once, Ki'ara was disinclined to do so. She sent a silent thank you to the magic instead for being here with her and, with a quick prayer, asked for help from her goddess. Digging out a coin, she was just about to place it in the receptacle. Suddenly, she froze.

A voice she knew only too well had caught her attention. Even after all these years, she recognized it instantly. The money, wholly forgotten, dropped from her nerveless hand and tumbled to the floor. Ki'ara was so stunned she never noticed.

⊱✦⊰

The StCloud! How could this be? He was not supposed to be here! Leana had mentioned that he was traveling far up north somewhere and was not expected to return for several months! Her maid was usually very up-to-date on all the events, and her information could be trusted. This was something she had not been prepared for!

Ki'ara had not dared to ask any of her brothers about further details on the owner of Cloudshire Hall. Nothing good would have come from letting them know that she still had an interest! How was this possible? How could Conall be here? Ragnald would have never let her come had he known! He would have locked her up as he always did whenever the StCloud was anywhere near!

⊱✦⊰

Ki'ara was only too aware of how her oldest brother felt about this lord. Ragnald saw him as his archrival and nemesis. He blamed Conall for just about everything which had ever gone wrong in his and his grandfather's life. He even held the StCloud accountable for things that had happened before the man was born!

The young woman had always seen it for what it was, an excuse. As long as someone else could be blamed, Ragnald had to take no responsibility for his own mess, and he could continue to idealize their granddad Raghnall who had not been a very admirable person.

⊱✦⊰

Facing the council was going to be enough of a challenge, but Conall being present made Ki'ara even more self-conscious. Should she send someone to go find Gawain, so he could go in with her? The idea did not appeal to her, it felt like a cowardly thing to do. As a lord, she needed to meet challenges head-on and not hide behind others.

No, Ki'ara decided. She could do this by herself. If she set a precedent of allowing someone to hold her hand every time something became difficult, she would make a terrible ruler. Gawain was counting on her, and her clan needed help desperately.

⁓�֍⁓

In a meeting this small, it would not be possible to avoid the man Ragnald had strictly forbidden her to speak to, nor was she willing to continue to comply with those orders. The young lady no longer worried about her brother's fury since she had no plans to return to Seamuir Castle until she was confirmed as lord.

After the incident earlier that day, Ki'ara was done with respecting her sibling's draconian guidelines. Why should she obey his command to stay away from the StCloud when Ragnald hated her so much that he had found it amusing to see her in peril and had tried to take her very life yet once again?

With that cowardly act, Ragnald had utterly lost her loyalty, her allegiance, as well as the little respect Ki'ara had still felt for her brother. Whatever was going on with the MacClair, he was done running her life.

⁓✖⁓

Once again, THAT voice reached her ears. Ki'ara could feel a strange sensation in her stomach, like butterflies dancing around. Her knees grew weak, and she placed a hand against the wall to keep herself upright, drawing the guards' curious stares.

Part of her wanted to flee, the other part to throw herself in his arms, to allow him to take over and take care of her, to make everything better like he had always done in the past. How easy it would be to let him fight this battle for her! And, how tempting! Ki'ara realized, however, that she could not afford to do either.

Taking some deep breaths, the young sorceress calmed herself. In a way, Conall being here was perfect. She required him as her ally if she was going to succeed in taking over the realm somewhat peacefully. Since her father had left, the StCloud and her uncle Iain had been the two men she knew would help her against Ragnald if there was ever a need.

Now that she had clarified the situation in her mind, the feeling of excitement at seeing Conall again started to grow. It had been so long!

Suddenly, her entire abdomen tightened with anticipation, and she began to feel downright nauseous. Ki'ara was elated and anxious all at the same time. Her fight or flight response had kicked into high gear, and her heart was pounding so hard she could hear the blood rush in her ears.

The last time she had talked to him, she had still been a child. Now, all new sensations were spreading through her body at the sound of that resonant voice. No other man had ever made her heart sing, only he. Ki'ara would never forget the day the StCloud had been forbidden to her because of some ridiculous grudge Ragnald still held.

Ki'ara had been forced to avoid Conall. Her brother had threatened her with dire consequences for both of them if she dared to speak to the man. She had been barely a teenager and had seen no choice but to obey. Every time she had looked into the StCloud's eyes from across a room, it had broken her heart.

Suddenly, a strange notion came to her, and something clicked. Had Conall and the illegal spells been the only reasons Ragnald had kept sending her away, or had there been more? A vague reference made by Gawain during the coach ride popped into her mind. Now that she thought back on it, her sibling had chosen his words rather carefully, something that was not usually his style.

There was something else, she could sense it! Ki'ara decided that she would ask Gawain for more information when she saw him later that night and that she would not take no for an answer.

⁘

The gods had truly smiled on her this day. Ki'ara could still barely believe her good luck. If she played this right, she could be joining forces with a powerful ally, one who was definitely not a friend of Ragnald's!

The young woman was aware that her oldest brother hated the StClouds with a passion and not just Conall. Ragnald fervently despised the entire family. The only event she could think of which could have born such feelings was the disappearance of his beloved grandfather along with the then Lord of the StClouds.

As it was, Ragnald had a very distorted view of reality. He envisioned himself as the future leader of the other rulers, as their overlord. Conall was powerful, and Ki'ara suspected that in her brother's twisted mind, he saw the StCloud as his main rival for that coveted position.

The MacClair had been bitterly complaining for years now that the lords went to Conall for advice when they should have been coming to him. It infuriated Ragnald that his adversary managed to put himself 'above him,' as he put it, with no effort at all. It had been a frequent topic at dinner, and Ki'ara had been forced to listen to his grudges on many occasions during her visits.

From what she had heard from Gawain, every time Ragnald came home from an assembly or a chance meeting with the StCloud, he would rant for hours. He would call a family council to inform his siblings of his enemy's latest transgressions. The irate lord would make plans to improve his own standing and then discard them. He was 'THE MacClair,' after all, there was no need for HIM to work on getting people to like him. Under no circumstances was he going to stoop that low!

Their brother would grumble for half the night how unfair it was that the other lords preferred the StCloud's counsel over his every time. Did they not realize that they were being manipulated by that man? How could they be so blind? Did they not see that he, the MacClair, really had the better ideas? How much improved life would be for all Zidarians in the Highlands if they just listened to him?

There had been a few times when Ragnald had been even more angry than usual when he returned. On those occasions, the other lords had actually dared to laugh at her brother's ideas. After those meetings, he would be furious for weeks and plot the murders of each and every one of his peers.

Ragnald saw himself as the perfect ruler, but from what his sister had observed, he had no consideration or regard for anyone except maybe himself. That others had feelings or needs never occurred to him, nor would he have cared if it had. In Ki'ara's opinion, something was missing in her oldest sibling, and she had often wondered if he even possessed much of a heart.

No matter what time he got back to the castle after one of the rare assemblies he had been made to attend, if things had not gone according to plan, as they usually did not, Ragnald would call his siblings to the study. They knew better than to refuse, there was no reasoning with the MacClair when he was in that kind of a mood.

His captive audience did not dare to move or say anything on those occasions when Ragnald felt offended or slighted and was in a rage. Nobody wanted to become the target for all that hostility. It was best to let their brother and lord rant and listen politely.

As it was, all it would take was one moment of perceived inattention. Without warning, all hell would break loose. Ragnald had found his victim to unleash his wrath on. If she was home, it was usually Ki'ara who became the target of all that pent-up fury. While she was gone, it was Gawain who would end up as the scapegoat.

⁘

The way the MacClair saw it, nothing was ever his fault, and he never did anything wrong. Somehow, in the end, he would always find a way to blame Conall. Ragnald had convinced himself that all he had to do was to come up with a way to get rid of that man. Then the other lords would treat him with the respect he deserved!

With the StCloud gone, nothing would stand in the way of his ascension to the overlord position of the Highlands; of this, Ragnald was utterly confident. Therefore, he was continually looking for a ploy to do away with his nemesis.

All he needed was a good excuse. The MacClair reckoned that violating the explicit and publicly issued command to stay away from his sister would do. He, the dutiful guardian, could then step in and protect her honor, something no one could fault him for.

⁘

Ragnald had never come out and mentioned that ploy to Ki'ara, but he had used other threats. The young girl was very perceptive. It had not taken her long to figure out what her brother had planned. Out of fear for Conall's life, she had stayed away from him at all times. She had seen the hurt this had caused him, but at least he was alive.

The young woman loved the StCloud and had been determined not to be the one who caused her sibling to finally snap and put one of his murderous campaigns into action. Ragnald was just crazy enough to get lucky, not a chance she had been willing to take. She was good at sneaking about but had been loath to take the risk.

⊱•⊰

Since early childhood, Ki'ara had perfected the art of blending in. This had made it possible for her to overhear some of the remarks made behind her oldest brother's back. Ragnald was delusional if he thought the other rulers would ever like, respect, or accept him as their overlord. They enjoyed being equals and were opposed to going back to the former system.

Even if Ragnald managed to do away with Conall somehow, his situation would most likely not improve. If anything, it might become more difficult. The StCloud was usually the one who made sure that things stayed civil at the meetings, no matter how annoying her brother became.

Why was it impossible for Ragnald to let go of the past? Could he not see that their grandfather had brought his fate on himself by his actions? And, that he was following right in his footsteps?

⊱•⊰

The feud between the MacClairs and the StClouds went back many centuries. The two clans had been the two most influential, right along with the McCullochs, and had always jockeyed for the best and most prominent positions.

All this had changed when Mikael took over the rule of the MacClairs and made peace with the StClouds. Her father had worked hard on smoothing the waves. The marriage he had arranged between the two families would have further tied them together and assured a lasting peace.

Once Ragnald had become lord after Mikael departed, a number of the old resentments had been revived. It had not taken long, and if anything, her brother had managed to raise hostilities to a whole new level with his abrasive behavior.

One of the first things the new MacClair ruler had done had been to publicly invalidate and even forbid the union between the two clans. He had burned the contract of Ki'ara's engagement to Conall right there in the council chamber. Not even the protest of the rest of the lords had been able to get him to see reason. His conduct only deteriorated from there.

On several occasions, their uncle, Lord Iain Elvinstone of Ravenshire, had seen himself forced to step in. He had tried unsuccessfully to put a stop to some of his nephew's hostilities. No amount of entreating had been able to reach Ragnald, who cared nothing for what anyone else thought.

All the kind man had been able to do had been to alleviate some of the damage. After a while, the usually so patient lord had enough. When her brother continued to refuse to listen to reason, Lord Iain had all but disowned him.

Ki'ara had noticed that Ragnald had become progressively more delusional and more defiant. Every time she had come home, she had seen a further deterioration in his morals and an increase in his belief that the laws did not apply to him, that the rights of others did not exist. He felt entitled to do as he pleased, regardless of who was being harmed.

At one time, Ragnald had become so antagonistic that he had almost caused a war with the StClouds. Neither the fear of the Zidhe nor the rules of the peace treaty had appeared to impress him in the slightest. Instead, he had increased his aggression, had poured more fuel on the fire.

It had been the StCloud who had been instrumental in preventing an exacerbation of the situation. He had put a stop to her brother's antagonism by taking his case to the council instead of responding to Ragnald's blatant attempts to provoke him. The lords had stepped in and had dealt with the wayward ruler the only way they could. They had closed ranks against him.

Her brother had been beyond furious but had seen himself forced to improve his manners, at least in public, since the council of lords had given him the option to behave or face punishment by the Zidhe, the highest authority in the land. They handled occurrences such as this, which were outside the council's control.

Had the elves become involved, Ragnald would have either been replaced, or he might have disappeared just like his beloved grandfather before him. With her brother's reluctant compliance, a bloody conflict between the two rulers had been averted, and an uneasy peace restored for the moment.

The clan, however, was still suffering under their cruel and narcissistic lord. Ki'ara was hoping that by being proactive and bringing Ragnald's latest offenses to the attention of the council before it reached their ears through other channels, she could keep things from escalating and prevent the most severe consequences her brother might end up facing.

⚘

In a way, it was understandable that the two rulers did not like each other. Ragnald and Conall were almost opposite in their disposition. Ki'ara was glad that the StCloud was so dissimilar to her brother. Unlike the MacClair, he was kind, caring, and generous of spirit, a truly benevolent person who had the good of others in mind.

Ki'ara was convinced that he understood her reasons for ignoring him for years and refusing to speak to him. She hoped that Conall would be willing to help, he always had been. It was just in his nature.

One question which had little to do with the situation on hand kept going around and around in her thoughts. Did the StCloud still love her? Could he forgive all her family had put him through?

Ki'ara wished so with all her heart, but she could not blame him if he had moved on.

Chapter 46

A Grand Entrance

For a moment longer, Ki'ara stood by the shrine near the council chamber doors. Taking deep breaths, she reached out to the magic of the realm. It came to her willingly and instantly and filled her with calm. She could do this, of that she had no doubt now. Her clan and her life depended on it.

Making her case and keeping her thoughts straight would have been much easier had the StCloud not been present, but that was life. If everything went well, she would no longer have to protect Conall from Ragnald. That would be a most welcome change.

What Ki'ara's brothers had seen as obedience, had been her way to minimize the risk of reprisal to the man she loved and to herself. Also, as long as her guardian had believed that she was doing as she was told, her life at the castle had been at least marginally more bearable. The act had almost become second nature over the years.

Any disobedience on her part had usually been met with swift and severe punishment. Ki'ara had been grateful when the council reined in her brother and instituted guidelines for the treatment of his people and siblings. Ragnald had modified his behavior minutely, but even that small amount had made life a little easier for her as well as the clan.

❧⬦☙

Despite all he had done, Ragnald was her brother, and she did love him even if she did not like the way he behaved. The actions Ki'ara was going to pursue were not something she was looking forward to. She was about to bring charges against her sibling and become instrumental in taking everything he had ever cared and worked for.

Inflicting that kind of hurt on another went against her belief of doing no harm. Unfortunately, Ragnald had brought this onto himself. Ki'ara knew in her heart and soul that she was doing the right thing, but that still did not take away the sadness she felt.

❧⬦☙

Ki'ara had usually complied with what Ragnald asked of her, often against her own better judgment. Obeying voluntarily had been easier than being forced to do something. It had not taken her long to figure this out after he had become her guardian. The MacClair was good at making a point.

Deep down, she had always feared that one day she would have to break relations with her brother and possibly even the clan. Blood ties ran deep in the Highlands, especially amongst the Zidarians. To survive, they had always stuck together, it was part of their code and was indoctrinated into their children from an early age on.

What she was about to do went against everything her people believed in. This was also the reason Ragnald was still in power. Ki'ara knew that she would have to present a convincing case to achieve her objective. It was time to gather her thoughts and go over the facts one last time.

The young lady's mind flashed back to the earlier scene in the courtyard. Her brother's coldhearted laughter had sounded insane. She still could barely believe it. No decent lord would behave like that! Only Ki'ara's quick intervention had saved the ones in the fire's path from being burned worse. Had she not instructed the magic to dampen the straw around the edges, more injuries would have resulted.

Ragnald had done nothing to help. The lord of the clan, who was supposed to be its protector, had just stood there watching his sister run for her life and his people getting hurt. Even if he had not been responsible for the blaze in the first place, this inaction itself was an unforgivable crime. As the wielder of the realms magic as well as the caster of the foreign spells, one thought, one wave of his hand, could have doused the raging inferno.

Ki'ara was certain that this had been no ordinary fire, but she had no direct proof. The magic had evaporated, but she had sensed the two spells. The witnesses had commented that the courtyard should not have been engulfed that quickly and that the damp straw should not have burned that ferociously.

All those who had seen the conflagration get started had called it unnatural, and they had been right. Ki'ara had overheard the whispers while she was healing those who had been injured. She was confident that rumors would lay the blame squarely at her brother's feet.

The focus of the inferno had been around Ki'ara, she had been the intended target of this attack. Everyone else had just been collateral damage. What kind of monster would come up with a plot like that?

Ki'ara had come close to having to use more of her powers to save herself. This would have given away her connection to the land. Ragnald would have tried to find a way to kill her right there, of that she was sure, regardless of who would have been watching.

It was time to put a stop to his tyranny. Even the magic was fighting him, and she was now 'The MacClair,' not he. For her own benefit as well as the clans, Ki'ara would have to wrest the power out of his grip sooner than later. If she waited too long, more harm would be done.

Any further loyalty to Ragnald would be grossly misplaced. He had shown that he had none for her nor for their people. It was time that she stepped up and did what had to be done. She had been entrusted with a great responsibility and needed to consider what was in the best interest of the MacClair Clan as well as the magic.

The sorceress determinedly steeled herself. She pulled back her shoulders and straightened her spine. Now, how to best present herself? Which one of the many facets of her personality would be the most useful for this occasion?

After a moment's consideration, Ki'ara slipped into her finest 'I am the queen' persona. It was time to do battle and losing was not an option.

⚜

After one more deep breath, the young lady walked up to the doors. She smiled at the guards stationed at each side and nodded. She was ready to enter. The sentries had been waiting patiently for her signal. One of the men opened the doors wide and walked in ceremoniously to announce her.

The warrior stopped and came to attention just inside the chamber. His entry drew the curiosity of some of the lords who were standing at the far side of the hall having a lively discussion. The guard paused for a second for maximum effect, then knocked the butt of his lance on the stone floor. The resulting crack reverberated loud enough to cut off any lingering conversations. The gathered Zidarians were now respectfully silent.

From where she was standing, Ki'ara could see most of the suite, a magnificent hexagonal space with an adjoining cloakroom on its right side next to the gate. Nine large magic mirrors, one for each clan and decorated with their insignia, were affixed to the three walls facing the entrance. The Zidhe were able to project their image into the room and therefore had no need for such devices.

Subtly lit by magic and an intricate system of small reflectors channeling in light from the outside, the white marble walls gave off a luminous glow, both peaceful and warm. The center of the chamber was occupied by three tables arranged in a half-circle. This allowed everyone in attendance to face the mirrors as well as see each other. The very middle position was reserved for the head of the assembly.

The sound of the lance hitting the stone kept echoing around the chamber for a good minute. Once it subsided, the guard made the required introduction. "Her Highness, the Lady Ki'ara of the MacClairs!" he announced grandly with a voice booming with pride since he was announcing a fellow member of his very own clan.

Seeing her waiting outside the doors, the other lords quickly returned to their chairs. They sat as a show of respect, their hands on the table. This custom had been introduced by the Zidhe to assure the newcomer that all were unarmed and that it was safe to enter.

Ki'ara remained standing just outside the room for a brief moment longer. The guard knocked on the floor one more time, but this time, not as hard. With a formal bow and a grand gesture of his right hand, the soldier invited his lady to enter.

The young woman swept into the room with her head held high. She walked in like the queen she would have once been. For her, this was not very hard since many of the rituals and customs of the past had survived the forced abdications and were taught to the children.

The Zidarians were no longer kings and queens, but they had maintained some of the pomp and many of the ceremonies. Supposedly, this had been done for the populace who loved those old rites and venerated their leaders. Ki'ara suspected that it had made the bereft rulers feel better to keep some of the trappings of their former status after losing their crowns.

"Greetings, my Lords and Ladies, and my apologies for being late. I was unavoidably detained. Please continue your discussion," Ki'ara stated with great poise when she reached the table. Throwing that little comment in about being held up was bound to pique her fellow Zidarians' interest.

Ki'ara was outwardly the picture of calmness but inside a bundle of nerves. She had to play this just right, so very much was hanging on a positive outcome. Good thing the manners and phrases she needed at the moment had been drilled into her from very young on. She was functioning on autopilot and had brought out her public persona, a little trick she had learned to overcome her shyness and to hide how anxious she truly felt at being the center of attention.

A quick glance upon entering had shown her the location of the StCloud at the table. She was doing her very best not to let her eyes stray back to that spot lest she would lose her fragile composure. It had been so long, and she yearned to drown in those warm brown eyes and forget all her troubles. That, however, was a luxury she would have to save until later and depended on whether said lord was still willing.

The young lady just caught herself as her traitorous mind allowed her gaze to wander back towards Conall. No way was she going to let the rest of the lords see the effect that man was having on her! She was representing herself and her clan after all, and acting like a schoolgirl in love just would not do. What she needed to display right now were dignity and poise.

Lord Weatherlin was sitting in for Andrew McCulloch of Cambria. Since he was heading the assembly, he was installed at the center of the table, which was closest to her. He quickly jumped up to escort her to the cloakroom. The grandfatherly gent gallantly helped her out of her cape and handed it to a servant to hang up.

The old man had always been one of her favorites. With a sweet smile, Ki'ara thanked him for his assistance, and the lord's bright blue eyes started to sparkle with pleasure. She could not help but think how adorable he was with his white mane looking like he had been through some kind of a windstorm.

"Do not worry, you are not late, Lady Ki'ara," the lord assured her kindly. "It is our pleasure to have you! It has been too many moons since any of us have seen you! Welcome home to the Highlands!" he beamed at her.

Ki'ara returned his smile, thankful for the momentary distraction. Now, however, it was time to set events in motion. Leaning forward, she whispered. "I need to address the council, my lord. It is rather urgent." Lord Weatherlin regarded her sharply for a few seconds, then nodded.

Offering her his arm, the elderly gentleman guided Ki'ara back into the assembly room. She was glad to have his support. Her legs felt like rubber, and her stomach was doing all kinds of untoward things. The tension in the young lady's body was almost too much.

Against her will, her eyes were drawn back towards Conall as soon as they entered. Ki'ara quickly averted her gaze but not before noticing that, as if by magic, an empty seat had materialized next to the StCloud. Was that where they intended her to sit? How was she going to keep her thoughts straight with him THAT close to her?

If she did not get herself under control soon, Ki'ara feared she might faint or throw up. Her stomach was now doing flips. She had to force herself to keep walking and to appear as serene and composed as was expected of her. Pushing her anxieties aside, she continued on with determination. Conall being near made stating her case more difficult, but then again, had she not always loved a good challenge?

Sure enough, Lord Weatherlin led her to just that available chair. He courteously pulled it out for Ki'ara, who gracefully slid into the seat. After being properly situated, the young woman turned and thanked her escort. The polite gent happily returned her smile, and she acknowledged it with a brief bow of her head.

If she did not want to appear ill-mannered, Ki'ara could no longer postpone the inevitable. It was time to greet the rest of the assembly. She locked eyes and nodded to each of the gathered nobles. Most were men except for the two ladies who had been sent to represent their absent lords.

Getting to a meeting or even being available by mirror was not always possible for the head of a clan. Travel was easy because of the gates, but sometimes, things came up that required the lord to be away from the castle and his direct line of communication with the council.

Therefore, he or she had the option to send a delegate in their stead. The person had to be a Zidarian and able to use a magic mirror. On occasions, the envoys were even given a choice to remain in a region as the permanent representative of their ruler.

Shannon O'Leary was the local stand-in for Lorena Kirkcaldie of Argness, while Heather McClintok had been employed by Rowena Alistar of Islandia. Both were beautiful ladies, shrewd, diplomatic, and very astute. Not much got past these two, and they regarded Ki'ara with frank curiosity during the greetings.

Finally, only the StCloud was left to acknowledge. When she could no longer avoid looking at him without appearing rude, she turned and glanced up at him. When their eyes connected, the effect was instantaneous. Ki'ara could feel her face flushing and the heat rising inside her.

The young lady could not help thinking that a dunk in some icy pond was due about now! How had it gotten so hot in here all of a sudden? It took her a moment before she noticed that she was staring at Conall. His gaze seemed to mesmerize her, hold her captive like nothing else could.

Oh no! She was gawking at this handsome man like a lovesick teenager! Ki'ara could feel herself turn even redder. She quickly gave the StCloud a brief nod and then turned back towards the rest of the nobles. Slowly her heartbeat slowed, and her composure returned.

⚜

To her surprise, Ki'ara noticed that all nine heads of the Highland Clans or their representatives were present. From what she had been told, this was supposed to be a very small meeting with only the immediate neighbors appearing! What had happened to change this?

The young woman decided that she would find out soon enough. Since a member of every clan was now present, the meeting could truly begin. The law dictated that without all the lords' approval, no final decision could be made in any matter of greater importance. Everyone being here was definitely to her benefit.

Lord Weatherlin briefly caught Ki'ara up on the council's discussion and on the topics on the agenda. "Do you, Lady MacClair, have something you need to bring to the attention of your peers?" he finally asked her.

Ki'ara stood and bowed to him and the others. "I do have three issues to present to you. Would you please allow me the time to address you today? They are matters of great importance and cannot be delayed until the next meeting. I am happy to wait until everything else has been settled."

Affirmative nods all around approved her request. From the glances being exchanged, Ki'ara could tell that all kinds of speculations were going through the lords' heads. They were now more than a little curious, which might help speed up some of the other scheduled discussions.

Once the lords got to work, one issue after another was efficiently dealt with. The last assembly had been three months ago, and a number of large and small concerns needing the council's attention had accumulated. Each was introduced, discussed, and then voted on. With every clan being represented, the rulings took into consideration everybody's best interest.

Ki'ara was only too aware of Conall's nearness. Her entire body was reacting to him. To keep herself from getting thoroughly distracted, she studiously avoided looking at him. No way was she going to embarrass herself yet again. She did her utmost to pay close heed to what was being said around the table instead.

No matter how hard she tried, time after time, Ki'ara's attention wandered. Her thoughts seemed to want to flit all about this day. Mostly, however, they were filled with speculations about the StCloud. It did help distract her from her anxiety about her upcoming speech, but still! This just would not do!

The young woman's many years of training came to her aid yet again. Resolutely, she kept her mind on the subjects at hand and even added her own input on occasions. When the time approached for the first vote, Ki'ara had more than a vague notion of what they were deciding on despite her anxiety.

Ki'ara was proud to be representing her clan and determined to do the best job she possibly could. That was what her people deserved and would get from now on if she had anything to say about it!

Chapter 47

An Unexpected Advance

The council of lords was working their way through the agenda set down for the day. They had already dealt with a good number of matters, and everything had gone relatively smoothly until now.

The next topic, however, a longstanding dispute over grazing rights in one of the common areas between two of the clans, led to an especially spirited discussion. Even Ki'ara ended up getting caught up in the fray. Paying attention was not so difficult anymore all of a sudden.

The young woman had put her hands under the table and was resting them in her lap. She had not wanted any of the lords to realize how badly they were shaking. The act of taking the power of the realm from her oldest brother was not something she was going to enjoy.

To achieve her goals, it was essential that she appeared calm and composed. As a ruler, she would be required to deal with all sorts of situations with detachment and competence. The time to start using the skills she had been taught by her father and uncle were now.

Keeping her cool would have been a lot easier had it not been for the added distraction of Conall next to her. Ki'ara had loved the StCloud as long as she could remember. There had been a time when she had looked forward to their lives together. To be this near him and not be able to touch him or speak to him privately, was almost more than she could bear.

The StCloud was sitting in the chair to her right. When Ki'ara surreptitiously glanced in his direction, she realized that the distance between them seemed to have decreased in the last few minutes. Her already pounding heart started beating yet faster. Having him even closer was having an increased effect on her body and mind.

How much she wanted to talk to him, to explain her previous behavior. If only she had been able to find a way around her brother's orders, which would not have jeopardized Conall's life! Ki'ara had not been willing to risk Ragnald finding out about any disobedience on her part since he had made the consequences of such an infraction perfectly clear.

Would the StCloud ever be able to forgive her? Ki'ara sure hoped so! Should she reach out towards him? She should be able to do so unseen under the table! As if reading her mind, a strong hand wrapped itself around her small one. When she did not pull away, long, powerful fingers intertwined themselves with her ice-cold ones.

⁖⊱⋆⊰⁖

At his touch, Ki'ara had frozen completely. It took her a moment before she could even catch her breath. Had anyone noticed? Quickly, she looked around. None of the lords seemed to have seen anything out of the ordinary in the heat of the argument, which was still raging on. The young lady let out a soft sigh of relief.

Ki'ara was amazed. The contact with him felt wonderful, exhilarating but also comforting at the same time. Definitely distracting, however, which she figured might not be a bad thing at this time. Strange sensations were racing all over her body. She had only felt something like this when he had been in her dreams. Did she dare look at the StCloud with him being THIS close?

A quick glance around the table assured the young lady that the other lords were still sufficiently preoccupied. It was now or never! She decided that being a coward just would not do. It was not like her, she was usually much braver than this!

Pulling herself together, Ki'ara took a deep breath and turned her head just enough to meet the lord's eyes. This was the first time since she had entered the chamber that she had allowed herself to really look at them. She could not believe it! As she had suspected, these were the eyes from her dream!

Conall, in turn, was watching Ki'ara intently. It seemed he was very little concerned with the present discussion and much more interested in her. When he grinned at her reassuringly, she involuntarily smiled back. Her heart started to sing as it always had when he was near. How much she loved this man; how handsome he was!

The StCloud's stare intensified, and his eyes seemed to bore into her. Ki'ara felt like she was drowning in their hypnotic depth. It took her a moment before she could tear her gaze away. Her breathing came in rapid gasps, almost like she had been running. She worked hard on slowing it before someone noticed, but still, it took her several minutes.

Had being with him always felt like that? It had been so long that Ki'ara had seen him, had been this close to him. She could not really remember, but kind of doubted it. Then, she had only been a child!

All those years ago, Ki'ara had loved him and enjoyed being around him, but it had been much more innocent. The effect his gaze had on her just now had been incredible! The young sorceress realized that entirely new sensations had been added to her reaction to him.

⚜

Since the day Ragnald had broken their engagement, Conall had often been in her thoughts from the moment she woke up until she fell asleep. He was never far from her mind and had been in her prayers every night.

Ki'ara had been unable and unwilling to forget about him. The StCloud had even frequently visited her dreams, which had evolved over the years to grow progressively more vivid and filled with desire. Actual meetings, however, had been few, and even then, except on rare occasions, they had seen each other only from a distance.

For a brief moment and mostly out of habit, Ki'ara almost pulled her hand out of Conall's. The memory of the look in her brother's eyes and his vicious laughter when she had been in trouble, however, filled her with defiance. Never again would she allow Ragnald or anyone else tell her who she could talk to!

So instead of pulling her hand away, she tightened her grip on those wonderfully warm fingers. A wave of comfort washed over her. Slowly, her breathing grew calmer, and her heart stopped racing. She gave the StCloud another shy smile before returning her attention to the meeting.

⚜

During their brief interaction, the discussion had grown even more impassioned. Tempers were flaring, and the situation was getting out of control. Two of the lords were now shaking their fists and screaming at each other across the table. Beside her, the StCloud loudly cleared his throat.

Silence fell almost immediately. Only the combatants continued shouting at each other for just a brief moment longer. They cut off in mid-sentence, however, once they realized that Conall wished to address them. Both sat down and turned their attention to the StCloud, but they kept shooting angry glances at each other.

"My lords, please, there is always a compromise to be found which would benefit you both," Conall's melodic voice reminded them. "After all, have you not been friends for many years? Must I remind you of the snowstorm when your herds were lost, and you were out there together rescuing your sheep? You ended up losing just a few instead of all because your clans worked together!"

The two lords looked at each other sheepishly. Leave it to the StCloud to remind them that they were no longer enemies. The discussion was concluded rapidly after this. Once everyone began working together, they quickly came up with a solution that satisfied both landholders.

After that one unpleasant interlude, the council meeting continued smoothly. A few additional minor problems were addressed and dealt with to everyone's satisfaction. Then, Lord Weatherlin stood up and turned to Ki'ara. "Lady Ki'ara MacClair, please, state your case to the council!"

The young lady glanced over at Conall and then gave his fingers one last squeeze before releasing them. The StCloud immediately stood up and pulled the chair back for her so that she could rise and address the assembly.

Ki'ara gave him a grateful smile and full well expected Conall to retake his seat. To her surprise, he moved to stand beside her, letting everyone know that he was there to support her. Deep gratefulness flooded through her, along with a sense of relief. Having the StCloud on her side gave her cause a much greater chance to succeed. What had she ever done to deserve such loyalty?

After taking a moment to compose herself and to put her thoughts in order, Ki'ara addressed the gathered nobles. "I have three important matters to present to you. The first is a dire situation in Frankonia," Ki'ara began. Quickly and factually, she relayed what she had learned on her journey down the mountains and what she felt needed to be done to deal with this danger.

Due to the seriousness of the situation, it did not take long for the council to agree on immediately dispatching a delegation to assist Jacques in isolating and containing the threat. Argulf would most likely never even notice a new servant, and this would make it possible to keep a close eye on him. No further enchantments could be allowed to leave De'Aire Chateau.

After getting her first concern out of the way, it was time to deal with the matters closer to home. Briefly, Ki'ara relayed the information she had obtained from Mathus. The lords were outraged to hear that her brother had been collecting illegal spells. This made him even more of a menace than he already was.

A plan of action was devised to deal with those enchantments. All agreed that they had to be collected and soon. If her brother did not hand them over peacefully, the Zidhe would need to get involved.

⚜

This left the last of her concerns to present, her case for Ragnald's dismissal as lord. Ki'ara took a deep breath before commencing.

"My lords, I was late today due to an attempt on my life. It took place in the courtyard of Seamuir Castle. I escaped mostly unharmed, but several people and a horse needed to be healed. I felt that taking care of the injured took precedence over anything else," she began.

There had been gasps all around the table at her words, and her uncle's face had gone pale. He had a good idea of what was coming. On Lord Weatherlin's request, Ki'ara described the incident in more detail. She stayed as calm and dispassionately as possible but could see the effect her narrative was having on the assembled Zidarians. They were angry and did not care to hide their feelings.

Several of the lords had questions that Ki'ara answered honestly and to the best of her abilities. She did her utmost to avoid all judgments and speculations. It was not up to her to share those things unless she was specifically asked. She wanted to be awarded the rule of her clan without having to resort to manipulations.

Finally, everyone's curiosity was sated. With a nod, Lord Weatherlin let the young lady know that she could continue. Ki'ara's face was sad but composed. This was the moment she had hoped would never come.

In his effort to support her, the StCloud had moved even closer. Ki'ara could feel his hand in the small of her back, encouraging her to go on.

"My lords, because of this and other incidents over the years, I see myself forced to request the removal of Ragnald MacClair as the lord and ruler of the MacClair clan!" she continued calmly.

Ki'ara's words were met with approving nods all around, but the lords' faces were grim. Removing a Zidarian from power because of his actions had never happened before and was a serious undertaking. Since the disappearance of the two rulers, only Ragnald had ever dared to behave with such disregard for the laws of the Highlands.

This was definitely a special case, but everyone present felt that this was the right time to deal with the MacClair's offenses and indiscretions. All the council members had been waiting for was a suitable replacement for the wayward ruler.

Ragnald had been warned multiple times over the years. The assembly had been only too aware that he had committed one atrocity after the other. Due to their reverence for his father, Mikael, and the lack of a suitable substitute, they had given him more chances than many felt he had deserved.

Lord Weatherlin thanked Ki'ara and invited her to be seated. Seeing that his fellow lords were already in agreement, he called for a decision. Each representative of the other eight clans was asked for a yay or a nay. The young lady started to relax as one affirmative vote after the other echoed through the chamber.

"We herewith declare that we approve the early termination of the rule of Ragnald MacClair due to his own actions. I, Lord Weatherlin, propose Ki'ara MacClair as the next Lord!" The words were met with loud clapping. Once again, the vote was cast, and the proposition approved. This part was done!

Since this was a case without precedent, the elves had to be consulted. They would have the final word in the outcome, but everyone at the table felt that they would most likely concur since the Zidhe had also been concerned about Ragnald's behavior.

Ki'ara's case was significantly strengthened by the rare occurrence of all the assembled Zidarians agreeing for once. A member of Ragnald's own family asking for his abdication would carry some weight but not as much as the vote of confidence she had received.

The elves would be the ones to carry out her brother's removal should he refuse to give up the rule peacefully.

There was one more thing the lords needed to know. Once things settled down a little, Ki'ara got the assembly's attention and received permission to speak. "My lords, I need to inform you that the magic itself has had enough and has all but abandoned Ragnald. It has already chosen me as the new ruler..." that was as far as she got.

The din around the table had grown to deafening proportions as each lord demanded to know how. This was more momentous than removing Ragnald from power and had also never transpired before. None of the gathered Zidarians had been aware that it was even a possibility. Could this happen to any lord if the magic did not like him or her?

Could someone just come along and woo it away? Why had the Zidhe never mentioned that the power could take such actions? All of a sudden, everyone had a multitude of questions.

⊱✿⊰⊱✿⊰

Most of the rulers had not realized that the power of the realm possessed free will and that much of a consciousness. They had worked closely with the magic for years without being cognizant that it was truly alive and could assert its own wishes.

For a couple, this was not such welcome news, and they were quietly evaluating their own behavior to see if their position might be in jeopardy as well. These lords suddenly realized that they might have treated the magic just a little high-handed. Conall, on the other hand, was smiling and looked at Ki'ara with pride.

"Silence!" Lord Weatherlin shouted in vain. It was not until the StCloud stepped in that the voices finally subsided. "Lady MacClair, how do you know this? What has happened?" the old gent queried.

"The first night I was home, I thought I had this amazing dream of flying all across the Highlands, of seeing the leylines, of healing the land. I was encouraged to explore every nook and cranny of Eastmuir, both above and below the ground. I was allowed to see the realm's hidden inhabitants, and they actually came out to meet me. I had no idea what was happening until later," Ki'ara explained.

"You said you were flying above all the Highlands, all the realms?" Lord Iain inquired. "Yes, my lord, from coast to coast and down to the barrier. It was truly amazing to see the land from above like that!" the young lady responded candidly.

For the next few minutes, the lords peppered Ki'ara with questions. They wanted to know more about the magic and about her experience, they were curious about every detail of what she had seen. Patiently, she answered each query with complete honesty.

Finally, a stunned silence fell over the assembly. No one ever spoke of the ceremony of the 'Choosing,' it was kept absolutely secret. During that rite, the power of the land bonded with the next ruler. Only a select few outside the ruling lords, mostly healers, had been told what to expect.

The councilors exchanged stunned glances. They were confident that there was no possible way that the young lady could have known about the initiation or what took place when the power came calling. To describe it this accurately could only mean that she had experienced such a bonding.

That the magic had acted on its own was not the only unexpected aspect. Usually, during the 'Becoming' the new lord was just gifted with an in-depth exploration of his or her own realm. How had it been possible for Ki'ara to fly across the entire Highlands? None of the rulers present had managed to go beyond their own borders!

Had this really happened? Ki'ara had described what she had seen very accurately, but they had to be sure. No doubt could remain. There was only one way to find out.

"Lady Ki'ara MacClair, please show us the magic!" Lord Weatherlin demanded. The others nodded their approval to his request, even the StCloud. He was looking forward to his peers being amazed by this unusual young woman.

Conall realized that they needed to see for themselves that she was speaking the truth. He knew her well enough to have believed every word she had spoken.

Ki'ara stepped back from the table. Spreading out her arms just a little, she let the magic flow into herself. It came instantaneously as if it had been waiting for just this occasion. Globes of power appeared in her upturned hands. She was outlined by a shimmering light bright enough to be almost blinding.

"Could you please turn that down just a bit, my dear?" came the wry request from the StCloud. Ki'ara immediately reduced the intensity of the glow. As she stood there, she looked like a goddess bathed in divine light.

Every person in the room could feel the power flowing through this young woman, and they stared at her in awe. Mikael had always claimed his daughter was special, but none of them except Conall had even had a clue just how extraordinary she really was.

Ki'ara shot a questioning glance at Lord Weatherlin, who nodded. She let the magic ebb away. The room felt dim without the brilliance of her power, and a stunned silence persisted for a few more moments.

"Thank you, Ki'ara MacClair. You have convinced me that you have been speaking the truth. Let me welcome you among us as Lord of Fairholme as well as MacClair!

Do you all agree?" the old lord concluded, turning to the rest of the council.

Conall showed his approval by clapping his hands, and the rest instantly followed.

Ki'ara had been accepted and brought into the fold as a lord. Even in the unlikely event that the elves decided to keep Ragnald in place, she still was the ruler of her own lands and now a permanent member of the council. She sighed with relief, and some of the tension drained out of her body.

Once they were all seated again, the StCloud reclaimed her hand under the table. Ki'ara turned and gave him a grateful smile. "Thank you," she whispered. Having him stand with her like that had meant much to her. She was confident that he had her back, no matter what. How much she had missed that!

After a few more minutes of chatter and several more questions for Ki'ara, Lord Weatherlin called the meeting to a close. The rulers were very curious about the young lady's experience with the magic, but the festivities were waiting. The bride and groom were ready, and it was time for the wedding to begin.

Once the assembly had been officially concluded, all the Zidarians rose, Ki'ara MacClair and Conall StCloud hand in hand. The two houses, which had been enemies ever since Ragnald took over as lord, were peacefully together at last, at least for the moment.

What has fate in store for the pair? Will the long-overdue wedding finally take place? And, will Ki'ara take her rightful place as the lord of the MacClair Clan? What will become of her brothers? Why did Ragnald hate his sister so very much, and what will happen to him?

All these questions and more will be answered in the second part of the saga!

Read the exciting continuation of the story of Ki'ara MacClair and Conall StCloud in Book 2 of the Mystic Highlands Sagas scheduled for publication in the winter of 2019!

Appendix

The World of the Highlands

The Highlands are the most northern area of the Mystic Isles and are initially divided into nine clan areas, the realm of the Zidhe, and the border (see Map in front of the book). They are a cold and often windy place with a rugged beauty, which is enough to take your breath away. The land's interior is inhabited by the Zidhe. The elves reside partially under domes as well as in fertile valleys and in beautiful evergreen forests, which they keep alive with their magic.

King Richard McCulloch of Cambria acted as a guiding overlord over the kings and queens of the clans for many years until his death. He died without naming an heir and without children of his own. A distant relative, Patrick McCulloch, eventually assumed the rule over Cambria but did not have the presence nor the strength to fill the vacant position as the leader and advisor for all the Highlands.

This set off an all-out war amongst the clans for the coveted position. Each ruler felt he was best suited to govern over them all. The Zidhe finally had enough and intervened. As a punishment for their unacceptable behavior, they forced the kings and queens to give up their crowns and become part of a council of Highland Clans.

More of the history of the Highlands is woven into the story of Ki'ara and Conall itself.

The Nine Highland Clans

Clan Name	Clan Region	Clan Chief	Clan Seat
Alistar	Islandia	Rowena Alistar	Seacrest Tower
Blair	Larinia	Duncan Blair	Killinstone Castle
Elvinstone	Ravenshire	Iain Elvinstone	Birdrell Tower
Fairlie	Kendall	Hamish Fairlie	Kendall Hall
Kirkcaldie	Argness	Lorena Kirkcaldie	Middlesea Castle
Macgillmott	Caithyll	Niall Macgillmott	Gilmockie Tower
StCloud	Summerland	Conall StCloud	Cloudshire Hall
McCulloch	Cambria	Andrew McCulloch	Lockmair Castle
MacClair	Eastmuir	Ragnald MacClair	Seamuir Castle

This table shows the initial clans, their region, present ruler, as well as the names of the Clan Seats. Later, Ki'ara MacClair becomes the Lord of Fairholme and her people, the 10th clan.

Places

Arillia

Arillian Continent: a large landmass that includes the Mystic Islands. In times past, most of the population inhabited the warmer parts of the continent. The peaceful societies founded by the Zidhe ·predominated in these temperate regions. The cold and barren northern reaches were only sparsely occupied until the elves made them their home.

Espanira

Espanira: A country bordered by Frankonia to the north and Portugana to the west, mostly rolling plains with some mountain ranges at the border with Frankonia.

Frankonia

Frankonia: A country to the south of the Mystic Isles. Part of it is mountainous, but it also has a beautiful coast.

Frankic coast: The coastal regions of Frankonia.

Frankonian Mountains: A range of tall mountains situated between Frankonia and Espanira.

De'Aire Chateau: A small dilapidated fortress way up in the mountains of Frankonia. It is home to the wizard Argulf and his few remaining servants. Not much grows there, and the supplies have to be fetched from the lowlands and the harbor of Mercede. The place is completely isolated in the winter, and provisions have to be brought in during the summer. During freak storms, the castle is often cut off for days. The servants raise some goats as well as chickens to supplement their diet. It takes more than 3 days to travel from the castle down to the harbor and an additional 3 weeks to reach the Highlands.

Mercede: The busiest port in the southern region of the Frankic Coast. The sizeable sheltered bay of Mercedeas makes for a deep natural harbor suited for large ships. It provides a safe haven in even the fiercest of storms. The shipping industry has brought prosperity to the port and its people, but crime has increased right along with the wealth.

Bay of Mercedeas: A deep water bay used as a harbor.

The Mystic Highlands

The 10th Kingdom: Until Ki'ara becomes a lord, the elves' realm was known as the 10th Kingdom. After that, the elves domain becomes known as the 11th realm. The Zidhe occupy the center of the Mystic Highlands, a strip along the border with the south, and several valleys leading down to the sea. Rumors have it that it is a truly wondrous place, but not many outsiders get to visit or live there.

The Barrier: An area along the border to the Lowlands created by the magic of the Zidhe. It is designed to keep people from crossing into the Highlands and extends out into the sea. This region is inhabited by all kinds of creatures and has an area of sentient fog which leads intruders in circles and spits them back out far from where they have started out as well as the Zone of Death where nothing grows.

Caithyll: The realm of the Macgillmotts.

Cloudshire Hall: The home of the StCloud clan and its present lord, Conall.

Council Chamber: A magnificent hexagonal space with an adjoining cloakroom on its right side next to the doors. Nine mirrors, one for each clan, are affixed to the three walls facing the entry. The room is subtly lit by magic and an intricate system of small mirrors that channel outside light into the windowless room and provide a luminous light that perfectly sets of the room. A table is placed in a horseshoe shape facing the mirrors with the head of the assembly always seated dead center.

Deansport: The closest ship harbor to Seamuir Castle. To travel by boat from Deansport to the castle, one would have had to go all the way around the spit protecting the bay and then work one's way south along the coast. Usually, this turns out to be an uncomfortable trip since the waters close to shore are rough. Storms blow up without warning. The road to Seamuir, the seat of the clan, is a much faster way to go. It first heads inland to avoid the wetlands bordering the shore. Once past those, it curves and heads up the coast. It winds its way between the heather-covered hills and the deep brown moors. The use of the local gates cuts hours of this journey.

Eastmuir: The realm of the MacClairs. A deep fjord, cutting far into the interior, marks the border between the lands of the MacClairs and the StClouds. Tall mountains border each side of this protected inland waterway. Many a ship finds refuge here from the powerful storms which can develop so suddenly on the local waters.

Elvenhorst: The mysterious central city of the elves, built in the shape of a five-pointed star. It is located in an extinct volcano and covered by an energy dome.

Fairholme Castle: A whimsical castle granted to Ki'ara along with the land on her 24th birthday. It is located half a day's ride from Seamuir and not far from Cloudshire Hall. The small but delightfully playful and airy Fairholme Castle is a truly generous gift and one that had been long in the making by Mikael MacClair.

Nor'Dea: Created as a last refuge for the Zidhe just in the case that humanity overruns the Highlands. It is one of five spots they selected as sanctuaries and has been extensively terraformed. Nor'Dea was transformed from a place of snow and ice with little vegetation to a paradise of sorts that is a vacation spot for some of the more restless elves and those wanting a child. For some unknown reason, any female Zidhe spending time here is able to conceive. The birthrate among the residents is actually quite high for the Le'aanan, and even multiple births are not unknown.

Seamuir Castle: The home of the MacClair Clan located in the hills above the sea. It serves as a watch station over the adjacent waters as do all the other coastal fortresses in the Highlands.

Sea Witch: The ship, a clipper, which meets Ki'ara and Mathus at Mercede harbor to take them back to the Highlands. Ki'ara is the actual owner of the vessel, and her uncle Iain looks after the business first for her father, Mikael, and now for her.

Zone of Death: A part of the border area created by the magic of the Zidhe. Nothing grows here.

People

Frankonia

Amara: The Goddess of the Frankonian Mountains. She restores Ki'ara's magic after the young sorceress saves the dragon wraith and the ghost cat.

Milla: The housekeeper at De'Aire Chateau, a woman well up there in years. Milla took to treating Ki'ara like a cherished granddaughter. She was the one who always fixed those wonderful cups of hot chocolate for Ki'ara to restore her after working on the castle.

Argulf: An ancient sorcerer and master of De'Aire Chateau. He is a rather arrogant man who is firmly convinced of his own prowess. When he first meets Ki'ara, he tells her that it would take her at least a lifetime to learn what he knows. Her being immortal, that would truly be a very long time. It takes her less than two years to best the self-important man, something which he does not handle very well. When Ki'ara arrives, the old sorcerer tries hard to give off an air of dignity and grandeur. He wears shoes with blocks glued to the bottoms to make himself look taller and more majestic, his floor-length robes are marginally clean but so wrinkled that they looked like he had slept in them, and he is continually tripping over the hem. Argulf's stringy, greasy mane is dyed but, somehow, the magic went wrong, and the hair looks more purple than black. His mean, beady brown eyes are close to his beak of a nose, and the wizard's gaze is cold and calculating. His mouth with its thin lips is usually turned down into a frown, and his face set in a permanent scowl. Argulf goes out of his way to appear imposing but lacks the height to truly pull it off. The short, pompous man reminded Ki'ara eerily of an overgrown rat.

Brianna: The great golden dragon whose spirit was captured and enchanted by Argulf. The dark emanations of the wizard's dungeon turn the dragon wraith evil and into a genuinely frightening being.

Dragon Wraith: A fearsome creature brought into being through dark magic. It can be directed to some degree by its maker but will kill any who cross its path. It takes tremendous energy to bring such a monster into the world, and it will live only a few days or hours unless it feeds.

Hugo: The stablemaster of De'Aire Chateau and Ki'ara's guide up and down the mountains. He is also the one responsible for fetching his master's supplies up to the fortress and makes the long trip at least once a month.

Jacques des Montagnes: The leader of the bandits. He and some of his men are attacked by the dragon wraith and only survive due to Ki'ara's assistance. Jacques and his outlaws have their hideout in the mountains. He is well-mannered and the son of a nobleman.

Mikka: The ghost cat and Taryn's mate. The wizard Argulf finds her close to death and decides to use her for one of his unholy experiments. Planning for bigger and better things, Argulf is no longer interested in this enchantment once it is finished. After placing the enslaved spirit in a vial for safekeeping, the careless man decides to store it down in the dungeons where the malevolent emanations of past atrocities perverted it completely and turned it to evil.

Pierre: One of the servants at De'Aire Chateau, he functions as a butler when needed.

Taryn: A mountain cat, also called a catamount or ghost cat who befriends Ki'ara and becomes her constant companion.

The Highlands

Ulric: A southern lord's son who sets his sights on the Highlands. His name means wealthy, powerful ruler or Wolf Ruler.

Ziderians

The Zidarians are mix-breeds between elves and humans or one of the other races. They are almost immortal, living well over 1000 years. The more Zidhe blood a person has, the more magical powers they possess. Once despised by all the races, they gained status as lords after the battle with Ulric. To maintain pure bloodlines, the ruling Zidarians only marry each other. The families have magic in their blood and are intimately tied to the land. When a Zidarian reaches 21, their physical body stops aging, but they continue to mature emotionally. Their bodies remain strong and full of vitality until well after their nine hundredth birthday. Nine main families rule the clans.

The Clan of the MacClairs

The MacClairs: One of the ruling Highland families. Ki'ara is born into this clan.

Ali'ana Ard Cymru: The second wife of Mikael MacClair and mother of Ki'ara.

Gawain MacClair: The youngest of the MacClair men and also the most handsome. His hair is of a beautiful dark red color, almost mahogany, not too unlike his sister's copper-colored curls. He usually allows it to fall into his face and cover one eye giving him a rakish air. His features are open and pleasant and beautifully set of his stunning brilliant blue eyes. He is a stocky man with a barrel chest and in great form since he keeps physically active all the time.

Ki'ara MacClair: The daughter of Mikael and Ali'ana. She is tall and slender, and her waist-long, somewhat curly hair shines like bright copper in the sunshine. Ki'ara's startling green eyes, set into a face with clear skin and delicate facial features, are the color of a mountain lake with moonlight reflecting off its waves. Her inner beauty matches her appearance and is so evident that most people instantly like her. Ki'ara has just recently turned 24 when this story begins. By Zidarian standards, she is still considered a child. Her oldest brother, Ragnald, was her guardian until her birthday. Ki'ara was thirteen when her dad passed on the throne to his oldest son. Due to his misbehavior, the young lady is made Lord of Fairholme by the council according to her father's instructions. She becomes the 10th lord of the Highlands.

Lyall MacClair: This MacClair's bland personality is very much reflected in his drab looks. Beside his siblings, Lyall is strangely colorless with his mousy hair and pasty face. He also lacks magic and has very little connection to the land. Lyall has been Ragnald's puppet since he was a toddler. He is the least attractive of all the siblings with his mud-colored eyes, slumped shoulders, and plain facial features and moves without the pride in his steps common to most Zidarians. This sets him apart from his brothers. Lyall has never developed much of a character due to Ragnald's overbearing influence.

Mikael MacClair: The previous lord and father to Ragnald, Lyall, Gawain, and Ki'ara MacClair, a kind and fair ruler who sees the best in most people. The lord passes on the rule of the clan and its land as well as the magic to his oldest son when Ki'ara is 13 years old. He and his wife, Ali'ana Ard Cymru, also make Ragnald guardian of their minor child, Ki'ara.

Morena Elvinstone-MacClair: The first wife of Mikael MacClair and mother to Ragnald, Lyall, and Gawain. She never recovers fully from the birth of her youngest son, Gawain, and slowly declines over the years. Only the love for her husband and sons, and the intense desire to see her small son grow up, keep her alive for as long as it does. She dies from lingering complications from childbirth when Gawain is 18 years of age.

Raghnall MacClair: The father of Mikael MacClair and once lord of the clan, a harsh and bitter man. Ragnald was his favorite grandchild, and he filled his head with his poison from an early age on. The old man resented the loss of the crown and the rules laid down by the Zidhe. He held on to the old hostilities and enjoyed a good fight. Raghnall, along with Daron StCloud, disappeared one night as a punishment for starting a battle.

Ragnald MacClair: The present lord of the MacClair Clan and an immortal Zidarian who has the land's magic at his disposal. The oldest MacClair's hair is raven black and always immaculately cut and combed. His features are even and clean cut. He would have been handsome if not for the perpetual scowl, which mars his visage. The name Ragnald is a form of Raghnall and means 'world mighty' or 'great chief.'

Clans People

Arabella: Gawain's date and the owner of the "Seven Sailors" inn. A very smart and ambitious young lady who has her sights set on the young lord. Being the rebellious daughter of a distant relation, she has enough elven blood to qualify for marriage with a fellow Zidarian.

Berta: The rude housekeeper Ragnald MacClair employs. Her primary job is running people off, which she does rather well until Ki'ara comes along.

Gina O'Malley: A female riverboat captain and the mistress of Ragnald MacClair. Gina has terrible manners, she is a true sailor, cusses like a deckhand, and loves to get drunk and belligerent down at the pub. It is rumored that the MacClair is not her only lover. Since she is nothing but trouble, most of the castle's inhabitants avoid her like the plague. Gina is an attractive woman with dark, sparkling eyes and long black hair, but what she has in beauty, she lacks in coordination. She is well known for being accident-prone and getting people hurt. Ragnald uses her in an attempt to harm his sister, and she ends up getting injured by the blaze.

Leana: Ki'ara's maid who is, in reality, her aunt and Princess Le'anara of the Zidhe. She accompanies her sister Ali'ana to Seamuir Castle to protect her niece and does so first as her nurse and later as her maid. She can see many possible futures and block the ones she does not like, and she is fiercely loyal to Ki'ara.

Marcus O'Rourke: He is and has been the captain of the *Sea Witch* for many years. He is a competent but jovial man with whom Ki'ara has always gotten along well. Under his guidance, the ship runs like clockwork.

Mathus: This Lowlander is Ki'ara's tutor. Ragnald sends him along wherever she goes, and he acts as her watchdog. He is a lanky, gangly, obnoxious man who abuses his position and mistreats Ki'ara. He reminds the young lady of an ill-tempered stork. All the self-centered tutor cares about is his own comfort. It is not surprising that Ragnald's lackey has been fired from his last employment and had to flee to the north!

York: The carriage driver, hired by Captain Marcus to deliver Ki'ara to Seamuir Castle. He is a shrewd, middle-aged man who assists Ki'ara in her dealings with the unfriendly housekeeper Berta.

The Clan of the StClouds

Conall StCloud: The present lord of the StCloud clan. He was Ki'ara's fiancé before the young lady's parents set off on their journey, leaving Ragnald in charge of their daughter. He is a tall and very handsome man with dark curly hair and warm brown eyes. Ki'ara loves his smile and has never stopped loving him in all the years they were apart. Conall means 'strong wolf.'

Daron StCloud: Conall's grandfather, a stubborn, willful man who disappeared along with Raghnall MacClair. The two men had remained bitter enemies despite the treaty and could barely stand the sight of each other. They had been furious that the covenant forced them to keep the uneasy peace.

Other important Zidarians

Airon: A young Zidarian messenger who is sent by the council to bring Ki'ara the news of her change in status.

Heather McClintok: Is employed by Lord Rowena Alistar of Islandia to present her at meetings in Eastmuir. A beautiful lady, shrewd, diplomatic, and very astute. Not much gets past her or her friend Shannon.

Lord Iain Elvinstone of Ravenshire: The brother of the first wife of Mikael MacClair, Morena. He is not a blood relation to Ki'ara but treats her as his niece and is fiercely protective of her, even against his own nephew Ragnald, for whom he, like most people, does not particularly care.

Lord Niall Macgillmott: Lord of the Macgillmotts and of the Caithyll region. He is one of Ragnald's foster fathers and is the one who mentions the prophecy to Ragnald, sending him off on a desperate hunt for this proof that Ki'ara is a threat to their clan. He and Lyall search until they finally find that reference in an old book high up on a shelf in Lord Macgillmott's library.

Lord Weatherlin: An old gent who is very gallant and has always been one of Ki'ara favorite people. His white mane looks like he has been through a windstorm, and he has bright blue eyes. Lord Weatherlin, who is sitting in for Andrew McCulloch of Cambria, presides over the fateful council when Ki'ara requests her brother's removal as lord.

King Richard McCulloch of Cambria: The lord acted as a guiding overlord, as had his father before him. While the circumspect man had held this power, peace had reigned across all the realms of the Highlands.

Shannon O'Leary: She is the local stand-in for Lord Lorena Kirkcaldie of Argness at council meetings in Eastmuir. A beautiful lady, shrewd, diplomatic, and very observant.

The Zidhe

Geradian: He is the leader of the Zidhe and stayed behind during the exodus to call for a council of the races. The Zidhe is a tall, handsome man with long, dark hair and a slender build. His bright green eyes are piercing and seem to see right through to the very core of a person. Not much gets passed him. Geradian is highly intelligent and intuitive but also kind and compassionate. What made him so ultimately suited for dealing with the elves' once friends, however, is his ability as a shrewd negotiator and an astute reader of others' emotions. Many years of experience as a circumspect leader has taught him much. He is extremely powerful and surpasses his peers in magical strength and abilities. His connection to the land goes deep.

Jenna: Wife to Geradian and the leader of one of the expeditions into the polar regions. The team went in search of shelter just in case the Mystic Highlands were ever overrun by the humans.

Definitions

The 'Choosing' or 'Becoming': The process of the magic of the land binding with the new lord. Only a select few outside the ruling lords, mostly healers, have been told what to expect.

Council of Lords: The Zidhe establish a committee, the Council of Lords. It handles all major problems affecting one clan or more and acts as the primary body governing the Highlands. The Zidarians lords are allowed to manage the everyday business of their individual clans, but all decisions involving the other regions, no matter how small, have to be brought before one of the councils.

First Council of the Highlands: After the clan lords are declared kings by the Zidhe, they realize that they need to be able to protect what was theirs. Therefore, one of the first acts of the new kings is to call a gathering. Zidhe, dwarves, and human alike heed the call, and even a couple of giants attend. Many an idea is born and then discarded or gives rise to a brand-new proposal. Progress is slow but steady. The northerners are all aware that things cannot continue as before. The battle with Ulric taught them that. Their way of life has to change if they want to keep their lives and their homes. The Highlanders understand that it is vital that they band together. They need to learn from each other, be better organized. They have to be prepared to respond more quickly and the days of separate groups living here or there are over if they want to survive.

Gathering of Lords: Minor problems, affecting no more than three neighboring clans, can be discussed and handled at the 'Gathering of Lords', which are held before weddings, christenings, and funerals, and such.

Magic Mirror: A very effective magical communication device. Outside the realm of the Zidhe, these looking glasses are very rare and highly treasured. Each lord, the council, and every gate have one of these items to allow for efficient communication as well as for the attending of meetings from afar.

Magical Gates: Had it not been for the network of such doorways all over the Highlands, bringing people together would have been a logistical nightmare. The gates are located at strategic spots in each realm, easily reached but never too close to one of the castles. They are primarily used for official business and connect the nine kingdoms to each other and the council's main chambers. The shortcuts allow the lords to attend meetings and events no matter where they are held. To prevent sudden invasions, only one carriage can pass through at a time, and the travelers have to state their name and destination to the gatekeeper there. He or she will then dial in the desired location, lock it in, and open the portal. An alarm goes off at any nearby fortress whenever someone enters the realm. A magic mirror is then used to determine if friend or foe is on their way to their doorstep. The system was built by the Zidhe and has been functioning perfectly for many a year.

Afterword

I love to write, and even the tiniest little bit of an impression or glimpse can give rise to a story or poem. Sometimes, a new tale will pop into my head while walking, reading a book, watching a movie, or in a dream. Since I have learned how to look, stories are all around me, begging to be shared with the world.

I especially cherish the ideas coming to me in my dreams. The ones I remember vividly feel different. When I put them down on paper, more details flow into my mind, almost as if I had lived them. Some believe that there are many universes and many dimensions, who knows, maybe in one of those I did have a part in these adventures.

Many of my longer tales start with a dream, as did this one. In 2017, I was actually in the middle of working on the sequels to "Arianna- A Tale from the Eleven Kingdoms" when I had this incredible dream of two lovers kept apart by her brother. She/me was Ki'ara, and he was Connor MacCloud. He left quite an impression since he was positively gorgeous, smart, kind, honest, supportive, and just plain awesome. In other words, my ideal man.

At first, I thought this would be just a short story. I had no clue it would grow to this extent. The tale soon took on a life of its own and kept getting bigger at an amazing rate. New twists and turns were appearing all the time, which I had never even imagined in the beginning, but that is where the story led.

The lover's name had given me the setting but could not stay due to the Highlander Series. I finally settled on Conall StCloud. Also, Ki'ara's brother started out as Donald, but since I am not writing political satire, he became Ragnald.

The Mystic Highlands are loosely based on Scotland but have magic, all kinds of mystical beings, and customs of their own. The sitting down with the hands on the table in the council scene came straight from my dream.

All the unexpected ideas made writing this book incredible fun. The words would just flow into my mind. Sometimes I could barely type fast enough to keep up. If I was not in the right frame of mind or it seemed that I was flailing, I stepped back for a few days until inspiration once again sent me back to the computer to continue this continually expanding work.

For me, writing is just as exciting as reading. I know kind of where I am going, but, along the way, most of my stories manage to surprise me. Adventures, which I never even anticipated, flow from my fingertips, and I can't wait to see where this new notion is going.

The suspense is what keeps me enthralled and working away. It is almost like automatic writing or channeling, and I am always eager to find out just what happens next.

I had a fabulous time creating this book and hope you will enjoy reading it as much as I loved writing it for you!

Author's Biography

GC Sinclaire loves to write and could not imagine her life without it. Her inspiration comes from many places. One of these sources is Sinclaire's vivid dreams. When she commits them to paper, more facts emerge, almost like she has lived them.

Just like her first book, 'Arianna - A Tale from the Eleven Kingdoms,' this latest novel is the result of one of these dreams. Several other stories, including a sequel to this saga and 'Arianna,' are in various stages of completion and should be published in the next couple of years.

If you would like to read more about GC and her works, please visit her Facebook page, GC Sinclaire, or her web page at <u>www.gcsinclaire.com</u>. You can check on updates there and connect with the author.

Made in the USA
Columbia, SC
15 November 2024

46140808R00357